John C

A
FAR GONE
NIGHT

FpS

Greenville, South Carolina

Second Edition

Published by:

FpS

1175 Woods Crossing Rd., #5
Greenville, S.C. 29607
864-675-0540
www.fiction-addiction.com

ISBN: 978-1-945338-81-6

Cover & Book Design by FPS

Printed in the United States of America.

For Lisa
So many kisses, so little time...

Acknowledgments

I want to thank the kind, patient, and skilled people at Neverland Publishing for their help in this writing. That would be Maggie, Donna, and Joe. You're the best.

Also, with much acclaim, I would like to thank my Book Concierge, Rowe Carenen, for her dedication to help me get my stories out to readers everywhere and for promoting my work intelligently, effectively, and professionally.

Furthermore, thanks to Melinda Walker, Melissa Lovin, Kevin Coyle, and Dara Ross in the novelistas writers' group, as well as those in another critique group, The Write Minds, for their careful reading and wise feedback on *A Far Gone Night*.

And thank you to my colleagues at Newberry College (especially fellow author Dr. Warren Moore III, *Broken Glass Waltzes*) for their enthusiasm for *Signs of Struggle* and desire to see the sequel.

Finally, on a family note, thanks and appreciation to my long-suffering wife Lisa, for her faith in me and her daily encouragement.

And, if you've read this far, good for you, because I want to acknowledge Roxie, The Best Dog Ever, a purebred Zimbabwean Cattle Retriever–Crested, appearing on the back cover with me. Rest in peace, pupper. And thanks for the memories.

Rockbluff, Iowa

1. Bednarik's Books
2. Holy Grounds Coffee Shop
3. Back to the Future Consignments
4. Sole Proprietor Shoe Store
5. Rockbluff Opera House
6. Kathy's Kuntry Krafts Korner
7. Rockbluff Community Library and Media Center
8. Mulehoff's Earthen Vessel Barbell Club and Video Rental
9. The Grain o' Truth Bar & Grill
10. Bloom's Bistro
11. Christ the King Church
12. Shlop's Roadhouse
13. City Park
14. Arvid Pendergast house
15. Rockbluff Community College
16. Whispering Birch Golf & Country Club

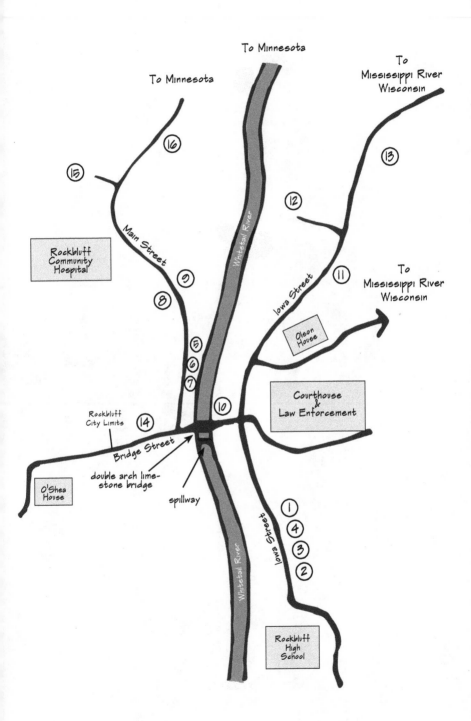

Chapter One

"To expect too much is to have a sentimental view of
life and this is a softness that leads to bitterness."

—*Flannery O' Connor*—

I knew immediately she was dead, half-spinning and languidly bobbing in the dark water. One arm appeared to be twisted behind her, but the other floated free, back and forth, back and forth, as if beckoning me to herself, like an Iowa Ahab, bidding me come see.

At first, I thought the drugs and alcohol were playing tricks on my eyes. Beset by insomnia, I had downed three Melatonin and three Three Philosophers Belgian ale and remained wide-eyed. So I had driven into town, walked out onto the double-arched limestone bridge spanning the Whitetail River seeking solace and looking for calm in the black water dropping down the small spillway, a smooth, uniform curtain, churning into brief curls of white water before calming and turning black again and heading on south.

I stared, thinking that maybe in doing so she might change into a mattress or a bunch of plastic wrapping or a cheap, abandoned Styrofoam cooler – anything else that would make me laugh at my first perception. But it was a body and the body was naked and it looked like a woman and I suddenly wished to God I had not seen it.

I looked away. I looked back. It was a body, alright.

My impulse was to flee, to just go back to my truck and go home and hope someone else would find her and be drawn into whatever drama awaited. But Sheriff Payne would hear and investigate and someone would mention they saw my truck parked by the bridge in the middle of the night and then I'd have to answer questions.

The only thing for me to do now, I realized, was to buck up whatever ethical and moral mettle I have in me and go to the woman in the water. How could I leave her?

I took off, slipped, went to one knee, then arose and scrambled full bore back across the bridge and down the grassy slope to the river's edge, my right hamstring nipping at me to slow down as I rushed to her, splashing into frigid, waist-deep water and reaching out to the body, not caring about crime scene forensics or damaging evidence. I just wanted to get her out of that damn water, and when I saw that she was just a girl, not even a woman yet, I charged to her side, slipped my hands under her cold arms from behind, pulled her free from whatever had snagged her, and lugged her out of the water. I placed her softly on the thick dead grass alongside the river.

The body was very cold, no longer supple, no longer anything but dead.

As soon as I set her down, I pulled off my sweatshirt and covered her above the waist, and then my t-shirt and covered her below the waist. The air was cold on my bare skin, and my jeans were wet and cold, too. I squatted down next to the dead girl and my shoes squished.

I said a quick prayer and rubbed my eyes hard with my palms. Her head was at an odd angle, so I slipped my right hand behind her head to move it a little, to make it more comfortable. I know, I know, but what difference did it make if she were dead? The point is, it made a difference to *me*.

It was then that my fingers found the two depressions in the back of her skull. Her long, matted hair nearly obscured them, but a little exploration was called for. Stunned, I let my fingers linger under her hair to be sure. I was sure, and then, for just an instant, I was holding another dead person's head—my friend's—in the streets of Sarajevo after we thought we had cleaned up that neighborhood, the sweet smell of cordite drifting in the air like a woman's fragrance on a breeze.

My attention rushed back to the girl. Wanting to disbelieve her wounds, I laid her head back down, slow and easy. Then I just placed my right hand on her dear, lovely forehead, and moved a tangle of drenched hair to the side, away from her face. For her. For me, mostly. That's when I noticed a slash of whiteness alongside her skull. There in the dark, at first I thought it was exposed bone, but when I touched it I realized it was just a blaze of white hair slightly forward of her left ear, an anomaly in her otherwise raven hair. It looked like a fat comma or that Nike swoosh sign.

It takes about ninety-seven seconds to patrol all of Rockbluff village, so I hoped a deputy sheriff would come by and investigate my abandoned truck up by the bridge. The law enforcement and EMS people know my truck, a mixed blessing. So I sat there on my haunches, keeping the girl company, waiting for someone to come along.

I had thought that a look at the river would make me sleepy. That's why I was in town. Or maybe a stroll through one of the solid, middle-class neighborhoods, ambling down darkened streets with pools of light at each corner from the Olde English streetlights. Thinking pleasant thoughts of couples cuddling spoons-like in a warm bed, breathing in and out in perfect rest; of children curled up with teddy bears and well-worn baseball gloves; of old white-muzzled, obese dogs snoring on downstairs sofas.

And then I looked down at the dead girl and realized my thoughts were maybe just so much romantic nonsense—that the couples cheat and the children torture baby birds and the dog bites. Still, I cling to my soft dreams like a congressman clings to a kickback.

I heard a car approach, pull over on the bridge, and cut the engine. I heard a door open and slam shut. Heavy footsteps. A tube of light played along the north side of the bridge, then the south side, finding us. I squinted into the beam in my face and shouted, "Get down here!"

I thought about calling out, "Got a floater here!" like they do in movies about crime in Philly or New York or Strawberry Point, but I didn't. She wasn't a floater; she was a girl.

Deputy Sheriff Doltch, an old acquaintance, a big guy, solid and true, started my way. He slipped once coming down the bank, then came up to us, shaking his head and keeping the flashlight on the dead girl. He was muttering something I couldn't understand, then he said, "That you, O'Shea?"

"Of course," I said, glad to have the flashlight off me. "Would you call someone, Steven? Please?"

Doltch handed me his flashlight and I shut it off, leaving us in darkness and the sound of the spillway. My knees burning and my right quadricep a little tight, I managed to stand up, by degrees. I heard Doltch talking to Sheriff Payne on his radio. Then he stopped.

"Sheriff's on the way," Doltch said.

"We gotta stop meeting like this, Steven," I said, remembering the Soderstroms.

Doltch ignored my remark. "What happened?"

I looked at him.

"How would *I* know? I was out for a walk and crossed the bridge and looked downstream and there she was."

"Sounds familiar," he said. "Like out at the Soderstrom place. Why is that, Thomas?"

"Just unlucky," I said, "but you need to know we're not talking about the Soderstrom place, Steven, so let's move on, pal." Something about my tone informed him of my displeasure with his comment and question. He shrugged his big shoulders and shifted his weight.

I changed the subject back to the girl. I said, "I have no idea how long she's been there."

Doltch seemed relieved to be back to the business of the moment. He looked at his watch. "You were out for a walk at two-thirty in the morning?"

"Gives me a chance to get acquainted with those who serve and protect."

"Always with the attitude, O'Shea." He shook his head. I thought I saw a little smile playing across his lips, but I might have been wrong. Might've been a smirk.

I said nothing.

"Was she there on the bank when you saw her?"

"Yes. She drowned; then, to make it easy on you, she crawled up here on the grass and took her clothes off."

Doltch, quick learner, ignored my insight. "Do you know her?"

"No."

We waited a couple of minutes in silence, the three of us. The wisecracker, the cop, and the corpse. Another cruiser came from the area of the courthouse, where the Sheriff's Department is housed in the basement.

"That would be Sheriff Payne," Doltch said.

"What took him so long? Doesn't he know Holy Grounds is closed? No doughnuts until dawn." Holy Grounds is a coffee shop not far from the high school, serving excellent coffee and a wide variety of baked goods, including scones, bear claws and, oh yes, doughnuts.

Doltch said nothing, walking away and up the bank toward the bridge, grunting with the effort. I continued to look at the girl. In the dark, she looked like she was sleeping, and I guess she was. She had a sweet, untroubled face and very dark hair except for that white mark. That's all I could tell. But I was sure that Rockbluff CSI would come through again and discover the truth.

"What is it about you and dead bodies?" Payne asked scrambling down to where I was standing, rubbing the back of my leg. My knees were on fire, too, but I wasn't going to mention it and ruin my tough guy mystique.

"I had nothing to do with it," I said.

Doltch piped in. "Said he was out for a walk and just *happened* to see this girl in the river."

I didn't care for the man's tone. The sarcasm again. "Steven, if you'd like to start something, I'm sure the sheriff would turn his back for those thirty seconds it would take for resolution." Getting snippy in my old age. Punk kids.

Doltch said nothing.

I looked back at the sheriff. Harmon Payne's a big guy, but not big like an offensive lineman. He's about six-four and lean and wiry, and I do believe he could take care of himself. Former Marine, law enforcement professional. All that lovely training. He said, "Those your clothes covering her?"

"Yes."

"Thank you, Thomas," Payne said. He walked over to the girl and gingerly lifted up my sweatshirt and looked, then set it back. He repeated the process with my t-shirt, shaking his head the whole time.

"God Almighty," he said, and stood up.

"Another suicide, looks like," Doltch said.

"*Another* suicide?" I asked.

"Don't you read the papers, Thomas?" Doltch asked, with the sarcasm again "There was a girl found out in northwest Iowa a few months back. Just like this. They take off their clothes and jump in and drown themselves. Boy trouble usually. They leave behind poetic notes."

"No point in bothering the coroner then, is there? Just sign her up as a suicide and look for family and forget about it, right?" I said, my own sarcasm back at Doltch, holding in check what I knew about the girl's wounds. Let the officials figure it out.

An ambulance pulled up, lights flashing but without the siren. No point in waking up the villagers. The EMS people came down, lifted my clothes from the body and gave them to me, seeing as how I was the only one standing around shirtless. Steel-trap minds. They took away the girl in a dark body bag.

"You been hittin' the weights, Thomas," Payne said. Not a question.

"Now and then," I said, slipping into my tee and sweatshirt. They felt good against a sudden, chill breeze that was just cranking up, but I was afraid everything south of my belly-button was trying to turn blue.

"Deputy, you can go ahead and call it a night after you mark this off with tape, take photos, and write your report," Payne said. Then he turned to me as Doltch hiked up to his cruiser. "Let's you and me have a cup of coffee, unless you're afraid it'll keep you awake."

"Coffee? Where? Everything's closed," I said as we turned and walked up the riverbank together. The sight of the dead girl was stuck in my head. I rubbed my hand across my face to stop the stinging in my eyes and nose. I hate it when that happens. I was just glad it was dark out.

"Coffee's up at my office. I got a pot just made when Deputy Doltch called."

"Your coffee? I'd have to be desperate."

"Which you are."

"Which I am," I said. "And I'm not worried about it keeping me awake. There won't be any sleep for me tonight."

"Indeed. Me either."

Sheriff Payne climbed into his cruiser and turned it around and drove back over the bridge. I followed in my pickup truck. I decided the next time I couldn't sleep, I'd just shoot myself.

CHAPTER TWO

**"Life is full of misery, loneliness, and suffering - and
it's all over much too soon."**

—*Woody Allen*—

I spent the next couple of hours hanging out at Harmon's office,
drinking bad coffee, discussing my discovery, and swapping bon
mots over old murders, suicides, and aggravated assaults from the
golden days a while back.

I filled out my statement, signed and dated it, after checking the
calendar on the wall to discover that it was now Wednesday.

Payne poured us each one last mug of coffee, and I threatened him
with charges of police brutality if he started another batch. As it was, I
had to pour in enough cream and sugar to allow the spoon to stand up
unassisted before I could get the fetid brew down my throat. I shoved
my statement across his desk and took my cup while he scanned my
short paragraph.

As long as I was filling out paperwork, I wondered if I should
go ahead and get with it and fill out an "Alienation of Affection"
complaint against Sheriff Payne, naming him as the principle since he
was now on intimate terms with my Last Chance to Go Steady, Liv
Olson, passionate English teacher at Rockbluff High School. Liv and I
might have had a chance, but she said I was a liar (true) and that scary

things happened around me (also true) and there wasn't much to build on there (debatable).

The good sheriff put my statement aside and took out a pint of Jack Daniel's from a desk drawer. I nodded and extended my cup. Payne dropped a dollop in each cup. "This might improve the flavor," he said as he poured. Enough said. I pulled back my cup, held it in both hands, and took a taste. Better.

"You wrote in your report that you were taking a walk because you couldn't sleep. That right?" Payne asked. He sipped his coffee.

"Correct."

"Why not?"

"Why couldn't I sleep?" I drank some of my coffee and held it up to Payne in a silent toast of appreciation for the added Jack.

He looked at me. "That's what I asked. It's not a trick question."

I said, "Covington."

"Excellent. That solves everything."

"I do what I can to cooperate with law enforcement professionals. Citizenship demands candor."

"Do I have to beat it out of you with a rubber hose? I have one, you know."

"I am familiar with rubber hose beatings. They're not so bad as long as one thinks of happy thoughts, like kittens mewing, puppies cavorting, the Red Sox hammering the Yankees."

"You've been beaten with rubber hoses?"

"Just a couple of times."

Payne looked thoughtful for a moment. Which made me nervous. Then he said, "Tell me about Covington. An old nemesis from your special ops days? A girlfriend's vigilant daddy? A coach who made you run 'til you threw up?"

"I don't know special ops."

"Right. My bad."

I said, "Covington was the name of the Georgia State Trooper who informed me that my family was dead. His name just popped into my head, unbidden and unwanted. And then a whole lot of other things popped into my head. And then I couldn't sleep. So I thought I might as well go looking in the dark for bodies in the Whitetail River since there wasn't anything on television."

"I'm sorry. I didn't mean to push it," the good sheriff said.

"It's okay. I can deal."

"Go home, Thomas. Go to bed," he said. It was 4:33.

"What are *you* going to do?"

"Probably have another pot of coffee. Think some about that dead girl."

"Want some company?"

"*Go*, Thomas. I'll see you sometime tomorrow. And, yes, I'll share with you what I've got, off the record, seeing as how you're such a stellar amateur cop, and I know I can count on you to not blab."

"Not even if that comely reporter, Suzanne Highsmith of *The Des Moines Chronicle* shows up and winks at me?" I finished my coffee and felt two kinds of warmth easing into my chest.

"If Miss Highsmith winks at me, I'll tell her everything she wants to know. She was certainly a pleasure to deal with before."

"Before what?"

"Say goodnight, Thomas."

I stretched my legs. Preparation for standing. And immediately regretted it. There are few things as rewarding as a good stretch, but the pleasure was offset by my hamstring twinge, a nemesis for the last couple of years. Ah, life. Ah, O'Shea!

So I got up and hobbled a few steps before falling into my manly, assertive, don't-mess-with-me stride of power and purpose. I drove home, the girl's face in my mind and the holes in the back of her head still alive on my fingertips. It was nearly five o'clock when I parked on the white gravel area in front of my home and went inside.

I don't lock the door anymore. It's a decision I made to help me get past the fact that, not all that long ago, two people broke in and tried to kill me. *And* Gotcha, which pissed me off, she being my only living family member. By not locking the door anymore, I am, supposedly, telling myself it's all in the past, that now is better, and the Hawkeyes will recruit a kid who'll run for 2,000 yards as a true freshman. The three psych courses I had in college have proven to be instrumental in my need for healing from time to time. And self-healing is the most satisfying kind. Cheaper than therapy. I mean, how complicated can it be?

At that weird hour, before it would be light enough for me to go for my daily run, too early for me to do a little carbohydrate loading before taking off, and much too early to go down to The Grain o' Truth Bar & Grill and harass Lunatic Mooning, I decided to get ahead of the curve and just go ahead and email Ernie Timmons.

Ernie was our pastor when we lived back down in Belue in south-central Georgia. He had baptized our daughters, and his son Matt had dated Annie. He had morphed from pastor to pastor/friend. His wife, Jan, had been a good friend of my wife, Karen.

I knew he would call as soon as the story reached the newspapers. Ernie assiduously scanned *The Des Moines Chronicle* online every day, something he had begun as soon as I left Belue. That's how he found out about the troubles last year. So, rather than have him harass me with a morning email, I decided to let him know first. I typed a succinct, accurate, and matter-of-fact message and hit the "Send" button. Then, since I was already on the computer and it wasn't beginning to get light out yet, I surfed around a while at some of my favorites: *The Boston Herald* Sports, "Black Heart Gold Pants" (Hawkeyes), and Dorothy Parker quotes. By the time I finished killing time and discovering there weren't any five-star freshmen running backs (yet) coming to play football for Iowa, it was time to go for my run.

Over the last few months, to go along with pumping iron with a focus and ferocity I did not fully understand, I had extended my morning runs from three miles to five with an occasional day off, an acknowledgement to Father Time. So I changed clothes and took off into a morning where the sun was just now rising, sending fingerlings of blue and pink light into the black, star-filled canopy overhead. A mile or so into my run, the sky took on a rosier hue and the stars began to fade.

I picked up my pace as I reached the two-and-a-half mile landmark, a twisted crabapple tree that had to be older than ignorance, branches snarled and misshapen, but alive. I turned and started back, pleased that I was still breathing easily enough to carry on a conversation had there been someone running with me, but I run alone.

Covington came to my mind again, but this time I just shrugged it off. The memory had lost its shock value, but I must admit I wondered how bad memories keep showing up like knee pain when you think they are no more. But the irony is that most of the good memories seem to slip away into the fog of forgetting. Sometimes I'd like to give life a two-finger "doink" in the eyeballs, like Moe used to do to Curly.

I finished the last fifty yards of my run with an all-out sprint, surprised that my hamstring did not yelp at me. That was a big plus to start a new day. I've noticed lately that I don't heal as quickly as I did a few decades back, so to have the hammy hold up was a gift from God. Not many of those lately, but I'm a patient man.

I walked up my driveway and shouldered aside the front door, still sticking a little since Gunther Schmidt repaired it after the shootout. Maybe I'd give Julie a call and she'd ask him to come out and shave off a thin layer of memory.

Gotcha was thrilled to see me return. She actually opened one eye and looked at me from her position on the recliner she likes to jump into and push against the back until it opens up for her. She is not a morning dog. She is not an afternoon dog. But she likes to join me on the deck in the late afternoons, even as it has grown cooler than normal this early November. Gotcha and I go out on the deck and I knock back a few Three Philosophers. She has a Fat Tire poured into her terra cotta bowl that stays out there just for that purpose. And we hang out together. She is good company and only bites really bad people, and even then she just bites once. And hangs on until I ask her to cool it.

The run felt good, putting an edge on my appetite. It was time to eat, so I asked Gotcha one of her vocabulary words – "Out?" – and she hopped down, eager to get started on her day, or at least the prelude to food. She rumbled over to the front door and stared until I let her out. I had Gunther build a doggie door for her in the back, one with a stiff, fringed plastic curtain she can easily push through for when I was going to be gone long, and a steel sheet when I was home. No point in having a wandering porcupine or skunk decide to explore Chez O'Shea. Gotcha prefers to have me let her out and in, but the doggie door is a good backup in case I'm late returning from the opera, or cross-stitch classes at the Rockbluff Community Center.

After I let Gotcha out, I set about fixing myself a breakfast fit for a champion. I started an eight-cup Mr. Coffee, serving up Starbuck's best ground coffee, took down the black bottle of Bailey's Irish Cream, and set it next to the coffee pot. I watched the coffee brew, enjoying the rich fragrance and finding small comfort in watching something reliable do what it's supposed to do. An oddity in my life so far.

I made a quick trip to the back door, where Gotcha always returns from her morning ablutions, and I let her in, presented her meds in a spoon of creamy peanut butter, refilled her water dish, and then poured dry dog food into another terra cotta bowl and set both bowls down on her little red eating mat with her name in cursive at the bottom. I watched her suck in her food like a shop vac going after debris, wondering if she ever actually tasted anything. But I know that when I toss her M & M's now and then, she always spits out the yellow ones.

I made myself a six-egg ham and cheese omelet, nuked a couple of slabs of hash browns and slathered butter over them. Realizing how much energy is expended detecting dead girls in the Whitetail River, I nuked a couple frozen waffles and drowned them in butter and syrup, then poured coffee into my big Harley-Davidson mug and added a serious glug of Bailey's. Gotcha joined me on the deck where I sat and worked my way through my training table fare, hand-feeding her bits of hash browns and waffles. Is there anything more glorious than a big breakfast on my deck in northwest Iowa, the chill of the November morning more effective than caffeine, and without the headache? I finished my coffee quickly before the cold air got to it.

Back inside, another cup of Bailey's with some coffee added in helped me through a few Psalms and Proverbs, but then I got sleepy, even though the coffee was not decaf, and suddenly I was more tired than I could remember. I set my Bible aside and wondered what God had in store for me. Previously, what He'd had in store for me was to uncover a murder, punch out a couple of bums at Shlop's Roadhouse, toss a man off the bridge downtown, gun down assassins, and get a friend and an innocent high school girl killed. Not to mention being shot myself and having Liv Olson wounded, too.

I gave up on trying to figure out God. Since He never asks for my advice, I decided to just mutter something like, "Your will, Lord, and not mine."

And then I stumbled off to bed, stripping down and then slipping on a pair of baggy black boxers before I tossed back the covers and climbed in. And climbed out. And locked all three doors. Someone had murdered that girl, and if they would murder a child, they might kill the person who found her.

Even knowing that, I was able to drop off quickly and sleep like someone who had been shot, which I have been, and probably would be again. My last thought was, why was Doltch so eager to call the girl's death a suicide? And why was Payne already in his office at that ungodly hour?

I decided that in the morning I'd shrug aside my desire for peace and privacy and go see what I could find out about a girl stripped and double-tapped and dumped in the river.

CHAPTER THREE

"Trust everybody, but cut the cards."

—*Finley Peter Dunne*—

It was almost two in the afternoon when I woke up. I guess the late night at the bridge, my early morning run, and a hearty breakfast had combined to render me comatose for nearly five hours.

You'd think I'd feel refreshed after such a nap. I was awake, for sure, but not rested. It was not a quality sleep. Karen and I used to call quality sleep "slumber" when we slept together all those years. Long gone, now.

I have noticed, over time, whenever I'm involved in an intense situation, I get hungry. It happened in Somalia when a buddy caught a round in the gut, and other places, and now it's happening here in Iowa, with a dead girl in the river. Most people get sick and throw up. I get ravenous. I tell myself my body needs fuel to face challenge.

Or, it could be that eating fulfilled a need to be involved in something predictable to bring stability back into my world. For that, I recommend Three Philosophers and a big plate covered in sausage. It is not gluttony; either, it's physiological fortification. You can look it up.

Now I was hungry again, and I decided that I needed to follow my own credo and refuel. I got up and walked to the foot of the bed. Gotcha opened both eyes from her sleeping position on her tuffet. She was, obviously, wild with enthusiasm for the remainder of the afternoon.

I stretched, dressed in skivvies, faded blue jeans, a black t-shirt and a heavy, black sweatshirt with IOWA in block gold letters across the chest. Socks and running shoes completed my ensemble. I can't remember the last time I wore a necktie. I guess it was for Horace Norris' funeral.

I let Gotcha out for her duties, brushed my teeth in case I ran into a beautiful woman unable to keep her distance, let Gotcha back in, gave her a medium Milk Bone, and left. Normally, when there's something eerie in the air, I carry along my new Mossburg, pistol grip pump shotgun, "L.C. (Law Clerk)," or "Elsie" for short, when there is trouble in the wind. But I wasn't sure my early-morning trouble at the river was *my* trouble, so I went without.

Elsie is kin to Lunatic Mooning's shotgun he keeps under the bar out at The Grain o' Truth Bar & Grill. Lunatic calls his weapon "Chief Justice." His backup, in the office in the rear of that fine establishment, is identical and named "Associate Justice." Chief Justice is an excellent firearm that helped me out one edgy evening a while back.

It was cold outside, and I was glad I was wearing the heavy sweatshirt. My truck, winterized a week ago, rumbled into life on the first try, and told me it was 24 degrees. Iowa heat wave. I strapped myself in and was on my way. The sun was bright and the sky was a brilliant cobalt blue, bereft of any clouds whatsoever. I found myself longing for the first snowfall of the winter as I cruised on into town at 93 miles per hour. I enjoy driving fast.

Arvid Pendergast, attired in a parka, was flat on his back just inside his front yard, his left leg hanging over the elaborate wrought-iron fence next to the gate, and I gave him a short beep to acknowledge his demise. He did not respond, of course. Arvid represents Lutheran Brotherhood Insurance and is preparing his wife and children for his eventual death, a near certainty according to all actuarial tables. So, he randomly falls over and acts dead. These spontaneous acts of mercy could happen anywhere – the yard, the kitchen table, his parked car. And they serve to prepare his family to take in stride the experience of coming upon his stilled form someday.

An unintended benefit of his fake death scenarios (he calls it "performance art") is that his business prospered and he has been a member of Lutheran Brotherhood's Million Dollar Round Table ever since he started playing dead. Seems that people seeing a dead body every now and then gets them to thinking about their own mortality, and subsequently, the financial effect it would have on their loved ones. People have been buying all kinds of insurance, and regularly upping it, ever since Arvid began his escapades into mortality reminders just a few years ago.

I just smiled as I drove on by, respecting Arvid's unique art form, and kept on into the village, turned left just before the bridge, drove up the street, and parked out front of Lunatic Mooning's place. He calls it "The Grain o' Truth Bar and Grill" because he says there's a grain of truth in every pint. The only question is whether that truth can be handled by the patron. Most of his customers seem willing to risk it. Again and again. Lifelong learners.

Just inside, I paused, as I often do, to take in the setting and the smells and the general ambiance of the joint. Cozy booths beckoned along the walls on either side of the front door. A few oak tables and chairs were scattered here and there. Two regulation-sized pool tables stood stolidly to the left, authentic Tiffany lamps looming low over the green felt surfaces. But the most unique element of the establishment is the U-shaped bar, a mission oak behemoth backed by an enormous mirror. Several barstools, the kind with backs, lined up around the bar, leaving an open space at one side where a flip-top counter provided a passway for the waitresses. They are not "waitstaff" because Lunatic hires only women to wait tables, usually women going through a hard time who need a job for a while. Moon is a softy, but if you call him that, be prepared to have him peel your face off for you.

I started toward the bar, glancing to the right at the booth historically inhabited by Horace Norris, now dead and buried. No one sits there as it remains perpetually vacant, a memorial to Horace. I returned my gaze to the bar, and the person behind it, the big Indian, Lunatic Mooning, so named after the first thing his mother saw after giving birth to him in the hospital in Mount Pleasant, Iowa.

Lunatic is built like a middle linebacker, a bit shorter than I but heavier, with bigger slabs of muscle everywhere. My guess is 6 feet and 245, but I don't know for sure and I'm not asking. His hair is black with streaks of silver, worn pulled back into a short, flat ponytail. He was wearing a long-sleeved, dark burgundy cotton sweater, the sleeves snug against his biceps.

My stomach growled as I approached the bar.

"I heard that, paleface. The white man's burden," Lunatic said, his deep voice a burly baritone.

"What white man's burden, Squanto? I thought the white man's burden was an exhortation to colonization and the Rudyard Kipling poem and all that."

"Your hungry belly is the burden. My people, the Ojibwa, also known as the Anishinabe, learned generations ago to discipline every area of their lives, including hunger, and how it manifests physiologically."

"And my people, the Irish, also known as the Wackos, learned generations ago that booze is the only answer, and that discipline is usually wasted effort," I said, sliding onto a barstool.

"You speak with forked tongue, white eyes. Navy SEALS are rumored to be highly-disciplined, even the ones who had to overcome Irish ancestry."

"I was never a SEAL," I said, scrutinizing the hand-lettered menu on the whiteboard behind the bar, on one side of the mirror, even though I knew what I was going to order when I decided to drive into town.

Lunatic gave a short laugh. "You continue to speak with forked tongue, yet I continue to accept you."

Actually, I am not speaking with forked tongue regarding the SEAL reference, but it's nobody's business that I washed out twice, very nearly at the end of training, both times with a broken leg forcing me out of training. After the second fracture, I gave it up and took the Navy's Medical Discharge, and training, with me. But I was noticed by the military, who found other work for me, every bit as entertaining as SEAL assignments. And those experiences helped me get a job in private enterprise when I left the Navy.

"I'm your best customer, you'd better continue to accept me," I said. "And, by the way, can I get some service here?" I said, looking around. "The help has an attitude."

"You forget. I am not the help. I am the owner-operator." He was polishing a glass with a bar towel, his biceps rotating inside the tightness of his sweater, the muscles bulging and smoothing out again.

"And a credit to your people," I added. "And with that acknowledgement of your greatness, sir, may I please have two Looney Burgers, an order of fries, and the first of three Three Philosophers, please."

"Thanks for saying 'please,' Thomas. I'll get right to it." He turned
to his work, placing the pair of 12-ounce ground round burgers on the
grill and dropping a wad of raw fries into a wire basket and then into
hot grease. My mouth began watering as he turned back to the bar,
drew a Three Philosophers, and poured it into a tulip glass. He pushed
the Belgian ale across the bar and I picked it up and drank half.

He said, "*Three* Three Philosophers? What's up, Thomas?
Something to do with a body in the river?"

Rockbluff, Iowa, is a small town. More like a village, really. News
travels fast, of course, but this was ridiculous. There was no point in
faking ignorance. Lunatic Mooning knew.

"How did you know about that?" I asked.

"The night has a thousand eyes."

"What do you know?"

"What do *you* know?"

I finished my drink and pushed the empty glass to Lunatic. He
took my glass, exchanged it for a clean one, and slowly poured another
Three Philosophers. The creamy head was a thing of beauty. He set the
glass before me. I took a sip. "I asked first," I said. "After you, Chief."

"I know that the tulip glass is required for full enjoyment of your
Belgian ale. The long stem is for the imbiber to hold in his, or her,
hand in order to keep heat from the fingers compromising the chill of
the drink, and the distinctive tulip-shaped top is so constructed as to
allow a full head to form, advancing both a visual and palate-pleasing
experience." He smiled at me. A rare thing.

"Thank you for that narrative," I said. "I knew that in fourth grade.
Now, omniscient one, what do you know about the body in the river?
Name? Age?"

"I will speak. I know that you discovered a dead woman south of the bridge around two or three in the morning. She was white, or at least, not African-American. EMS came and took the body away to Doc Jarlsson, probably for an autopsy."

"That's it? That's all you know? I thought you had a comprehensive, systematic, and sophisticated network of Ojibwa operatives who know everything. The night has a thousand eyes alright, but that's not much information. 'Woeful' pretty well describes it," I said.

"Give us time, I will know more."

"I'm sure you will – by reading the newspapers. The key thing is that I know more than you do, and you're a native, while I'm an outsider, from downriver, Clinton. Maybe you should sign up for remedial information-gathering systems at the juco."

"Okay, I lied," Mooning said. "Something that's rubbed off on me from being around Caucasians all the time. I also know that Harmon Payne was there, and that the two of you went to his office after the body was removed. I know Steve Doltch took pictures and roped off the area with yellow tape. Maybe it was an accident, or a suicide. Someone upstream getting in too deep, or too despairing of this vale of tears."

"You are unusually chatty this morning, oh Native American."

"I am loquacious from time to time. Never, as you put it, 'chatty.'" He turned and attended to my order. My stomach growled again in anticipation of the food. The fragrance of my meal cooking was almost as wonderful as puppy breath. Lunatic brought me a big ceramic platter with two Looney Burgers on it and another, smaller dish with the fries, the best on the planet. I finished my second Three Philosophers and Lunatic brought me my third.

"Another thing," he said, taking a rag and wiping condensation off the bar. "You're involved."

"And that alone should make it a crime scene."

"There is a history with you, this town, and crime scenes. Not a criticism. We're all better off since you came our way."

"Thank you."

"I didn't mean to intrude on your feelings, but you must be keeping something back about the girl in the river," Lunatic said. "You don't trust me?"

He had a point. After all, he saved my life once when he shot a professional killer closing in on me. I leaned over the bar toward the big guy and motioned him closer. He inclined his head toward me after looking around the bar and grill, which was doing a decent business for mid-afternoon on a Wednesday.

"In confidence, Lunatic, I can tell you that the girl was young and unclothed." I sampled my Three Philosophers. Every bit as good as the first one. And the second.

He was silent, looking thoughtful. Then he said, "Sounds like a ritualistic suicide. There was one just like it in LeMars a few months back. Girl left a Shakespearean sonnet in iambic pentameter as a suicide note, shed her clothes, and walked into the river."

"That's what Doltch said. A good-bye poem. Sad."

I had no intention of telling Lunatic about the two bullet holes in the back of the head, a fact that ruled out suicide unless she was a highly-motivated self-destructive type. Information would leak out, but I wasn't going to contribute anything about the murder. I wanted to see how the coroner and Sheriff's Department handled the case. I'm conservative when it comes to trusting people. The three people I trusted with my life are all dead, so there you go.

"Probably, yeah, could be a ritualistic suicide," I said, enjoying being non-committal for a change. Lunatic gave me a look that indicated he suspected I was up to something, but I let it pass, and so did he.

I was beginning to acquire a soothing buzz. Two ales on a mostly-empty stomach, my breakfast notwithstanding, were working their magic. I felt good, and began humming the James Brown hit by the same name. I began grooving a little as I bit into the burger, swaying my shoulders.

"Another white man's burden," Lunatic said.

"What?"

"Inability to dance."

Stung, I finished chewing, and said, "You need to know that I was voted 'Honorary Soul Brother' for my dancing skills. My African-American buddies in the Ultimate Special Forces Annihilation Unit granted me that honor when we were partying after freeing three major nations of dictatorships one weekend. So there." I returned to my food. And quit barstool dancing. "Everyone's a critic," I muttered, feigning hurt feelings.

"Not a criticism. A *critique*," he said.

"And by the way, my critique of red men's dancing goes something like this – toe, heel, alternate feet, toe, heel, repeat. All the while chanting, 'Hey-ya, hey-ya.' Stunning."

"You mentioned the news media a few moments ago," Lunatic said, ignoring my racist remarks, "as one of my anemic sources of information."

"Yes, I did. I suspect that's where you get all your inside stuff, like most of us, after someone else has done the legwork."

"Well," he said, looking over my left shoulder, "speaking of the media, *and* legwork, guess who just walked in the door?"

I was enjoying the smoothing-out benefits of the Three Philosophers, which began to quickly erode when I understood to whom Mooning was referring.

So I took another swallow of my ale and turned around, rotating my barstool, and there she was, ubiquitous and nosy and frequently hyperbolic ace reporter of *The Des Moines Chronicle*, the talented and lovely Suzanne Highsmith.

She looked my way, waved with great vigor and apparent delight in seeing me, hung up her fur jacket on a coat tree, and started my way. I turned back around to face Lunatic, whose face was a combination of controlled merriment and faux sympathy. "How did she find out about the body in the river? That happened only twelve hours ago!"

Lunatic shook his head. "Only The Great Spirit knows. But you can ask her yourself. Here she is, Thomas." And with that, he turned away.

Chapter Four

**"Man does not control his own fate. The
women in his life do that for him."**

—Groucho Marx—

Suzanne Highsmith is a beautiful woman. And she knows it. She can also be a monumental pain in the ass, a too-frequent character weakness of beautiful women. Nevertheless, I decided to slide off my barstool and greet her.

I looked around. There wasn't a client in The Grain who wasn't looking. Suzanne is the kind of woman who turns heads. Women turn their heads out of envy and jealousy; men out of lust and admiration. But lust can only get you so far. But admiration can go on for a lifetime. I admired Karen until the day she died. Still do.

So far, I am not an admirer of this woman.

She said, "Hello, Thomas, and, oh, may I call you Thomas, given our history?"

"Feel free," I said. "May I buy you something to drink. Or eat?"

She smiled that smile and flipped her trademark braid, long and thick and dark, a singular rope of style and sexiness of which she is well aware. She turned to Lunatic and said, "Nice to see you again, Mr. Mooning. May I have a Diet Coke, and maybe an antipasto salad, please, bleu cheese dressing on the side?"

Lunatic nodded. "Nice to see you, too, Suzanne."

"Diet Coke and a salad?" I asked.

"One has to watch one's body," she said, "because it goes south in a hurry, although it doesn't seem to apply to you, Thomas. You look better than ever. Steroids from Mexico? Lance Armstrong Specials?" She leaned back and gave me the once-over.

"Actually, it's beeroids and hard work. But let's get to the point," I said, already knowing, "why are you here in beautiful downtown Rockbluff, Iowa?" Suzanne lives in West Des Moines.

She took my arm and began steering me toward a booth. I grabbed my pint in one hand and plate in the other, abandoned my place at the bar, and allowed her to be the designated driver. She started to sit us down in Horace's booth, but I cut her off and angled for the next one.

"What's with that? That booth looks perfectly fine."

"No one sits there anymore," I said. She didn't know. She'd think it was stupid and illogical. Another reason not to cooperate with her. No heart. I maneuvered her into the next booth, then scooched in the seat across the formica tabletop separating us.

Almost immediately Lunatic was there with her Diet Coke and salad. He winked at me and strode back across the middle of the room that served as a dance floor on weekend nights. I hadn't tried it out yet, but there's always hope, I thought. But Lunatic would critique, so there you go.

After taking a birdlike sip of her drink and picking at her salad, she said, "You go ahead. Eat. I think it's cool to watch a big man eat."

"What are you doing in Rockbluff, Suzanne?" I asked in a loud whisper, leaning toward her and securing eye contact despite a desire to take in the front of her purple cardigan, open quite a ways down, revealing stunning cleavage and the edges of a snow-white, lacy camisole. I didn't fool her.

"There are some wonderful views around here," she said, an impish smile on her face.

I said nothing. Looked up. She went on.

"For instance, gazing downstream from that beautiful centerpiece bridge, one might see all kinds of interesting objects. Like a dead woman," she whispered. She picked up her fork and diddled around with her salad, then selected one small piece of lettuce and placed it delicately in her mouth. She was not wearing lipstick. No need.

"Who told you that?"

"You don't have to raise your voice, Thomas. But it's interesting," she said, "that you didn't question my remark. Just," and then she lowered her voice to sound gruff and masculine, "just 'Who told you that?' You crack me up, Thomas."

"*Interesting,*" I said, "that you didn't answer *my* question."

"I never divulge my sources. Without them, I wouldn't win all those awards and receive accolades from all over the country for my story about you and all that interesting stuff that happened here a while back." Then she dug into her salad.

I understand what passes for journalism these days. A writer has to have sources she won't give up, even to the point of being jailed for withholding names. I get it. I also have to admit that she did a credible job on all the troubles I ran into over a year ago and, even though I didn't cooperate with her, enough people did, and she took it to the bank. Awards, keynote speaker gigs at big conferences, and interviews on all the networks followed. A big book deal soon after the fireworks ended.

The sensationalism of her coverage sold papers and her book. I heard that she even got to sit on the curvy couch with the hosts of *Fox & Friends*. A brief big deal nationally until the next rock star overdosed. Time enough to get rich and independent.

"Okay," I said, after starting in on my second Looney Burger, "so you know. What's so newsworthy about a simple suicide? As far as I know, she wasn't famous."

"What's *newsworthy* about a simple suicide is that it happened in this crime-infested, quaint village. What makes it *sensationally* newsworthy to me is that *you* found the body, in the middle of the freaking night, Thomas. When everyone else is sleeping! There be intrigue about, boy-o, for that simple reason."

And then she giggled, snickered, and laughed out loud.

"What?"

"You're a real piece of work, Thomas. So close-mouthed and such a lousy liar."

"I didn't lie. I believe I just mentioned suicide, just because that's likely what it was."

She stopped laughing. "Look, you know me, and you know I'll get to the bottom of this. I'm already ahead of the local constabulary, far ahead of your little weekly newspaper, and miles beyond the national media. I'll get this 'suicide' figured out, and I'd love to work together with you in finding out what exactly happened."

"Who told you about the body?"

"None of your beeswax, bub," she said. "But knowing you, you'll find out eventually."

She gave up on her salad and pushed it away, took a sip from her soda, leaned back and stretched up her arms, and locked her fingers behind her head. Her lovely topside lifted in a kind of poetry that goes beyond any poor language to describe. She unlocked her fingers. Her hands returned to the table separating us. She was wearing a dazzling opal ring. New, I think. All that fame. All that income. Next thing I know, she'll have a tan in February.

"You know, Thomas, this little town of Rockbluff, jewel of the Whitetail River, is making me famous. How the hell are you people able to generate so many luscious stories in such a small place in such a short period of time? This is like that old TV series *Murder, She Wrote*. I learned one thing from watching those reruns: stay away from Jessica Fletcher—wherever she goes, murder follows. And you're just like her.

"And, by the way," she said as I continued to work on my meal, "I have looked into your past, and imagine, I discovered there are little security blocks everywhere other than the fact that you sang in the junior church choir in Clinton, rescued stray cats and dogs, played football and basketball for the River Kings, and got thrown out of school once for fighting in the hall. Oh, and you enlisted in the military right after high school and went to some kind of Navy boot camp in California.

"Then, imagine this," she said, lowering her voice again and propping her bosom on the table, nearly brushing her salad aside, "I can't get any deeper into your past. And considering my resources," she went on, shifting her weight, "that's saying something."

"Once again, your sources are inaccurate. Remember when the troubles took place last year, and you said your sources said I called in the nine-one-one call? Remember that?"

"Yes." Attitude. Petulant.

"And it turned out that the caller was Mrs. Soderstrom? Not me?"

A look that would chill a serial killer.

"Well, you need to know I was never in my junior church choir. Another error in your reporting. And I don't rescue cats."

"I wasn't being *literal*, Thomas. Jeez, lighten up a little."

"But I've improved on hospitality, haven't I? I mean, I bought that lunch you're ignoring and I'm talking to you, aren't I?"

"Yes, but that's your beer talking.'

"Ale talking. Belgian ale." I finished off my final Three Philosophers.

"Let's change the subject," she said, leaning back against the booth and folding her arms under her chest. "I could make you famous, you know. If we worked together, we might make things happen. It could be fun, Thomas."

"I had my taste of fame after you wrote your stories about me. I couldn't step outside my home without some nutjob wanting an interview, or a photograph and an interview, or money, or even some endorsements for shotguns. Look, all I want is peace and quiet and to be left alone, and you damn near ruined it for me. You DID ruin it for a while. And now you're back." I finished my second Looney Burger.

She raised her hands in surrender. "Alright, alright, I apologize, Thomas. I'll admit I got a little pushy with the story, and I'll even admit I might have emphasized some elements of the story that would have been just fine by themselves, and . . . "

"You *sensationalized* parts of the story! You made me sound like a death machine – not a person. I've had three men at different times come into this place and want to fight me, and when I told them to go away and they didn't, Mooning had to throw them out, all because of that charming little line in one of your follow-up reports about, 'if there were a Tough Guy Contest for northeast Iowa, Thomas O'Shea would easily win.' That brought 'em out of the bushes, Suzanne. Thank you for that."

"I'm sorry."

"And when those guys went outside, they waited for me. Each of them, weeks apart, waiting for me in the parking lot outside."

"What did you do?"

"I defended myself. What do you think I did, call for help?"

"Did they end up in the hospital?"

"That's beside the point. They were just young punks, wanting to make a rep by working me over for some kind of street cred. They didn't even know how to fight. And you put them there. Shame on you."

"I said I was sorry, and I am."

"Why do you suppose I don't believe you?"

"History. Which is just that – history. I really do think we could work together, but I can let that go. For now," she said.

"I am not one bit interested in working with you. *Reporters*," I muttered, tossing in a little contempt in my tone.

"I'm not a reporter any more. I'm not even an investigative journalist, Thomas. I'm a *writer*. Nothing more, nothing less."

"I saw your book on display in Bednarik's Books. I think everyone in town bought one."

A smile broke brightly across her face. "What did you think?"

"I didn't read it."

Her smile drifted away. "Did you buy it?"

"No."

I looked out the window. A rich, vivid, red and orange sunset was showing off, its vibrant colors a backdrop for the trees denuded of foliage, their stark outlines against the burning sky like a Japanese print. I looked back at her face and saw the disappointment there and understood once again despite her hurt feelings, maybe *because* of hurt feelings, that she was a beautiful woman.

"If you buy a copy I'll sign it for you," she said, the hurt lingering in her eyes. I was suddenly ashamed of myself. No need to be mean.

"Okay," I said. "I'll go down to Bednarik's Books in the morning and pick up a copy, if there are any left."

"Thank you, Thomas. I do hope you'll enjoy it. Read for yourself, then, if you must, condemn me, but not from second-hand knowledge."

"How long are you going to stick around looking for a sensational story to write a book about?" I said, shifting attention from personal topics.

"Until I find out, for sure, what happened to that poor girl. Maybe get a look at the Medical Examiner's report. You *do* have a coroner in this town, don't you?"

I just smiled at her thin condescension.

She said, "May I count on you for some help with this story?" Suzanne has beautiful eyes, I noticed again as she pinned me down with her question.

"You may not. You're on your own, ma'am," I said. I tried not to squirm as she continued her penetrating eye contact.

"*You* found the body, Thomas, so *you* are already in the story. Might not hurt to be an asset instead of an ass. I think we could work together. Pleasantly. You just might discover that I've toned down my attitude a good bit."

"Money helps with that, I guess."

She smiled an I'm-not-getting-anywhere-with-this smile. Then she dug into her purse, pulled out a business card, and slid it across the table between us. It was cream-colored with dark blue writing on it, telling me who she was, that she was a "Writer," and her email and cell number.

"Tasteful," I said.

And with that, Suzanne Highsmith, manipulator of the media, grabbed her purse, slid out of the booth, smiled, and said, "When you step down from your high horse, Thomas, I'd love to get together. I'm warning you that I can be persistent, but without the 'bitch' part in my past."

Then she marched over to the coat rack, tugged on her coat, and rushed out the front door to the parking lot as if she had a million better things to do. I watched through the window as she climbed into her blue Toyota 4Runner, and exited in controlled haste.

While I was watching Suzanne's leaving, Lunatic Mooning came over to my booth and picked up the barely-touched salad and half-gone Diet Coke. "Did you say the wrong thing again?" he asked, his face blank, impassive.

"Apparently."

"She seems like a nice lady. So did the others who thought you were hot."

"Yes, they were," I said, thinking of Liv Olson and Ruth VanderKellen, both appealing and both beyond my ability to try again with them. "I'm beat, Lunatic, so I think I just might mosey along back to the house. Gotcha will be hungry."

"You know," he said, "I told you that Gotcha will always be welcome here. If she were with us now, you could stick around, shoot a little pool, fight off some more beautiful women who ache to get to know you in a biblical sense. I would feed her good meat back in my office and she would like that."

"The Board of Health would strip you of your license for having a dog in here, even one as delightful as Gotcha."

"I'm not sure you really have a dog. You have spoken of her, I have asked you to bring her by any time, and still, nothing. Time passes. Many snows, many moons."

"Many Indian cliché metaphors."

"Is she your imaginary friend?"

"She's not imaginary, and she is a great friend. I'll bring her with me next time if you'll give her a beer on the house."

Lunatic Mooning nodded his head. "I assume she prefers imports?"

"With a few exceptions, yes. Now, I must adieu," I said, handing the Ojibwa owner-operator enough to cover both tabs and a hefty tip.

"Miss Highsmith's staying at The Rockbluff Motel. She's always been straight up with me, Thomas. That's all."

I left, climbed into my giant F-150, and drove home, Suzanne Highsmith on my mind as I pondered two questions: was she maybe lonely in her room at the Rockbluff Motel; and second, where was she getting her information?

CHAPTER FIVE

"Middle age is when you're sitting at home on a
Saturday night and the telephone rings and
you hope it isn't for you."

—Ogden Nash—

I must be getting old. Certainly old-*er*. Genuine fatigue was shoving its way into my body and mind by the time I started out for my little home in the woods overlooking two rivers. It had grown dark while I hung around The Grain. Now, the dark was deeper. And colder. And since I had kept my eyes mostly on the road as I drove past the Rockbluff Motel where I noticed Suzanne's 4Runner parked, all I wanted to do was rest. I drove on home, parked, and went inside.

But my cell phone rang. My cell phone never rings. It knows I hate it, but it's a necessary evil. Like dental floss.

I enjoy the idea of ignoring my cell and just waiting for the person to leave a message. Or call back. Or not, which is best of all. Then I can decide what I want to do. I hadn't even had a moment to mess with Gotcha, or sit down and put up my feet, and there's that interruption from the first few notes of "Three Blind Mice."

It was a brass monkey night. I was well fed. Pleasantly lightheaded from the Belgian ale, but a bit too much on my mind to be able to relax and just go to bed. Suzanne. Dead girl in the water. The Hawkeyes basketball team at Iowa State.

The phone quit ringing.

I walked from the living room into the kitchen and picked up the cell. The call was Ernie. I hit the button to call him back and he picked up right away.

"Thomas! Why aren't you down at the river looking for bodies, man? Or is that what you were doing when I called?"

"You got my email, I see."

"And I read the story in *The Des Moines Chronicle*." I thought I could hear Ernie chuckling.

"I didn't read it. Didn't realize it was in print already." Here we go again.

"Tomorrow's edition on line. Says you and violent deaths are, let me see how they put it, oh yeah, you and violent deaths AND Rockbluff, Iowa are 'inextricably, tragically united'."

"Who wrote the story?" Suspicion lurked.

"It says, just 'Staff'."

"Such B.S.," I said, excoriating journalists in my mind. Then, "Is that why you called, to harass me about my bad timing ever since I moved up here?"

"No. Not at all," Ernie said. "I'm calling to invite you to Thanksgiving dinner wherein we provide all the food and you provide all the wine." He sounded triumphant.

"I'm not sure I can get down there for Thanksgiving, Ernie. That's just a few days away, and I expect I might need to stick around and answer questions from the coroner or some more from Sheriff Payne. Maybe even a legitimate journalist if there's one out there somewhere."

"No problem. We're inviting you to Thanksgiving dinner at *your* place! Thanks! You are such a wonderful paragon of hospitality, something you picked up in the South, no doubt. And your home is well appointed for entertaining, too. I have heard it is stunning, and the view so breathtaking, well, we couldn't turn down the opportunity to have you host the feast."

"Let me talk to Jan."

"Be like that. Here she is."

I could hear fumbling and movement and faint voices, then Ernie's wife, Jan, came on the phone.

"It's my idea, big boy, so you might as well accept it. It's been years since you invited us over, and that was here in Belue, so we're going to help you continue to reassimilate into the wonderful world of the living."

"You have a point. I've been spending much too much time associating with the dead."

There was brief silence from Jan. "Some of whom you appropriately placed in that category, I must say. And a good thing, too. *Now,* start shopping for a nice dinner wine and perhaps a fine brandy for after when we sit on the deck or by the fire, depending on the weather, and reminisce about your glory days in Belue."

"Yes, ma'am," I said. "I'm glad I thought of this."

"So am I, Thomas. You have special gifts and talents, and we've missed them. We'll come by the Tuesday evening before Thanksgiving. That way we can settle in, get a tour of Rockbluff and environs the next morning, including an introduction to that wonderful man, Lunatic Mooning. Then I'll start cooking. I trust that your kitchen is well-appointed?"

"I have a steel sink, a hand pump, and a Swiss Army Knife."

"Everything I could ask for," she said. "Now, I'll give you back to Ernie. Just remember, Thomas, we love you and miss you. I'm excited just thinking of seeing you again. And Gotcha, of course."

Jan Timmons was sniffling when she handed over the phone to Ernie. Italian-American women can be emotional.

He said, "I suspect you'll have everything wrapped up concerning this girl in the river situation by the time we show up on your doorstep."

"If not, I know I can count on you to bring a degree of probity to the proceedings," I said.

"I'll bring my Bible," he said. And with that, we hung up after brief good-byes, looking forwards, and stay warms.

I spent most of the next couple days trying to lose myself in my routine. Morning run, time on the internet, hard workout at the Earthen Vessel Barbell Club and Video Rental, and spending lots of time reading. Susan Boyer, Mark Mustian, and Robert B. Parker mostly. Some Sheri Reynolds. And waiting to see what the authorities in Rockbluff would come up with regarding the girl in the water. I heard nothing but a mention on the local radio saying, "The investigation of an apparent suicide continues."

Two days after my Wednesday discovery, I decided to sleep in and skip my morning run to give my aching knees a rest. I started the coffee and walked with Gotcha down my drive to the blacktop county road where the week's edition of *The Rockbluff Recorder* waited in my mailbox. I tucked it under my arm and walked back up to the house, a few sharp pings of pain in my left knee, probably that pesky ACL that got injured on a mission in Jordan. I don't recommend jumping out of helicopters, even if they are hovering just a few yards from the ground.

Gotcha ambled alongside me except for an occasional foray into the brush to attend to her duties, sniffing and squatting and sneezing.

The morning was crisp and cold, 21 degrees according to the thermometer outside my kitchen window I had glanced at first thing, a habit from childhood and inherited from my mother. All Iowans are required to have thermometers outside their kitchen windows. I liked the air so sharp and brittle that one could almost break off a shard and save it for July, and I found myself enjoying the simple beauty of what's left of my life. I have significant resources, good health, a beautiful place to live, and a few friends I've made over the last year or so.

And I continue to sleep alone. Unless you count Gotcha on the foot of the bed, or on her tuffet on the floor at the foot of the bed. Snoring. I guess for me Romance has become a vagrant on the town.

But I have nothing I really have to *do*. To some, that would be a good thing, and for me for a while, it was. Lately, however, I found myself considering adding something to my predictable routine of eating, sleeping, working out, running, and hanging out at The Grain. Of watching sports on my giant TV and movies I rent from Mulehoff's.

That need to expand my horizons was probably just one of the reasons I couldn't sleep a few nights ago. Probably God getting me ready for craziness. Like finding a murdered girl in the river one night when I went for a walk because I couldn't sleep because I had nothing important to do and God was pulling me into another set of "troubles." God saying, "Here, Thomas, you wanted something to *do*? Try this!"

I am strong, rested, and pretty much recovered from the Soderstrom situation eighteen months back. Why shouldn't I tiptoe into some more yuckiness?

The only problem is that every episode of trouble and pain brings with it, long after everything has been sorted out, a kind of residue of regret that the disasters leave behind. My family gone from me, all those people dead in Rockbluff because I moved up here, and now this murdered child.

I was curious to see if the "suicide" made it to our local newspaper. Apparently *The Des Moines Chronicle* mentioned something about it.

Might even be a coroner's statement by now. I doubt if there was anything else on the agenda of Dr. Jarlsson, County Coroner. Small town. Quiet place.

Back up at the house, I let Gotcha in, filled her water dish, dipped a soupspoon into a jar of creamy peanut butter, placed her meds in the middle of the goop and held the spoon low for her. I watched in amusement as she worked through the peanut butter sticking to the various caverns inside her mouth and chops. Once that was accomplished, she went to work on her food as I filled her water bowl and set it down beside her food dish. I made coffee.

Satisfied that my best bud was taken care of, I pulled out two tubes of hot sausage from the refrigerator, opened them up, dumped them into a big Teflon frying pan, and began browning them, pushing the meat around with a wooden spoon, breaking it into smaller pieces. While that was happening, I stepped away and reached up on top of the refrigerator and pulled down a box of powdered doughnuts and ate three while waiting for the meat to cook. I got out the Bailey's and set it beside my big coffee mug and coffee maker, then returned to the sausage. When it was ready, I turned the pan at an angle over the sink and pressed my spatula on the meat and squeezed out as much grease as I could, running hot water all the while to keep it from coagulating in the pipes leading to my septic tank.

Next, I poured the meat onto a big platter, withdrew a big jug of ketchup from the refrigerator, and set the platter on the small kitchen table. The coffee was ready, so I filled a hefty mug, dumped in enough Bailey's to make the liquid a toffee color, and sat down. After a brief prayer of thanksgiving, I dribbled ketchup over the meat and began eating, unrolling the newspaper that caters to Rockbluff County High School news, yard sales, Help Wanted ads, auctions, bake sales, church bazaars, free kittens to a good home, and blocks of advertising.

But this morning I was looking for news about the girl in the river. And there it was. I took in a forkful of browned sausage chunks and fully opened the paper, then folded it down to the relevant story.

The headline read, "Suicide in the Whitetail." And it went on to state that the nude body of an unidentified, white female of about fourteen years of age had been pulled from the Whitetail River. By Thomas O'Shea. That would be me. It went on to state that, according to Dr. Prentice Jarlsson, Rockbluff County Coroner, there was "no evidence of foul play," and cause of death was drowning. A suicide. The writer of the story asked that anyone with any information about the identity of the girl, or any other details about the suicide, to please contact Sheriff Harmon Payne.

The other front page stories included warning of an unusually-cold winter and a report on two farmers whose feeder pigs had been stolen during the night. Hog rustlers! Bad weather! And a suicide.

I should not be surprised by surprises, but I am. I had assumed Dr. Jarlsson would discover the bullet wounds in the back of the head during a routine examination of the body. I mean, if I could accidentally find them, wouldn't he find them under the scrutiny of a bank of powerful lights that expose everything? Had he no training? No medical degree? No experience?

Of course he had those things. He also had a lie to explain.

I began shoveling in the chunks of sausage with ketchup glaze, interrupting my solid food fueling with long swallows of rich, supplemented coffee. Gotcha had finished her breakfast and come to my side and sat longingly at my feet, her big brown eyes looking up at me in sorrow induced by underfeeding. From my fingertips, I fed her a few chunks of sausage that she took gently. An occasional fembelch followed.

Dr. Jarlsson had lied about the dead girl. Why? To what purpose? Or was he incompetent, simply assuming that the girl had stripped off her clothes in some kind of ritual, eschewing all things worldy, and plunged into the icy Whitetail River to end it all? But two bullet wounds in the back of the head? Did he even check? Of course he did, and now I was so awake I decided to *give up* sleeping. I could kiss it goodbye until I had some answers.

My pendulum of pondering about Dr. Jarlsson swung slowly from ascribing to him incompetence to being engaged in something nefarious. But if the latter, what was behind it? I was itchy to take a little stroll down to the Coroner's Office, so I forced myself to slowly consume my breakfast, carefully dress for cold weather, and then calmly leave the house and lock the door behind me after giving Gotcha a small "going-away" Milk Bone to ease her chronic separation anxiety.

Then I trotted to the truck, climbed in, and drove more rapidly than usual into town.

Although I wasn't positive where Dr. Jarlsson's office was located, somewhere in the back of my occasionally-logical mind I had the impression it was in, or very near, the Rockbluff County Courthouse. I crossed the bridge without looking over the side for another body, then circled the block upon which the courthouse was situated.

It was behind the courthouse in an unassuming, architecturally-ugly single-story red-brick building painted yellow a long time ago with patches of original brick showing through. It looked sterile, and functional. And deserted.

There were no cars or trucks in the four-car parking spaces, one of which had a little sign that read "County Coroner."

Four parking places and he needed his own? Are there that many people who need to see the coroner on a regular basis? I glanced at the clock on the dashboard and then I understood. It was only 8:30. Too early. My desire to learn more about Dr. Jarlsson's findings, and why he came to such bogus conclusions, had urged me to fast forward.

So I pulled into the slot next to Dr. Jarlsson's appointed space. I could make out the sign on the door, which gave his hours as MWF 10 – 2. Not bad. Happy it was Friday, not Tuesday or Thursday.

Since I had an hour and a half to wait, I decided to grab some breakfast at Holy Grounds. I wasn't hungry or thirsty, but some strong coffee and three or four assorted doughnuts would help me pass the time. Balancing my breakfast protein with mid-morning carbs.

And, oh yes, I could swing by Bednarik's Books and pick up a copy of Suzanne Highsmith's book. I had forgotten to ask her the book's title, but I'm sure "Boots" Bednarik would know. I backed out of the parking space and drove away, impatient to talk to Dr. Jarlsson, but not without some trepidation. It's not easy to call someone respectable a liar.

Chapter Six

"No man is old enough to know better."

- Holbrook Jackson

My experience at Holy Grounds bordered on the spiritual. Dark coffee with plenty of cream and sugar along with four doughnuts (two sour cream and two lemon-filled) helped me pass the time until I could go talk to Dr. Jarlsson.

Of course, while I was at the doughnut shop, I ran into two officers of the law. The man was Marty Landsberger, with whom I was familiar. Landsberger, like Steven Doltch, looks like one of those assembly-line Scandinavian/German men who model skiwear and endorse snowmobiles.

The woman was not Scandinavian. She was short, dark-haired, brown-eyed, and looked like someone who might model makeup and fashion accessories. She wore small, silver earrings of an indeterminate design and a red headband that pushed back her curly black hair, the ebony locks and accessory complementing each other. The officers sidled over to my booth after they got their coffee and doughnuts (one for her, three for him), to say hello.

"Morning, Steven," I said. "Have a seat. Who's your chaperone?"

"Good morning, Thomas. I want you to meet Deputy Penny

Altemier, new to our department. Deputy, this is Thomas O'Shea, a citizen good at finding bodies."

I stood and took her hand. Strong, confident grip. I said hello. She gave me direct eye contact with brown eyes that might be the most intense and beautiful I have ever seen. "Stunning" is the word. We all sat down at my booth. I asked Penny where she was from since it was obvious she was new. She took a tiny bite from her plain doughnut, which she had cut in half with the plastic knife on the plate. Then a bird-sip from the coffee, black.

"I'm from Dubuque, originally," she said.

I don't think she was twenty-five, but she had the confidence of someone much older and more experienced. Her lips were full and sensuous, her nose a bit prominent, her chin strong. Her field jacket, like Marty's, was unsnapped and I noticed that her figure looked proportional, at least what I could see.

"Did you go to Dubuque Senior or Wahlert High?"

"Senior. Played soccer, not too well, and tennis, badly."

"So, did you ever run into Mike Mulehoff? He tells me that's where he works," I said.

"Well, actually, I had Mr. Mulehoff for American History. Both sections. Great teacher," she said. "Like Marty here," she said sweetly, serving a glance in Landsberger's direction. He caught it and pulled it in.

"Where have you served before?" I asked. I took a bite from my sour cream doughnut, enjoying the heft.

"This is my first job. I'm right out of the Academy. Before that, a couple of years of community college, criminal justice major."

"Well, I'm sure you'll bring justice to any criminals around Rockbluff County," I said.

"From what I understand," she replied, "you pretty much cleaned them out, Mr. O'Shea."

"An exaggeration, I'm sure."

"Well, we'll scoot along," Landsberger said. "Don't want to invade your privacy any more than we have already, O'Shea. You might get annoyed and shoot us."

"Always a pleasure to interface with symbols of power," I said.

The two deputy sheriffs slid out of the booth and stood. Penny said, "A pleasure to meet you, sir," and winked.

I love it when women wink at me.

"Give us a call if you spot a crime," she said, turning away. Marty smiled at her and then they left. She took his arm in hand as they departed, Marty munching on his second doughnut and Penny glancing up at him in admiration, I guess. Friendly.

When it got to be 9:30, I got up, left five dollars on the table, and took my bill up to the cashier. Her name is Margo and she's a well-rounded lady with frizzy red hair and a big smile squeezed out from between chubby cheeks. Her complexion is florid and I worry about her blood pressure.

"Have a blessed day," she said, taking my left hand in her right, and pressing my change into my other hand.

"Same to you, same to you," I replied.

I walked two doors down, past a second-hand clothing store ("Back to the Future") and a shoe repair shop ("Sole Proprietor") and enjoyed the high cultural literacy rate of Iowans. Next was "Bednarik's Books" and it was a small relief to have such a straightforward name to a bookstore.

The outside of the store looked like it belonged on Dagon Alley from the Harry Potter stories. It had a window with several displays of best-sellers and regional books, a couple of handbills inviting citizens to a reading by a local poet, to be followed by a wine tasting and autograph opportunity, and a t-shirt that one could purchase. The t-shirt was bright blue with gold letters with the exhortation: "So *Be* Stupid; Don't Read."

When one strolled inside, a little bell jangled over the door. The interior of the shop had shelves of books neatly divided by category – Used, Best Sellers, and Paperbacks in Fiction, then other areas marked off for poetry, travel, religion, and so forth. It was a little dark inside, and Boots had situated several overstuffed chairs in various locations with reading lamps on small tables nearby. A little nook had coffee and tea available for a small donation.

I waited a few feet away from the counter behind which stood Bednarik, next to a cash register, waiting on a customer. A tall wooden stool was also behind the wooden counter, and an enormous tortoise-shell cat slept on a thick, embroidered pillow on a shelf. A hand-lettered sign near the cat read: "Pet Bartleby At Your Own Risk."

I had been in Bednarik's twice before, and was impressed with his inventory. He had paperbacks, hard covers, classics, and a few rare books, which he called his hobby. On my first visit I had bought or ordered every Robert B. Parker book I did not already own, and my second time I had just browsed, purchasing only a used hard copy of *Catch-22*.

The customer, a man in his sixties wearing a gold and black Hawkeye stocking cap, a worn leather jacket, and wool trousers, had just asked, "Where can I find the self-help books?" to which Bednarik replied, "If I told you, that would defeat the purpose, wouldn't it?" Both men laughed and I found myself smiling as the store owner pointed in a direction toward the back. The man turned and walked by me, smiling. I nodded and he went on by.

"What'll it be, Thomas O'Shea?" Bednarik asked, demonstrating his habit of calling people by their full names. His first name was Benjamin, but everyone called him "Boots" because he had been an all-state kicker in football for Rockbluff High School, then kicked for Coe College in Cedar Rapids.

"I guess I need to pick up a copy of Suzanne Highsmith's book."

"Ah-ha! I was wondering when you were going to stop by for your own copy of *Something Rotten in Rockbluff*. Hate the title, but I love the sales. I thought maybe you bought one from Amazon or one of those outfits. Or a Kindle version."

Boots was wearing a blue shirt with a button-down collar and a darker blue cardigan, buttoned over his small paunch. The cuffs of his shirt stuck out from the sweater's sleeves. The cuffs were white around the edges where they were frayed.

"I saw Suzanne Highsmith the other day and promised I'd buy the book," I said. Boots reached into a cardboard box behind him and produced a hard-cover copy of the book.

He handed the book over. "I'll bet she promised to autograph it, too." I reached for my wallet. "That'll be two hundred fifty-seven dollars even," he said with a straight face.

"All I have in cash is twenty-seven dollars," I said, seeing the price on the sticker.

"That'll work, seeing as how you're one of the principals in the story. I have a copy Suzanne signed for me. Would you kindly sign, too, right next to her autograph?"

I paid for my copy and tucked it under my arm. "I've never been asked for my autograph before," I said, trying to figure out how I felt about it. I really couldn't turn Boots down. Too nice a guy. "But I'll be happy to sign for you."

Boots grinned, reached under the counter, and produced his own copy, handing it over. He handed me a Sharpie, then studied my hand as I opened the book to the second page and wrote next to Suzanne's signature, "Best wishes to my friend, Boots Bednarik," and signed and dated the comment. Suzannes' signature included the inscription, "Thanks for the memories, handsome" and the date. I handed the book and Sharpie back over the counter.

"I'll put this on E-bay today!' he said. I gave him a look. "Just kidding! Just kidding!"

"See you around, Boots," I said, heading for the door.

"If you don't turn square."

I jangled the doorbells and strode over to my truck, tossed the book onto the passenger's seat, fired up the engine, and drove over to have a chat with Dr. Jarlsson. His car was parked in his reserved space. No other cars. That was good, I thought, because our conversation needed to be private.

I parked and went in. The office was tidy and spare. No receptionist, just an open office with file cabinets and a big oak desk, a refrigerator, microwave, and a handful of framed photographs of family, I guessed, given their strong resemblance to each other. Dr. Prentice Jarlsson sat behind his desk, his head in his hands. His hair was unkempt and his tie was loose. Jarlsson looked up with fear in his face which remained when he saw me.

"Hello, Prentice."

"Oh, hello, Thomas. What brings you here so early in the morning?" He ran his fingers through his thinning, brown hair and adjusted his glasses. Twice.

"I was curious about the dead girl I found in the river. The paper said it was a suicide. That right?"

Jarlsson's shoulders slumped and he stood up from his chair, touching his fingertips to the edge of his desk, as if for balance. He looked up at me from above his glasses. He said, "That's right. Clear case. Water in the lungs."

"When you examined the body, did you find anything peculiar that might have led you to believe she had *not* drowned herself, Prentice? Just wondering."

His face visibly reddened and his body trembled. "I know what you're up to, Thomas, and I'm telling you to leave it alone. I've taken care of the poor girl's Cause of Death and that's it. That's legal. I don't need you coming around here stirring things up. Why the hell can't you just leave well enough alone?"

I like Prentice Jarlsson, so it bothered me to see him so much on the defensive, but I couldn't let it go. Not after what I knew.

"I can't leave well enough alone because that girl had two bullet holes in the back of her head, Prentice. I guess you just overlooked it."

Jarlsson looked down at his desk and moved some papers around, then back to where they were. Then he rearranged them. Alphabetically or chronologically? He readjusted his glasses again.

"I'd like to see a copy of her autopsy report, please," I said.

"Unless you're family, which you are not, I can't do that. Privacy issues," he said, seeming to be fortified by escaping into regulations.

"Okay, Prentice, but you can release a summary of your findings. That's public record."

He gave me a severe look, angry, and afraid. He spun around in his swivel chair to his computer on a side table, moved the mouse around, clicked on something, and hit a button. His printer whirred and produced a piece of paper. He stood and stalked over to me, looked at me for a long time with an expression I could not identify, then shoved the paper at me and said, "Now get out, Thomas. Please."

I looked into his eyes and said, "If there's something going on with you, I can help, Prentice. Seriously."

"Everywhere you go, Thomas, there are bodies. I don't want mine counted among them," he said. Then Dr. Prentice Jarlsson turned and left the room, disappearing into the interior of his domain.

I looked at the paper he handed me. It was an official Coroner's Report dated 12:30 AM today, Friday. It read:

The body of an unidentified white female was removd from the Whitetail River by Thomas O'Shea, passerby, at approximately 2:30 AM on wednesday, November 17. The deceased was naked when she was found and brought to my office at 3:30 AM by EMS staff. The leceased appears to be approximately fifteen years of age. There areno identifiable marks on the body and there was no jewelry on the body. No tattoos. A thorough examination revealed water in her lungs which indicates clearly that the cause of death was due to drowning. **No indication of fowl play.**

There were no personal effects except for one very small silver earring taken from her left ear, identifiable as a tiny eagles head figure with an attached selver feather.

Fingerprints were taken of the deceased for purposes of identification.

Signed, Dr. Prentice Jarlsson, D.O.
Rockbluff County Medical Coroner

I thought about the "Fingerprints were taken of the deceased for purposes of identification" note and decided to go see if Sheriff

Payne had run them yet. And I wondered about all the spelling and mechanical errors in the report. And why the bold font on the "No indication of fowl play" statement with "fowl" instead of "foul"? Was he exonerating poultry? Not to mention the "no jewelry" and "one small earring" contradiction. I didn't remember Jarlsson as having problems with clarity because I had seen his Medical Examiner's Reports on the two men I shot and killed in my home thirteen months ago. In fact, I remember the reports as being meticulous in presentation, succinct, professional. And another thing; his signature on the report he handed me was illegible. I remembered it from before as readable, at least for a doctor's signature. I looked around the office one more time. The place was neat and orderly and business like. There was a photo of Jarlsson shaking hands with the Governor of Iowa, and another photo of him posing with Ernie Banks, still in his Cubs uniform. A couple of plaques for meritorious service from the Elks and the Kiwanis Club.

I decided to go see Harmon Payne.

As I turned to leave, I opened the door to the minimalist parking lot and met Suzanne Highsmith, writer. "Saw your truck outside, Thomas," she said. "And how are you this fine mornin', and what are you doing here, may I ask?"

Apparently she'd been sleeping well. There was a glow about her, and her breath, which I could see in the cold air, was sweet.

"I was wondering when you'd show up again. Heard you were still in town," I said, holding the door open for her, yet standing in her way.

"I've been holed up in my motel room, writing, Thomas. And again, I ask, what are you doing here?"

"I have the same question for you. There haven't been any gunfights, no shootings downtown, nothing like that."

"Oh, I just thought I'd see what the Coroner's Report said about the floater you fished out of the river the other morning."

"She was a young girl," I said. "Not a floater, please."

Suzanne's eyes lost a bit of their fierce hardness. "I know. Sorry. I wasn't there."

"Well, let me get out of your way. Dr. Jarlsson is in, but he's not in a very conversational mood. What did you want?" I asked, folding his report over in my hand and sliding it into my hip pocket.

"What's that!" she said, her eyes locking on where the report had gone. "Thomas, what is that?" She tugged at my hand and it felt nice, even through her leather gloves.

"It's the Coroner's Report Summary signed by Dr. Jarlsson. I doubt he'll give you a copy. As I said, he's a bit of a grump today. But I wish you well."

"I'll buy you dinner if you make a copy for me. There's a copy machine in the Rockbluff Motel Office," she said. "A very *nice* dinner."

"There's a copy machine in my house, too. But I'm keeping this one to myself."

"You know I'll get my own, don't you?"

"But not as quickly as I did."

"He has to give me a copy. Public record. I'd hate to threaten him with legal action," she said.

"That would be tacky."

"Let me through, Thomas."

"He's retreated to private areas."

"I can be very patient," she replied, and slipped on by me.

"Good luck, Suzanne."

She just waved a hand behind her as she entered the offices. I continued on out to the parking lot and climbed into my truck. While

I was re-reading the note, Dr. Jarlsson emerged from a door at the side of the building, gave me a grave look, jumped into his four-years-old gray Camry, and took off, bumping my fender. We did not exchange insurance information.

I knew Suzanne would be rushing out the door, so I put away the report, started up my truck, and left, heading over to have a conversation with Sheriff Payne. I decided to share what I knew and see what information he could offer. No point in tailing Jarlsson. He'd probably drive into a tree out of nervousness.

In my rearview mirror, I saw Suzanne burst from the front door, throw up her hands in frustration, and wave at me to come back. I pretended I didn't see. That's all I need, saddled with Highsmith while trying to help figure out what the hell was going on in peaceful, bucolic Rockbluff, Iowa. I headed for the courthouse, and Payne's offices underneath, troubled greatly that I had forgotten to get Suzanne's autograph on my copy of *Something Rotten in Rockbluff*.

CHAPTER SEVEN

"You can't trust anyone with power."

—Newt Gingrich—

"I'm glad you're sitting down," I said as I entered the offices of the Rockbluff County Sheriff's Department.

Harmon Payne looked up from behind his desk. Deputy Steven Doltch, who was standing with a sheaf of papers in his hand, looked at me with a kind of smirking expression and then looked at Payne. Then sat down to his computer.

"Now what have you done?" Payne groaned. "No, wait! You've solved the case of our young suicide. THANK YOU, Thomas!'

"There's no time for sarcasm." I walked over to his desk. He used his foot to push out the banker's chair next to his desk. I am more familiar with that chair than I'd care to admit. I sat down. Doltch shook his head and turned to his computer.

"Coffee, Thomas?"

"No. I'm about to burst as it is. Did you see Dr. Jarlsson's Medical Coroner's Report on the dead girl?"

"Of course. He faxed it to me in the middle of the night. Why? What's wrong with it?"

I took a deep breath. Might as well be truthful right up front. Time's winged chariot waits for no one. "It's a lie."

Payne sat up straight. Doltch froze at his keyboard. I had their attention.

Payne made a give it to me gesture with his hand. "Talk to me."

"The report says she drowned. Not so. She was murdered."

"And you know this because . . . ?" Payne asked.

"When I pulled her from the river, Harmon, and set her on the bank, I repositioned her head to a more, I mean, well, a more *comfortable* position. And when I touched her head, I found two bullet holes in the back of her skull."

Doltch snorted. He said "You made a corpse's head more comfortable? A freaking *corpse*? That takes the cake."

I ignored him.

Payne asked, "Why would Prentice lie, Thomas? He's a good man. A friend of mine. Decent, hard working, fine family."

"You tell me."

Payne paused. "Are you sure about the bullet holes? Could it have been places where she hit her head coming downstream? It's a bit rocky on the northern reach of the Whitetail."

"I know a bullet hole when I see one. When I feel one."

Payne slowly nodded his head. "I believe you do."

"This is so much bullshit!" Doltch said from across the room. "Dr. Jarlsson's report said the girl died of drowning, not from gunshots. It was a suicide, not a murder. That's good enough for me. O'Shea, you are just so full of it. Are you going to believe this guy, Sheriff?"

"I believe he believes the girl had been shot in the head, murdered," Payne said. "But let's not get our panties in a wad before we know anything for sure. I'll give Prentice a call and see if I can take a look at the body."

"Dr. Jarlsson took off right after I talked to him this morning," I said.

Payne looked pained. "There you go again, Thomas, jumping the tracks and going out on your own investigation. We've talked about that. I respect you, but you do burn my butt when you go charging off. Now, dammit, leave this to me. A simple phone call, or just stopping by here for free coffee and a chat about your suspicions would have been fine. First you moved the body when it wasn't your place, and now you're nosing around in law enforcement business when you aren't authorized. So, please, go home, or stop by and see our friend Moon at The Grain. Drink some beer, take up macramé or something. I'll check things out and get back to you. Got it?"

"It makes me nervous, but I'll submit to an authority greater than I."

I ignored Doltch as I left the office. He was fuming, but he'd get over it. One thing I'll give him, though, that overrules his emotions, and that is he is loyal to his people. First at the Soderstrom Farm months ago when he resented my remarks about the dead Hugh Soderstrom, Doltch's friend and former teammate, and now, with the County Coroner, with whom he probably had a good relationship, too. I admire loyalty.

So I left, fully intending to obey Payne's directive. I drove back over the double-arched limestone bridge that had become so dear to me, and headed for the Hy-Vee to get wine for Thanksgiving, and to visit the small liquor store next door for that bottle of brandy Jan wanted.

I took a long walk on Saturday, watched three college basketball games, and began reading Ken Follett's latest 1,100-page novel. And mostly, I behaved myself, even though Harmon Payne had not called, e-mailed, or spoken to me about his promised conversation with Dr. Jarlsson. I stayed away from Rockbluff's environs except for Sunday worship services at Christ the King Church. Carl Heisler preached a grace-filled sermon surrounded by praise songs that bring tears to my eyes, if I let them. I spoke with Carl and Molly briefly after the service, turned down their invitation to Thanksgiving dinner and told them why.

After Sunday worship, I swung by Subway and ordered a foot-long meatball sub and took it home, sharing the last bites with Gotcha. After a nap, I just whiled away the afternoon. Still nothing from Payne.

I tried everything to get my mind off his lack of communication. Around ten-thirty Sunday night I decided just riding around a bit in my truck was irresistible, so I put on a sweatshirt and my Navy pea coat, gave Gotcha a going-away treat, got in my truck, and drove into Rockbluff.

My plan was to simply drive around town, enjoying the ambiance of a lovely little village on a quiet early-winter's night, maybe drift by the Coroner's Office in my meanderings. When I actually drove by the yellow-brick building, it looked to me like the front door was ajar. So I turned in and shone my headlights on the door and, sure enough, it was open just a crack.

Well, if God didn't want me to go investigate, why else would the door be beckoning me to have a little innocent look-see? One has to be spiritually discerning to interpret signs and wonders, and I am. Sometimes. Depending on the weather.

I killed the lights and shut down the engine and got out of my truck. I crept up to the front door of Dr. Jarlsson's office and pushed open the door with my fingertips, wishing I had brought Elsie the shotgun with me.

The office was dark. I swept my open left hand against the wall, searching and finding a switch. I flipped it up and light flooded the office. There were papers all over the floor, desk drawers wrenched open and bent or broken, and broken picture frames strewn about.

The two file cabinets were tipped over onto their twisted metal drawers, and the computer that I had seen just a couple of days before was gone.

I decided to take a look into the lab. Its door was slightly ajar as well, and there was no light shining from within. I crossed the office, crunching broken glass underfoot and nearly slipping on papers. There was enough light in the office projecting into the lab for me to find the light switch. I turned on the lights. More of the same.

The first thing I noticed was the metal examination table in the middle of the room, but then I saw to my left the wall of compartments where bodies were kept in refrigeration until their disposition to families, or friends, or the State. Three of the doors were open and empty. The other two were closed.

I've been around plenty of dead bodies, so I was not fearful of peeking inside the closed compartments. They were empty, too. The body of the murdered girl was gone. It was enough to make me think maybe something was amiss. Hard to fool an astute observer like me. I walked deeper into the examination room to see what else I might discover before the sound of glass crunching underfoot behind me disrupted my thinking.

"Stop right there, don't move. Raise your hands high over your head!" I recognized the booming voice of Deputy Steven Doltch. Still, I obeyed. Sometimes I can follow instructions. I turned around. Halfway in my rotation to greet The Face of the Law, Doltch shouted, "Don't turn around!"

Then he recognized me at the same time I recognized the Glock pointed squarely at my chest. Upon seeing who I was, I had hoped he would lower his weapon. He did not. A twisted smile crossed his handsome face.

"It's the curious Thomas O'Shea, is it now?" he said with a decent attempt at an Irish brogue.

"As I live and breathe, Deputy."

"What are you doing here—in the middle of an obvious crime scene?"

"Would you please lower your gun? You make me nervous. I have no idea if you're proficient in firearms or not, and I'd hate to have it go off in order to learn that you are not."

"Always with the attitude," he muttered. He did not lower the weapon. "Turn around. I'm going to cuff you."

I lowered my arms. "Is that really necessary?"

"Hands back up! And don't move!"

I complied and Doltch came over, holstered his weapon, spun me around in a rather rude manner, pulled down my hands and jerked them behind me, shooting pain through my shoulders. I grimaced but he didn't see. What a relief that was.

Then he handcuffed me. I have an irrational fear of having my hands immobilized behind my back because just about every time it's happened, something bad follows. But not always, so I tried to mask my nervousness.

"You're under arrest for breaking and entering, trespassing on government property, and interfering in a police investigation." Then he read me my rights.

"I didn't break and enter. The door was already open."

"Let's go, dickhead."

Doltch put his hand on my shoulder and shoved me, but I shoved back in protest of his unnecessary use of muscle.

"Oh, boy," he said, "you thinking about resisting arrest? I wish you'd give it a shot."

"Even in my restricted condition and advanced age, you don't want that," I said.

Doltch chuckled, not realizing that in five seconds I could have him in pain on the floor. A knee to the groin, another knee to the face when he bent over in pain, and a sudden half-turn and stomping on his right instep, collapsing the arch, would do it. Tempting though it was, I resisted the impulse. He was just doing his job, albeit a bit overboard.

He turned out the lights and shut the front door to the office as we left. Shoving my head down, he put me in the back of his cruiser, and we drove in silence to the Sheriff's Department in the basement of the Rockbluff County Court House. I leaned forward and looked at the clock on the dash. It was 11:15 PM, way past my bedtime.

Doltch parked in the official parking lot behind the Court House, pulled me out of the back seat and, hand on arm, marched me around front to the limestone steps leading down to the Sheriff's Department. At the top of the stairs we hesitated, then a hefty shove in the middle of my back got us started again.

Was he trying to push me down the stairs? Did he want me to fall? In any case, I was able to resist, grateful that I was in good shape. I wondered who would be on duty so late on a Sunday night, but I quickly found out as Deputy Penny Altemier got up from her desk and came around as we entered the lavish offices of the Rockbluff County Sheriff's Department.

"Caught myself a little lawbreaker, Deputy. I think we should book him and let him enjoy the hospitality of our jail overnight," Doltch said. He turned to me and said, "Sit down!" I did, leaning forward to keep pressure off my shoulders, which were screaming.

"Thomas, what did you do?" She cocked her head to one side in amusement.

Doltch said, "B and E, Trespassing on Government Property, and Interfering With An Official Investigation, for starters. Maybe Resisting Arrest. Let's go ahead and book him."

Deputy Altemier actually giggled. "Don't be silly, Steven. I think a few questions on site and asking Thomas to come by in the morning would suffice. I'll call Harmon to be sure," she said, picking up her cell before Doltch could protest, and working her thumbs faster than the eye can follow. Ah, youth.

"Harmon, it's me. We've got a situation down here," she said, and went on to review the events.

"Could you get these handcuffs off me, sir?" I asked Doltch, oozing subservience and good manners. I wanted to distract him from the conversation going on between Harmon and the female deputy. I caught Altemier's eye and she gave a little wink and nodded. Doltch didn't see, but he set me loose anyway. I refused to rub my wrists, which were hurting. My shoulders ached, but I didn't let on.

Doltch went behind his desk and began filling out paperwork just as Deputy Altemier buttoned off her phone. I gave her a better look, the Queen of Accessorizing. She was wearing different earrings, diamond studs, and a bright yellow headband that showed off her dark hair.

"Harmon will be right down," she said.

"*Sheriff Payne* is coming down?" Doltch asked.

"On his way," she said.

"This is bullshit," Doltch said.

I slumped a little in my chair, suddenly feeling tired. She noticed.

"Would you like some coffee, Thomas?"

"No, but thank you."

"Coke? Mountain Dew?"

"Nope. But you are very kind."

Deputy Altemier came around from behind her desk, over to me. She put her hand on my shoulder and moved it up to the base of my neck, an intimate touch that surprised me but I didn't resist. In a soft voice she said, "Harmon will be here shortly and we can get this taken care of." I fought the urge to ask her to rub a little lower and to the left. She drifted her fingers along my neck and moved back to her desk.

Five minutes later Payne showed up. Furious. He questioned Doltch in a calm voice and told him to go home, that another deputy would be coming in for the end of his shift and the beginning of the next one. Doltch got his things together and left, shooting me a scalding look, breaking my heart.

Next, my friend Harmon read me the Riot Act, ripping into me for being nosy where I didn't need to be, and threatening to put me in jail. Then he settled down and asked me what happened. He was clearly disturbed about the missing body and the ransacking of Dr. Jarlsson's office, promising to send investigators over to the Coroner's Office first thing after he went down himself and secured the area.

"That girl's body will never be found, Harmon."

"And you know what that means."

"No proof of the double tap to the back of the head."

Harmon made a face and slowly nodded his head. "So what do you think they were looking for, besides the body? I mean, if all they wanted was the corpse, and what evidence might be there that she was murdered, why tear up the place? You say that the computer was gone?"

I nodded. "I think, bad as it is, this goes beyond just a murder. I hate to think. Any idea who the dead girl was?"

He shook his head. "No missing persons reports that come close. All I have are the photographs Deputy Doltch took that night."

"That's it! I forgot all about the photographs. Couldn't we just post them all over the place, in Iowa and Minnesota and Wisconsin. Wouldn't someone see her and identify her? That would get our investigation off dead center! I can't believe I forgot about the photos!"

"Old age," Payne said. "But you're right. *My* investigation might just get things rolling so that *my* people can get to the bottom of all this—dead girl, coroner's office trashed."

"Are you going to get in touch with Prentice? Were you able to find him to talk to him?"

"That's another thing. I can't get him on the phone, just a recording, so I went by his house several times, including odd hours. No sign of life inside, car still in the drive. No sign of Julia, either. I contacted their two daughters and they haven't seen them."

"Yikes."

"Yeah, 'yikes'. Well, I've got some work to do, more calls to make in the morning. We have a situation on our hands, and I want you to stay out of it, except to come in tomorrow and write out a report. We can add it to our collection. You keep this up, we'll have to build a new room just for your crap."

"I'm going, but I just want you to know that, if I find anything, I'll let you know."

"You're a prince among men, Thomas."

"And it's a blessing to be recognized," I said. "And if I shouldn't see you before the holiday, I hope you have a Happy Thanksgiving, Sheriff."

"Get out of here."

So I left.

Chapter Eight

"If you're going through hell, keep going."

—Winston Churchill—

I went home after my arrest and mistreatment from Deputy Doltch, my assistance and comforting from Deputy Altemier, and my interrogation and forced collaboration from Sheriff Payne. After locking my doors, I loaded my shotgun and laid it next to my bed, said my prayers, and went to sleep knowing that my early alert system, Gotcha, was ever vigilant for bad guys in the neighborhood. The sound of her snoring from her tuffet assured me that all was well.

That was my Sunday night.

On Monday morning I got up early and went out on my five-mile run in 23 degree cold. And enjoyed it, getting into a smooth pace, warming up after just a half mile or so, no sharp pains in the knees. And plenty of time to think about the terrible things that were happening once again in Rockbluff, and how I could have sidestepped the icky stuff I knew was headed my way if I had just resisted pulling that girl out of the frigid waters of the Whitetail River. I understood and realized that I could not avoid the future, so I needed to be ready to deal with it, ideally with honor. One must aim high, after all.

I finished my run and let Gotcha out for her duties, then let her back in and fed and medicated her. My four-legged protector and defender taken care of, I fixed myself a light breakfast of sausage links, hash browns, and an eight-egg ham-and-cheese omelet. A big mug of Bailey's Irish Crème and coffee, half and half, served me well as I sat down at my kitchen table and ate, looking out the window over the river valley below. When I finished breakfast, I let Gotcha polish my plate while I rinsed the dishes and then placed everything in the dishwasher and cleaned the Teflon fry pan. Finally, anticipating the arrival of Ernie and Jan Timmons the next afternoon, I dusted, vacuumed, freshened up the two rooms and bath upstairs, and mopped all the tile and hardwood floors.

The house was clean and shining by one in the afternoon, so I showered and dressed and decided to go have lunch at The Grain and touch base with Lunatic to see if he'd learned anything from his heathen network. I didn't expect to bump into Liv Olson.

She was seated at the bar, enjoying some frilly sandwich with lettuce fluttering from the sides of the bread. No French fries were visible. It's sad to see people with unbalanced approaches to nutrition, but there's only so much one can do by example.

I decided to be bold and sit next to the woman I might have loved and who was shot protecting me from an assassin several months ago. Never a dull moment in the Rockbluff dating scene. She turned to see who was approaching her space, and when we made eye contact, I saw several expressions in quick succession spread across her lovely face— surprise, warmth, then a kind of stoic resolve.

"Hello, Liv. Long time no see."

She had been conversing with Moon. He inclined his head toward me and said, with great sadness in his deep voice, "Paleface phrasing?

'Long time no see'? What kind of language is that? Injun in movies?"

We both ignored him. She said, "Nice to see you, too, Thomas. It's been months. Hiding again?"

"The heart is a lonely hunter," I said, "and typically requires isolation. I thought you would still be in school today. When do classes let out for Thanksgiving?" Liv teaches English at Rockbluff High School. She is a petite blonde in her early forties and looks like she could still be a cheerleader. She is divorced, which initially encouraged me, but she turned down my affections for superficial reasons: She thinks I'm a liar and dangerous and not exactly forthcoming about my past. She has moved on to Harmon Payne, fellow divorcee.

"To answer your question, Thanksgiving break begins Wednesday, but I'm taking a couple of personal days to tie in with the holiday. Use them or lose them."

Lunatic said, "What may I fix for you, white eyes? You must be weak with hunger after expending all that energy rummaging through government offices at night."

I groaned.

"Moon and I were just talking about you and, shazam!, here you are. What do you have to say for yourself? Is it true? Did you get arrested by Steve Doltch in the wee hours?"

"Obviously, you know about that. My arrest was temeracious. And obviously, I did not get tossed in jail."

"'Temeracious'?" Lunatic asked.

Without taking her eyes off me, Liv said, "He means his arrest was reckless, or rash."

"I knew that," Moon said, "just testing the English nerd."

"Deputy Altemier let you go?" Liv asked. "She can be persuasive, I suspect."

"To tell the truth, she laughed at Steven's desire to put me in jail overnight, then called Harmon and he came right over. He gave me a tongue-lashing that has scarred my self-esteem, then reverted to being a nice guy and asked me a few questions."

"So what were you doing in Jarlsson's office while the rest of the county was sleeping?" Lunatic asked. "And while you're making up a story, I'll get started on your order. You look hungry." Lunatic turned away after providing a pint of Three Philosophers. He headed for the grill after sliding the tulip glass toward me.

"What do you think of Penny Altemier?" Liv rotated her barstool in my direction. Her question alerted me. There was something female going on. I had a wife and daughters once, and I learned things.

There was a definite chill in Liv's tone, and her eyes suggested an ice storm behind them. Oh. A loaded question; one woman asking me about another woman I had barely met. Tread softly, O'Shea.

"She seems nice enough," I said.

"Jeez, Thomas, you really put yourself at risk of character assassination with that one."

"Why the fishing expedition? Have you met her?"

"Yes, I have, a couple of months ago when Harmon hired her."

"And . . . ?"

Lunatic returned from the grill where my lunch was sizzling on the hot surface and my fries were burbling in hot oil. He said, "Olivia is reluctant to evaluate a woman from a younger generation."

"She *is* young," I said. "A mere child, as it were. Seems friendly enough. She actually winked at me over at Holy Grounds the other day when Marty introduced us."

"I suspect she did. She seems to be attracted to older men."

"What's that supposed to mean?" I asked.

"I think I hear your order calling," Moon said. "I must take my temporary leave."

Just then several customers came into The Grain. One of them was Sheriff Payne, who came up to the bar and stood between Olivia and me. Again. I nodded at him and she smiled at her steady guy, but the smile was lacking something. Warmth. But maybe it was the weather.

"Let's grab a booth," he said. Liv slid off her barstool in a manner I can only describe as "reluctant." Something was going on between them and it was not quite chummy enough to rise to the level of "cordial." Good.

"Have a nice lunch," I said.

"You're invited, too." Payne sounded distracted, maybe even worried about something. Surely, he was about to tell me. From his expression, I suspected it wasn't going to be good. At least I could look at Olivia, which is a good thing. Very good. Especially up close to each other in a booth.

They sat on one side and I was on the other. No one said anything, but when Lunatic brought my two Looney Burgers, fries, and a fresh ale (although I hadn't finished the first one), Harmon invited him to join us. He set down my food and made a signal to Rachel Bergman, his fifty-something chief waitress, she of the flaming red hair and proclivity for patting me on the backside now and then. I like it when women pat me on the butt. She nodded back. I scooched over and Lunatic squeezed in beside me.

I finished my first ale and started in on the second one, cautiously dipping one thick, lemon-peppered, garlic-salted French fry at a time into the stainless-steel vat of ketchup that came with the order. Liv had brought her sissy sandwich with her—and her Perrier.

I looked around the table and thought if someone wanted to paint a picture of us and name it "Apprehension," it would work.

"What is it?" Lunatic asked, putting his big forearms on the table top between us.

"If it weren't for bad news I'd have no news at all," Payne said, echoing the old Hee Haw staple.

"Deputy Altemier has resigned to start her own escort business?" Olivia said.

Payne raised his eyebrows and projected a bit of anger in Olivia's direction. He said, "I can't find any sign of Prentice or Julia, but you knew that. It's like he's disappeared into the ether or something. Not only that, the photos of the deceased girl are not to be found, not in our evidence room, not in any files, not in any desk drawers or under the coffee pot or in any of the patrol vehicles."

"No body. No photo. No Dr. Jarlsson," Moon said, shaking his head. "This dead child becomes more and more obscure. Very sad."

"More bad news," Payne muttered. "Since we can't find Prentice, we don't know if he took the girl's fingerprints. We couldn't find any in his office or exam room."

"Isn't it routine to fingerprint the deceased as part of the autopsy?" I asked rhetorically.

"I'm sure Prentice fingerprinted the girl, but we can't find any record of the fingerprints," Harmon said.

"So how are we going to identify this girl if no one's reported missing, we have no body, no photo to distribute and now no fingerprints?" Liv asked.

"We need something personal to I.D. her," Payne said.

A thought flashed into my mind, a fairly rare occurrence for me, so I couldn't ignore it. I said, "I might have something."

Immediately I had everyone's attention. By the way, it was nice to see Liv looking at me with something other than indifference. Payne looked skeptical. Lunatic was looking straight ahead, so I couldn't read his expression. I heard that he had a facial expression in 6th grade but was immediately chastised for it by the ruling elders of Anishinabe Nation.

"What?" Payne asked.

"I have a copy of the Medical Examiner's memorandum. You do, too, Harmon, and remember how jumbled and scattered and error-filled it was?"

"Yes, not typical of Prentice."

"And remember how he said there was no jewelry, but that there was a tiny earring? That's a clear contradiction, and so is the memo itself with all those misspellings and errors and the illegible signature. I think he was trying to tell us something that he could sneak by whomever it was looming over him to make sure he falsified the report."

"Falsify the report?" Lunatic and Liv asked at the same time. I was amazed they hadn't heard, seeing as how Payne, Altemier, and Doltch had all heard my theory the night before in the Sheriff's Department.

"How falsified?" Liv asked. "Cause of death?"

"You might as well know," Harmon said, squirming in his seat. "Thomas here swears that the dead girl has two bullet holes in the back of her head. That she was murdered."

Liv slumped in her seat and I could feel Moon squirming just a little bit next to me. Then he said, "Prentice said suicide. She'd have to be strong willed to commit suicide by shooting herself in the head. Twice."

"Keep going, Thomas," Payne said.

"Someone murdered that girl. It was supposed to look like drowning, so someone screwed up at the scene of the murder, somehow the body got away from them in the river and she slipped downstream. I don't know. They waited and watched and checked out the news and when they heard that the body had been found here, they knew what they had to do. Find out where the body was, and the local paper told them it was here, and taken to Dr. Jarlsson's lab. Next, they had to get the body back so they could destroy evidence of the murder, and then intimidate Prentice into writing that false report before taking Dr. Jarlsson and his wife 'away.' No body, no fingerprints, and an official report that the girl committed suicide. I fear for the Jarlssons."

"But what about the missing photographs? How did they disappear?" Lunatic asked.

"No idea," I said.

"Thomas," Payne said, his voice low and serious. "You said you might have something. What is it?"

"You have it, too, Harmon. She had a small silver earring. Actually a pair. The report said it was a tiny silver eagle's head with a silver feather."

Moon made a sound. We looked at him.

"What?" Liv asked. "What, Moon?"

"I gave someone in my family an earring like that, one I made myself."

Liv shot me a look and said, "There are lots of earrings out there, Moon. This doesn't mean this girl is someone you know."

"Pretty sure," Moon mumbled.

"It's not enough to go on," Payne said. "If there were only something else, some other way to be sure whether this is your person or not. Something definitive."

My stomach sank as I recalled the swoosh of white hair on the left side of the girl's skull. For a moment, I considered not saying anything, then I had to. Lunatic Mooning is my friend, and I owe him the truth. After all, he saved my life once. So I said, "There was something else that was not in Dr. Jarlsson's report."

"What?" Payne asked.

I said, "The girl had very dark hair, but there was a patch of white on the left side, looked kind of like a Nike swoosh. Prentice didn't have that anomaly in his report. Should have."

Moon slumped and dropped his head. "That girl is my niece. She is Ojibwa," he said, his voice breaking.

CHAPTER NINE

**"Sometimes I go about pitying myself, and all
the while I am being carried across the sky by beautiful clouds."**
—Ojibwa Proverb—

"**M**y niece's name is Cynthia Stalking Wolf. Cindy," Lunatic began, his voice barely above a whisper. "I gave her that earring when she was ten because she was now a big girl, I told her. Two years later, she ran away, and I never heard from her again."

Liv, tears in her eyes, reached her hands across the table to take Lunatic's hands in hers.

"There is only one earring like that," he continued. "I made it for her. It was silver and in the shape of a tiny eagle's head. A symbol for Mi-Ge-Zee. A tiny silver feather was part of the earring. And she's had that streak of white hair since birth. The dead girl is Cindy."

"Does she have family we can contact?" Harmon asked. "Where do they live?"

"Her mother was my sister, Harriet Red Wing," he said, straightening up in the booth. I glanced sideways and saw the face of a man of great sorrow. I looked away. "Harriet was Anishinabe. She died three years ago. Cirrhosis of the liver. Her husband, Lawrence Williamson, was Chalaka, and was killed in a knife fight outside the casino on the Chalaka Reservation about four years ago. He was no good. Susan was an only child, ignored, likely abused, a three-year-old walking alone along the gravel roads of the reservation."

"What do you mean by 'Chalaka'?" I asked. "You're Anishinabe, and Susan was your niece?"

Moon said. "The Anishinabe made alliances with other tribes, such as the Ottawa and Potawatomi. The Chalakas are like that. Some intermarrying among tribes." He took in a huge breath of air and let it out haltingly. Liv and I exchanged glances of pity.

Harmon looked sad as well, but he continued to ask questions. "Was Lawrence Williamson an Indian? Where is the Chalaka Reservation? Up in Minnesota somewhere, isn't it?"

"Lawrence was also Chalaka. He chose a white man's name. The reservation is just outside the small town of Red Oak, about forty miles northwest of Winona," Lunatic said. "The Whitetail River passes through it."

"Why would anyone want to kill Cindy?" Liv asked, squeezing Lunatic's hands. Olivia and Moon have been friends since middle school.

He shrugged his shoulders and shook his head, a hopeless smile passing over his face. "I can imagine scenarios," he said. "She was a runaway, a street kid. Didn't care for the ways of her people, and I can't blame her. Poverty, drugs, alcoholism, and then the casino coming onto the reservation, and you know what that can bring."

"Not much good," Harmon said, sitting upright. "Lots of money, but, inevitably, prostitution, corruption, gambling addiction, drugs."

"Mitigation payments," I added.

"What are mitigation payments?" Liv asked.

"An open door to corruption," I said. "Mitigation payments are monies paid from the casino to local authorities to 'mitigate' the impact of the casino on the local government. The casino goes in with a contract to pay the locals for infrastructure – roads, power, water, additional law enforcement. It can be millions of dollars annually."

"That would be hard to turn down," Liv said.

"Yes," I said, "and the typical response from the locals goes something like this: 'I hate to see a casino come in, but it's hard to turn down the money.' Of course, the casinos provide lots of well-paying jobs for not only Indians but quite a few non-Indians, too."

"It's enticing," Lunatic said, his deep voice soft, "because who really wants to work all day in a fish processing plant, or making souvenirs for tourists and casino customers when you can pull in a good paycheck, and benefits, from the casino's owners?"

Liv said, "Why would the Indians have to make those payments if the casino is on their land?"

"The reservations have a kind of sovereignty, protected by the federal government, it's true," I said, "but they still need local support and the roads need to be built to the casino and building permits, and, again, a need for local law enforcement. Casinos usually have their own security, which is serious stuff, but they need to coexist with the local sheriff's department or police department. And guess who gets the bulk of the mitigation millions? Usually, it's the local District Attorney's office and the local law enforcement budget."

"And that opens the door to a sweetheart deal between the officers of the law and those they are supposed to supervise," Harmon said.

"Uh-oh," Liv said.

I continued. "Of course, those monies go into beefing up the numbers of deputies needed because of the riff-raff that come into the area to feed their addictions, and to the D.A.'s office for more lawyers to prosecute cases arising from the casino traffic."

"And maybe lavish 'professional' conferences in Hawaii," Payne said. "I believe that most of those arrangements are on the up and up, but temptation can be powerful when you're talking about millions."

Lunatic turned his head toward me, looked me in the eye, and asked, "How do you know so much about casinos and mitigation payments?"

"I read a lot."

A brief, rueful smile crossed Lunatic's face. He said, "I must do something to find out who killed Cindy Stalking Wolf. And punish them."

"Let's amend that statement to substitute 'we' for 'I'," I said.

"It is not your place," Moon said.

"I agree with Thomas," Liv said. "We are friends, all of us, and even if Thomas has only been here a little while, he's the one who pulled your niece, Cindy, from the river, and if it weren't for him, her death would be a suicide and not a murder and those scum who shot her would be laughing up their sleeves having gotten away with it."

"What Olivia said," Harmon interjected, "but this has become a murder investigation and a missing persons investigation now that we're searching for the Jarlssons, and even though I would really appreciate your help, please step aside and let me get after this. I know that, no matter what I say officially, you two will probably want to nose around on your own. Don't do it."

"Sorry, Harmon, but I can't leave it to you. This will be handled by me, my people, and you know why," Lunatic said, leveling a look at the sheriff.

"What?" Liv asked. "What? Why not?"

Sheriff Payne leveled a look at Moon and said, "The Ojibwa, the Chalaka, do not trust the white man's legal system. That's why there was no Missing Person's Report coming to my desk, no social workers' intervention, no communication from law enforcement up there."

"I guess I can see why trust is lacking," Olivia said. "Just watch the news. Corruption abounds."

"But you know I'll do what I can to find out everything about this girl, Moon," Payne said, glaring at Olivia.

"I know you will," Moon said, "but you're just part of the white man's system. It is corrupt as a system. Nothing personal."

"Moon," Liv asked, "do you think Cindy might have been involved in some of that yuk that goes along with casinos? Those things Harmon just said—drugs, prostitution?"

"Maybe," Lunatic said, "but that isn't more important than finding out who killed her, why, and where that goes."

"I agree," Harmon replied. "And you are beginning to sound like a law enforcement professional. But we need evidence to prove what happened to her. Keep that in mind."

"Thank you, Harmon," Moon said. "But this girl is family. I can't let it stand." He turned to me, not an easy accomplishment given his bulk and the restraints of space in our booth. "And I am grateful to you, Thomas, for what you have already done for Cindy. Perhaps we can work together to gather information, although as an outsider, you won't get far."

"Why not? I have my ways," I said.

"You're what those on the rez call a 'Chi-mook,' slang for white man. Not a compliment," Moon said.

His voice was recovering from the earlier brokenness, and I could sense a kind of resolve building in his mind. I said, "We'll get those guys. Who can withstand the might of an Anishinabe-Irish confederation?"

"Who, indeed?" he said.

"I must reiterate," Harmon said, "that this is my job, and my department's. We've had this conversation before. Stay out of it, gentlemen."

"I need to get back to work, business is picking up," Moon said.

He started to slide out of the booth but a woman appeared in his way. Suzanne Highsmith said, "This looks like a combination Tribal Council, Sheriff's Department, and 'Concerned Citizens' meeting. What did I miss?"

"Your ride out of town," I said.

Lunatic said, "Excuse me, Suzanne," and headed for the bar.

He held out his hand, and without hesitation, she slipped off her full length blue wool coat and handed it to Moon. He moved away.

Underneath the coat was a pale blue cashmere sweater, a bright blue silk scarf, and snug charcoal slacks. High-heeled black leather boots completed her ensemble.

She slid in beside me and sat down. "Ooh, a nice, warm seat. I'll have to thank Lunatic." She looked around at us, smiled, tossed her long, black braid over her shoulder. "What are you eating?" she asked Liv.

"Heartbreak," she said softly, dabbing a napkin at her eyes.

"We were just leaving," Harmon said, and they both left.

"This is nice," Suzanne said. "Alone at last, and hip to thigh," crowding me a little. I didn't mind. "May I?" she asked, reaching for my second Looney Burger. I nodded. She took a knife, cut the sandwich in two, and slid her half onto a double napkin she'd assembled for the purpose. "Looks scrumptious." And she dug in. She rolled her eyes and mumbled a sound of satisfaction.

"You've never had a Looney Burger before?"

"I've been tempted. They sounded too big, but half of yours is just right."

"That's ambitious of you, eating my food."

"Oh, yeah. I'm hungry after my morning stroll and then writing about what's going on with you since late last night. By the way, did you know, Thomas, that the Rockbluff Motel has *suites*? Three of them. Mine has a roomy bedroom with a very comfy queen-sized bed and big screen TV and a bath with a freaking Jacuzzi! The main room also has a big boob tube and really nice furniture along with a teensy kitchenette. Who would have thought?"

"I stayed there for a few days when I first came to town, but it was just a very plebian single room and bath. I'm not surprised Harry Goodell has suites."

"Who?" she asked over a small bite of her sandwich.

"Harry Goodell. Owner."

"Oh, that cute little darling man! Harry Goodell! He is so *nice* to me!"

"What do you want, Suzanne?" I asked, picking up the remains of my second Looney Burger.

"So much for small talk. Sheesh, I'm trying to be conversational and gregarious, you know, building my relationship with you and accommodating your nutritional oddities, and you try to brush me off. Not very *Christian*, either, if I may."

I ignored her jab at my faith, fighting off the urge to lay hands on her forehead. Suddenly.

I continued chewing my sandwich. I do love Looney Burgers. Between bites, I grabbed a French fry, dipped it into the ketchup, popped it into my mouth. Suzanne was eating rapidly. She reached over and took my Three Philosophers and drank a little. Getting a little brazen now. Risking injury.

"You continue to amaze me, Thomas. I mean, how do you do it? You're just ambling along in the country one day, enjoying the scenery, and you stumble onto the Soderstrom murder and all the garbage that went with it. And you were just trying to help someone. Of course," she said, touching her fingertips to her mouth to push back a little morsel, "the fact that Wendy Soderstrom is a gorgeous woman had nothing to do with it. Then, once again, just minding your own business, in the middle of the freaking night, you see a naked dead girl in the river and haul her out. But, you can't stay out of it. You discover something about the suicide," she said, putting quotation marks in the air with her fingertips around the suicide word, "and you just can't help yourself. You need to nose around when you should be in bed, ostensibly alone, sleeping, or whatever if you're not alone. Next thing I know, you're getting locked up and tossed into the slammer for a few hours for breaking into the freaking County *Coroner's* office, tearing the place apart. You are a bloody wonder!" she exclaimed. "I'd think you'd learn, big guy."

I had finished off the violated remains of my Loony Burger, and the fries that went with it, while Suzanne was rattling on. I had finished off my Three Philosophers, too.

"May I say something?" I asked.

"You just did. But go ahead, be my guest."

"Actually, *you're* the guest here. You ate my food and drank my ale."

"The way you say that, 'You ate my food and drank my ale' sounds very intimate, as if there is some sort of proprietary relationship here. Man. Woman. Food. What could possibly follow?"

"Dessert?"

Suzanne laughed, and it was genuine. It's cool when I can make a beautiful woman laugh. Karen laughed a lot.

I went on, admiring the beauty of the woman whose right hip was pressed firmly against my left thigh. It was a wonder I could utter a coherent sentence, but I did.

"Once again, dear Suzanne, your sources are in error. How in the world did your book find publication with all your inaccuracies? It's a miracle."

"Speaking of which, I peeked into your enormous motor vehicle and noticed my book in the front seat. Would you like for me to sign it?"

"After we leave here. Please."

"Thomas O'Shea said 'please'? See, you *can* be nice!"

"As I was saying, your sources are in error. I was never thrown in jail and I did not break into the County Coroner's office."

"Big deal. You *were* arrested and handcuffed, though, and you were messing around late Sunday night in Dr. Jarlsson's office. Why? Oh, wait! I'll bet it had something to do with that poor girl you found in the river! Obviously murdered, otherwise there'd be no fuss. Aren't you impressed with my deductive skills? Positively Holmesian. So, the girl was murdered, not a suicide. The plot thickens, and I'll bet that little congregational meeting I just crashed was about the details of the murder. So, who did it?"

"No one knows."

"But you suspect. Why would someone murder a young girl and throw her in the river? I am going to find out, and I'll bet you a steak dinner that I find out before you *or* Sheriff Payne. This is going to make another great story. God, people will start coming to Rockbluff, Iowa, booking rooms and suites at the Rockbluff Motel just to see what mayhem you're going to unearth the next time. People will come and follow you around like groupies. If you help me with my book, I'll be sooo grateful, Thomas."

Was that a little pressure I felt from her hip on my thigh? Probably not. Just my imagination. Yes, that.

"I won't help you with your book, Suzanne," I said, "and now

I must bid you adieu." I pushed against her to get her moving as I dropped thirty dollars on the table in front of me. She slid out ahead of me and stood.

"May I sign your copy of my book now? It's handy, right in the front seat of your truck."

I waived at Lunatic as we moved toward the front door. He inclined his head in our direction. His countenance looked better, recovering from the shock of knowing that the dead girl was kin. I took Suzanne's coat from the hook by the door where Moon had hung it. I helped her into the coat while she got up on her tippy-toes and whispered in my ear "Thank you" and smiled, then I opened the door for her and we stepped out together in the sunny, cold, Iowa afternoon.

"It's right over here," I said.

"I know. I told you I peeked."

She followed me to my truck, which I unlocked and then retrieved her book. I looked at the back inside flap to her photo and bio. I said, "This photo doesn't do you justice."

"Oh? Why is that? I was pretty pleased with it."

"You're much more beautiful in real life."

"Thomas, how *sweet*! Thank you! You really can be a nice man!

"I am not a nice man, but sometimes I do nice things."

I handed over the book and she whipped out a Sharpie from somewhere in her little purse. I guess writers always carry a Sharpie so they can sign the occasional book thrust upon them. I don't get the whole autograph thingy. A desire for connection? That, I understand.

She wrote more than just her name, I could tell. Then she blew on her writing, closed the book, capped and shoved her Sharpie back into the depths of her purse. She handed the book back with another big smile.

I said, "Thank you."

"You're most welcome."

"Have a nice day."

"Ta-ta, Thomas!" she said, and walked briskly toward her 4Runner. I watched her walk for a while as she got in and drove slowly away. She waved and winked and I waved back. It was then, when she was out of sight, that I checked out her autograph.

It read: *For Thomas, in memory of all those wonderful nights in Rockbluff, ever yours, Suzanne Highsmith.*

CHAPTER TEN

"Maybe eventually winter will finish our job
for us and end the world in ice instead of blood."

—*Isaac Marion*—

The snow came first as a rumor, then a whisper, finally, a warning. And I embraced it, taking comfort in the beauty of the first snowfall of the winter, and that I was seeing it with Jan and Ernie Timmons safely ensconced in my house.

They had made it earlier than expected, arriving Tuesday mid-morning, inspired to haste by the previous night's weather report at their motel. The leaden sky had begun to puff out an occasional snowflake, delighting them both, south-central Georgians.

I gave them a brief tour of Rockbluff, everyone admiring the double-arched limestone bridge over the Whitetail River. We drove by Christ the King church and they both remarked on its architectural beauty and then said how much they looked forward to meeting Carl and Molly Heisler.

Ernie wanted to see Shlop's Roadhouse, so I drove down that way and turned around in their parking lot, looking lonely with only two pickup trucks parked there. I suggested we grab our lunch right then, service would be faster with so few customers, and Ernie could meet the alluring Bunza Steele, head barmaid and aspiring pro wrestler/med student. Jan shook her head and smiled an exaggerated, threatening smile at my suggestion, so Ernie and I swallowed our disappointment.

"Maybe later tonight, Ern," I whispered, "after Jan's asleep. We can slip away." An elbow to the ribs from Jan.

"We can pray about it," he said, fighting off another elbow.

I sighed and turned my big truck back downtown, driving by the high school, Bednarik's Books, Sole Proprietor, and Holy Grounds Coffee shop.

"How 'bout lunch at The Grain o' Truth Bar and Grill?" I asked.

"Of course," Jan exclaimed, "we need to meet your friend Lunatic Mooning!"

"After present company," Carl said, "the person we are most interested in seeing. I want to see if the man matches the voice on the phone."

"I forgot you have had conversations with the man, invading my privacy," I said.

"And a good thing, too," Ernie laughed. "Now, let's go eat some Looney Burgers."

I found myself looking forward to the weather on its way, picking up a bit, the fragments of snow steadily coalescing and turning into a genuine snowstorm. With a bit of wind to go with it. The big, wet flakes stuck to the windshield so I directed some of the heater there and turned on the intermittent wipers. I wanted the Timmons to meet Lunatic, of course, but I was also eager to hurry back to my house so I could watch the woods fill up with snow, could hear the wind and the sound of flakes against each other in the air and, maybe if the storm was as hearty as predicted, see gentle drifts here and there.

All went well at The Grain, where attendance was a bit down, probably due to the impending storm. I introduced Ernie and Jan to

Lunatic, Rachel, and a bunch of other people, including Gunther and Julie Schmidt (who had given birth to a big boy several months ago); and Olivia Olson, who was sitting with Molly Heisler. Arvid was there, lifelessly slumped over against a window and ignored by Clara, his wife; as were the Deputy Pals, Landsberger and Altemier, and a few acquaintances. We sat in a window booth and had Looney Burgers, fries, and one Three Philosophers each for Ernie and me. Jan had a glass of Coppola Rosso after taking a sip of Ernie's Belgian ale and shaking her head. "Too strong," she said. I explained Arvid.

Our food arrived promptly and that's how it was consumed, amid grunts from Ernie and a steady, "Mmmm" of appreciation from Jan.

"We really should get going," I said, looking out the window. The ground was now covered, white and smooth, unblemished in a thin, pristine blanket. And there was no letup in the storm. In fact, it had picked up in intensity and volume.

"I wouldn't mind waiting it out in this wonderful establishment," Jan said, finishing her second glass of Rosso, "but we might have trouble getting to your drive and then making it up to the house."

"You Southerners," I said, "this won't slow me down, but I don't think we should tempt fate."

"You've done enough of that," Ernie said, nodding at me. "So, let's go."

I left a big tip for Rachel Bergman, then we all drifted over to the bar and shook hands again with Lunatic. He directed his comment at the Timmons. "Please try to keep my pale friend out of trouble."

Without hesitation, Carl said, "Prayer helps, Lunatic."

With that, we stomped out through snow in the parking lot and headed for the truck, climbed in, and started for home. Seeing where the road was presented a minor challenge. The snow plows weren't out yet, and where the road ended and the shoulder began was up for debate. Already, there must have been three or four inches on the ground. The blanket had become a quilt, and quickly.

The snow squeaked as the big tires and serious weight of the truck pressed down on the storm's fresh thickness. We heard the wind howl and Jan scrunched her shoulders like a little kid and exclaimed, "I love it!"

I knew I would have good traction, but the trouble with getting back home now became the problem of dealing with the thickness of the storm, the snow swirling and pouring out from the heavens like a ripped-open goosedown mattress. Visibility became the issue.

"Pretty hard to see," Ernie said.

"This is a beautiful storm," Jan whispered reverently as we slowly met another truck edging down the street. He flashed his headlights as we passed, and we exchanged brief nods, the wildly-extroverted means by which Iowans say hello while driving. My heart soared like the hawk at his demonstration of brotherhood. I flipped on my headlights and flashers in response to his signal. Good to see, but good to be seen as well.

"The first snowfall of the winter," I said, and then I remembered another first snowfall of the previous winter, and Ruth VanderKellen's request.

Jan, who was sitting between Carl and me, said, "What?"

I glanced to my right. She looked worried. I asked, "What 'what'?"

"Something passed across your face. Sadness, when you said this was the first snowfall of the winter. Why sad?"

So I told them about Ruth and her leaving for California just as we were finding each other, and her gift of a cell phone and a note asking me to call her when the first snowfall came to Rockbluff County so I could describe it to her, and her promise to come back the following spring, and stay. Then I changed the subject before the interrogation could begin.

"So, how are Matt and Aaron doing?" I asked, referring to the Timmons' sons. Matt had dated Annie regularly. Mine wasn't the only pain from that accident south of Atlanta.

"They're good," Ernie said. "Matt's at Georgia, thinking about pharmacy and Aaron's a sophomore at Belue High. He talks about seminary."

"You've got to stop him!" I said, panic creeping into my voice, keeping my eyes on the road ahead. "Look what it's done to you!" Everyone laughed. That was a relief, too, believe me. I congratulated myself for steering the conversation away from Ruth VanderKellen and last year's first snowfall, but I knew Jan would come back around to it, circling, looking for clues about the state of my heart, preparing to minister to me like some theological vulture.

We continued to creep along. An old Buick approached us and went on by, the driver raising two fingers from the steering wheel. Another Iowa greeting. The sound of his chains making a steady chink-chink-chink sound.

Ernie leaned over and looked at me. "Was that chains I just heard?"

"Oh, yeah. They work in this stuff."

"Do they leave them on all winter?"

"Nah, just for weather like this. When the streets get cleared later, they'll take them off again. Useful in this kind of storm. By the way, remember Arvid?"

Jan said, "Yes, the guy pretending to be dead in The Grain o' Truth."

"That's his house over there on your right. You can hardly see it, though, the yellow one with the wrought iron fence."

The Timmons looked. The Pendergast mansion was barely visible. The storm was turning into a whopper and I was glad to see it, but I preferred to see it from a warm room with a pint of dark ale or glass of wine in my hand, a roaring fire in the fireplace turning into glowing coals later, the pattern true love takes over time. I slowed to thirty miles an hour and tapped the brakes. No sliding. Good.

"She didn't come back, did she?" Jan asked.

It was easier to talk as I drove the truck into the teeth of what might now be a blizzard. I could not risk eye contact, and I realized, once again, that the Lord does provide what we need at the proper time. In this case, the need to keep my eyes on the road instead of Jan's face. I didn't think I could look into her dark eyes and keep a grip, so I wasn't going to risk it. I hunched forward a little, pretending that it helped me see better into the snowstorm. If we were driving at night, that would help. But we were close to a total white-out, so leaning closer to the steering wheel proved no advantage. Except socially. The wind howled and lightly rocked the truck.

"Thomas?" Jan again. I was going to have to deal with it, something I knew would come up when the Timmons thanked me for agreeing with them for me to host Thanksgiving.

"Alright, I know when I'm cornered," I said. Jan squeezed my arm. "There are three, three-word phrases that have great impact on me. One makes my mouth go dry, elevates my blood pressure, and makes me weep in agony." I went quiet. Several seconds passed.

Ernie broke the silence inside the cabin of the truck. "Alright, I'll bite. What three words are those? 'Pizza without meat?'"

"Close, very close."

More silence.

"Thomas." This from Jan. "No more of this. I know what you're doing, and you know I can be as determined about something as Gotcha. So give it up. What three words cause you pain and fear?"

"The ones that state, 'Some Assembly Required.'"

Both Timmons laughed, but briefly.

I went on. "There are three more that are definitely better, especially spoken by a woman to me. I'm talking about the simple phrase, 'I love you,' and I've been blessed to have heard it for years before it stopped."

"I love you, Thomas," Jan said softly.

"Thank you, Jan, but I'm not talking about agape love, necessarily. I'm talking about eros love, among others."

"Can't help you out there, *brother*," she said, laughing.

"Thanks, dear," Ernie said.

"Well," I said, "*that's* the one I had hoped to hear from Ruth. If things worked out. Which I thought they would, but she substituted three other words when I called her and she picked up the phone." I paused for dramatic effect, of course. And also to help me swallow.

"What did she say?" Jan nudged me with her shoulder, a soft nudge, a kind nudge.

"That would be, 'I found someone,' which is what she said when I dutifully called her to describe that first snowfall about this time last year."

"I'm so sorry, Thomas," Jan said.

"In this context, that's a nice three-worder, even though it includes a conjunction. Thank you," I said. "When she picked up the phone out there in Southern California, she was laughing and didn't know who it was, too busy to check caller ID, and I could hear a man's voice in the background, and I knew, you know, what was going on and then I guess she checked her phone and said, 'Hello, Thomas?' with the kind of nervous, false interest that can mean only one thing. So I went ahead and told her I would like to describe the first snowfall, as she had asked, and then she was quiet. I heard the man's voice in the background asking 'White or red?' and she was shushing him to be quiet."

It was dead silent in the truck except for the steady whooshing of the heater/defroster, and the slapping of the wipers shoving heavy snow off the plane of the windshield.

"She sounded like she was sniffling a little, you know, and then she said, 'I've found someone' and I said to please be happy and she started apologizing and I just quietly closed up the phone. I did, however, keep the phone. Silly to be impractical by throwing it off the deck when it might come in handy sometime, like when wackos call and invite themselves up for Thanksgiving. If I had tossed that phone away, which I more or less considered seriously doing, you couldn't have gotten in touch with me. On second thought, maybe I should have tossed it."

"Oh, Thomas," Jan said. No one spoke again as I nudged slowly through a full-blown blizzard with heavy snow and whipping winds, howling here and there. The truck's instrument panel said it was 22 degrees, so all three elements of an official blizzard were in place – heavy snow, high winds, and sub-freezing temperatures.

The State Road blacktop on my left finally showed up and I slowed down, negotiated the turn, and drove in silence the next mile until my mailbox and driveway appeared in the dense white gloaming, again on the left. My truck easily handled the incline, the gravel surface offering more traction than asphalt. We got out and trotted to the front door, leaning into the wind with our coats pulled up over our heads, protecting our ears and faces. I found myself slowing to look around at the stark beauty of black trunks and branches of the trees in silent silhouettes against the white backdrop.

The house was warm and welcoming, and so was Gotcha. Jan got down on her knees on a thick throw rug covering a section of the polished red oak floor and Gotcha bumped into her again and again, licking her face, nearly knocking Jan over. Gotcha is seriously powerful. Then it was Ernie's turn to remind Gotcha of how beautiful she is, and what an outgoing personality she bestowed on everyone who knew her.

We took off our coats and hung them on a coat tree. I said, "I'll start a fire and let Gotcha out. She won't hang around long in this weather," and I was right. She came back in almost immediately after attending to her needs.

The Timmons hurried upstairs to slip into jeans and sweaters and I fed and medicated Gotcha, leaving her to her dinner, and walked over to the sliding glass door that led out to my deck. I slid the door open and snow that had drifted against the glass fell inside. I bent down and scooped it up, or most of it, and pitched it back outside. Then I stepped onto the deck and slid the door closed behind me.

I live in a beautiful place, and I am grateful to God for it. I am also grateful to Gunther for building the house and Lunatic for telling me about Gunther. I crossed over to the far railing and looked out over the Whitetail River Valley below me and could see almost nothing except the storm and close-by trees, the snow now thick and furious and beautiful. I knew the two river valleys were beyond, hidden by the snowstorm.

I stood there until I was uncomfortably cold, then turned and went back inside. Ernie and Jan had come downstairs. He was looking at the few family pictures on the bookcase in the foyer. She was standing in front of the fireplace, watching the flames lick into the dry wood that had been seasoned for over a year.

"Can I get you guys anything while we're recovering from a few snow flurries?" I asked.

I took orders and came back with brandy for Jan and Ernie, and a glass of red wine for me. Then I went back and gathered up some crackers and a couple of tubs of Pub Cheese, a spreading knife, some Trader Joe's cheese sticks (acquired in Dubuque), and a wooden bowl filled with roasted almonds and cashews. We sat around in front of the fire, pulling comfortable chairs together so we could look at each other and the fire as well. It was cozy, and I felt blessed.

We could not resist talking about the weather. "Jeez, you guys, we haven't seen each other for a long, long time, you drive up here for hours on end, and what do we talk about? The freaking *weather*," I said.

"That's because it's new to us, and it's beautiful and fierce and dangerous," Jan said, sipping her brandy, then sipping again.

"Those last three adjectives describe my bride," Ernie said.

Jan blew him a kiss and patted his leg.

"When Philip Roth came to Iowa as a visiting writer a few decades back, he said one thing he liked about Iowa was that the weather can kill you. He said it made him feel more alive," I said. "You know, every year it's in the news about some old person on a farm, living alone, goes out to check the mail, falls down, can't get up, and freezes to death."

"Sayyyy," Jan said, "how 'bout those Dawgs!"

"I think she's changing the subject," Ernie said as Jan took another sip from her brandy. The snifter was getting low.

"Let me freshen up your brandy for you," I said. "I want a little more wine myself."

"Pleash, I mean 'please'," Jan said, smiling, her face exuding benumbed satisfaction.

I came back with more brandy for her, more Rosso for me, and a fresh package of cheese sticks.

"I like Olivia Olson!" Jan said suddenly. "I liked her on first sight at that delightful pub, The Grain o' Mooning. She just seems so genuinely pleasant, friendly, but there's a lingering sadness in her eyes, just barely there. Is that because of your problems together?"

"Jan, give Thomas a break," Ernie chided with a smile. He knows his wife.

I said, "No, I think she's having problems in her relationship with Sheriff Payne, her romantic interest. I'm not sure what."

"I think she misses what y'all had," Jan said. "Just a woman's intuition. In the meantime, I'd stay away from that girl deputy. How old is she, eleven? Anyway, she's a little *too* friendly, if you get my drift."

"I don't get your drift," Ernie said. "What did she do to make you think that? She seemed perfectly nice."

"Men," Jan said, rolling her eyes. "Ernie, did you see that girl hug Thomas and not you?"

"Yes."

"That's because you are obviously married to me and Thomas is single." Jan turned to me. "Are you two lovers? Young as she is, you can't be old friends."

"No," I said.

"There you go," Jan said. "She's prospecting. Now, may I get us all some brandy?"

An hour or so later, everyone was sleepy, especially Jan, whose empty brandy snifter was resting on the floor by her chair. Ernie took her hand, pulled her to her feet, and started toward the stairs.

"Say goodnight, darling," Ernie said.

"Goodnight, darling," she said, grandly waving her hand over her shoulder as they took the first steps.

Ernie turned to me and said, "Goodnight, Thomas. Hope you sleep well."

"Feel free to sleep in. I don't think I'll be going for a run."

"I think we'll all benefit from a good night's sleep, especially herself," he said, nodding toward Jan.

"I am not 'herself.' I am Jan DiBella Timmons. Night-night, Thomas. And Olivia's the word."

And with that, Ernie and herself went on upstairs and into their room.

Chapter Eleven

"Walls have ears.
Doors have eyes
Trees have voices.
Beasts tell lies.
Beware the rain.
Beware the snow.
Beware the man
You think you know."

—Catherine Fisher, *Incarceron*—

Beautiful snowstorms should not be seen alone. They beckon softly for two to watch, side by side, holding each other close, silent and snug, gazing out into deep cold and white fury just beyond the window pane. One should be intimate with another when there's a blizzard going on.

I went to bed hoping Ernie and Jan were looking out their upstairs east bedroom window, arm in arm, loving and secure and cozy in my home. Is that me being envious?

The blizzard continued into the night, and I finally fell asleep, the howling of the wind and the sandy pattering of sudden snow gusts against my windows somehow comforting in that it was out of my control, reminding me that I am not God. Which would come as a surprise to Gotcha. The big, brindle and white Bulldog was sound asleep on her tuffet on the floor at the foot of my bed, and had been shortly after I closed the door to my bedroom. Her snoring sounded like someone softly and slowly tearing stiff cardboard boxes into strips, and it escorted me into sleep.

My sleep was as deep and dreamless as the snowdrifts I saw when I woke up and glanced out my window. The day was gray and looked cold, and I was glad it wasn't sunny. A bright day after a blizzard, like stark truth, can hurt the eyes. Too much light can sometimes blind, Emily Dickinson said, and it's true in more ways than one.

The strong smell of coffee awakened me, startling me, and then I remembered Jan and Ernie were in my house. I made myself get up, grumbling a little. I didn't want to get up just yet, but I couldn't sleep with someone out and about. Still, I needed to arise. Maybe I would hear some good news about Cindy Stalking Wolf's case.

As much as I wanted to, I couldn't go hunting bad guys right away because the snow had brought just about everything to a padded pause. Damn! I might as well do what God told Job to do; that is, man up and quit whining. Still, just for the record, I prefer to be alone since losing everything that mattered. And *still* losing, I thought. Ruth VanderKellen. Olivia Olson. Christina Hendricks in eighth grade who told me to "Drop dead" when I offered my love.

Maybe the longer we separate ourselves from other people, the stranger we become. Lots of stories about hermits in the mountains with long, ratty, bug-infested beards; shotguns at the ready; and limited skills in both hygiene and conversation. Something to which I might yet aspire.

Since the Timmons were going to be with me for at least today and tomorrow and Friday morning, I would have to finesse Ernie to keep him from knowing too much about my plans. Otherwise, he would insist on staying to help me out, and I couldn't have that. As good a guy as he is, he would be in the way, and I like to travel light when I'm on a mission, and what lay ahead of me was most definitely a mission.

I dressed in jeans and a heavy, royal blue cotton sweatshirt. Then I slipped on a pair of battered moccasins I have owned for over a decade that I bought in Banff. Gotcha was not on her tuffet and it threw me off a little. Along with that coffee smell.

I opened my door and stepped into the kitchen to find Jan working over the stove.

"Where's Gotcha?"

"And good morning to you, too," Jan said, smiling over her shoulder. "I just now let her out. I suspect she's close to coming in. I peeked in a little while ago, saw you sleeping like a sloth, and when she got up and came my way, I let her. Then I closed your door. Gotcha actually *grinned* at me when I spoke to her this morning. Kind of a horrid yet endearing expression – all those jaws and folds and spikey teeth, and her grinning. A bit unnerving if I didn't know her. Actually, a bit unnerving even though I *do* know her."

"You peeked in on me?"

"Yes-s-s," she responded warily.

"Knowing I sleep in the nude?

"No, you don't!"

"How do you know that?

"Karen told me. Years ago. You booger!"

I walked past Jan and touched her shoulder on my way to the back door. I opened it to a cold blast of air and an annoyed-looking dog. She came in and gave herself a shake and proceeded to her bowl. Then she looked up at me, clearly impatient with the whole process being behind schedule. I fed and medicated her, then she headed for the sofa in the front room and hopped up. She is not a morning dog and she is not a winter dog. She prefers mid-day in the Spring and Fall. There's only so much I can accommodate for her.

"So how're you liking Iowa so far?"

"I like it just fine, Thomas. This snowfall is breathtaking. Have you looked outside?"

"I have, but I can't help but wish we'd had a *real* snowstorm yesterday and last night. This hardly qualifies. Disappointing. I wanted you guys to see the real thing, and all we get is these flimsy flurries."

Jan gave me a look.

"Ernie sleeping in?

"Indeed. The poor guy just couldn't handle the blizzard and the brandy and the . . . ," she caught herself and actually blushed. "Actually, he's in the shower, and by the way, I like your house more and more. That bathroom is stupendous – all that Italian marble."

"I do what I can to honor your heritage. I hope you slept well. So, what are you doing in my kitchen? What's cooking?"

All three of us had carried in boxes of groceries when the Timmons had arrived yesterday morning, and all of it was food Jan had judged to be essential and that she didn't think she'd find in a small town in Iowa. She'd said she *had* to have ricotta cheese for the lasagna she was going to make and leave for me—she simply could not substitute with the cottage cheese I suggested—an unpardonable sin. Jan can be an inflexible woman when it comes to Italian cooking.

"I'm preparing Italian sausage and cheese grits. Coffee, too."

"Italian sausage and cheese grits? You are a gift from God, Jan. I smelled the coffee. Woke me up. Great way to start the day."

"Here, have some," she grabbed my big Harley-Davidson mug that waited, upside-down, on a towel spread out on the counter. She poured it half full and handed it over. "I couldn't remember if you took sugar and cream, or neither, or just one. Or even if you wanted this big of a cup. I remember you liked it strong. How is it?"

"Thanks," I sipped some. "Good. Perfect coffee." I scooched around her and reached up into the cabinet above the stove and retrieved a big bottle of Bailey's Irish Cream. I poured it into the mug, bringing the liquid to the brim and turning the coffee several shades lighter. I got out a spoon and stirred.

"Having a little of my coffee with your Bailey's, I see."

"I do like a little cream with my coffee."

"Didn't used to, did you? Seems early in the day."

"Things change," I said. " Bailey's is a kinder, gentler way to start the morning. Besides, it's afternoon in Ireland." I leaned forward and kissed her cheek. "You make great coffee, Jan. Do you have a sister somewhere?"

"You know about Sophia in Brindisi, but she's married. But there are other women around, and some of them you know back in Belue. Laurie Pendleton and Marie Pitts still ask about you. Handsome women. Are you even looking? Are you ready to move ahead? Isn't that what you and Karen agreed to do if anything happened to either one of you? You know you really should by now. It's been over two years, Thomas."

"I know how long it's been, Jan."

I walked across the kitchen and looked out the window.

Ernie saved me from Jan's questions by coming down the stairs. "Did I hear the dulcet tones of my beloved?" he asked as he entered the kitchen. He was in corduroy pants, a thin sweater, and loafers with red socks. Ernie always wears red sox, even though he's a Braves fan. He even wore them on his wedding day, and says he wants to be wearing them when he's buried. He just likes the color. Iconic.

"I have dared to take liberties with another person's kitchen," Jan said. "I woke him up with the smell of coffee, sneaked Gotcha outside, and started breakfast. All this in *his* kitchen. I think it made him edgy, having a broad in the joint."

"Je regret, Jan. Mi cacina es su cacina."

She started laughing and the tension broke like a brittle Christmas bulb.

"You just spoke to my wife in multiple languages, Thomas," Ernie said. "Trying to impress her?"

"Yes," I said, coming back across the kitchen. "Now she needs to impress *me* with her cooking, which is always an iffy endeavor."

Jan smacked me with the spatula, leaving a greasy little swipe on my shoulder.

"Shug," Jan said to Ernie, "you should take a look at this man's refrigerator and freezer. It's pathetic, and a wonder he is alive. I guess Moon's place is where you eat most of the time, right?" she asked, turning to me.

I smiled my most innocent, youthful smile and said nothing.

"What's wrong with his refrigerator?" Ernie asked.

Jan replied, "Well, before I helped stock it, there was nothing in there but beer, white wine, bacon, brats, cheese, and peanut butter. Some milk. Butter."

"*Natural* peanut butter, Jan. Don't leave out the adjective," I said.

"And his freezer had nothing but hash browns and sausage patties! Lord!"

"Don't forget the ice cubes," I added.

"What's wrong with his food supply?" Ernie asked.

The day passed slowly. I couldn't get out and about because of the snow, even with it starting to melt in mid-day sun and temperatures in the upper 30's. I couldn't do anything to help Moon, yet. Nine inches of pure snow had struck Rockbluff County, and not many people were venturing out.

After breakfast, Jan was in and out of the kitchen. When she wasn't in the kitchen, we all hung out in the front room and caught up with what was happening in our lives when we weren't getting up and going to various windows to admire the outdoors that Jan said looked like God had squished out shaving cream all over the countryside.

From time to time I went into my room and turned on the local radio station. No news about the murder of Cindy Stalking Wolf or the disappearance of the Jarlssons and the trashing of Prentice's office. I checked every hour. Sometimes I cranked up the internet to see if there was anything in any other papers. I checked local weather, forecasts, and conditions around the area. Several times.

During one lull in conversation I strolled outside with Gotcha, took my snow shovel I had set out the night before, and pushed some of the wet snow off my deck. Ernie and Jan joined us and admired the view while listening to the water dripping from the roof and trees. I told them about the eagles I had seen off and on since my move, and that Lunatic Mooning had told me the Ojibwa believe the eagles were the spirits of those I had lost, and that all was well with them in the world of the Great Spirit.

"You have been through a lot, Thomas," Ernie said, gazing out over the white landscape beyond the deck. "See any benefits?"

"Not yet," I said. Jan took my arm in her two hands. I could not look at her.

"Well then, what benefit have *others* derived from your steadfastness through your trials?" Ernie asked.

"You want me to say that my exposing the evil and corruption and fraud around the Soderstrom murder benefitted others, don't you?" I said.

"Didn't it?" Ernie continued.

I paused, not because I didn't know the answer, but because I didn't want Ernie to have the satisfaction of my quickly agreeing with him. So I paused a little longer. Then I said, "Yes."

"You haven't lost your faith," he said.

"No," I said. "I still love God. But it's no fun. Well, there is some fun in putting on my white hat and righting wrongs. I do so enjoy smacking bad guys, Lord forgive me."

"So, through the testing of your faith, you have remained steadfast through it all – losing Karen and Michelle and Annie, losing Liv, losing Ruth, losing your friend Horace," Ernie said.

"I don't feel very steadfast, though."

"You can't trust your feelings," Ernie said.

"Thank you!" I said. "That's why I don't *have* any feelings."

Jan punched my shoulder, then stood up on her tiptoes and whispered "You are *such* a dweeb" in my ear.

"Let's go back inside," I said. "I'm getting cold."

We hung around the fire in the fireplace, dozed intermittently, looked in on a couple of football games on TV, and pretty much consumed the day. When the moon came up through the clouds, the snow stopped melting and shone in glittering blue glory, and we simply turned out the lights and stepped outside and took it in.

An occasional sheaf of snow slipped from a branch and sifted to the ground, pulling more snow from other branches and making soft little avalanches. The woods had, indeed, filled up with snow. I thought about Lunatic Mooning and his loss.

At one point in the day, while I was seeking a little piece of privacy, looking out my bedroom window into the deep woods with the black trees outlined against the white land, that was when I resolved to not include Harmon Payne in my snooping.

He has this annoying habit of always wanting to do everything by the book. I have a different book, employing dormant skills last year to defend myself from nefarious types who tried to discourage me, beat me up, blow me to bits, and have me snuffed by a pro. Getting back in "the game" pulls me in, and I go with it.

Besides, there was the look on Moon's face when he realized the dead girl was his niece. His usual stoic manner had slumped for a moment, and I am compelled to do something about it. There were questions that needed answering. Who had murdered Cindy Stalking Wolf? Why was she naked? Why shoot her in the first place? Was it a message of some kind? Where did she come from, besides upriver? Who would I need to talk to? What happened to the fingerprints and photographs of the girl? What happened to the Jarlssons?

Moon and I would investigate and introduce the killers to a streamlined, direct, and lawyer-free justice system. We would head north to the reservation, the "rez." I was counting on Lunatic Mooning to get us into places by dint of his Ojibwa-Chippewa-Anishinabe blood. I had a hunch he could be effective in motivating recalcitrants, and I wanted to be there when he was. In the meantime, I had to let time pass. I had no choice, but I didn't like it.

Thanksgiving Day began with a light breakfast, then football games followed by dinner at 3 PM. Superior food, good wine, and entertaining conversation flowed like pure joy until late in the afternoon when we finished and Ernie and I took care of the dishes and kitchen cleanup. Jan had prepared huge amounts of food, with multitudinous leftovers already in the freezer for my future meals. She is a precious woman.

Outside, the snowmelt continued, and little pockets of bare ground began to appear like spots on a Dalmatian. We could hear big chunks of snow falling from the roof and the nearby trees, punctuating the warmer weather, although it had still not reached forty degrees.

Once, I found myself jiggling my truck keys in my hand, not knowing how they had gotten there. I quickly put them away, but Ernie noticed. He just smiled and looked away. I hate to embarrass myself, but I have had lots of practice. One would think I could overcome it.

Just as it was growing dark, Carl Heisler called and asked if he and Molly could drop by. He said the roads were fine and he wanted to meet my friends, since Molly had described them to him so delightfully when they met at The Grain. In short order they showed up and joined us in the living room in front of the fire and near the television after I had given them a brief tour of the house since it was their first visit. As I have said before, I value my privacy. Maybe a little too much.

I was glad to see them for reasons other than my growing friendship and respect. Carl had been at the shootout during the Rockbluff County Pork Festival a year ago last summer, and I appreciate him. Molly is simply a delight, and another member of a marriage to be admired. Having them in my midst now was useful in diverting conversations from me and my problems, and more toward theological discussions intermixed with commentary on the football games we were watching with the sound turned low.

I suspected the Heislers hadn't come by just to say "Happy Thanksgiving!" and chat about football, and I was right. When there was a brief lull in the conversation and a series of lame commercials on the television, Molly looked around the living room and into the foyer and said, "I really like your home, Thomas."

"Thanks, Molly," I said, "but you know I killed two men in this house."

That remark dampened conversation and season's greetings for a few seconds. Carl said, "One of the old German hymns we sang in church this morning, Thomas, was 'Stricken, Smitten, and Afflicted.' There's a line that ends, 'was there ever grief like this?' and I thought of Jesus on the cross, of course, but I also thought of you. You have born up well through everything, and yes, I even know about Ruth and what happened there. Molly told me. Yet, you do not lash out at people, you do not seem self-pitying, and I believed you when you told me during one of our sessions at The Grain o' Truth that you retain your faith."

"Steadfast. That's what he is," Ernie said.

"Exactly," Carl said.

"And by the way," Molly piped up, "if you hadn't killed those two men, they would have killed *you*. I've never taken a life, yet I know it's a big thing, but sometimes necessary. I hope you can get past it, and I think you probably have. But what encourages me, and one reason I love you, is what Tim Keller wrote about trials."

"Which is?" I asked.

"When you face trials, you can disobey and or disbelieve, or you can believe God. It seems to me, to *us*," she said, gesturing to the Timmons and Carl, "that you believe God."

"I do believe God," I said, "but I'm hoping now that my share of trials is played out. Maybe He will parcel them out to somebody else, present company excepted."

"I'm afraid maybe not," Ernie said. "There's something about this dead girl you found in the river that makes me edgy. I know the authorities are investigating, but you're the one who found her. That means you're involved."

"I agree," Jan said. "I just have a feeling about that, so you know I'll be praying for you to just be wise and safe."

Suddenly everyone was nodding their heads and I was saying thanks and turning the sound up for the football game, a hint to stop talking about me. What I really wanted to do was go for a long run on the wet blacktop at the end of my drive.

I want people to pray for me. I *need* people to pray for me. But it makes me uncomfortable when they do it in my presence. Pride, I suspect, but there it is.

A short time later the Heislers bade us good evening and, soon after, everyone went to bed; Ernie and Jan together, me alone.

I did not immediately fall asleep, even though Gotcha did her best to lead the way, slipping into soft snoring shortly after I closed the door to my bedroom. With food and friends and football no longer center stage, my mind drifted to the life and death of Cindy Stalking Wolf, a girl in the approximate age group of my dead daughters. I couldn't shake that thought.

The last time I looked at the clock, it was 3:15, and I know I didn't fall asleep right after. But the next morning the smell of coffee once again nudged me awake. I looked at my clock again. It read 6:13. I heard Gotcha snoring at the foot of the bed, got up and dressed, and padded barefoot past my slowly-awakening Bulldog and into the kitchen. Jan was cooking breakfast again, cheese grits and bacon. Too bad she's married.

"Good morning, Thomas." She handed me a big mug of light-colored coffee. "Fifty-fifty, coffee and Bailey's, right?"

"Yes. I thought you two might sleep in this morning. We were up fairly late, minds numbed by football, bodies stuffed to the gills, and a snowy night outside the windows." I sipped my coffee. Perfect.

"Normally, yes, but we need to get on the road. We're going to drive straight through. Already packed the car and ready to go while you were snoring. Ernie checked the weather channel and the roads are clear everywhere. We hate to leave so quickly, but we really miss our boys."

"And I'll miss you guys."

"BUT, you have things to do. Things to check out. In this dead girl's case, maybe a calling."

I didn't say anything. I looked out the kitchen window. Snow was still melting. Good.

Jan took my hands in hers and looked into my eyes. "Thomas, we love you. And I want to tell you that maybe you should just go ahead and live. All is not lost, and when I say 'live,' you might consider spelling that word with just three letters. I saw how she looked at you."

"Aaaand," Ernie said, coming in through the front door and stomping snow from his feet, "we need to turn you loose so you and Lunatic Mooning can help bring those killers to justice forthwith."

After a quick breakfast, prayers for travel mercies, a handshake from Ernie and a kiss from Jan, they were out the door.

"Call me if you need backup, Thomas!" Ernie shouted after Jan slid into her seat and he went around the car and opened the driver's side door, "even though I know you won't. We'll pray for you – strength and protection and effectiveness."

"Shalom!" I shouted, waving, grinning in spite of myself.

"Shalom!" he called back, got inside, shut the door, and slowly pulled away and down the drive.

I love Jan and Ernie.

As their car disappeared around a stand of trees down my drive, my one thought was that, now I could get to work. Actually, there was another thought, about Liv Olson, but I shouldered it aside. For now, anyway.

Then I went inside and called Lunatic Mooning.

Chapter Twelve

"It is impossible to suffer without making someone pay for it;
every complaint already carries revenge."

—*Friedrich Nietzsche*—

The big Packard rumbled smoothly northward, as if the very automobile had purpose and focus and intent to provide correction. It was driven by more than Lunatic Mooning: It was driven by blood.

The roads were clear, even though it was still early morning. The blacktop that stretched and curled ahead of us like a blacksnake had an occasional frosty patch, but the heavy car forged ahead with nary a slip.

Moon's '51 Packard is in mint condition, his means of transportation and a diversion from his business, not to mention the demands of women in various small towns he is rumored to be courting. An escape and a source of pride.

In silence, we drove on, taking a state highway for miles, then departing for blacktop roads shortly before we reached the Iowa-Minnesota border. We drove into forest filled with oak and elm and tamarack trees, lakes every few miles glinting in the sunlight. A few family farms appeared here and there, lonely outposts in the world of corporate farming, eking out a living from crops and livestock on dwindling acreages, the last of a dying breed. We passed several abandoned farmsteads as well, houses sagging, skeletal barns where paint had long since disappeared, and empty feed lots.

Growing up as a boy in Clinton, my friends and I made fun of farmers, characterizing them as dumb, nonverbal, and unsophisticated. Unlike us, of course. As I grew and learned and observed, I realized they are typically intelligent, well-educated, and solid businessmen who use computers and spreadsheets to operate their lands.

We said nothing for miles. Then, as we crossed into Minnesota, "The Land of a Thousand Aches" I used to call it, Moon, keeping his eyes on the road, said, "I know the dead girl is Cindy."

I didn't say anything for a couple of minutes, then I spoke. "I do, too."

Moon said, "Thank you for not condescending and offering false hope. We both know."

A mile later, I said, "Yes."

Worn out from so much idle chatter, we didn't speak for a while after that, allowing our vocal chords to recover from the constant yammering.

After a few miles, Moon slowed down as the forest grew deeper, thicker, and closer to the road. He was looking for something, and he finally found it; an old gravel road leading off to the right into the woods. Three or four miles later, we came upon a rusty sign that proclaimed, "Chalaka Reservation of the Ojibwa-Anishinabe Nation."

"Why don't they include 'Chippewa'?" I asked. "You used that when I first met you."

"It is a white man's term, a corruption of 'Ojibwa.' I should have left it out, but, since you knew nothing about my people, I used it to ease you out of your ignorance."

"You are a kind and thoughtful man."

"And you are discerning."

We crunched on for several miles and then the woods opened up into a clearing where a half-dozen homes were scattered around a small lake. The homes were wooden and small, in various stages of disrepair. Newer SUV's were sprawled out in the unkempt yards, and every home had a satellite dish. We pulled up in front of a small, unpainted wooden house with smoke curling out of the chimney. Moon put the Packard in park and cut off the engine. A pair of mixed-breed behemoths, half pitbull and half chainsaw, came around from behind the house, growling and walking stiff-legged, roughs up.

"Are you packing?" I asked, eyeing the dogs, then the houses.

"Not this trip."

"That does not comfort me."

Moon ignored my comment and spoke. "This man is a Ruling Elder in the Tribal Council. He is old and wise, and knows much about the Chalaka Reservation. I respect him. He will tell us things. We must not push. Do not offer to shake hands. Do not look him in the eye."

Moon opened his door. "The dogs will not bite me."

"Great. What about me?" I asked, sliding out on my side.

"Fairly good odds," he replied, and swung out of the car.

"Which way?" I asked over the top of the Packard, keeping an eye on the dogs, each of which was in the 130-pound range. They looked like they could use Gotcha for a volleyball. If she let them. In the distance, near each house, other dogs looked our way and began barking. Moon said nothing.

I decided to follow Moon's lead. I felt awkward, completely out of my element, a ham sandwich at a bar mitzvah, an honest politician in Congress.

Moon and I approached the house, walking slowly. Both dogs came up to Moon and sniffed and began wagging their tails. Then they came up to me, sniffed, but did not wag their tails. Of course, they didn't drag me into the woods for the fun of it, either.

The front door opened and an old man stood there. I expected an ancient prophet with shoulder-length white hair, a blind man with milky eyes, softly chanting and shaking a stick with feathers and bones on it. A bear claw necklace. Maybe wearing a buffalo robe across his stooped shoulders.

"Anin!" the man said, smiling at Moon, looking over Moon's left shoulder. I followed his gaze and saw nothing but trees.

"Anin!" Moon replied, nodding to the man we had come to see.

"Boozhoo," he said to me, glancing over my shoulder. I wondered what he was looking at besides me, but decided to not ask; then I remembered Moon's instruction about eye contact.

The man's name was Fire Bear, "Ishkode Makwa" in Ojibwa. His hair did not disappoint. It was shoulder length and white. My preconception died there, however. He was wearing a purple Minnesota Vikings sweatshirt, faded blue jeans, and cowboy boots. The man's age was hard to ascertain, but my guess was late 70's. A little on the plump side, his eyes were black and lively from what I could tell, since, true to Moon's information, he did not give me eye contact.

He invited us inside, and there I found a tidy, humble, well-kept interior. I could smell bacon in the overheated room as my glasses fogged over. An enormous, high-def television was tuned to a college football game and a big, leather recliner was positioned eight feet from the screen. There was a coffee cup and a bag of Doritos on a small table next to the chair.

Fire Bear found his remote and buttoned off the TV. He and Moon spoke in Ojibwa for a while as I cleaned my glasses with the hem of my sweatshirt, and then we went outside, to a small firepit ringed with flat pieces of rock stacked about a foot high. We pulled together blue, plastic Adirondack chairs into a tight circle and sat, facing each other.

Fire Bear pulled a pack of Camel cigarettes from inside his sweatshirt, broke open one of the cigarettes, and tossed bits of tobacco into the air, addressing each of the four directions briefly, muttering in Ojibwa. He passed the pack to Moon, who took out a cigarette, then offered the pack to me. I took out another cigarette and passed the pack back to Moon, who returned it to Fire Bear. We lit up from a matchbook that Fire Bear withdrew from his sweatshirt. We smoked slowly in silence.

Since quitting smoking in fourth grade, I had not had a cigarette in my mouth. Once, after a particularly edgy op in the mountains of Turkey, I had smoked hashish and didn't like it, or the nightmares. Snakes. And, again, deep in the Peruvian mountains after a particularly bloody "intervention," I had taken a joint offered to me by a native ally and smoked. But when I found myself giggling while looking at the corpse of an enemy who had been shot to pieces, I put out the dope and haven't smoked anything again until now.

I fought off a couple of shallow coughs and managed to smoke my Camel. It did not taste good, it did not make me light-headed, it did not sooth my nerves, which were pretty steady to begin with, even with the two dogs eyeing me from their position at Fire Bear's back door.

After we finished smoking, Lunatic spoke with the old man for a few minutes. They stood. I stood. They headed back to the house. I followed. At the back door, Moon said, "Migwech," which I took to mean thanks or so long or something like that, so when Fire Bear looked toward me, I said "Migwech," too, and he nodded. Then Moon and I walked around the outside of the house while Fire Bear went in the back door. The dogs followed closely. We got in the big, gray Packard.

I let out a sigh of relief.

"You have questions, Thomas?" he asked, starting the engine and turning the car around, pointing it back down the road.

"Hell, no. I am copacetic with the meeting. Seemed pretty much up front to me. Clear, concise, and coherent. Why would I have questions?"

"Thomas, you are amusing."

"I'm a natural-born entertainer, Moon. I appreciate your recognizing it."

Lunatic nudged the Packard forward and we rolled slowly back down the road, tires grinding on the gravel. He took a deep breath and said, "Most people on the rez have dogs. My people like to have warnings when someone is approaching. Defense. My people do not usually look others in the eye. We see it as a penetrating intrusion of the soul. He did not shake hands with you because that is a white man's custom, not Ojibwa."

"Okay, so what about smoking? I didn't see a peace pipe. I mean, Camel cigarettes?"

"We smoked biindaakoojige, tobacco, because of our belief that the smoke carries our prayers to the creator, Kitchimanidoo."

The car carried us through the trees which clung close to the road. Very little shoulder if one needed to pull off the road. Dusk was descending. Moon drove slowly, deep in thought. Neither one of us said anything until we were nearly to the end of the reservation. Then I took a chance.

"Does Fire Bear know anything about Cindy?"

"He believes she is dead."

"Why?"

"Last week he felt what he called a 'lack of her presence' in his spirit, and so he sang to help guide her onto the Path of Souls."

I took that in for a few minutes. It was a little eerie, to tell the truth, but I had seen other examples of eerie religious beliefs, many of them in rural Georgia. "Does he know what happened to her? How she died?"

"No. One thing, though. He said it was not white men. He said it was a magimanidoo, a devil spirit of the Ojibwa."

I wasn't about to disbelieve. Neither was Moon. I could tell by his darkening mood that he believed, and that he would do something in response.

"Who would know the details," I asked. "I mean, who do we talk to next?"

"A bad man."

I lit up. "Where?"

"Here on the rez, but the other side. There are over seven thousand square miles on the Chalaka Reservation. It will take a while to get there."

"Who is he?"

"He is Ojibwa but calls himself Henry Thurmond. He has a bar on the edge of Crow's Wing. That's a village of just a few hundred people. Not far from the town, Chalaka, where the casino stands. Deals drugs, favors, protection. Might be linked somehow to the casino, but hard to prove."

"What's the reputation of the casino?"

"It's spotless. No charges ever brought, no complaints except from a few sore losers. Maybe on the up and up," Lunatic said, "or very smooth." We pulled onto the blacktop and took a right, speed increasing to an easy sixty-five as darkness fell..

We drove in silence for the next forty-five minutes, the big car's headlights throwing beams of light before us. We took another right down a state-maintained road into the reservation and, ultimately, the village of Crow's Wing. There was a gas station/convenience store, a hardware store, a small grocery, a non-denominational church, a Mexican restaurant called "El Lobo," and a burger joint – The Pow Wow. We drove slowly through the town, passing just a few side streets, dilapidated houses with new cars parked outside and the omnipresent satellite dishes on the roofs, and then out of the village.

About two hundred yards on the other side of town, we pulled over in the gravel parking lot of "The Tomahawk," according to the big, red, neon sign blinking on and off. Another sign, purple and not blinking, proclaimed "Ladies Welcome." The cinderblock building had no visible windows. A big glass door beckoned us inside.

We got out of the Packard and headed for that big glass door. "You know this Henry Thurmond guy?"

"Yes."

"Tough guy? Truly?"

"Yes"

The gravel shifted underfoot as we continued across the parking lot. I said, "Tougher than you?"

"Don't know."

And there we were, heading into a bar probably filled with tough guys, an establishment that just might make Shlop's Roadhouse look like a daycare center. That glass door, however, was way better than the tattered Army blanket that indicated the way into Shlop's. It gave "The Tomahawk" a certain panache that Shlop's could not match.

And there I was, probably the only white guy in town, starting to channel General George Armstrong Custer. I thought of the Chinese curse, "May you live in interesting times."

Moon stopped just as he put his hand on the door, turned and looked at me and said, "Why are you smiling, white eyes?"

"Adrenalin," I said, "body fluid of champions."

Moon just shook his head, pulled the door open, and walked inside. I followed, starting to enjoy the rush that comes with intense activity. I asked the Lord to forgive me – only later.

CHAPTER THIRTEEN

**"The world needs anger. The world often
continues to allow evil because it isn't angry enough."**
—Bede Jarrett—

"The Tomahawk" was properly named. The first thing that made
it edgy, at least to me, Mr. Token White Eyes, was the fact that
the place went quickly but steadily silent the minute we walked in. No
music, no backdrop of convivial conversations or even cursing, and
no one moving around, either. No women speaking. Human activity
just falling away. In a bar. Just pairs of dark eyes staring at us in dim
lighting. Freeze-framed life on the rez. The only thing moving was an
eight-ball that had just been struck on the nearest pool table. I watched
it fall into a pocket.

"Reminds me of your place, Lunatic," I said.

"And how are you getting home?" he asked, scanning the clientele.

We moved over to the bar, tended by a young woman who was
really quite pretty in the limited lighting. The closer we got, though,
I could see that she'd once been stunning, but repeat trips down hard
roads had eroded her beauty. Her eyes were black and suspicious. She
was wearing a Timberwolves sweatshirt. Apparently more authentic in
her sports faves than Fire Bear and his affinity for big blonde warriors
with blunt instruments and horned helmets.

"Henry here?" Lunatic asked.

She studied Moon for a moment, then pushed away from behind the bar, sighed as if she'd been assigned the weight of the world, and disappeared through a door behind the bar. The fragrance of frying steak, onion rings, and beer wafted around me. My mouth watered.

"Anin, Lunatic Mooning," a voice boomed out from behind us, cracking the silence like focused thunder, a deep voice with challenge in it. "So who's the chi-mook?"

I remembered Moon telling me that word was not a complimentary one for white men. I also knew it was a token insult, like any racial slur used by various cultures to start intimidating or challenging an outsider, or someone known but not liked. I had heard varieties in places like Malaysia, the Philippines, Jordan, and Kazakstan, among others. It did not intimidate. Or anger. Of course, if he had called me a "bingawallasala" I might have snapped, but we weren't in Central Australia.

Moon turned, as did I, and faced a pig-tailed man in his early thirties, bodybuilder's physique, eyes that bored into mine. Must be that younger generation of Ojibwa or Chalaka who don't respect tribal traditions and beliefs.

"Boozhoo, and he's with me, Puking Cat," Moon said.

The man smiled sardonically. "I told you not to call me that, Lunatic. Did you not listen?"

"No one with brains listens to you, Puking Cat," Lunatic said.

Puking Cat? Puking-for-real-*Cat*? I wondered. While I wondered about the genesis for his name, the young Ojibwa hesitated, as if he were considering getting physical. If he really were a cat, his butt would be wiggling. His eyes did not show fear, but they did show respect. He turned to me.

He said, "What's so fucking funny, chi-mook?"

"I don't know," I said, feeling my old competitive juices perking, forcing the point, expediting the confrontation he wanted. I'd seen it all before, and I just don't have patience anymore to go through all the steps. So I didn't. "I was just thinking about how silly your tough-guy persona is. I mean, you *look* tough, but there's a certain wimpiness about your character that just doesn't go with how *you* think you are perceived. I mean, you obviously work out, but I have just a teensy hunch that you wear white girls' panties."

His hand went behind him and suddenly there was a knife coming up low at me. Predictable. Close to boring. Maybe he pulled it to be menacing, maybe prelude to attack. All the same to me. No time for a focus group to process the data. I caught his knife wrist and forced the blade low and down with the cutting edge away, grabbed Puking Cat by the back of his wool shirt, pivoted and pulled. Using his momentum, I propelled him face-first into the bar. There was a crack of bone and a cry and the knife fell to the floor. Moon bent down and picked it up, as if it were nothing more than a cigarette butt.

Puking Cat, his face a bloody mask, turned from the bar, where he had briefly slumped, and lunged at me. I had to give him credit. I had mistakenly assumed that the facial into the bar would have calmed his waters and persuaded him to smoke the pipe of peace. Every time I'd used that move before, it had always worked. There goes the flaw in that word "assumed" again.

This time, I grabbed him by the front of his shirt, pulled him up to get a better grip, then spun and dragged him toward the front door, giving him a little hitch to pick up speed and then slamming him into the wall. He was supposed to slump to the floor, but he didn't. He staggered, then got his legs under him and stood, taking a deep breath. Uh-oh.

Snorting and blowing a fine spray of blood, he grinned, ducked down and came at me again, cautiously this time. Quick study. He adopted a boxing stance, leading with his left, shaking his head sharply to get the blood away from his eyes. A boxer? Heck, I could do that, too, I thought. It was growing more intriguing by the minute as he swung wildly with a left roundhouse that I ducked. I planted my feet, and delivered a hard right to his ribs. His heavy wool shirt helped cushion the blow, but he grunted in pain and launched a right cross which caught me just above my left ear, a solid blow that hurt and set the bells to ringing in my head.

I faked a punch to his face, and when his arms came up in defense, I drove another hard right into the same ribs I had hammered before. This time he yelped, and I quickly slugged again, getting my weight into it. His arms came down to protect his ribs, and that was when I brought another right, an uppercut, to his chin.

Puking Cat's teeth rattled, chipping against each other, and I saw something small and white fly into the darkness. He sagged, I stepped back, and when he didn't fall, I provided a left jab to straighten up his face, followed by a hard right to his jaw. He went down as if he'd been kissed by a cobra. Tough guy, but victim of the old one-two.

The bells in my head had stopped as two men about the same age as my attacker came forward, gave me a look, bent down, picked up Puking Cat, and carried him out of The Tomahawk. A friend will help you move a body, especially if it's yours.

Breathing a little too hard for my self-respect, I quickly recovered, grateful that I had been lifting and running. I noticed that the noise level in the bar had changed. Someone had put money in the jukebox and I heard Harry Connick singing. Surprised me, not the kind of music I expected. Muffled conversations flowed again as I turned back to Lunatic Mooning.

A big man with a nose that had been broken more than once was now leaning across the bar, grinning at me. He was not there when the fight started. His grin was not pleasant. The word that came to mind was "sinister." His face was fleshy, and even in the dim light of The Tomahawk, I could see that the ravages of acne had left his skin pitted, as if his face had caught fire and someone put out the flames with a track shoe. The girl we had spoken to was gone.

"Henry, this is Thomas O'Shea. Thomas, Henry Drummond," Moon said.

Henry Drummond surprised me as he reached across the bar and offered his hand. There were big rings on each of his fat fingers. I took his hand, noticing the thickness of the flesh and obvious strength. He did not try to crush my hand by way of intimidation. We shook and let go. Henry, like Puking Cat, had clearly drifted from the Ojibwa way.

"Let's go back here to my office," Henry said, exchanging his slumping posture for an erect carriage, turning away and beckoning for us to follow. The man was tall, maybe six-three, and built heavy going to fat. Maybe fifty years old. Something feral about the way he moved. We followed him into a large room. He shut the door.

There was a battered oak desk and matching desk chair in the middle of the room. A couple of nicked-up naugahyde recliners and a rickety coffee table, a pair of gray folding metal chairs, and a floor lamp completed the furnishings. There were posters of nude, sultry women adorning the unpainted walls, a crucifix on the wall opposite the nudies, and an official-looking photograph of John F. Kennedy behind the desk. Boxes of potato chips and beef jerky were stacked everywhere, along with cases of beer, Coca-Cola, and Mountain Dew. Shelves held bottles of whiskey, gin, and vodka. A flickering three-tube neon light provided most of the illumination, which was faint. A red lava lamp slow-mo'ed on top of an Army-green file cabinet.

Moon looked at the shelves and said, "Didn't know your license included hard stuff, Henry."

"Yeah, right," he said, going around behind his desk and sitting down. He did not offer us a seat, so we stood. "What can I do ya for?"

"I want to know what happened to my niece, Cindy Stalking Wolf," Lunatic said.

"Yeah, I heard that she took off, two, three years ago."

"What else did you hear?"

"She was mixed up in some bad shit." Henry pushed a stack of papers around in front of him. He did not look up.

"What was it?" Moon asked. "Anything yours?"

Henry looked up, the tone of Moon's voice lifting Henry's head. He looked at Lunatic. In the background I could hear the jukebox playing "You Can Do Magic."

"You know me, man. I do drugs, life insurance, a little this, a little that. Low-level corruption and traditional fraud, you know, payoffs and bribes and such. Most of the classics. The American Dream. I don't do girls. I got a daughter."

Moon said, "You're a prince, Henry. Was Cindy into prostitution?"

"I heard things, here and there, but I'm not the one to ask," Henry said.

"Who then?" Moon asked.

Henry looked left, then right, but not at us. He seemed a little conflicted. "Ask around," he finally muttered.

"That's what I'm doing with you," Lunatic said. "So you know the person who can tell me about Cindy, and yet you're hesitating?" Moon asked, his voice rising a little. I could tell he was, how shall I put it? Yes, Lunatic Mooning was *vexed*. He started around the desk. Henry stood up quickly, the desk chair scooting back behind him, wobbling, turning over. I expected a cataclysm of some sort.

"If I don't tell you," Henry said, his voice low and even and unafraid, "seein' as how you're talking family, you would probably assault me, I would put you in the hospital, that would provoke questions from law enforcement, and I'd have to pay more hush money to keep my license. So, fuck you, Lunatic Mooning. Go talk to that chi-mook Ted Hornung. He's got a club down the road from the casino. Calls it the Pony Club. He runs girls. Maybe he knows something about your niece. I don't."

"Migwech, Henry. I guess I can do that." Lunatic stepped away from Henry, turned and headed for the door.

"Buy you a beer?" Henry asked, laughing.

"Next time, Henry," Moon said.

"Always welcome, brother, but don't bring your rowdy friend. He is not welcome. Bad for business," Henry said.

I blew a kiss in Henry's direction as we left. He gave me the finger. We went out into the bar and, once again, experienced a hush, although not as profound as the first time.

Back outside, in the cold air, there was no sign of Puking Cat or his buddies as we walked across the gravel parking lot to the Packard. I half expected it to be damaged, or at least keyed, but it was not. We got in, Moon started the big engine, fiddled with the heater controls.

"Puking Cat?" I said. "Really?"

"No. His name in English is 'Panther Claw,' which he prefers. I call him 'Puking Cat' to get under his skin."

"It worked. He seemed a little sensitive to his nickname. Still, he's a tough guy."

"Was." Moon glanced my way. "He did give you a bloody ear."

"Gave me a tidy little headache, too." I would have touched the side of my head, but restrained myself. Someone might see.

Lunatic put the Packard into gear and we slowly pulled out of the parking lot and headed back onto the road, turning right on the highway, opposite direction from Crow's Wing. The night was dark and cold, and snow that had warmed to water was now freezing into ice where once were puddles. Slush that would harden overnight and contribute to skidding cars and ankle sprains if you tried to walk on it unaware.

"Where we going?" I asked.

"The Pony Club."

"You must know where it is."

"Forty, fifty miles from here," Moon said, his eyes straight ahead.

We drove on into the night woods, seeing very few cars for miles. It was warm in the car. After fifteen minutes or so, Lunatic said, "You acquitted yourself well."

"Thank you."

"SEAL training?"

"I was never a SEAL."

"I forgot."

"I've *had* SEAL training," I said, feeling like maybe I should have kept that to myself. Still, I felt as if Moon maybe had a right to know, if for no other reason than to stop his hectoring me about my skill set. Plus, he saved my life that time.

"But you're not a SEAL. Did they throw you out? I can see where you might have trouble taking orders."

"I nearly finished training before I broke my right leg," I said. "When an injury or illness forces discontinuing training, they make you start all over again if you're still committed. They do not let you pick up where you left off. Disrupts the value of the training if I jump right in, all healed and fresh and join a class that's exhausted and hanging on by their fingernails."

"Makes sense."

"So, after my leg healed, I went back in again. Same story. Broke the other leg helping carry a boat."

"You didn't drink enough milk as a child," Moon said. "I would not try a third time."

"I did not. Besides, each leg broken and healed helped me balance physically. Otherwise I'd walk around in circles all day."

"You learned much."

"Indeed," I said, and shut up.

"Harmon told me he saw you take on those two guys on the bridge last year. Said he was impressed, that you're what he calls a 'manhandler.' You are a bad man, Thomas O'Shea."

"Indeed," I said. "And before we finish up with Cindy's story, I might have to be badder."

"Indeed," Moon said.

We drove on in silence, verbally benumbed, two motormouths riding together in the cold, black night of the north woods, looking for girls.

CHAPTER FOURTEEN

**"I believe sex is one of the most beautiful, natural,
wholesome things that money can buy."**

—Steve Martin—

"**Y**ou know Henry probably called this Hornung guy before we left the parking lot," I said.

I could sense Moon's head nodding as I looked straight ahead into the dark tunnel of trees that was the highway leading to the town of Chalaka, and the Pony Club.

"They might not be interested in answering our questions," I continued.

"Maybe we can help them."

"Yeah, work with their reticence."

"I thought you were straight," Moon said.

I laughed silently so as not to encourage him. He laughed in silence at my silent laughing. We were having a whiz-bang time on our road trip.

Fifteen minutes later a dull light appeared in the distant sky, barely discernible over the treetops. Shortly after that sighting, we came to a sign that read, "Chalaka, pop. 2,384" on the top line and "Headquarters for the Chalaka Branch of the Ojibwa-Anishinabe Nation. Welcome!" on the next two lines.

In town, there were a half-dozen mainline motels, all of the two-story variety with rooms opening to the outside. There were also two seedy looking roach traps boasting of hourly rates and free adult movies. We continued on through Chalaka with its meager, predictable amenities for the world travelers: gas station-grocery places, a hardware store, a handful of souvenir shops, three liquor stores, several grungy bars, two fast food joints, and a church – flavor unknown.

We passed the "Chalaka Community Center" building on our left. Its sign boasted of an indoor pool, game room, basketball court, lending library, and Tribal Offices. The Center was nicely-landscaped and appeared to be well maintained. And closed, probably for the white man's holiday weekend. The yellow brick and stone building offered a cleared blacktop parking lot with fresh white paint lines, and a pair of tennis courts out back in the dark, bordered by dormant light towers. No one was serving aces tonight.

Two blocks later, the Pony Club loomed up on the right. Its bright blue neon sign was written in script, and the red neon silhouette of a well-endowed woman jerkily gyrating loomed above everything. The parking lot was dark, but the entrance to the business, trimmed in river stone, was brightly lit. A small, green neon sign by the door proclaimed "Ladies Welcome." No sexual discrimination on the rez.

We pulled into the parking lot and slid into a spot in the middle of a handful of other cars. Friday night and not many cars, but in a way it figured. Day after Thanksgiving, everyone thankful and staying home.

Moon parked the Packard. We got out and ambled up to the entrance. Inside, we were immediately confronted by a wall directly in front of us with a sign advertising mud wrestling and a "Special Holiday Performance" by Lola the Pole. We were forced to turn left, heading down a long, brightly-lit hallway with two security cameras eyeing us. Halfway down the hall, three men eyed us, too.

They were all young, beefy, and black, dressed in black, long-sleeved tees and black slacks with black belts and black shoes. Hell, their underwear, if they were wearing any, was probably black, too. They had the look, the cultivated, squint-eyed, head tilted back and disdainful look that freezes the tee-tee in most men. But Moon and I are not most men. Besides, I didn't need to tee-tee. We kept walking until they stepped in front of us.

"You Lunatic Mooning?" their obvious leader, a gleaming-headed elder statesman who might have been twenty-five asked.

Moon nodded.

"Funny fucking name, Lunatic Mooning," a subordinate thug, maybe nineteen years old, snorted. His coarse language and derisive tone were shocking.

The leader looked at me. "And you, whitebread. You O'Shea?"

"No, I'm the Imperial Wizard of the Ku Klux Klan of the great state of Iowa. Of course, I'm O'Shea. Jeez, pay attention."

"Fucking smart-ass Irish," said the third member of what must have been The Pony Club's security force, also in his late teens, poking his finger in my chest. Which I don't like, so I pushed him back with my left hand and, with my right hand open flat, I jammed my palm into the tip of his finger. This, of course, took only a small percentage of a mini-second and, of course, jammed his finger, like when one catches a baseball on the fingertip. It smarts, and the finger swells up and become stiff and might even be broken. There's at least a small tissue fracture resulting.

"Ow! Ow! Ow!" he yelped, dropping his hand and cradling it with his good hand. Big baby. My confidence soared like the hawk.

"I want to speak with Ted Hornung." Moon brushed past the three men, me right behind.

The leader nodded, hurried to get ahead of us and then beckoned us down the hallway. With every step, the noise escalated. It was music and people shouting over the music. I turned around to see what the rest of the homeland security detail was doing. The one I had jammed looked sullen, sucking his damaged digit as we began walking. He looked stupid. The third guy was working on his scary look, and failing, his expression coming across like someone suffering from indigestion and willing to sell his kingdom for a Beano. We moved ahead, shouldering our way through swinging double doors into The Pony Club itself.

An albino who looked like Jabba the Hut was seated at the door. His shaved head was covered in tattoos, some in dirty language. A variety of obscene tats adorned his big, flabby bare arms, neck, and much of his face. His eyebrows were white, his eyes were pink, and the few patches of ink-free skin looked as pale as a fish belly. After he jabbed a thick thumb at the sign over his head that stated his demand, we each paid him the twenty bucks cover charge

"Make yourselves comfortable. I'll get Mr. Hornung," the security detail leader said. His associates shot us more testicle-withering glares and shuffled off.

Moon and I took seats at a small table deep inside the club. Clouds of blue smoke hovered over the gathering, but I did not detect the odor of weed. Just tobacco, beer, fried food, and booze. Now I was really hungry. First The Tomahawk's exquisite cuisine tantalizing me, and now this.

We had situated ourselves between the mud wrestling pit and a lonely-looking performance pole, waiting patiently, no doubt, for Lola the Pole and her amazing repertoire of salacious moves. A dim blue spotlight was trained on the empty accessory to her performance art.

The mud wrestling was going on. Two fleshy women in bikinis were slipping and falling and grappling in the ooze, which looked like melted chocolate. A big-bellied male referee in a black-and-white striped shirt trotted around the roped-off pit, occasionally leaning over or squatting, searching for infractions. I wondered what possible rules might accompany the sport. The crowd of men, and a few women, hooted and cheered, and when one contestant ripped off the bikini top of the other woman, then pushed her down in the ooze, the place erupted in cheers. The topless woman tried to get up, but her opponent immediately unleashed a flying tackle that pinned Ms. Topless helplessly in the mud. The referee beckoned the winner over to the side and raised her hand in victory while the loser gave everybody the finger, screeched salty Anglo-Saxonisms, and slunk away into the crowd's insults hammering her ignominy.

A man in jeans and a gray sweatshirt emerged from the crowd waving a hand-held microphone. "The winner of the first semi-final match of the evening is Dorie O'Dowd, queen of the double-breasted pushdown!"

The crowd cheered and hooted some more, and Dorie, wiping her upper body and face with a wet towel, waved triumphantly. She was maybe thirty and a little soft-looking, understandable since she was easily thirty pounds overweight. A patch of purple hair adorned her scalp. Of course, the coating of mud would have obliterated any muscularity, but she just did not have the look of a fine athlete. She glared at the crowd and tore the microphone away from the announcer.

"I came here tonight to take names and kick ass, and the next victim of Dorie O'Dowd is gonna be YOU, bitch!" she snarled, glaring at someone in the crowd. Then she gave the mic back to the announcer and stalked off.

"Ladies and gentlemen, there will be a short break to allow our two finalists time to prepare for the title of Minnesota Mud-Wrestling Champion AND the five hundred dollar cash first prize. So have a drink and eat some wings and be prepared to enjoy the showdown between two unbeatens – Dangerous Dorie O'Dowwwwwd and the enigmatic Bunza Steeeeeeele!" And then he exited at the same time my jaw dropped.

"My God," I whispered.

Moon looked at me.

"I know Bunza Steele," I said.

"How?"

"Nice Injun lingo, Moon, but she's the barmaid at Shlop's Roadhouse back in Rockbluff. I've had a dozen conversations with her, back when I was trying to get information on Larry Soderstrom."

"Oh, *that* Bunza Steele." He flashed a little smile. I started to say something, but I was interrupted.

"I seed you!" a familiar voice screeched. And then I was looking up, and over, into Bunza Steele's blue eyes and natural silver hair pulled into a French twist. "Remember me?" she asked, leaning over to put her face close to mine, nearly falling out of her skimpy black bikini top that might have been immodest on a five-year-old. She had smears of mud caked on her body, but I would have recognized her anywhere. The "eyeball" tattoo around her navel was a dead giveaway.

Bunza is *not* flabby. She told me back in Rockbluff during our conversations that she worked out regularly and it showed, and she really did have buns of steel. Her boss, Shlop, had once been a pro wrestling entrepreneur before going into the fine dining world of Shlop's Roadhouse and its Hendigits Specials, and he had begun training her for a pro career that would finance her dream to become a neurosurgeon.

"Have a seat, Bunza," I said, privately enjoying my play on words and reaching behind me to drag another chair to our small table. "Let me introduce you to my friend, Lunatic Mooning."

"A pleasure," she said, reaching across the table as Moon stood to shake her hand.

"An honor," he said, and sat back down.

She looked at Moon for a moment, her face blank, then animation returned. "You stayin' for the championship? We're goin' at it in about ten minutes. My victim has to suck in some air so she can dream about stayin' with me. She has NO CHANCE."

"This is cool, Bunza," I said. "I mean, you told me you were going into wres . . rasslin' and here you are." I gestured grandly around the big room.

"I ain't doin' this forever," she whispered. "After I win tonight, I'm movin' up into *real* pro rasslin', TV and stuff. This will give a little weight to my introduction when they announce me as, 'Bunza Steele, Minnesota Mud-Wrestling Champion.' Shlop says paradin' around in this tiny top and thong an' gettin' all slithery with another woman will be good for my rep. He says doin' this in front of men will help my boner fries."

Moon produced a minor choking sensation and beat gently on his chest. We ignored the big Ojibwa.

"You mean your 'bona fides'?" I asked.

Bunza shrugged. "Somethin' like that. Anyway, Thomas, what are you boys doin' here tonight? This is a long way from Rockbluff. You gonna start comin' reg'lar, like that blonde depity you got down there?'

"Blonde deputy sheriff? From Rockbluff? Who would that be?"

"I don't know. Sounds like 'dope' or 'mulch' or something like that," she answered, shifting in her chair and looking toward the ring. "He's here nearly every time I am. Practically a regular."

"Doltch?" I asked.

Bunza spun around on her chair, jiggling. She adjusted her top. My right eyelid began twitching. "That's the one!" she said. "He might even be here tonight. I saw him earlier, I think, but not lately. Musta left about the time I noticed you boys. He comes by here and has a few then heads up to the casino. Maybe that's where he went."

Moon and I exchanged glances.

Bunza continued, looking me in the eye. "If you ask me, he's gettin' in deep with the craps. If you're winnin' at the tables, seems like there'd be a smile on your face. Even if you're breakin even or just losin' a little. But his face gets longer ever time I see him."

She leaned forward and whispered, "I think he's in over his head. Can't even pay for private lap dances anymore. It's that's serious."

"Wow," I said.

The announcer came back to the side of the ring. "Ladies and gentlemen, I welcome you to The Pony Club's exclusive extravaganza to determine the Minnesota Mud-Wrestling Champion. To the winner goes five hundred dollars in cash and any other folding money, Ben Franklin's or better, please, that you, our discriminating audience, can tuck into the winner's thong."

Whistles added to the earlier song of hoots and hollers. And boot stomping, too. The crowd, which had doubled in size from the earlier match, whipped into a frenzy of mud wrestling cognoscenti, anticipating the festival of flesh about to be offered up to their eyes and libidos. The announcer broke into the raucous cacophony of eager fandom. "In this corner," he intoned, beckoning to an emerging

Dorie O'Dowd, cleaned up and wearing a new orange day-glo bikini, "The Undefeated. The Dangerous. The Delightfully-Endowed. Dorie. O'Dowwwd."

Dangerous Dorie put her hands on the top rope surrounding the mud pit and attempted to vault over and into the ring in a flagrant display of athletic intimidation. She did not quite make it, her trailing leg hanging up on the rope, but she saved herself from total embarrassment by clinging to the top rope and planting both bare feet in the mud, after which she strutted around the mudpit, performing bumps and grinds that would shock a lobbyist.

When the noise abated, the announcer continued. "And in this corner, also undefeated, I present the voluptuous, the erotic, the lovely-limbed Bunza Steeeeeele!"

Bunza, who had left our company to stand by the mud pit, accepted her introduction by placing just one hand on the top rope and vaulting into the ring, executing the maneuver the delightfully-endowed Dorie O'Doud had failed to perform. Score one for Bunza, who adjusted her top again.

The crowd erupted into an avalanche of adoration for Bunza, the obvious fan favorite of Minnesota mud wrestling. They began chanting, "Bun-za, Bun-za, Bun-za!" I felt compelled to join in, yet restrained myself, drawing on my reserved upbringing as an Iowan. But I nearly lost it when she paraded to the center of the ring, spread her legs to shoulder width, looked over her right deltoid at our part of the crowd, and flexed her glutes together, then one at a time, then together again. She repeated the moves three more times, once to each quadrant of the crowd. I was immediately reminded of Fire Bear and the tobacco thingy, something I did not understand. But I understood what Bunza was up to. And so did she.

The decibel level in The Pony Club began to reach painful levels, experienced only once or twice before in my lifetime, and only in combat.

When she had her back turned to Dorie, the doubly-endowed one made a move, rushing toward Bunza to deliver a blind haymaker to the back of Bunza's head. But the inimitable Ms. Steele sensed the charge and dropped to all fours, tripping Dorie and sending her headfirst into the slop. Bunza came to her feet and laughed and pointed at her opponent. And that was only the beginning of a performance that is burned into my memory forever, to be retrieved and enjoyed from time to time for the rest of my days, when life seems gray and gloomy.

Bunza toyed with Dorie, much like a cat messes with a mouse, flipping it into the air, batting at it, letting it "get away" only to be caught from behind and dragged back into a vortex of humiliation and, ultimately, defeat. When Bunza had given the crowd a lengthy performance that had the crowd begging for even more, she pulled off Dorie's top and, simultaneously delivered a vicious clothesline across Dorie's throat, dropping her into the slime, coughing and struggling for breath, her hands clutching at her throat. At that point, still holding onto Dorie's bikini top, Bunza reached down and yanked off her rival's thong, stood up, and then tossed each part of the bikini into a different section of the salivating crowd. Then she turned, placed her foot on Dorie's bare chest and held her there while the ever-vigilant referee counted to three.

As the berserk crowd heaped praise on Bunza, she reprised her four corners glute flexing, adding in a double-biceps pose that rivaled anything that Arnold Schwarzenegger performed in his Mr. Olympia prime. The announcer beckoned her over to the side of the ring, proclaimed her championship, and handed over five one hundred dollar bills, which Bunza accepted after giving the announcer a significant, and lengthy, deep kiss. Then she paraded around the edge of the mud pit and allowed men to tuck folded Franklins into the front of her thong while she stashed her cash in her bikini top. I was having trouble breathing at this point. Bunza stepped through the ropes amidst wild applause while the announcer, barely recovered from her affections, announced that Lola the Pole would be performing in thirty minutes. Bunza disappeared into what must have been the ladies' dressing room.

"Your friends are interesting," Moon said as I turned back toward our table.

"An eclectic array of individuals."

"That, too," he replied.

I was going to add to our lengthy verbal exchange, but just then a man approached our table, more or less gliding across the room to where he now stood.

"My name is Ted Hornung," he said. "I own The Pony Club. What can I do for you gentlemen?"

Chapter Fifteen

**"Where there is mystery, it is generally
suspected there must be evil."**

—*Lord Byron*—

Ted Hornung wore gray flannel slacks, a pale blue shirt with button-down collars, and a black and blue-striped silk necktie pulled into a perfect Windsor knot. Fit-looking and trim, his short blonde hair clean and professionally cut, and his round, Harry Potter eyeglasses emphasizing bright blue eyes, Ted Hornung came across as an earnest Rotarian. Clean shaven, white-toothed, and a winning smile all worked together to make me dislike him immediately.

"My niece was Cindy Stalking Wolf," Moon said.

Hornung's face showed no recognition. He said, "And who are you?"

Moon stood up. "I am Lunatic Mooning, and you know who I am. My associate is Thomas O'Shea."

His *associate*? We would have to chat about that, I thought. Maybe get on the payroll.

"Of course, I do know who you are, *now*. Your *name* comes to mind. Perhaps it would be more, um, *private* if we talked in my office? Would that be okay with you gentlemen?" Hornung's voice was soft, mellifluous, the voice of a radio announcer.

Moon looked at his associate. I shrugged. He nodded at Hornung and the man set off with us trailing along behind his shiny, tasseled loafers.

Hornung's office was even more pleasantly appointed than he. And I realized as he closed the heavy, oaken door behind us, that the office was sound-proofed. No noise from The Pony Club invaded Hornung's private space. We walked into a thickly-carpeted room with a desk; two love seats; a pair of upholstered chairs, one gray, one blue, facing his desk; and a giant, blank HD television screen. The walls were paneled with solid wood I did not recognize. I strolled about, absorbing the ambiance.

Oil paintings that looked like original landscapes adorned two walls, along with a love-me wall with a framed B.A. from the University of Minnesota and an M.B.A. from the Wharton School. Several awards from various civic clubs were also framed. A "Man of the Year" for two years ago from the Chalaka Tribal Council was prominently displayed under a tasteful little spotlight. While Moon took a seat, I wandered over to a book shelf loaded with hardbacks next to a baby grandfather clock in working condition. I saw volumes by Dumas, Shakespeare, de Sade, and even James Patterson before Hornung interrupted me.

"Not enough time to read, unfortunately," he said, noticing my perusal of his bookshelf. "Work keeps me busy, and of course, my small activities for the betterment of our community."

"Of course," I said. "I have the same problem. Little league, Toastmasters, quilting bees. One simply must do what one can to enrich others' lives."

"Please have a seat, Mr. O'Shea," he said, his voice warm and friendly.

"No pictures of family," I said, sitting in the other upholstered chair, the blue one next to Moon. Hornung reclined behind his desk and looked at me.

"I have not yet met the right woman," he said, a hint of sadness in his voice.

"Maybe this isn't the best place to find the bride of your dreams," I said.

"You have a point," he replied with a short, practiced laugh. "Now, as to your purpose. I do not know who Cindy Stalking Wolf is. Why should I?"

Moon said, "She's from here. Ran away a while back. Murdered and dumped into the Whitetail River. Found in Rockbluff, Iowa a few days ago. You know everything that goes on up here. Tell me what you know about my niece."

I wished Moon hadn't said "murdered" even as Hornung extended his hands and held them out, palms up. They looked soft. "Boys, you flatter me. I wish I could help, but I don't even recognize her name, whatever," he said in a sing-song voice that could only be interpreted as "mocking."

"I don't have time for this," I said, "so let's expedite things."

I got up, stepped past Moon, walked over to the seated Hornung, and slapped him hard across his smug face. His Harry Potters shifted. I removed them and tossed them onto the desk. Then I picked him up by his Windsor knot and slapped him again and shoved him back into his pricey desk chair. He looked stunned, even as his right hand moved slightly forward and started to slip under the edge of his pretty desk.

I grabbed his arm and pulled it back, then pushed his hand onto his desk and pinned it there with my right hand. After that, I brought my left forearm down across his right forearm. His scream of pain would not be heard out in the Pony Club.

"You broke my fucking arm!" he screamed. I slapped his mouth, then bent low and looked under his desk. The little button was there, alright. I looked back at Hornung. A serious rivulet of blood was slowly sliding down the corner of his lips and onto his chin. Pretty soon it would mess up his shirt.

"I have no patience with people like you," I said. "I have no interest in going through a little verbal dance while you stall us. Life is short and I want you to understand that I am going to be direct with you until we know what you know about my friend's niece. I'm not even going to ask you if you understand. Now, tell us what you know about Cindy Stalking Wolf. Did you make her into a prostitute? Hook her on free drugs, treat her nicely, pull her in, give her money? Maybe offer her to men who like young girls?"

Teddy's face had gone sullen. He had his left hand on his right forearm, I guess trying to protect it from further encouragement from me. Moon stepped forward, coming around the chair and taking up a position on Teddy's left.

"This is going to be a painful evening for you, Teddy," I said, "unless you open up, because you have lots more bones that can break, and I swear to God, I'll break every one until I hear what I want to hear."

"Okay, okay. You'll find out anyway. Fucking thugs. Shit! Okay, besides what you see out there," he began, starting to gesture with his right hand, yelping in pain, pulling his arm back against his body, "I run prostitution. *Nothing with young girls*. Traditional stuff, you know, women for men or women and anything they want to do and both agree to. Softer stuff, like lap dances, private massages, pharmaceutical-enhanced encounters." He glared at me. *Nothing* with underage girls. Nothing like *that*! Is that expeditious enough for you?"

"What do you think, Moon?" I asked, keeping my eyes on Hornung.

"I think he might be holding back," he replied. He slowly reached across Ted and took the broken forearm into hand. Hornung yelped and lost a little color in his face.

"I haven't even applied pressure yet, and he's acting hurt," Lunatic said to me. "Imagine what he'll do when I give him a good squeeze and quick pull." He turned to Hornung. "So, Ted, *if* what you say is true, and you don't know anything about my niece, who would? Surely someone knows what happened to her."

Hornung looked at Moon, then me. Neither one of us was smiling. I think he could tell that we were concerned. Hornung looked defiant, angry. His hesitancy to provide information used up the last of my patience. I slapped him again – hard. His chair spun to the left. Moon stopped it, turned it back toward me. Ted's mouth was bleeding freely now. The lovely shirt was a lost cause.

"Marty Rodman," he said.

"Tell me about Marty Rodman," Moon said while I placed Hornung's spectacles very gently back on his face.

"He recruits young girls." Hornung wiped his hand across his mouth, looked at the bright crimson smear on his palm. "He takes runaways, treats them nicely for a while, gives them things – clothes, nice dinners, earrings. Shit like that. He sells them to chimooks who want a little 'strange,' if you get my drift."

I said, "'Strange'?"

"You know, something different than the fat wife, or the frigid bitch, back home. Rodman hangs around the casino and talks to men and pretty soon finds out if they're interested in a Chippewa girl. If the tourist is interested, Marty takes it from there. Cheap hotel usually, but he has a brothel back in the woods – nice place for the more classy clientele and more attractive girls," Hornung said. He wiped his face again. "Shit! You've ruined my shirt now," he said, looking down his front.

I looked at Moon. "I'm starting to like Mr. Hornung more and more. He's a great source for elusive information, and that's so cool."

"Are you going to fuck off now?" Hornung asked, his voice petulant and pissy.

"One more question," Moon said. Ted looked at Lunatic.

"What's that?" Hornung asked, grimacing as he moved his right arm a little, still cradled in his left.

"Do you know what happened to Cindy Stalking Wolf?" Moon asked.

"I told you I don't even know who the fuck Cindy Fucking Stalking Wolf is! Fucking morons! Coupla assholes! Don't you listen, man?" Hornung said. He was starting to really interest me. Typically, people I rough up tend to lose their attitude, display a little healthy concern about their well being and future prospects. This guy was turning into one pissed-off smartass.

"I do not like your tone." Moon clamped down hard on Hornung's broken forearm.

"SHIT!" Hornung shouted, leaning his body toward where Moon had the injured extremity in what I imagined was an impressive grip. Moon let go. Hornung held his arm against himself, rocking back and forth and moaning and muttering. His mutterings were shocking, drifting into profanity. He took a deep breath. "Last I heard, Rodman had his hooks into her and she wanted out of the life."

I took a quick step toward Hornung and drew back my right hand. He started to put up his hands to protect himself, but that only made his broken arm hurt more. Guess he forgot it was fractured.

He said, "Please, that's all I know! I promise!"

I looked at Moon. Moon looked at me. We both looked at Ted Hornung, sitting erectly now in his nice desk chair. We believed him.

"Thanks for the tip, Mr. Hornung." I stepped back. "And thank you so much for saying 'Please'. I knew you would eventually revert to your Ivy League background."

Moon came around the back of Hornung's chair and stood next to me. I continued. "I'm a little concerned about you, though. Your complexion, where it isn't bleeding, is a little pale. Are you okay, Teddy?" Hornung said nothing, but his look probably needs to be registered as a weapon. The dude was not contrite, not one bit.

Moon said, "If you touch that little button under your desk before we're long gone, we'll come back and abuse you."

"And no fair calling Marty Rodman. That would push me over the edge if you warned him. And when I get pushed that far, I tend to be rude," I said.

Hornung nodded weakly and looked down. We left his office and walked across the Pony Club floor toward the main door. The big albino held out a hand as we approached and pointed off to his right. Bunza Steele was waving at us from across the room, coming our way. We stopped. She had cleaned up and was dressed in a leopard-skin body suit. It looked like a second skin. Men were watching her. Women were watching their men watching her. She walked like she knew she was being admired. She came up to us.

"Leavin' so soon?" she asked, smiling. Nice smile.

"Places to go, people to see," I said.

"I wish you boys would stay. We could catch up, Thomas," she said, lightly punching my shoulder. "Old times at Shlop's. Remember the time Bob and Ray tried to mess with you?"

"I do," I said. "Maybe we'll catch you later. You swing by The Grain where I tend to spend my money these days."

"I'll do that!"

"We really do need to get going, Bunza. We have irritated Mr. Hornung and worn out our welcome. Check ya later," I said, patting her shoulder and turning away.

"Okay," she replied. "Maybe we could get together down in Rockbluff. You could come see me at Shlop's and I could show you some holds."

"Be still my heart," I said.

"You talk funny, Thomas."

Moon and I left. I felt a sense of trepidation and urgency to split, not believing Hornung would be able to resist calling for some reinforcements, and I was right. As we stepped out into the cold night air, we noticed three big men, all Indians, hanging around Moon's Packard. One was sitting on the hood, heels resting on the front bumper. Another, a very tall man with a shaved head that was steaming in the cold night air was thumping the barrel of a baseball bat in the palm of his hand. The third was picking his nose. Honest.

Moon muttered something and took off across the parking lot. I matched him stride for stride. Three more men, our initial greeters, burst forth behind us from the front door of The Pony Club. Two of them had baseball bats. Do they manufacture them on the rez? I had no idea hardball was so attractive to the thug class.

"Get off the car!" Moon shouted as we came up to the Packard.

The man laughed. Another man produced a tire iron and smashed the windshield and Moon became agitated. And then something came loose in me and I rushed toward the Packard, Moon on my left.

I stopped suddenly and spun around, facing the men closing in on us from the club. They didn't expect it. They stopped. I looked around and saw Moon catch the man in mid-air, the one who had been sitting on the Packard's hood, and who had launched himself at my companion. Moon head-butted Skywalker and threw him into the tall man with the shaved head and they both went down and began scrambling to regain their feet.

Overall, it was a wonderful fight. Six of them, some with baseball bats, and then me and Moon. The odds were with us. I felt the composure and confidence that comes when I am about to do something at which I excel. And, for his part, Lunatic was fighting for family. We had a good shot, especially since I suspected these guys were three-for-a-penny pussycats.

Moon had quickly dropped the guy who had shattered the Packard's windshield, taking away the tire iron and laying out the guy with a blow to the side of the head. He had another, the tall guy, in a headlock, delivering hefty uppercuts to the face. His other adversary, bloody forehead from where Moon had butted him, baseball bat in hand yet now tentative, was circling Moon and Moon's headlock victim, looking for an opening. I would have taken him on but my hands were full as the three security guys from earlier strode my way, looking confident. Strength in numbers.

Their leader, the taller, older guy, stepped up close to me, taking a martial arts stance, then going into a spin to deliver a kick, but his speed lacked, um, well, *speed*. He had beginner's speed, which isn't really speed. So I stepped forward as he went into his move, closing in on him when his back rotated away from me. When he came around and actually kicked, I was too close for him to be effective. I grabbed his kicking leg with my hands on his ankle while stepping down hard on his anchor foot, pinning it to the pavement. And then I shoved his kicking leg as high and as hard as I could.

Three distinct, wet, popping sounds of ligaments and tendons tearing in the groin were accompanied by screams from the attacker. He went down, legs akimbo, hands clutching his groin, which had to be on fire.

The other two jumped me then, and it was time to go all elbows and knees. I accepted their blows, some significant, as the cost of doing business in a world beset with sorrows and heartache. I believe I gave a good bit better than I got.

They soon abandoned the fight, retreating quickly, each grabbing their burning-groin companion by an arm and dragging him back toward the Pony Club. I turned to Moon just as I heard him grunt in pain. Two of his attackers were down, moaning and struggling to get to their feet, but the shaved-head giant had gotten loose from Moon, found a bat, and had struck Moon in his left arm, above the elbow. That arm was hanging a little loose at his side. And now Lunatic was being circled by that man, a man who felt he was going to win.

I trotted over to Moon's side and engaged the batboy's eye contact.

He said, "One down, one to go," and grinned; then, waving the bat around, he came for me. I caught his first pass and ripped the bat out of his hands. He looked stunned, noticed the second group slinking back to the Pony Club, observed his two friends on the ground, then took off running.

I could have let him go, but he didn't have any mementos from our introduction, so I crouched and slung the bat hard, spinning, at his legs. The bat skimmed along the pavement and caught up to him, taking him down there in the parking lot. He scrambled to his feet.

I ran up, recovered the bat and, tossing it behind me, moved in on the guy. I kicked at his knee, dropping him. I considered a head shot, noticing for the first time that his bare skull had several tattoos on it, something like eagle claws and beaks. I fought off the urge to punish, so I went to work on his ribs, breaking some. I am an effective body puncher, I'll admit, and there are so many ribs to hit.

Then I dragged him with one hand, cursing, to his feet, and kicked him in the butt, sending him limping and lurching forward, a stumbling giant, toward the Pony Club. Moon's other assailants struggled along after him. I started back toward Moon, picking up the bat. I looked at the barrel. It was an Ichiro model. Diversity on the rez. I broke it over my knee and tossed the pieces away and went to Moon.

He was holding his left arm with his right, gritting his teeth. His pallor was evident.

I said, "You have a pale face."

"Shameful," he replied, "and I also have a broken arm. Let's get out of here before a war party shows up."

"Can you drive?"

"No one but me drives my car. I will steer, you will shift," he said.

"Okay." I glanced again at the departing thugs.

"Let's go, Thomas," Moon said, striding over to the Packard, opening the door and sitting behind the wheel. He looked over his shoulder toward the front door of the Pony Club. No one was there now. They had all gone inside.

It was a cold drive with the wind coming through a few broken places in the windshield, and difficult to see through all the cracked glass. But the night was clear and that helped, and after a long time on lonely roads, I pulled up to the Emergency Room Entrance at Rockbluff Regional. It was nearly 3 AM.

An X-ray revealed that Lunatic Mooning had a broken humerus, non-displaced. The doctor on call, Dr. Brandenburg, who still had pimples, put Moon in a blue sling and told him, "No mobility for two weeks, sir." A followup visit to check progress was scheduled, at which time specific exercises would be given to increase range of motion. Dr. Brandenburg, who looked like a vegan addicted to running long distances, also gave Lunatic pain pills. Then he looked at me. "Let's take a look at that eyebrow."

What eyebrow? I declined and we left. We shared driving skills again for the short ride back to The Grain. It was fun shifting gears, something my father allowed me to do one time when I was a little kid. One time.

"I'll sleep in my office," he said as we pulled up at The Grain.

I dropped him off, got in my truck, and headed home, hesitating a little, slowing down as I passed the Rockbluff Motel and the parked, blue 4Runner. Then I gunned it and left Rockbluff behind, already planning my next trip, solo, to the Chalaka rez.

I was looking forward to helping Mr. Ted Hornung through a remedial course in following instructions. I hadn't decided yet if I'd kill him.

Chapter Sixteen

"Revenge is sweet and not fattening."

- Alfred Hitchcock

I didn't sleep much. Too many questions rolling around in my head about the murder of Cindy Stalking Wolf. And side issues. What was it with Steven Doltch and his trips to the Chalaka rez, the Pony Club, and the casino? Bunza indicated he was in trouble with his gambling, which was his business; that is, unless it had something to do with the body in the river. What was the connection, if any?

And I thought our confrontation with Ted Hornung would have intimidated most people into being candid with us. But even after slapping him around and breaking his arm, he didn't seem afraid, just angry, and, obviously, he ignored our threats about pushing his emergency buzzer after we left. It didn't take long for his thugs to come after us.

Given those circumstances, it dawned on me that he was probably lying about not being involved in underage prostitution and, if that was the case, he had to know who Cindy Stalking Wolf was. The man's conservative appearance and businesslike demeanor indicated impressive confidence that comes from money. I had heard from impeccable sources that money can buy power, but I have found that to be a particularly cynical observation that is also absolutely true.

These were some of the thoughts tumbling around in my head all night. I'd doze a bit, aided by Gotcha's soft snoring on her tuffet on the floor at the foot of the bed, and then I'd wake up with another question. And I came to the conclusion, around five-thirty in the morning, that I needed more information about those who might be responsible for Cindy's murder and the Jarlssons' disappearance. And I might need to continue snooping more effectively, especially with Moon banged up and only partially effective in any kind of tussle, as Bunza would call brawls. I needed to know more. It can be helpful sometimes to research those one plans to kill, but I remember times when I was okay with knowing nothing about my targets.

I was hungry when I got up. So I put on my glasses, glad they hadn't been knocked off, never mind lost, in the rumble last night. I let Gotcha out and in and fed and medicated her and watched her go jump up in her favorite recliner, push the top part back to stretch out the chair, then stretch out herself. She didn't seem to be angry with me for not feeding her the day before, especially after I doubled her rations this morning. A day without meds wouldn't hurt her, either. I was glad Gunther had installed her doggy door just for situations like yesterday. Sometimes I surprise myself by planning ahead.

I showered, letting hot-hot water play on my back and chest where I'd been punched and kicked. Out of the shower, I toweled off and slipped on skivvies and checked myself in the mirror. My face was a little puffy, and a black eye was building. My right eyebrow was hanging a little loosely, so I got out my box of Band-aids, pushed the brow back into place, and applied three butterfly patches. I needed stitches, but I wasn't in the mood. Besides, the eyebrow would adhere over time if I kept bandages in place. In addition to everything else, my lower lip was just a little swollen, and my ear looked fine with the dried blood washed off in the shower.

At no time did I remember a punch in the mouth; but then, there were a lot of punches thrown, most of those from my scuffle mates wild and ineffective. My teeth were all in place, undamaged, and I was glad about that, because I didn't want anything to mitigate eating. I was ravenous and my stomach was growling. I decided not to shave, mainly because my right hand was fat and stiff and sore.

I fixed myself eight sausage patties and six of the whole wheat pancakes Jan Timmons had prepared and frozen for me. It was Saturday mid-morning and a new day and I needed calories. When the sausages and pancakes had been nuked and the pancakes drenched in butter and maple syrup, I ate my breakfast, gave half a sausage to Gotcha, who had hopped down from her chair and given me her "You never feed me" look, and drank my coffee with Bailey's. And then a second cup, taken in standing up out on the deck, where a clear, cold day revealed the Whitetail River Valley below, and beyond that, faint in the rising mist, the Mississippi River Valley. I went back inside after a quick prayer, thanking God we hadn't been killed, and for the progress in finding out who killed Cindy Stalking Wolf and disappeared the Jarlssons. I went back inside, my coffee cup empty.

After tidying up, I used the blasted cell phone to call Harmon at the Sheriff's Office. He picked up right away, said hello, and asked what he could do for me. Caller I.D. His voice had an edge of stress to it, and his words were abrupt, as if I had interrupted something important.

"Harmon, I was just wondering if there's anything new on the Cindy Stalking Wolf case, or if you've been able to find anything on the Jarlssons yet."

"Christ, Thomas, maybe if you wouldn't harass me with stupid questions I could get more done. You know damn well if I heard anything I'd call you. I always do every time you stumble onto an accident that turns out to be murder. Jesus!"

"Have you had your caffeine yet?"

"Yes."

"So what's with the attitude?"

I heard a deep sigh. "Sorry, Thomas. I'm just a little on edge. No progress and I'm starting to get pissed, and frankly, worried about the Jarlssons. It's been ten days. I have a bad feeling about this. It's out of character to act the way Prentice did with you, then disappear. Out of character."

I decided to push a little. "Is Doltch doing okay?"

"What do you mean?"

"He just seems a little more uptight than usual, at least with me," I said.

"What do you know about Steven?"

I decided I might as well go for broke. "I heard he had some issues with gambling."

"At the Chalaka Casino?"

"Yes."

"How do you know that? Never mind. Obviously you've been up there recently, you and Moon, which explains his broken arm. I just left The Grain. He was close-mouthed about the blue sling. Who's your source about Steven?"

"That's confidential."

"You piss me off, Thomas. Just keep messing around in these investigations and you could bite off more than you can chew, even given your big mouth."

"Harmon, let's just change the subject. So, how's your new deputy working out? The cute one, Deputy Altemier?"

It was silent on the sheriff's end of the conversation. Then Harmon said, "Have a nice day, Thomas," and hung up. Loudly.

Well, shoot, if some people didn't have emotions, wouldn't it be a boring world?

I got on the internet to check emails. There was one from Ernie. It read, "Good trip back to snow-free central Georgia. Thanks for the hospitality. Good to catch up in person. I'll be scanning the on-line *Des Moines Chronicle* for your next adventure. You and I both know it's going to happen. We pray for your safety. Jan wants to know how's Liv Olson doing? Have you called her yet? And so on. Blessings, brother!"

The email was dated early this morning. They must have just gotten in.

I responded to Ernie and Jan. "Everything swell," I typed, and signed off.

I checked two other emails and deleted them, then visited my favorite sites to find out the Hawkeyes had defeated Clemson in basketball, the Red Sox were looking to trade for pitching at the meetings in December, and there was corruption in politics.

After my internet activities, I sat down and read some from the Old Testament and happened randomly onto Psalm 68 which read, in part, that we should thank God for our salvation and escapes from death, a clear signal to proceed into troubled waters, or Indian reservations. Then I prayed for myself because, even though I can handle conflict pretty well, I also know when there just might be more than I am up to, and recognize the need to call in air power. It was nine forty-five when I looked up and decided to drop by one of Rockbluff County's better venues for information.

I dressed up a little (clean white shirt under a navy sweater) and left the house and drove over to the Whistling Birch Golf and Country Club.

Even though I was wearing bluejeans, the maitre 'd allowed me into the dining room, where brunch was being served. Walter is flexible with me ever since the events of last year; in fact, for a stuffy and formal man, I think he likes me. He personally led me into the area set aside for brunch and I thanked him.

Brunch at the Whistling Birch Golf and Country Club does not consist of a buffet line. No, it is a time to be seated and waited upon. If you want seconds on anything, the waitress will get it for you on a clean plate. And so on.

Grace, my favorite waitress, greeted me and offered to take me to a table for one, but I saw the person I wanted to talk to, and so declined her offer. She smiled and walked away to assist someone else.

The room was redolent with the fragrance of coffee, scrambled eggs, bacon, and other intoxicating smells I could not identify, but longed for. I searched the room and saw Jurgen Clontz at a table for two, by himself. He looked at me and I raised my eyebrows, even though my right one objected. He beckoned me forward with his left hand.

"May I?" I asked as I put my hand on the back of the vacant chair at Clontz's table.

"Please," he said. "May I order something for you?" He snapped his fingers and a waitress appeared, one of the three African-American females in the county, an attractive young woman with elaborate braids in her hair and a full figure stuffed into her white blouse.

"Our friend would like to order, Karisma, and please put it on my tab. Thomas, what will it be?"

"I'd like a double. I mean a double Diet Coke, or Pepsi, either one.

"A double Diet Coke okay?" Karisma asked.

"Okay, *sir*!" Jurgen said.

Karisma's head dropped a couple of degrees. "Double Diet Coke okay, sir?" she asked, a smile returning to her face.

"Yes. Thank you."

Karisma left and Jurgen Clontz looked at me, dabbing at his mouth with the linen napkin. The remnants of toast, Eggs Benedict, and cottage cheese with chives remained on his plate. Jurgen is not a friend, although he is one of the people who participated in saving my life a while back – that is, he was able to discover that the person being sent to kill me was a woman, which gave us a serious advantage in crime prevention.

I had uncovered during the course of my snooping back then that he was involved in a fraudulent scheme to secure the highest bid for the Soderstrom Farms that eventually went for forty-four million bucks. And change. Jurgen is a land glutton. The license plate on his Jaguar reads "MY LAND." He owns thousands of acres of Iowa land, some in Wisconsin, and quite a bit in Illinois. He wants to own America and won't stop until he has it – it's a hunger that cannot be satisfied. Sort of like me and sausage.

Anyway, there was no way to prove he was involved in the fraudulent scheme, just a he- said-she said kind of thing, but he had the dignity to withdraw his offer and slip out of the arms of the enforcers of the law. It was a close call, and Sheriff Payne decided not to push it since Clontz had used his considerable resources to provide us with a heads up regarding the woman who wanted to put me at room temperature. Although she wasn't the first woman who wanted me dead, she was the first professional to attempt to separate my body from my soul.

I appreciate what Jurgen did for me, even though his reason was that any more violence in Rockbluff would negatively impact land values, and his net worth, so he didn't want me shot. I'll take what I can get. Since then, we've been on speaking terms when we meet at Grange meetings and tractor pulls.

I looked at the departing Karisma and then back at Jurgen and said, "Still berating the help, eh?"

"Still the Chairman of the Board of Directors, ever vigilant for transgressions of the help that might lower our rating from four stars. It looks like you've been fighting again, Thomas. When will you learn?"

"I've already learned. Hate to admit it, but sometimes I enjoy it."

"And I must say, you do it so well. Now, what can I do to provide you with more fights?"

After securing his promise of secrecy, I briefed him on what was going on with the murder of Cindy Stalking Wolf and our visit to the Chalaka rez. He already knew about the Jarlssons. Not surprisingly, he knew Ted Hornung. He did not know Martin Rodman. That told me a lot. I asked his assessment of the principles. He just started to speak when Karisma came by with my Diet Coke. I smiled at her and she smiled back and left.

"Thomas," Jurgen began, adjusting his white shirt cuffs extending from the sleeves of his navy blue blazer, "I have bad news for you."

Jurgen is a dandy, a fastidious dresser, and a misogynist. So much to adore. His silk tie was a deep orange that shouldn't have looked good, but somehow did, complementing his sandy hair and ruddy complexion.

"Is this the bad news before the good news thing?" I asked.

"Nothing but bad news. Let me advise you, and there's no charge this time: Stay away from Ted Hornung. He is powerful and he is rich, and he is connected to a large criminal entity. You cannot win this one. Let the law take care of it."

"The casino is a criminal entity? The Anishinabes?"

"*Everyone* is a criminal in this life. Everyone has a mob. Or a union. Not just the Italians and Irish and Columbians. I guess these Indians do, too, but that's not the point. It's not the casino *per se* that is criminal. I hear it's on the up and up. It's the businesses *around* the casino where one bumps into nefarious, and powerful, organizations. Prostitution, loan sharking, illicit gambling, protection. You won't be able to beat them, even given your talents obtained in that nebulous background of yours. Stay away, Mister O'Shea."

"What would *you* do if your friend's niece were murdered? How would you proceed?"

"First, your premise is flawed. I don't have friends. They only weaken you, make you vulnerable. That's why kidnappers never kidnap loners. But, if I were in your place, I'd probably hire somebody, or somebodies, to take them out."

"Where's the satisfaction in that?"

"Dead enemies. Fewer enemies."

"Anything else?" I asked.

"No. Just don't do it. You can't cut off the head of the snake. You'll never get to it."

"Maybe you're right, but maybe we can make the snake lose interest, count its losses, and slither on, a sadder but a wiser snake."

"You are an idiot, but one I admire a little. By the way, would you like to sell me your land? I'll pay you double what you paid."

"Thanks, Jurgen. I appreciate the offer, and the information about Mr. Hornung. Helpful."

"Lunatic Mooning has a broken arm. That should tell you something about the quality of the opposition."

"That was just a numbers issue. You should have seen the other guys." I got up, drank half my Diet Coke, put the glass down on the table, and thanked him.

"You're going to just plunge ahead, aren't you?"

I gave him a big smile and left him there at his table, shaking his head.

My next stop was The Grain o' Truth Bar & Grill. Lunatic's Packard was not in the parking lot, but there were many other cars and pickup trucks. Lunch crowd. I parked, crossed the slate patio with shallow puddles of melted snow, and pushed my way inside. Moon was behind the bar. Sinatra was on the juke box, singing about reasons why a lady was a tramp. Moon likes to enlighten his clientele about good music. I approached the bar.

"How ya doin', Moon?"

"Fine. Why?"

I rolled my eyes and ordered a Three Philosophers and a bratwurst. He poured my ale into a tulip glass and set the brat on the grill, then turned back to me, performing all the functions easily with one hand. The blue sling was in pristine condition.

"So when do we go back and clean up?" he asked.

"Patience, Crazy Horse. I'm gathering information on the opposition. It looks like we'll have our hands full, but I can't wait to go back."

"Not today, then?"

"No. A day or two. Maybe three."

"Ugh," he said, and tended to my brat, rotating it one-eighty on the grill.

"Packard in the body shop?"

"Of course. They picked it up this morning at dawn. It will be in rehab for three days."

"When we go back up, let's take my truck."

"I'm ready to go now."

"I need more information about our adversaries. Harmon doesn't have anything yet, on Cindy or the Jarlssons. We know more than the cops. I pestered him on the phone this morning and he's strung tight, and he knows about Doltch. And there's something going on with Penny Altemier, too. I tried to change the subject, just to see how she's doing and he hung up on me."

"Harmon is busy, and now Liv's mad at him. His waters are turbulent," Moon said.

"Love the metaphor. You are waxing eloquently for a stoic."

"I am not stoic. I am Ojibwa."

"And Anishinabe."

"That, too."

"And a poet," I continued.

"Injury invites introspection."

"You are one profound dude," I said.

He retrieved my brat and brought it on a ceramic platter piled high with French fries, a stainless steel vat of ketchup, and a squeeze bottle of Dijon mustard.

I said, "How do you know Liv's mad at him?"

Moon gave me a look and I understood. Childhood friends. He then inclined his head toward a booth in the back. "Go to her," he said.

I followed his eyes. Liv Olson was sitting by herself, studying a glass of white wine. I thanked Moon, took my lunch and Belgian ale with me, and strolled over to Liv's booth. She looked up and smiled, rubbing her palms against her cheeks, where there had been tears.

"Got room for a friend?"

"A friend? Sure," she said, shrugging. "Why not?'

"You okay, Liv?" I asked, sliding into the booth and setting down my food and drink.

"Just dandy," she said, reaching across the table and taking my Three Philosophers, then draining half. "Oops," she said, sliding the glass back. She chased it with a sip of her wine.

"Is this about Harmon?"

Liv took a deep breath, let it out slowly, her chest magnificent even under a heavy green RHS sweatshirt. She fixed her gaze on me, her blue eyes intense and stormy, and said, "You know, Thomas, I'm not attracted to women, God knows. And I'm not much impressed with some of the men I've run into. *Lately*. Do you suppose there's another sex somewhere I could try out?"

I took a sip of what remained of my ale, smiled, and waved my right hand back and forth saying "Me, me!" like a kid trying to get the teacher's attention. Liv teaches English at Rockbluff High School. We have a short, but intense and appealing past.

Liv snorted. A dismissive snort that hurt my feelings. Then she leaned across the table, took my face in her hands, studied what she saw, cocked her head, and let go, sliding back onto her bench seat.

"You *might* work out, but it's a remote possibility. You're too obviously a man. And men simply cannot be trusted. So, Thomas, what happened to your face? Fighting bad guys again? With Moon?"

"Very bad guys. They lost."

"Such a competitor," she said, slumping. Her eyes were leaking again.

"Is this about Harmon? Something he's done?"

"Harmon. And Deputy Altemier. I caught them in *flagrante dilecto* two nights ago."

"That means 'in blazing offense' doesn't it?"

"How did you know that?"

"I read a lot. You know that," then, before I could consider my words, I said, "Are you sure?"

She glared at me and I apologized. I said, "So Harmon was bopping Altemier. That stinks."

Liv looked at me. "Yes. It does."

I tried to ease away from the topic. "Jan Timmons wanted to know how you were doing and whether I had called you yet. In this morning's email from Georgia. She likes you. She loves me. I guess I won't tell her how you're doing."

"Thank you. Tell me about your latest fistfight. I'm thinking you should have asked me to go along with you guys last night. For adult supervision."

"I try to keep the innocent out of my problems with bad people." As soon as I said it, I wished I hadn't. History.

"Tell me, how's that principle working out?" she asked, pulling at the neck of her Rockbluff High School sweatshirt, exposing where the bullet had gone through her left trapezius. The pucker scar was obvious.

"No need to rub it in. You probably saved my life. But you know I didn't want that to happen, your being shot I mean, and you also know I'm sorry. And," I went on, "you were right about bad things happening around me. It's happened again, but it's not like I'm seeking them out."

"The hell you don't! So you and Moon were kidnapped last night, dragged up to the Chalaka rez, and forced to fight?"

"We can't ignore the fact that someone murdered Moon's niece, stole her body, and probably murdered the Jarlssons. Can't leave that alone, Liv. And I'm not going to apologize for it. Official Law Enforcement isn't getting anywhere. Too many rules, too many protocols, too much timidity about lawsuits. The Jarlsson's daughters have filed Missing Persons Reports, which brings in the state and federal people, but they have hundreds of those reports to deal with. I don't expect much. So I'm not going to ignore what's happened. Moon and I were compelled to go up to the rez. It's the right thing to do."

"The right thing to do is help law enforcement, as objectionable as that thought is to me personally," she said, "not go beat up a bunch of Indians and get pounded yourself. Moon's arm is *broken*, Thomas! And your eyebrow makes you look stupid, which somehow seems fitting."

I ignored her observation. "This is an exception needing attention. It's personal. Besides, we didn't just beat up Indians. We also beat up several African-Americans."

"But you do this *all the time*," she said, exasperated, ignoring my inclusion of the black guys. "It's *always* personal, Thomas. It is."

"You exaggerate. I only do this every eighteen months or so. Before last year, I hadn't done anything like that for over twenty years. Truly."

"Thomas, you shot and killed two men in your house. You wounded another. You put those two thugs from Dubuque in the hospital. You tore up a couple of rednecks out at Shlop's Roadhouse. And now, look at you! You're messed up again from another incident. On a freaking *Indian* reservation! In another freaking *state*! What's wrong with you!"

It was a fair question, and I thought about it. But then I realized she probably couldn't handle the truth about me and violence, so I just smiled my winning smile and said, "I think it's dietary. Vegetable overexposure."

She didn't get it.

"Thomas, you aren't always funny. You sit there making wisecracks and I'm here across from you and my life's a freaking *typo*, Thomas, and I can't delete it and I can't use white out to make it better. My husband left me for a man, then I fall for you and you lie to me and get me shot, and now Harmon's dumped me for a bimbo from Dubuque half his age. I am not having fun, and there you are, shooting people and getting in fights over and over, fighting off Suzanne and Penny, and you're just cruising along having a fine old time. We've had this conversation before."

"Liv, I don't think you want to compare your downers with mine," I said, my voice low.

She looked as if I had just pushed her, hard, in the chest. Her shoulders sagged, then she took my Three Philosophers and drank the rest of it. At least I'd had a taste. Then she looked at me, and there was some of that fire in her eyes I had seen before, and I knew she was going to speak with fervor.

"You know something, Thomas, you can always pull out your dead family and trump everyone else's troubles. You can. What happened to you is the worst that can happen to a person. I am sorry it happened. Everyone in this town is sorry. People in *other states* are sorry. But that doesn't mean other people can't hurt, too. When I just now told you my life was a typo, you immediately shot me down with your trump card. Well done. You win. You always win, so good for you. Just continue being what you are, whatever this is besides 'all about you.' Have a good time with it. Me? I'm tired of it all. You just wear me out. I'm just not strong enough to deal with you. Sorry."

Moon showed up with another Three Philosophers, noted Liv's facial expression and stiffened body language. He set the ale down in front of me, took the empty glass, and departed with some degree of Ojibwian haste.

Liv had gone quiet, dropping her eyes. She picked up her wine glass and finished the few swallows left. "I'm sorry," she said again. "I shouldn't have said that. Your family is off limits. I'm sorry, Thomas."

"No, *I'm* sorry. I should have listened. Please talk to me."

"The moment has fled." She started to slide out of the booth.

"May I call you? May I ask you out to dinner when I call you?" I asked, relying on what had worked once before.

She offered a small, sad smile, said, "I don't think so," and left.

I was encouraged. She did not give a definite "No" to my offer. I turned to my brat and ale, mildly comforted by the reliability of good food and drink, something positive about our "I'm sorry" fusillade.

CHAPTER SEVENTEEN

"A man's got to know his limitations."

- Clint Eastwood, as Dirty Harry

After listening to Jurgen Clontz's assessment of the adversary, and knowing that Moon was badly banged up, and there were lots of folks working for Ted Hornung up in Chalaka, and even more muscle behind them, it seemed prudent to attend to the strengthening of my hand. The fact that I'm getting older never once figured in to my calculations. No way. Or the fact that I took some pretty good shots I might have evaded in earlier times during my pre-Karen years.

So Monday morning Gotcha and I drove to Iowa City and were lucky to find a vacant parking place within two blocks of the University of Iowa Student Union Building down by the Iowa River. I went around and opened the passenger door, Gotcha hopped down from the cab, and we set off. It was the first day of classes after their Thanksgiving Break, and students were drifting here and there, every last one of them using a cell phone as they strolled in the achingly cold, sunlit morning. A few who looked where they were going saw us walking along toward the SUB. One was a pretty girl.

"What a beautiful dog!" she exclaimed, walking right up to us. We stopped. Gotcha was not on a leash because I had taught her to be obedient and to follow voice commands.

"Sit," I said. Gotcha sat. I stood next to her.

The girl had smart gray eyes and was wearing a nice, full-length lavender cloth coat, a white scarf around her neck, and a lavender knit cap on her head that matched her coat. She asked, "May I pet your dog? What's his name?"

"Her name is Gotcha, and yes, you may pet her. She likes people, unless they are bad," I said. "If you're a bad person, she'll bite, so take your chances."

The girl looked at me with an impish smile, assessing my words, then she laughed. "I'm not worried," she said, and came to a full squat in front of Gotcha. The girl held out her hand in a fist, palm down, for Gotcha to sniff. Gotcha sniffed.

And then Gotcha started wiggling her little root of a warped tail, came to her feet, and bumped into the girl, licking her face, and putting her on her backside. The girl laughed loudly and Gotcha pounced, slurping the helpless girl's face.

"Gotcha, no!" I said, and she desisted. I told her to sit again and she did, all the while eyeing the student and hoping for another opportunity to slurp her face. The girl got up, laughing.

"What a fabulous dog," she said. "That's the hardest I've laughed in some time. I guess there's nothing too bad that can happen when there's such a fine creature on the planet. That was terrific therapy."

"I'm glad. My name is Thomas," I said.

"Of course you are," she replied, and I noticed for the first time a faint English accent. "And I am Chelsea. Pleased to meet you. This is wonderful, and thank you so much for allowing this encounter, but I must be off. Thank you so much! Bye-bye, Gotcha, you wonderful girl," she said, patting my dog's big shoulders and head. Gotcha remained sitting and looking very proud of herself.

The girl, a marvelous and astute young woman, briskly marched away, humming something, heading in the direction of the English-Philosophy Building. Made my day, and that's for sure. Good therapy for me, too, to have such a wonderful encounter in the midst of everything else going on in my life – murder, kidnappings, Liv Olson mad at me.

We proceeded on, Gotcha and me, entering into the SUB by the front doors, noticing as we sauntered along that male students tended to look askance at Gotcha while female students, generally speaking, smiled at her.

Inside, we meandered about until we found a bank of pay phones. Gotcha and I approached, and I made a call to a number that would lead to another number and so on, most messages untraceable, many by word of mouth in dank habitats of dangerous people on maybe more than one continent. Almost certainly more than one continent, and eventually reaching the ears of Clancy Dominguez.

I finished my brief call and stood and, just as I turned around, a young man in a shirt, tie, and blazer with the University of Iowa seal emblazoned over the left breast came up to me and said, "You can't have a dog in here unless it's a guide dog, sir."

"Sure I can. I just did."

"But you can't. You need to leave," he insisted, looking a little nervous when I stood close to him, seeming to lose his resolve. "It's against the rules," he added.

"We were just leaving, Spoilsport." I brushed by him, saying, "Gotcha, come." Which she did.

Once outside, another fine thing happened regarding Gotcha. Three girls walking together stopped and asked the same questions Chelsea had, and got the same answers. And then they swarmed over

Gotcha, petting her and rubbing her ears and massaging her shoulders. A look of bliss came over the Bulldog's face, and I had to smile.

"We all have dogs at home, and we miss them," one of the girls said, smiling up at me.

"I understand," I said.

For a full five minutes Gotcha received the love of three girls, evoking jealousy from me, and then they were on their way. Gotcha looked up at me and actually grinned, a horrid yet beautiful sight, and we set off again, charged up by one of the best parts of people – that they love dogs, too. At the same time, I couldn't help but think that the girls were about the age Annie would have been.

Back in the truck, we drove around town for a while as I reminisced about places where Karen and I had lived. Gotcha slept. Down to the 900 block of Iowa Avenue, over to Hotz Avenue (between Parsons and Clapp – a story right there) and out to Emerald Avenue by Finkbine Golf Course, I allowed myself the luxury of living for a while in fine and pleasant memories of when Karen and I were in town and bursting with dreams and plans and love.

But then my stomach growled, waking up Gotcha, so I found a drive-through Burger King near I-80 and ordered two Whoppers and fries for me, a cheeseburger for Gotcha, which she ingested with the sound of a sump pump starting up, devouring the sandwich in less than ten seconds. Then she belched and flopped down on the shotgun seat and fell asleep again, her thick tongue hanging out to afford better breathing.

We took our time driving home, avoiding the interstates and sticking to back roads, just enjoying the morning and the small towns as we motored through Mount Vernon, Prairieburg, and Greeley. The humble beauty of the small towns, small farms, and rolling hills gave me a kind of pleasure that's hard to explain other than to say I felt at home, even though I am all alone and stripped of my family I would have gladly died to protect.

Life doesn't knock us down, it holds us up with one hand and slaps us back and forth with the other.

As we approached rural Rockbluff, I thought about what might come from my phone call earlier in the day.

I had not seen Clancy for over twenty years. He had disappeared into Costa Rica eleven years ago and was living off the grid, surrounded by beautiful, brown-skinned women no doubt, and living the good life. However, I suspect that his skills had not eroded very much. He was not one to take it easy, develop hobbies, play golf every day, or retire. Too much energy and too much joy in high-risk situations for him to settle down for very long. To Clancy Dominguez, adrenalin junkies were just half a step above assistant librarians in life's excitement hierarchy.

Clancy had been in my SEAL Training Class, my first one, and became a legend, setting records in virtually every physical challenge presented. Further, he emerged as a unique combination of lunatic and leader, always willing to do extra at every juncture of training. He would be laughing and shouting as we jumped out of helicopters at midnight into the Pacific Ocean with a five-mile swim, with gear, to the island where our assignment waited. Everyone else was silent, meditating, praying, concentrating on the exercise, and Clancy would be chanting, "Let's go! Let's go! Let's get rolling!" He went on after I broke my leg, finished first in his class, and shipped out. We kept in loose contact even after I broke my other leg and received a Medical Discharge from the Navy.

We had become buddies in training, friendly competitors to see who would finish first in our class, in a dead heat when my wimp leg broke. It was one of those, "If you ever need a little help with something . . ." relationships. When the government contacted me to do some contract black ops for them (apparently I had done something in training to get their attention), I jumped at the chance to pick up considerable income and stay sharp doing my best to screw up the lives and organizations of people who hated the United States. I was good at it, and when Clancy was Honorably Discharged from the Navy with a chestful of ribbons and a reputation out of a Quentin Tarantino movie, I hired him and we collaborated on several lucrative missions. Oh, and Clancy Dominguez is the best I have ever seen with a knife, and even better with explosives.

Clancy is a person who would not rate a second look if you saw him on the street. He is five-ten or so, maybe 170 pounds, lean and loose-limbed. His face is unremarkable unless you look into his eyes and notice that one is pale blue and the other is dark brown, and they are intelligent and intense. But he usually wears sunglasses, so you wouldn't notice. He is not built like a bodybuilder, but he is strong, possesses excellent coordination, and 20/10 vision; that is, he sees at 20 feet what most of us can see at 10 feet. And he can hear a cat walking on moss two blocks away, his auditory gifts are so extraordinary.

I stopped by the house, let Gotcha out to do her duties, and then we both went inside where she sought out her favorite recliner, jumped up, pushed it open, and stretched out. I changed into my workout gear, black Umbro bottoms, black cross-training shoes, a gray t-shirt with NAVY in block letters, and a blue sweatshirt. Then I got back in the truck and drove into town.

I arrived at Mulehoff's Earthen Vessel Barbell Club around four-thirty, a little later than I prefer, knowing that there would be a good number of people there, something I try to avoid by usually hitting the weights around one-thirty, between the lunch crowd and the after-work gang. But it was the best I could do right then, so I stretched and got into my upper body routine, starting with incline dumbbell bench presses, blocking out the dozen other members moving around, chatting, lifting.

After a warmup set with a pair of 60's, I pyramided to a set of six reps with one hundred pounders. Dumbell flyes followed with eighties, and then I went to work on my back, doing machine pulldowns with one-eighty, a few dumbbell rows with a hundred-pounder, seated behind the neck presses with two hundred, and so on, sweating like hell and loving it all. Then I hopped onto the elliptical trainer and began that smoothing out part of my workout, and came face to face with Suzanne Highsmith.

"Hiya, big boy," she said, fluttering her eyelashes and wiggling the fingers of her right hand as a greeting. She was wearing black short-shorts that could have been a second skin, and a purple tank top, under which I could discern a sports bra working overtime to fulfill its calling.

"Hello, Suzanne."

"You and Moon should have invited me along on your little trip Friday. I knew something was up when his car wasn't at The Grain o' Truth, and you weren't home. I should have figured out you'd head for the Chalaka Reservation. Dumb me. By the time I figured it out, it was too late to go looking for you guys."

She looked closely at my face. "So Moon wasn't the only one who got bumped around."

"Are you in here to work out? Did you join the Earthen Vessel?" I asked, continuing to work on the elliptical.

"Yes. You remember what I said about the body going south. I'm trying to slow that down a little, plus I just had my chance to see how strong you are. Really. Pretty impressive poundages, Thomas. No wonder you're the toughest man in northeast Iowa."

"Don't start with that."

"Just teasing. Anyway, why don't you buy me dinner tonight? We could meet at The Grain and harass Moon about his broken arm."

I was tempted, but then I realized I couldn't accept. I thought of Liv Olson. I said, "Thanks, Suzanne. But I don't think so. Besides, no one harasses Lunatic Mooning. Trust me on that one."

"Are you messing with me?" She reached down and tugged at the bottom of her short shorts. When she leaned forward, she kept her eyes on me and I let mine slip to the remarkable cleavage her tank top offered. When I looked back, she grinned.

"I am not messing with you," I said, "but I'm flattered that you asked. What do you want from me? Just ask. Maybe I can tell you what you want to know without going to the trouble and expense of taking you out to dinner."

"You are a rude and inhospitable man," she said, then flounced off to her workout.

So now I had two beautiful women mad at me. I shrugged my shoulders and finished my thirty minutes and 350 calories from the elliptical. That nullified about twenty percent of a Whopper, I think. I stepped down and pulled my towel from the handle. And there was Suzanne again.

"Sorry I snapped at you," she smiled. "My bad. It's okay. Maybe I'll see you at The Grain later. Now, I have a question for you. About working out. Since you're knowledgeable about the body, what might I do to build up my chest?"

"Nothing," I said, glancing down. "I think it's already happened."

"You are *such* a nice man," she said, smiling.

"No, I'm not," I replied, "but sometimes I say nice things." Suzanne went back to her workout and I watched her go, admiring from the back her choice of workout attire.

I draped my towel around my neck, and walked over to a row of coat hooks along a wall next to the counter where one could purchase protein powder, energy drinks, muscle magazines, and high-protein candy bars. The DVD selection was next to the cash register. I took my sweatshirt off a hook and shrugged it on, reached into the pocket for my keys.

Just then Mike Mulehoff came into his gym. He had a funny look on his face, as if I were amusing him by working out, or he had just heard an entertaining joke. But neither was the case.

"Why didn't you guys invite me on your trip up to the rez?"

"Well," I said, "I didn't think we'd need any help to just ask a few questions."

"And that worked out how?" he asked.

"Not so good, obviously. Too bad about Moon's broken arm."

"And it looks like you might have walked into a door," he said, eying my face.

"Actually, the door jumped out at me, just as I was getting ready to go into an authentic Anishinabe souvenir earring shop."

Mike smiled. "He's more upset about the Packard being trashed than his busted arm. So, now that Lunatic's on the injured-and-unable-to-perform list, next time you head north, give me a call."

"Unless it's a school night."

"Unless it's a school night," he replied, laughing. "Therefore I wouldn't suggest any more fact-finding expeditions other than Friday or Saturday nights. So what did you find out? Moon wasn't too forthcoming. He did say you guys have a lead on some guy named Marty Rodman."

"Just how good a lead it is remains to be seen. I doubt much will come of it."

"You think he killed Moon's niece? Or ordered it?" he asked.

"Who said the girl was killed? Where did you hear that?"

"Small town, close friends," Mike said.

"Of course," I said, "that."

"Well, I've got some papers to grade," he said, turning away. He turned back quickly and said, "Did I mention that I have a Bible study in my home on Wednesday nights?"

"No, I never knew, but thanks for the heads up," I said as he headed for his little office. Mike has been trying to get me to come to that Bible study for more than a year now, and someday I'll actually go. Honest.

CHAPTER EIGHTEEN

"Life is too short for self-hatred and celery sticks."

- Marilyn Wann

I took a long shower, leisurely shampoo, and a close shave after I got home from the gym at six-fifteen. And then, after slipping into bluejeans, hiking boots, and a heavy sweater, I headed for The Grain. My workout had left me cleansed. And hungry. And I was ready for some serious food. I could hear the siren song of a brace of Loony Burgers.

On my way over to The Grain o' Truth, I began to have second thoughts about turning down Suzanne. No need to be rude to her, which I guess I was, implying she wanted something from me.

Moon's place was quiet, subdued. I nodded at a few regulars who nodded back. Moon was behind the bar and it was good to see him at work. I approached him as he was handing over a tray with a pitcher and three glasses to a new waitress, a little thing with bootblack hair and a hank of it hanging over her face. Fashionable and annoying. She looked tired and drained even though she was probably in her twenties.

"Misty, meet Thomas O'Shea, my friend," Moon said. The girl gave a little curtsy and a small smile and nodded. Then, with Rachel

Bergman beside her, she took away the tray and headed across the room to a booth occupied by three gray-haired women.

"New employee," he said. Moon hires females with backgrounds of abuse, alcohol, and drugs, and works with them to help get them back on their feet. They usually respond to his offer and, with Rachel's supervision, turn out pretty well, moving on most of the time to better lives, strengthened.

"Good kid," he said. "Now, what can I do for you, Thomas? You look hungry."

"I *am* hungry. Just finished working out. Pumping iron. You should try it." Moon never works out that I know of. He's one of those rarities with great genes and a body that benefits from hard work. He wrestles with kegs and wholesale food deliveries and who knows what else, plus hustling pitchers and stacking chairs at the end of the day, and occasionally escorting out the door some obstreperous customer.

"My Zumba instructor forbids it. Now, as to your order?"

I ordered two Loony Burgers and a pair of Three Philosophers and asked Moon to join me. To my surprise, he accepted, acknowledging that it was time for his dinner break, which is usually taken standing up while filling orders. He asked Rachel to take over behind the bar and she smiled and agreed.

She said, "I wish *I* could have dinner with Thomas" and gave me a wink. I like it when women wink at me. Sometimes Rachel pats me on the butt in passing. I like it when women pat me on the butt.

Moon brought my order and I took a booth near the back that afforded a good view of the bar and the front door. Someone had played Andy Williams' rendition of "Moon River," the song that launched his career independent of The Williams Brothers, Iowans all. My guess was one of the gray-haired ladies had approached the Wurlitzer.

I waited for Moon before starting in on my food. He appeared quickly with a thick sub packed with meat and cheese. I silently blessed our meal and we began eating, focusing on the food. Halfway through my second Loony Burger, Moon looked at me and said, "Your eyebrow is off center. Makes you look quizzical."

"Liv said it makes me look stupid."

"You looked that way before."

"True, but I *am* quizzical. I'm quizzical about a lot of things, but I'm going to eventually be unquizzical when I get some damn answers about Cindy's murder."

"Me, too."

"We're going to have to make things happen. Stir things up."

He nodded. "Which we did, but not enough. Let's go back."

"Let's."

Nothing more was said for the rest of our meal. No need, both of us worn out from our extensive verbal exchange. We finished and got up, I bussed the dirty dishes and glasses, and Moon headed behind the bar and back to work. I decided to hang out for a while and just enjoy the genuine ambiance of a subdued Monday night.

I shot a few games of pool, picked up a few friendly bucks from a retired farmer in for the evening, stuffed my winnings into the "TIPS" jar by the flip-top counter, and played some tunes on the big, antique Wurlitzer jukebox in the corner. Then I ordered another Three Philosophers and just lounged at the bar for a while.

And then Suzanne Highsmith waltzed through the front door.

She stumbled, slipped off her short fur jacket and tried to hang it on the coat tree by the door. She missed the hook on her first two tries, succeeded on the third, and ambled over to the bar, smiling crookedly. She plopped onto the barstool next to me, exhaled loudly, blew a kiss at Moon, and ordered a dirty martini.

"I jus' love those drinkies," she said. "And how are you tonight, big boy?"

"Fine," I said. "Are you okay, Suzanne?"

"I am seriously sherenpipidus. Sherendoofusis. Sheren something." Her head dropped and lolled from side to side.

"Serendipitous?" I asked. Moon brought her dirty martini.

She slumped a little and pointed a finger gun at me, dropping the thumb. "Tha's it, Tommy. Now, I have a confession to make."

"Do I look like a priest?" I asked.

She exploded into laughter that tapered off to giggling sprinkled with snorts. Rachel passed us, trailing Misty. And patted me on the butt while shaking her head at Suzanne's antics.

"Tha's funny, Tommy. You, a priest? Might as well be, though, since you won't sleep with me." Before I could say anything, she continued, "Anyway, my 'fession is about to come out. My God, it's hot in here." She tugged at her sweater, pulling at the neck then letting it go.

"Your confession better not be about business," I said. Her eyes were a little swimmy and her smile just a bit on the naughty side. I wondered how much she'd drunk before she found Moon's place. And where she'd loaded up on 'drinkies'.

"It is not about business, at least, not about *business* business." The naughty smile became naughtier.

"What then? I love other people's confessions."

She lowered her voice. "I am not wearing any frilly underthings."

I leaned forward and said, "Neither am I."

She smiled and said, "I am not wearing *any* underthings."

"And why is that?" I asked. "Didn't pack enough for your stay in Rockbluff?"

"No, it's because I didn't want anything to slow you down after you take me back to the motel." She sat back, folded her arms beneath her breasts, nudged them up a tad, then leaned with her elbows on the bar. Moon found something to do.

I said, "Did you drive yourself over here? From where?"

"I was out at The Wishful Birch place."

"You mean The Whispering Birch Golf & Country Club?"

"At the bar. And I drove myself there and I drove myself here, although I did leave a couple of smudgies on some other cars badly parked out there."

"I'll take you back to your room." I put money on the bar and a few singles in the TIPs jar.

"Indeed," she said, and I came around and helped her to her feet and led her out of The Grain, grabbing her coat and slipping it over her shoulders. Several older men gave me a smile and a thumbs up.

It was frigid outside. In the truck, Suzanne tried to bridge the gap between me and her side of the cabin, scooching and twisting around the console until her head was on my shoulder and her right hand rested on my right thigh.

I drove slowly, thinking my way through the situation, endeavoring to take the high moral road and not take advantage, then telling myself that Suzanne was a grownup woman of great allure that wanted me to sleep with her, then telling myself that I needed to be true to Liv, then telling myself that maybe nothing would ever come from my relationship with Liv. And then I thought all those thoughts again. Twice more. Three times. I asked myself what would Dietrich Bonhoeffer do? I did not ask myself what would Kobe Bryant do.

By then, I was pulling up in front of the Rockbluff Motel and Suzanne was asleep on my shoulder, her mouth open, a little thread of drool leading from her lovely, full lower lip to her chin. I eased her to a sitting position while I started to get out and go around and help her down.

She woke when I maneuvered her upright in her passenger's seat.

"Oh my God, I must have fallen ashleep!" she muttered loudly. "How embarrashing is *that*?"

"Don't worry about it, Suzanne." I quickly slid out of the truck and went around to her door. I opened the door and took her hand and she kind of slithered backward and out, her body like a liquid. I grabbed her purse.

I supported her as we walked to door number 38, which was locked. Of course. I fished her key out of her purse and tilted her against me as I worked the key and opened the door.

Inside, she went slack as she passed out again, so I carried her into the bedroom, dumped her fur coat onto a chair, pulled the covers back from her bed, and gently deposited her there. I slipped off her shoes, put a pillow under her head, and pulled the covers up to her chin, congratulating myself for not peeking at her body. She began snoring, effectively snuffing out any impure thoughts I might have had regarding my next step. Years ago I would have awakened her with kisses and then spent the night. Now that I am a nearly-completed candidate for sainthood, I did the right thing, aided by the twin realities of advanced age and experiences with weird women half a bubble off.

Once I was sure she was asleep, I walked through the entire suite, checking to make sure no one was lurking around to cause trouble. I looked behind doors, in the shower stall, under the bed and sofa. Then I turned out all the lights except a night light in her bathroom and a small table lamp in the living room. I left the door to the bedroom open a little so there would be enough light from the lamp for Suzanne to see when she woke up. I tossed her key on the coffee table and left, making sure the door locked behind me.

That was Monday night. On Tuesday, she was nowhere to be found. I worked out at Mulehoff's, lower body day, and mostly stayed home, except for a side trip to the library to study satellite photographs of the area around Chalaka. I called Liv Olson and, when she didn't pick up, I left a message for her to call. I figured she was grading papers.

On Wednesday I worked out and later dropped in on Mike Mulehoff's Men's Bible Study. He and Gabby have a beautiful stone house that they renovated and upgraded. It's on a quiet side street as the end of a cul-de-sac. When he opened the door, he did not look surprised. He invited me in and led me to a book-lined study where I said hello to Gunther Schmidt, Arvid Pendergast, Harmon Payne, and another man I did not recognize. He got up and came across the room and said, "I'm David Elmendorf, Thomas" and we shook hands.

"He's Doctor Elmendorf, family practice," Mike said. Then we all shook hands and took seats. Shortly after, Gabby, Mike's wife, came in with a tray of heavy hors d'ouvres, setting them on a side table. Mike took drink orders, offering beer, cokes, hot chocolate, and water. Arvid asked which beers he had, and Mike said he had Heineken. We all voted for Heineken except for Harmon, who went with hot chocolate "In case my pager goes off and duty calls."

In a moment, Mike was back, handing out frosted glasses of Heineken and a big mug of hot chocolate for Harmon, then we all moseyed over to the side table loaded with pigs in a blanket, chips and dip, and pimento cheese sandwiches on white bread cut into halves with the crusts removed. I went last and was pleased to see that everyone before me acted as if they had not eaten in a while. I followed suit. We all sat down, nibbled and sipped. Mike spoke.

"I want to welcome Thomas to our group," he said, and everyone nodded. Then he said, "Let's continue with our study of the Book of Acts, Chapter 28, written by Luke, the physician. The Kingdom of God is the theme of this book, and it is clear, which is good, and steps on our toes, which we can't avoid if we're honest with ourselves."

"If the Word of God doesn't step on our toes, something's wrong," Dr. Elmendorf said, "and I'm not even a podiatrist."

From that point, the study went forward and then it was time to stop at the appointed time of 9 PM. I said nothing all night, trying to get the lay of the land and not make a fool of myself. After a prayer by Gunther, the meeting broke up with a few hugs that I avoided, some backslapping I accepted, and see you Sunday's. I hung around at Mike's request after everyone else left. I don't know where Gabby was, but I could hear a television in a distant room.

"I'm glad you came, Thomas," he said as we hung around the closed front door. The air was cold from all the men leaving into the night. "I hope you got something out of it. This is a good group."

"I wasn't too crazy about asking God to reveal to me the truth about myself," I said.

Mike laughed. "Nobody likes that one. Anyway, glad you came. Hope to see you later."

I thanked him and left, trudging out to my truck as others were driving away. He stood in the door and watched me go until I was in the cab and the engine was running. We waved at each other and I drove off, glad I had been there, especially for the heavy hors d'ouvres. And glad Mike hadn't made a big deal out of my being there for the first time.

That was Wednesday. And Liv Olson was still not returning my calls. More papers to grade, I suppose, and they had a play they were putting on, which I understand she was directing.Thursday had me back again at the gym, but mostly staying home, watching basketball games and reading Hemingway for the first time in years. *A Farewell To Arms*, and the saddest closing line in literature.

On Friday, I had dinner at the Heisler's house, the manse behind Christ the King church. It was a late dinner, eight-thirty, so the children could introduce themselves beforehand and say goodnight. I bought a big bouquet of mixed-color roses – eighteen of them, and a nice bottle of Stuhlmuller Vineyards Cabernet Sauvignon 2004. Molly had told me the fare would be Swedish meatballs, so I guessed the wine was okay for the occasion.

It was cold, in the low 20's, when I left Gotcha snoozing on her favorite recliner and drove over to the Heislers. I parked in the four-car parking space behind the church, between the van I had seen over a year ago at the Soderholm tragedy, and a Honda Accord with a Luther College bumper sticker. The porch light was on and many of the downstairs windows shone brightly, and I thought about the last time I had approached that front door. It had been with Ruth VanderKellen at my side, and we had kissed, and I had allowed myself to dream that maybe there would be a future for us together. But then she had left town for California, leaving a note for me with Lunatic Mooning, the note about the first snowfall, and her return to Rockbluff in the springtime. To stay.

Hoping she was now rejected by that boyfriend, suffering from shingles, and thirty pounds overweight, I squared my shoulders and marched up to the front door. Before I could knock, the door opened to reveal Molly Heisler, aglow with health and happiness. I could hear Carl in the background thumping around with squealing children.

"Welcome to our home, Thomas," she said. "We are so glad you could come over tonight."

"Thank for inviting me," I said, extending the roses. Her face lit up.

"These are beautiful, Thomas! Thank you! I'll put them in some water right away."

"Amazing what they can do with silk flowers these days. They don't need water," I said.

Molly gave me a quizzical look, then sniffed the flowers, than looked at me and shook her head. "You had me going there, Thomas, but these are real and they smell great."

Another squeal of delight emanated from within. Molly shook her head and said, "That Carl, he's always charging up the children just before they go to bed instead of calming them down. Course, he then reads to them after tucking them in, and that helps them ease off to sleep. Please, come in out of the cold!"

"Here." I handed her the bottle of wine. "I hope you like this."

"Thank you, Thomas. You are so thoughtful."

Molly led me into a formal living room littered with children's books and plastic toys – one a music box of some sort and the others superheros action figures. Carl came in with two children in tow.

"Thomas, glad you're here!" he said. "I want these two to meet you. Go ahead, children."

A blonde girl, maybe seven or eight, stepped forward, extending her hand. "I'm pleased to meet you, Mr. O'Shea. I'm Dahlia. May I get you something to drink?"

"Nice to meet you, Dahlia, and that's a gorgeous name. But no, I don't think I'll have anything right now, but thanks for asking."

Dahlia grinned and looked up at her dad.

"How was that, Dad?"

"Nicely done," Carl said. Then he turned to his son, and nodded. The boy, dark haired, lean like his dad, maybe four years old, turned to me. "I'm pleathed to meet you, Mithter O'Thea. I'm David. Would you like to wrethle?"

"Spoken like a true Iowan. Maybe we can wrestle another time, David, but thanks for asking," I said.

"Well done, children," Carl said, "and now it's to bed. Say goodnight!"

They did, and then Carl took one in each arm and carried them away upstairs. In the meantime, Molly had decanted the wine and poured three glasses, offering me one. And suddenly I was choking back a stinging feeling in my nose and a clutch in my throat, surprised, then angry at the sudden takeover that Molly noticed.

"Are you okay, Thomas?"

I nodded my head and sipped the wine. It was good. I felt better.

"What was it?" she asked, pausing, "Oh. Family."

I nodded again and took another sip and tried to think about Iowa's chance in the Big Ten basketball season. The senior power forward was destined for first team All-American, but could he carry the team until the younger players coalesced into a seamless unit? I decided he could. I felt better then. Carl came into the room and announced that the children were tucked in and it was time to eat, which we did. In addition to the Swedish meatballs, there was curried fruit and mixed vegetables along with homemade bread. The wine went perfectly and I drank too much and then Carl opened another bottle - Kendall Jackson cabernet sauvignon. Mince pie completed the meal.

We moved to the study, where a fire was burning in the fireplace. Carl and Molly sat together in a love seat and I pulled up a leather upholstered chair across from them. Carl said, "I'm glad you could come over tonight. We've been wanting your company here for some time. Something always seemed to come up."

"But you were able to come visit me at my place," I said, "so that was good." I had the sense that I was going to be ministered to, and I didn't really want it, as much as I cared for Molly and Carl.

"Your house is beautiful," Molly said. "And so was your family. I saw the pictures. Karen was beautiful, and so were Annie and Michelle."

"Thank you. Forever young," I said.

"I heard you were at Mike's gathering of revolutionaries this week," Carl said.

"Yes."

"You know Gabby's not Mike's first wife," Carl said.

"Really? I didn't know that."

Molly smiled and stood. "May I get you guys some coffee? Thomas? Carl? I'm having some. No trouble."

"Thank you," I said.

"Irish?" Molly asked.

Carl and I both nodded. "I do have some Jameson's," she said, and headed for the kitchen.

"So Mike's divorced?" I asked.

"No, his first wife, Ellyn, was a farm girl. She was helping out at harvest a few years back, there was an accident at a silo when they were pouring grain into it for storage. She was up at the top and slipped and fell but they couldn't immediately stop the conveyer from continuing to fill. By the time they did stop all the machinery, they couldn't get to her. She was buried alive. She suffocated."

Carl paused. "Mike was the one who dug the body out. He was grief-stricken. I, *we*, worried about him a good long time, prayed for him, talked and counseled him. You'd never know it now. God's comforting."

Molly came into the room carrying a tray with three cups of coffee on it. The aroma of strong coffee and Irish whiskey was welcome on a cold night in northeastern Iowa.

I took the coffee and so did Carl. Molly sat down, taking the last cup into both hands, cradling it. She said, "Mike met Gabby at church. Her husband was killed in Iraq, but she grew up here before she married him and they moved away, serving all over the place. When he was killed, she came home and then she and Mike found each other."

The coffee was good, warming my belly in a couple of ways. I didn't say anything at first, and neither did they. Then I spoke.

"So, when do you want me to ask Liv Olson to marry me?" Might as well come to the point.

Carl looked surprised. Molly pulled back, paused, and grinned. "Well, since you asked, how 'bout tonight?"

"I'm having too good a time here to go get turned down." I forced a smile.

"Thomas," Molly said, "Liv and I are good friends. *Good* friends." She gave me a look that told me maybe Liv had told her about our night together way back when. "She might turn you down, but I wouldn't bet on it."

"I got her shot, you know," I said, "and since you're such good friends you must know she thinks of me as a liar, and she's afraid to be with me, and said there wasn't much to build a relationship on. So there you go."

"That was then, this is now," Molly said with just a hint of an impish smile.

Our conversation fumbled a bit after that, and then I said I needed to get home or Gotcha would worry and thank you very much for dinner and your children are wonderful and I love you guys, I really do, and I'll be fine.

When I got home, Gotcha was not worried. She was asleep. It was after ten, much past her bed time. And that was my week as November faded away and December bulled its way into my life, three evenings of fine food interspersed with workouts, avoiding Suzanne Highsmith, and trying to get Liv Olson to answer my calls on that blasted cell phone.

I was getting more than antsy by the time Saturday came and went, so my decision to take another trip north to the Chalaka Reservation was an easy one. And it was a trip I was going to make on my own. Private. No one would know. I couldn't help but smile at the thought of being back in the game again.

CHAPTER NINETEEN

"The violence between women is unbelievable ... women try to make each other crawl so that their knees are bleeding."

- Tori Amos

It was Sunday morning. I got up and showered and noticed that my bruises from the set-to at the rez were gone and my ear was healed. I pulled the butterfly patches from my injured eyebrow. It tilted a little, providing my face with an inquisitive look that I decided I liked. Do it yourself plastic surgery.

I ate cold pizza left over from the night before when I had taken a meat lovers' pizza out of the freezer and embellished its surface with loads of pepperoni slices and three kinds of shredded cheese. Not wanting to overdue the cholesterol stuff, I left off the extra bacon. I let Gotcha out and in, medicated and fed her, and dressed for church in my cleanest bluejeans and a heavy wool Irish fisherman's sweater Karen had given me years and years ago. According to the thermometer outside my kitchen window, it was nineteen degrees.

Church was good. A solid sermon from Carl Heisler lifted my spirits a little after I realized my spirits were down, thanks to people at church who kept asking me, "Are you okay, Thomas?" which bothered me because I thought I looked pretty good. Maybe they were asking about my spiritual well-being.

The sermon was entitled, "In Whom Do You Trust?" I realized I didn't completely trust God, which made me feel guilty, so I vowed to myself that I would invite Him into my decision-making, but not just yet. The only three people I totally trusted were all dead, and had been dead, for almost two years. But God was not dead, so I took comfort in Carl's sermon. I didn't see Liv. She usually sits middle left with Harmon. I sit in the third row, center. Fewer distractions. After the service concluded and I shook hands and chatted briefly with Carl on my way out of the sanctuary, restating my thanks for Friday night dinner, I headed for Bloom's Bistro since The Grain o' Truth isn't open on the Lord's day. Moon's idea of appealing to spiritual diversity.

Bloom's is cool. It's a fine little bar and restaurant with a big deck hanging out over the Whitetail River. Since it was so cold outside, I didn't expect to find the deck open, so I just edged into the establishment, slowed in front by a bunch of Methodists and pushed from behind by a crowd that looked like they'd be comfortable with Druids.

A perky, blonde, blue-eyed girl in a red ski sweater and charcoal slacks met me. It was Beth Gustafson, my favorite Bloom's waitress.

"Hiya, Mr. O'Shea," she said. "We're pretty crowded. Do you mind sharing a table?"

"Yes, I do mind," I said. I wanted to think about what Carl had said from the pulpit, not engage in small talk with people I didn't know. Or be rude and ignore them.

"Well, then, I guess you'll need to come back in a little bit," Beth said.

I turned to go. Beth touched my shoulder. "Say, would you object to sitting with someone you do know at a table for two?"

"That depends. I know several people I wouldn't want to eat with."

Beth smiled. "I understand. But would being seated with Ms. Olson work out for you?"

I looked away from Beth and out over the crowd. Scrunched in the back at a table slightly larger than a frisbee was Olivia Olson. I decided that would work, and nodded in the affirmative to Beth, who smiled and began leading me to Liv's table.

On the way, Penny Altemier reached out and took my hand. My eyes on Liv, I hadn't noticed Penny. She was sitting with three older men I'd seen around the Rockbluff County Court House, mostly county employees. I didn't recognize her out of uniform. I stopped, told Beth to go ahead, and said hello to Altemier since she hadn't let go of my hand.

"You must be off today," I said, glancing Liv's way. Liv was studying the menu even though she had been in Bloom's dozens of times in her life. She did not look up or see me.

"You look wonderful, Thomas!" Altemier said in a voice better suited to a cheer at a sporting event. Her hand let mine go, then brushed up against my hip, slid upward a few inches, and came to rest on the small of my back. There was a kind of electricity in her touch, and it was the kind of electricity that can light up more than a bug lamp on the porch.

"Thanks, Penny. Same to you."

"Hope to see you again," she said, her voice now low and conspiratorial, almost a whisper. A little husky, nearly breathless. Minor league Marilyn Monroe imitation. Yikes. She pressed her fingertips gently into my lower back and let her hand drop, brushing my hip again. Her eyes were smiling and she was looking at me as if I were a 50% Off The Sale Price item.

I just nodded and produced a quick smile at her and the men she was sitting with, then turned toward Liv Olson's table. She had looked my way, probably when Penny had offered up her high-decibel observation about my appearance.

I found my way to Liv, maneuvering around people coming and going, and tables in close proximity to each other. Bloom's Bistro is popular year 'round, and it deserves the attention. The food is excellent, although sometimes slow to arrive, but worth the wait. And the overall ambiance is friendly, comfortable, and enjoyable. Somehow, Penny Altemier didn't help promote that atmosphere.

"Mind if I join you, Liv?" I said as I arrived at her table.

"Don't mind if you do," she said, her face impassive. "Have a seat, Thomas."

"Thank you." I sat down. She was wearing a white blouse under a blue cardigan that underscored the beauty of her eyes and complexion. There were frilly things at her throat and sleeves. Her makeup was spare, I guess, because I didn't notice it. There was none of the raccoon look so prevalent with women who think makeup reverses the aging process. Just fresh and clean and wholesome. I wanted to touch her.

"Have you checked your voice messages lately?" I asked. "I've been trying to reach you, but I know you've been busy with grading papers and directing the play."

"I did, but I *have* been busy. Much to do."

I decided to change the subject. "Did you order yet?"

"No. I'm indecisive this morning."

"You? Indecisive? Hard to believe. What's your indecision about?"

"Well, I can't decide to order the Belgian waffles or take this butter knife and go over to that woman and see if I can generate enough force for the dull blade to penetrate her skin and sever a carotid artery." She shrugged. "Belgian waffles sound good."

"Okay then, good decision."

Olivia gave me a long look, cocking her head to one side, scrutinizing my face.

"Your face looks better than the last time I saw you, but the eyebrow needs professional help. I could recommend my cosmetic surgeon. He does all my implants. He's excellent."

"You don't have a cosmetic surgeon. You don't need one. Besides, it would go against your fine character."

"Thank you for that. You're right, I do not have a cosmetic surgeon. But the jury's still out on my character."

"*This* jury isn't, not that I would judge. I know your character to be beyond reproach."

"Shoot, you're just being kind to a lady who doesn't have the strength of character to return phone messages. I know how much you hate cell phones, and I appreciate your interaction on my behalf with that vile tool. I really do."

"That's okay. I've got you face to face right now, and that's so much better than a voice over the atmosphere."

Beth showed up then and we ordered Belgian waffles and a Mug o' Bloom's each of coffee. A Mug o' Bloom's is coffee for sure, but in a 20-ounce pottery mug. It has enough caffeine to keep me functioning at a high level until Spring. I ordered a side dish of sausage patties. Beth smiled and left.

"So, now that you've got me, what were you calling about?" Liv asked. She was looking at me with a neutral, but attentive, facial expression.

"I want to take you out to dinner. Whispering Birch if you want, or a little side trip to a place I used to visit in Iowa City. Or I could cook you dinner at Chez O'Shea."

"Chez O'Shea has a nice ring to it. I'd like that, but I must decline. I am so ashamed of myself for what I said to you, I don't think I could be in your home again, your family pictures, all that. I would be an intruder into your privacy. Very uncomfortable. For me, for sure. Maybe for you."

"Maybe we can get past that. Maybe you'd be very welcome in my privacy. That would be peachy."

"That's very sweet of you," she said, and I knew she was going to lower the boom. Whenever a guy is in love with a woman and it's not going to happen, she always precedes with the bomb by saying, "That's very sweet of you." Followed by, "But."

Liv followed form. "But I think not. Too much water under the bridge. Oh! I didn't mean a particular bridge. I mean, I wasn't alluding to Moon's niece. I just meant it as a figure of speech. Sorry."

"And a cliché," I said. "You can do better than that, English person," I said, stinging a little from her put down. "But I would think that my working with Moon would make it *more* likely that you could carve some time out of your exhausting schedule to let me take you to dinner some night, maybe when the play is concluded, and allow yourself to talk my ear off. After all, he's your friend and I'm helping him."

Beth Gustafson showed up with our orders. The fragrance of the coffee preceded her and started my juices percolating. The waffles were huge. I smothered mine in butter, syrup, and jelly. No point in offending any of the food groups by leaving them out.

Liv took a careful portion of her Belgian waffle and ate it, then a big sip from her coffee. I attacked my side order right away, assuaging my prickliness with warm sausage. It isn't good served cold, unlike revenge. I drank coffee. It was good.

"Yes, you are helping him, and it looks like you helped him acquire a broken arm."

"That's right. I said, 'Moon, let's go up to the rez and get you a broken arm. How's that sound, big guy?' Liv, that's exactly how it went down, and Moon was all for it. Said he'd never had a broken arm and was pleased that I was going to help him get one."

Liv shook her head slowly and a faint smile crossed her lips. "You and Moon are pretty formidable. I can't imagine someone whipping him. He won't elaborate on the adventure. I asked him for the details. He just admitted the broken arm."

There was so much background chatter and dishes banging and silverware scraping that I had to lean forward to continue the conversation. When I leaned forward, I got a good whiff of the sausage's aroma and it settled my nerves. A little.

"A gigantic guy with a baseball bat smacked Moon. Shaved head, spooky tats on his skull, a desire for combat," I said. "There just might be a rematch at some point."

"What happened to the guy? Did he lay out Moon and go have a beer?"

"Actually, I was able to show him that he made a poor decision when he and his pals decided to rough us up. You know Moon's car was damaged. Windshield broken out, key marks."

"Those guys had a death wish, didn't they? How many were there?" Liv asked, looking up, chewing. She smiled and took another slug from her coffee mug. I finished off my two sausage patties, wishing I'd had the foresight to request a double order. I guess Liv's fresh beauty had distracted me. It usually does.

"Just six," I said.

"Just six, huh? I see," she murmured, nodding her head in fake approval. I know sarcasm when I see it. "Did you ever think that you might have gotten *killed*, Thomas!"

"How's the play coming along?"

"Oh, just dandy, Thomas! We have some *talented* kids. 'Our Town' is going to be a *hit*. It always is, every four years at your Rockbluff High School Drama Club presentation. Get your tickets early. A hit, I say."

I could see that the conversation was shifting all over the place. Every time there was an opportunity for either of us to get serious, the subject shifted, with Liv the obvious perp, but me accommodating the dialogue and adding to it. Or taking from it.

We finished the meal at about the same time, polished off the big coffees. I took the check over Liv's mild protestations, left a nice tip for Beth, and we walked out together, going a different way to avoid Octopus Arms Altemier. I offered to give Liv a ride, but she said she'd rather walk.

"May I walk you home, then, Miss Olson?" I asked. Her house is just a couple of blocks east of Bloom's Bistro.

"Suit yourself," she said, and strode off. I caught up right away and fell into step with her, heartily encouraged by her passionate desire to have me attend her. We didn't say anything over the two blocks, and the silence pushed down on us.

When we got to her house, she swung open the gate in her front yard and we ducked under the rose arbor. I walked with her up to her door.

"Thank you, Thomas, for lunch and the walk. Nice of you to escort an old maid to her home."

I decided to ignore the tone of her remarks, so I just said, "May I come in?"

Liv opened her unlocked front door just a crack. "I don't think so. Not today."

"I remember the last time I came by your home," I said, harkening back to an evening months before which had led to her bed. And bliss.

"Me, too," she said, "and that's why I'm saying no this time."

I touched her chin and lifted her face to mine. She was blushing, and I thought, what a great thing that there are still women with enough modesty to blush over such things instead of putting it on Facebook.

"Look, I apologized for being insensitive, and I'm not going to do it again," I said, beginning to resent the cold shoulder

"I don't expect you to. Now, really, I must . . . "

"Liv, I was wrong to apologize," I went on. "What I should have done was asked you to *forgive* me. So now it's totally up to you what happens next with us. The ball is in your court."

She pulled her face away from my hand, opened wide the door, and stepped inside, closing the door behind her and leaving me on her front porch, feeling better than I expected. Short of sacrificing a burnt offering of fatlings on her front steps, there was nothing left for me to do to return to her good graces, and all that went with it. But I had a hunch Moon could tell me where I could purchase a fatling or two.

Chapter Twenty

"The belief in a supernatural source of evil is not necessary;
men alone are quite capable of every wickedness."

- Joseph Conrad

I did not sleep well Sunday night, haunted by images of Liv Olson's face, her body, our strong affection for each other manifested in various scenarios that were both beautiful and baffling. I found myself dreaming how remarkable her bare flesh had felt under my hands months ago, the exquisite sounds she made, and the deep peace when she slept beside me. And then the sweet dreams would be dashed by images of her turning away from me forever, with nothing to build on.

Glad to wake up after a particularly unpleasant dream, I went ahead and got up early in order to avoid falling back to sleep and dreaming more. It was Monday morning. It had been a couple of days since I had gone for a run, and I was antsy to get back to that part of my conditioning. So I took off, even before first light. The road was clear and empty, almost as if it, too, had been sleeping but was now awake as I got into an easy rhythm. I pushed myself, continuing past the twisted crabapple tree that marked the two and a half miles down the blacktop from my house.

I ran until I was thinking about being tired but enjoying a new tableau of woods and rocks and a gentle curve in the road I had not run before. Splashes of snow were scattered around the woods, survivors of the post-snowstorm melt, dark patches of ground testament to the reality of heat.

I turned when I came to a big, mossy boulder that had slid down a hill, maybe centuries before, and had come to rest in a gully near the road. My new farthest point. I started back, forcing myself to maintain my pace, ignoring the burning in my lungs and legs as I approached the house. I sprinted the last fifty yards and stopped at the front door, waving my arms and walking circles around the front of the house, blowing plumes of breath into the cold air. Then I went in.

After my morning ablutions and Gotcha's routine with meds and going out and coming in, I fixed myself a leisurely breakfast with twelve sausage links and six of the whole wheat pancakes Jan had made, two slabs of hash browns, and a big mug of Bailey's coffee. I took my time, enjoying every bite and sip. I cleaned up and put my dishes in the dishwasher, which was nearly full. I poured in detergent and turned it on, enjoying the soothing shush-shush sound of the machine at work.

I checked my emails. Nothing. I checked on the Hawks, who were playing in a tournament in the Bahamas and had won their first game against Syracuse. Good sign. Nothing happened with the Red Sox, but there were plenty of trade rumors. Pitching needs, always pitching. I avoided the news sites. I looked at the clock. It was past nine and time to launch.

I dressed in jeans and a heavy cotton t-shirt and a black sweatshirt with a hood and put on two pair of heavy socks and hiking boots. I pulled a pair of fleece-line gloves from a bottom drawer of my armoire, stepped to my hall closet and brought out my Navy peacoat and my Mossburg pistol grip, pump shotgun (Elsie) and two boxes of shells. I stuffed a black wool watchman's cap in the pocket of the coat and set the coat and the shotgun on a sofa near the front door. Back in my bedroom, I took out my sheathed black Ka-bar knife from post-Navy days, with the 8 inch blade, and strapped it to the calf of my left leg. Gotcha watched the entire process.

I fished out a New York Public Library tote bag from under the bed, then tossed in a few items that I have learned, over time, can be useful in friendly interrogations. Two rolls of duct tape, a pair of pliers, an awl, a butane lighter, and a couple of other items I hoped I wouldn't need. I set the bag by the front door.

I read my Bible for a few moments and said a prayer for effectiveness, efficiency and protection for my trip north.

The day was clear and cold as I took on the drive to Minnesota. There was little traffic and no snow or ice on the road, but I drove slowly, the fifty-five speed limit. I wanted to take my time with the day, learn what I could, do what I could after I learned what I could, and enjoy the pace. And I didn't want to do anything to be noticed, like picking up a speeding ticket. My word for the day was control. Also patience. Not my strong point.

As the road stretched out before me, through bleak farmland and frozen fields of harvested corn, bare stalks bent and broken, I thought about Liv Olson. She no doubt knew by now that I had taken a drunken Suzanne Highsmith back to her motel. And did it matter that I had been a gentleman and rejected Suzanne's obvious attempt to seduce me? What I had done by taking her back to her suite was what the theologians would call "making provision for sin."

But I couldn't call her a cab. Rockbluff does not have cabs. She had admitted scraping a couple of other cars in the parking lot, so I couldn't let her drive. Maybe I should have asked Moon if Rachel could take her home. Better yet, I should have had Moon call Liv to come get Suzanne.

That would have been worth seeing.

Now Suzanne had disappeared. She did not leave town because I would occasionally see her scraped blue 4Runner in the parking lot at the Rockbluff Motel. Was she ashamed? Probably. Was she writing all this time? Maybe. Would I see her again? I guess it didn't matter at that point. My thoughts left Suzanne and returned to Liv.

Liv had not invited me in after I walked her home from Bloom's. She did not even indicate she wanted to kiss me at her front door. She was not interested. I wondered if I should have just taken her into my arms, but there was not even a hint of her willing to give in. It had been over a year since we had slept together, and it saddened me to think we'd never share a bed again. But I decided not to give up. I would adopt a siege mentality and try to wear down her resistance. It would give me something to do, I thought, and then I turned my attention to the tasks before me.

I passed into Minnesota around mid-day and continued, ignoring the gravel road Moon had driven when we went to find Fire Bear. I drove on and on as the land shifted from fields to forest. I passed through a couple of small farming villages, and then, mid-afternoon, I came to a four-way stop. One of the signs pointed east and read "Chalaka 31 miles." I turned right and drove on, wondering why there was no sign announcing the reservation in that direction. Twenty miles later, I drove right by a big, solid wood sign with indented yellow letters that read, "Chalaka Reservation of the Ojibwa-Anishinabe People." A few miles farther on, I came to the outskirts of the town of Chalaka.

My plan was to scout out the area in daylight, snoop around, see what I could see. My training years ago and my experience after that training had taught me, whenever possible, to look things over carefully before initiating trouble. In Chalaka, I figured I'd get around to maybe asking a few questions that might lead me to Martin Rodman, then politely ask him about Cindy's murder. If he were reluctant to provide information, I knew he would eventually respond to the incentives I had for him. I truly enjoy gathering information. Knowledge is power, President Bush said.

I followed the signs to the casino. The casino/hotel complex was situated at the end of a mile drive with established trees, now leafless and barren, on both sides of the drive. The building was five stories of architectural beauty with extensive glass and lighting and landscaping. As I drove slowly around the circle drive in front of the entrance, I noticed uniformed staff parking cars and opening doors for people. I did not see a speck of litter. A neon sign announced a singer with a vaguely familiar name performing in The Torchlight Theatre. The sign changed as I drove by and the message announced complementary drinks in the casino from 7 – 9 PM. I drove away from the entrance and took a well-marked sign to the parking lot. Again, an immaculate area with lights everywhere.

There were plenty of cars in the lot, and most of them were upper end. A few clunkers here and there attested to the lure of easy money. Sections closest to the casino/hotel were marked off for various levels of membership with "Eagle Feather" being the most prestigious designation. After my quick cruise through the parking lot, I drove back down the mile-long approach and took a look at the town. I knew where to find The Pony Club.

I saw several motels, a post office, two supermarkets, five gas stations, and a large city park with yellow and red playground equipment that tempted me to try it out. There were also a couple of bars, one lacking windows but making up for its lack of decor with a trashy front yard. Several skinned up pickup trucks were already in the parking lot, which was strewn with litter, just like out front. The place, "Mike's Asylum," according to the buzzing neon sign by the front door, intrigued me as a place where, with a few dollars wisely offered, I might learn things I couldn't get any other way. Like how to find Martin Rodman.

I continued to drive around town, making a side trip down a street with a sign pointing the way to Chalaka High School. The buildings were beautiful and the student parking lot had a variety of nice cars. The athletic fields were kept up, and a big sign announced that this place was the "Home of the Chalaka Warriors!" I wondered if they could be a little more creative than "Warriors." I think something like "Screaming Scalpers" would be more effective in striking fear into their opponents' hearts. And what a cool mascot they could have, too!

By then I was hungry, so I decided to go back to Mike's Asylum, sample the menu, and see what I could learn. I parked in the lot, tossed my pea coat over my shotgun on the passenger's seat, got out, and locked my truck. In the raggedy parking lot, I sidestepped a few crushed beer cans, and moseyed on inside the Asylum, enjoying the music even before I opened the door.

Johnny Paycheck was declaring that someone could take his job and shove it, and I thought that was too bad, that I really enjoyed my work, and my job that day was to learn things and maybe even act on them. I slid onto a revolving barstool four seats down from a pair of rough-looking gentlemen in flannel shirts, insulated vests, dirty jeans and work boots half unlaced. Each had a bit of a beard going, and they were hunched over pint glasses of beer half gone. They looked at me and I was reminded of a tussle I'd had at Shlop's Roadhouse a while back. But I wasn't going to do anything or say anything that might lead to a tussle. I would be slow to anger if they decided to pick on me. I looked at them. They looked back. Then they dropped their eyes and studied the glasses of beer in front of them.

The bar smelled like stale beer, cigarette smoke, and fried everything. Half a dozen tables and chairs were scattered about, some occupied, mostly by men, and a few booths were situated against a wall opposite the bar, which itself was nondescript. Two pool tables were occupied. One was taken by a single young man, the other by couples playing eight-ball in pairs.

"What'll it be?" A man's voice, deep and rumbly. I turned my gaze from the bar's layout to the man behind the bar. He was a medium guy – medium height, medium weight, medium length brown hair, three-day growth of a medium, patchy beard. His eyes, though, were not medium. He looked intelligent.

"What's good? I'm hungry."

"Everything's good, bud. Need a menu?"

"No, I'll go with a couple of cheeseburgers and an order of fries. And a pitcher of Miller's," I said. "You must be Mike."

"The one and only. Coming up," he said, and turned to preparing my food. Mike was wearing jeans and a baggy brown sweater that had either a random pattern or a lot of splatters, dribblings, and spills. When the burgers and fries were going, he produced a pint glass and a pitcher. A new song, one about former wives living south of Oklahoma, made me smile. It was a clever song, concluding with "That's why I reside in Tennessee." I couldn't remember the artist's name.

"Saw you smiling at that song. You must be divorced," Mike said as I poured my first pint. "How many times?"

"Three," I said. "There was Margarite from Milwaukee, Darla from Des Moines, and Sally from St. Paul." Off the top of my head. A gift.

"Funny guy," Mike said. He turned to poke at my food and came back after flipping the burgers and shaking the wire basket of fries before dropping them into the bubbling grease again. I wondered how long the vat of grease had been there. "So that's how you remember them? Seems like I'd want to forget about 'em."

"I do want to forget," I said, "but remembering their names helps remind me not to get married again. How 'bout you?" I asked. "You divorced, too?"

"Just once." He retrieved my food and brought it to me. I was surprised. It looked and smelled good. Hard to improve on greasy burgers and fries. "I think everyone's allowed a mulligan. Good wife now. Works at the casino, dealing blackjack."

"You're a lucky man," I said, digging into the first burger. Not as good as Moon's, but not bad, considering it wasn't very big or thick. Still, it was fuel.

"*Very* lucky," he said. "Got this bar, which I keep from fixing up on purpose. The décor brings in a dependable clientele. My wife and I make do. What's your work?"

"Oh, this and that," I said. "Semi-retired, disability check."

Mike nodded and looked down at the men at the end of the bar. One of them had called his name and held up his empty glass.

"Send them a pitcher of whatever they're drinking. On me," I said.

Mike nodded and produced a clean pitcher, then filled it with Budweiser from the tap and took it down to them. He said something and they looked at me. I nodded and they nodded back, overjoyed. It's fun being a philanthropist. Mike came back.

"You headin' over to the casino today? Not much else to do here in Chalaka. It's a nice place," he said.

"And I'll bet they have outstanding blackjack dealers."

"That's true. If you do go over to play blackjack, look for the redhead with "Clarice" on her nametag. Tell her I said hello, but you won't get any special cards. She's honest. In fact, I'm pretty sure the casino is honest, too. A good thing for the Indians and a good thing for other businesses, including me."

"I guess in a town this size, everyone knows everyone else, right?"

"Pretty much that way with most small towns. You lookin' for someone?"

"How did you know that?"

"You're not the type to come into a place like this unless you're after more than food. I'm guessing information. What do you want to know?"

"I'm looking for a gentleman named Martin Rodman."

A small smile flitted across Mike's face. He said, "You don't look like someone who'd have to pay for it."

"I don't. I'm just wanting to talk to the man."

"Marty's not a bad guy for a pimp. He's a pimp, he admits it, and that's that."

"Does he work out of the casino?"

"Oh, hell no. They wouldn't allow it. But he does operate on the fringe, if you get my drift. He has links with a couple of the scuzzy motels, you know, the ones that rent rooms by the hour, and he has a cathouse north of here. I understand it's pretty much on the up and up, like one of those legal places in Nevada, which is where he came from about eight years ago."

"What's the cathouse like?"

"I've never been there. Paul Newman once said, when asked about how he'd stayed married to Joanne Woodward for so long despite all the temptations of Hollywood, 'Why go out for hamburger when you have steak at home.' Course, that reduces women to meat, a product, and dehumanizes the fairer sex."

"But he had a point."

"Yes. And that's why I have never been to his place of business. I'm one of the few."

"If everybody knows about his business, why hasn't he been busted and shut down?" I asked.

Mike smiled and raised his eyebrows.

I said, "Oh."

"Now, I'm not saying he's never been in the casino, but they don't encourage him unless he's actually gambling. They keep a close eye on him. Still, it's possible for him to acquire clients inside the casino, but when he's caught, they make him leave and stay away for a couple of weeks."

I finished my burger and some of my fries and drained my pint glass. I poured myself another from the pitcher.

"So I need to go out to his emporium of negotiable affections to talk to him?" I asked.

Mike laughed. "No, sometimes he comes in here to relax about this time of day. We're friends, actually." Mike looked toward the door and waved. "In fact, he's here now. Like I said, he's pretty regular. I'll introduce you."

I turned sideways to see a man, probably in his 50's, dressed in slacks and a heavy sweater, glide through the front door. He came up to Mike at the bar and ordered "the usual." Mike set to work on the ingredients for a Philly cheesesteak, dabbing at the meat and onions with his spatula. Once he returned from the grill, he poured a double vodka and said, "Marty, I want you to meet someone who wants to talk to you. Marty, this is, wait, I didn't catch your name."

"Ryne Duren." I reached across and to my left. We shook hands.

"I'm Marty Rodman. What kind of questions?"

"Let's go over to that booth." I gestured toward a booth in a corner of the room, not near anyone. He agreed, and so I took my food and pint glass and he took his vodka and we sat down.

Once we were situated, he said, "Are you interested in companionship?"

"No, just questions about something that happened in the neighborhood a few days ago."

"And that would be . . . ?"

"Murder."

Rodman's face went from curious to frightened. "I had nothing to do with that."

Mike brought Rodman's cheese steak and another double shot of vodka and left.

"I had nothing to do with anything you're asking about. I regret that I must leave right now. I'm not hungry anymore. Nice meeting you."

He started to slide out of the booth, but I had my Ka-Bar out and pressed it gently against his right leg. He looked down as I drew the knife back a little, slicing open the material. My knife is very sharp. Rodman stopped. He slid back into the booth. I laid the side of the knife on his leg, leaning forward, telling myself that I just might be eye to eye with Cindy Stalking Wolf's murderer, and the kidnapper and killer of the Jarlssons.

"I'm here for Cindy Stalking Wolf. You pulled her into prostitution and you, or someone under your direction, killed her when she wanted to get out of the life, and then you had her dumped in the Whitetail River. She ended up downstream, in Rockbluff. I'm the one who found her."

"Who told you that crock of shit?"

"Ted Hornung."

A string of rich epithets flowed smoothly from Rodman's mouth. He knocked back his double vodka and gestured to Mike for another. Mike delivered and turned away after asking Rodman if he was okay. Rodman said he was, even though his face was contorted with anger. Mike gave me a look and left. I wondered if he had a shotgun under the bar.

"I run girls, I admit it," Rodman began, "but I am small potatoes. I hire girls, *women*, who come to me for work. Some of them are out for a thrill before settling down in the suburbs with a husband and children. Some work for the money, and it's good. I only take forty percent: they get the rest. And no one is forced to stay or do anything they don't want to do. Understand? I sell straight sex between consenting adults. No threesomes, no lesbo shit, no underage crap. Ted Hornung is the one who pulls in damn children and sells them to creeps who come up here for gambling and sex. And that's the truth. And *he* decides when they can leave the life – *they* don't. I had nothing to do with Cindy's murder, but I heard about it. You'd be better off talking to Hornung about that, the sonuvabitch. I hate his guts, man."

"I already talked to him. He put your ass in the sling over Cindy's murder."

A look of realization came over Rodman's face, then a smile. "You're the dude! The one who busted Hornung's arm and kicked the butts of his boys. Man, I'd kiss you if you wouldn't think I was kinky."

"You're mistaken."

"There you go, lyin' again. You told me you were Ryne Duren, but I happen to know he was that wild fastball pitcher for the Yankees back in the 50's. Now, tell me what else you want to know about Ted Hornung."

"Who killed Cindy Stalking Wolf? She was only fourteen, Marty. I don't like that, and her family doesn't like it."

"My guess is Hornung did it. He definitely takes in underage girls and sells them to weirdos who come here to gamble and get some. Picks them up off the rez where they're just kind of hanging around, or working in the fish processing plant, or school dropouts. He flatters them and gives them nice clothes and takes them to dinner and concerts and such, and then he eases them into drugs and talk of big money being 'nice' to older men. Women, too."

Martin downed his vodka and nodded at Mike. "God, he's one sick mother. No conscience. Cold bastard, I can tell you that. But you can forget about going back to him. Since you and your buddy busted him up, he's doubled down on personal protection. He's hired a couple of shooters from Chicago to go with his usual boys."

Mike delivered another double vodka and left.

"Where does he live?"

"I don't know. Honest. Might as well live at the Pony Club, but I've heard he's got a place in Florida and another over the border in Wisconsin. And I heard there's big syndicate money behind him. You're messing with some serious shit, Ace."

"So who can give me the truth about Cindy Stalking Wolf?" I asked

Rodman looked thoughtful, twitching his mouth around, jumping a little when I removed the blade from his thigh and put it back in its sheath on my calf. I was okay with him, mostly from Mike's introduction, and I liked Mike. Plus, Rodman just didn't look the part of a killer. He relaxed a little once the Ka-bar was put away, then looked me straight in the eye and said, "I know who knows. One of Hornung's best guys, Ivan something. I call him 'Ivan the Terrible' because he's a bad dude. A freak. He's a giant, man, shaved head, weird tats, mean streak. And he's smart. I've heard that he reads books. Weird. But I heard he got busted up some when you and your buddy took them on. Another reason to give you a kiss."

"Lighten up on the affection," I said. "I know the guy. So you think he might know what happened? Would he be willing to talk to me?"

"Ace, I wouldn't be surprised if he wasn't the one who wasted the girl. Sounds like something he'd do. But I don't know how you'd get him to spill."

"Leave that to me. Where could I find him?"

"As far as I know, he still hangs at the Pony Club. You might try there, but you'd better have some weapons grade backup. That place is like a fortress now, thanks to your previous visit. You're going to need more than that serious pigsticker you cut my pants with."

"I think you're telling me the truth, Marty," I said. "And I know for sure you're not going to tip off Hornung, or Ivan, that I'm in town."

"Hell, no. Frankly, I wish you'd grease them all. Bad for my business. Gives prostitution a bad name."

"If you think of anything else that might help me square things over Cindy's murder, let Mike know. I'll be back from time to time until this is settled. He can tell me."

"I'll be glad to be your eyes and ears in Chalaka," Rodman said. "Damn straight."

I thanked Rodman, left a wad of money on the counter, got up, nodded at Mike behind the bar, who seemed to relax a little, and left The Asylum, just tickled pink with my lead on the killers of Cindy Stalking Wolf. And a new respect for a pimp.

Chapter Twenty-One

"Bitterness is like cancer. It eats upon the host.
But anger is like fire. It burns it all clean."

—*Maya Angelou*—

When I exited Mike's Asylum I was amazed at how cold it had become. I hopped into my truck and cranked the engine and the dashboard told me it was twenty-two degrees. That meant it would be in the teens tonight. Good to know.

I drove over to the Pony Club, circling the block and watching. It was too early for the club to open, but there were two cars in the Employees' Parking area. One was a Jaguar and the other was a Honda Civic. I made the decision to wait for Ivan because the Jag was clearly Ted Hornung's wheels and Ivan would not fit in the Civic. I figured employees would start showing up before long.

I parked two blocks from the club by a wooded, vacant lot, got out, shrugged into my peacoat, and hid my shotgun inside the coat, secured upside-down by a loop I had sewn in for just that purpose years ago. I pulled my hoodie down over my head and sauntered over to a place in some bushes across the street from the Pony Club. It was cold, and I was not much interested in waiting around, but I had a hunch Ivan would show up before long. I slipped on my gloves.

He did appear, but not before three other vehicles came, parked in the Employees' lot, and disgorged their passengers. I recognized them all from the rumble Moon and I had had a little over a week ago. They were the black security force. They went inside.

When a big Chevy S10 extended cab pickup truck came around the corner, I stepped behind a tree to avoid being seen, but allowed myself an angle to observe who was driving. It was Ivan. He pulled into the parking lot even as I quickstepped in his direction, pulling my hoody down over my face, hiding me from the cameras in the parking lot. Ivan shut off the engine and sat there, behind the wheel, for a couple of minutes, probably meditating on his past sins and seeking forgiveness, giving me time to slip up nearby out of sight from his mirrors. When he gingerly eased himself out of the truck, obviously still a little tender from my applications of force a little over a week ago, I was waiting for him.

He looked surprised when he saw me, said, "What the f . . . "

By way of greeting, I punched him hard in the ribs on his left side where I had struck him with the baseball bat. Ivan yelped and bent over, trying to cover up. His face was a rictus of pain and I was glad. If Marty Rodman's information was accurate, I had found the key to solving Cindy's murder. I punched him in the same place again, bringing his head down to my level. The man was huge, but I had him.

I said, "Get back in behind the wheel and do what I say. I'm going to get in with you and then we're going for a little ride. Don't even think about messing with me or I'll kill you."

As a means of encouragement, I shoved him back against his truck, jamming my hands against his broken ribs. This time he cried out in pain. But he followed instructions. I hurried around and got in the passenger's side, unlooping Elsie from inside my pea coat. Ivan turned his head and saw the shotgun pointed at him. I admit it, Elsie looks malevolent and terrible, a weapon built for close quarters killing.

"This gun can go off at the slightest pressure, Ivan, and if you try anything, slam on the brakes, drive into a tree, I promise you she will go off. You'll be a mess. Just an explosion and tremendous noise and a great sense of pressure, then knowing that you're going to die quickly; that is, if you live long enough to have a thought."

"How do you know my name, and what the hell do you want?" he asked, his right arm snaking across him, holding his side. His face was pale.

"I want you to do as I say, *Ivan*," I said as I cinched in my seatbelt. "Turn on the ignition and follow my instructions."

He cranked the engine and it roared into life. I glanced at the interior of the cab. It was messy with candy wrappers and bits of food, a couple of empty Miller Light beer cans, a bottle of water. A heavy, hooded sweatshirt slung between the seats. A pack of Winston Lights had fallen to the floor on my side, matchbook tucked into the cellophane. I told him where to drive and he did, and in minutes we were heading north out of town, then into the deep woods. Ivan drove in silence with an occasional, furtive look in my direction.

I was glad I had broken his ribs because a healthy Ivan in that cab would have been a potential problem for me if he decided to be noncompliant. But he was broken up and in fresh pain and I had the shotgun pointed at his belly. At that point, I was pleased with my position.

"There's a dirt road coming up shortly, just a few miles from here. Turn there and keep going," I said after we had driven a while.

Ivan grunted and nodded his head, slowing as we approached the road. He turned left, the only direction available, and continued. The road looked neglected. It had a grassy spine and no indication of traffic in a long time. There was no snow on the ground now, melted away by a couple of days in the upper 30's. But it was cold today. We rode in silence, a potentially rough ride smoothed out by the big truck's weight and shocks. Another road, no more than a nearly-invisible path, led off to the right. I told Ivan to take it. He hesitated, then turned.

"You forgot your turn signal," I said. "Time for a citizen's arrest." Then I laughed.

Ivan shot me a worried look. "Where are we going, man?"

"Shut up and drive, Ivan. We're going someplace people don't go, and probably never will. It's very private. I don't think you'll like it."

After another mile or so, I told him to stop next to a white birch tree I pointed out. He did. I told him to get out. He did. I got out, bringing my tote bag with me, and walked around, looking in the back of his truck. There was a gas can and a large metal tool box, tire chains, and a pair of jumper cables. Good to know that Ivan seemed resourceful. He would need to be.

"Okay, Ivan," I said approaching him, "go stand against the tree and put your hands at your sides."

"I ain't doin' nothin' like that, you fuck!"

I set my bag down and walked up to him. As I got within reach, he did what I knew he would do. He grabbed for the shotgun. Anticipating that, I swung the gun around and cracked the barrel against the side of his head as hard as I could, staggering him. Then, while he was still dazed, I slapped the barrel up against his head again, same place, and he sat down hard. I pulled off his sweater and tossed it aside. He was wearing a threadbare gray t-shirt with "Property of Chicago Bulls" in black print across the chest. An orange basketball was centered below the printing.

"Get up. Do what I said." I gestured toward the white birch tree with a diameter of about a foot. Big enough. Ivan struggled upright, glared at me, touched his fingers to his head and looked at the blood on his fingers.

"You're crazy, man," he said. I pointed Elsie at his face. He wobbled over to the tree and stood up against it, his back against the trunk.

"What're you gonna do?" he asked.

"Maybe nothing. Maybe kill you. Maybe something in between. It's up to you. You're in charge, the master of your fate, the captain of your ship. I have some questions and you're going to answer them correctly or die." Then, sotto voce, I said, "Some of the images involved in your situation may not be suitable for children." I laughed again, a short, hard laugh. "That good enough for you?"

Nothing.

I ordered Ivan to put his hands against his sides and stand still or I'd kill him right off. He looked convinced.

I fished out two rolls of duct tape from my New York Public Library tote bag, got the duct tape started, pressing it against the back of the tree, then, all the time training Elsie on his gut, I quickly made several circuits around his gut, binding him to the birch. I finished that roll of duct tape, took out the other roll and taped his legs to the tree, then more tape on his torso. He looked snug when I finished.

"Thanks for helping!" I chirped, wiggling my eyebrows like a demented Groucho Marx.

Ivan looked troubled.

"What happens next, Ivan, depends entirely on you. I am not going to waste time and dance around. It's too cold out here. Below freezing, and the sun is going down and it's gonna get *real* cold real soon. Street people will be spending the night in meat lockers just to stay warm. So don't impede my progress by saying dumb stuff, like 'I don't know' or 'I can't remember. You're not a member of the government. You can't take the Fifth Amendment. You're just a man out here in the middle of nowhere with someone who is really pissed off about what you and your pals did to my friend's niece. Understand?"

"Fuck you."

"I had a hunch you'd say that. You are choosing to not cooperate and, in a way, that makes me happy, because now I can use some of my cool ideas to see if they work. Remember, what is about to happen to you is for entertainment purposes only. My entertainment." I faked another giggle, pulled up my left pant leg, and unsheathed my Ka-bar knife. I walked up to Ivan and spoke. I said, "If you go wiseass on me again, I am going to cut something off your body. It won't be your ears, that went out with Viet Nam. And it won't be your scalp, that's something reserved for you Indians. Guess what I'm going to cut off?"

Ivan looked down.

"No, Ivan, I won't cut any of your manhood away. I'll CUT OFF YOUR DAMN LIPS!" I screamed. I feinted with the knife toward his face.

The big Indian startled and pulled his head back, banging it against the tree and said, "I'll be good," as if he were a little child. I had a hunch I was getting inside his noggin.

I stepped back. "That was wise, Ivan, because if I cut off your lips, no amount of plastic surgery will help fix it. You'll look like a leering maniac the rest of your life. No more kissy-face with beautiful women, no more smacking your lips after eating pumpkin pie, you won't even be able to do this." I gave him a Bronx cheer. I couldn't help but laugh, genuinely so. I was starting to have fun as I morphed into my sadistic side. The look on his face was beyond any price, and my laughter just reinforced it. "So, now that you've agreed to be civil, we can proceed. Okey dokey?"

"You're crazy, man," he said.

I said, "You have no idea," and then I chuckled a little, then a lot, then threw back my head and cut loose, laughing my head off. When I stopped, I noticed in his dark eyes the look of someone who was wrestling with basic life issues, instincts, and permutations on his situation.

"Now, Ivan, this is the *big* question. Your lips, your miserable life depend on your answer. Who killed Cindy Stalking Wolf?"

"I don't know, man. I don't!"

I said nothing. I walked up to him, took my knife, and sliced away his right pants leg from high up on the thigh, then I slit it down the side and cut it into two strips. I tossed them aside. Superficial scratches appeared on his bare leg where the knife had barely grazed him. A little bit of blood beaded out from the marks.

"What are you going to do?" he asked. He didn't realize he was bleeding.

"I'm the one who asks the questions. But, since your question was politely provided, I will tell you. I'm making tourniquets for you."

"What?"

"How tall are you, really, Ivan? Six-six, six-seven?"

"I am six-eight and a half," he said, pride in his voice, as if he had decided, when he was in third grade, if he got that far, how tall he was going to be, then achieved it through willpower.

"You won't be that tall in just a little bit because I'm going to take my shotgun here and shoot your feet off just a smidgeon up from the ankles. Don't worry, you'll still be tall, but your dancing days will be done for. No more soccer, no more pirouettes on the dance floor. No more walking tippy-toes when you sneak up on innocent girls to turn them into whores. The tourniquets will be applied to the bottom of your legs so you won't bleed to death. You'll live, but you'll be much shorter. Now, tell me who killed Cindy Stalking Wolf?"

"It wasn't me."

"I wanted to know who *did*, not who *didn't*. Jeez Louise, Ivan, you are getting under my skin." I walked over to his truck, looked in the bed, pulled out the gas can and wiggled it. It sloshed around inside. I set it down, then got inside the cab and pulled out the big, half-empty bottle of water. I carried them both over to Ivan.

"What're you gonna do?" Genuine, old-fashioned fear now edging into his voice.

I adopted a pose and pointed a finger in the air and said, "Some say the world will end in fire, some in ice, the poet once wrote, and I think I'll see which is better." Then I poured gasoline on Ivan's left leg, and dribbled water over his bare right leg. His eyes were becoming just a little bit wild.

I grinned, sharply saluted him, did an about face, and marched off to his truck, making trumpet marching sounds as I went. In the cab of his pickup truck I found his Winston Lights and the matches. I took the matches and marched back to stand in front of Ivan. I did a little hop and stomped both feet down in a snappy military manner and saluted him again.

"If I leave you out here just as you are, you will freeze to death. But fear not, those who have nearly died from hypothermia declare that, once the shivering stops, a kind of peace comes over the mind and body and sleep ensues. Not bad, huh? Let's hope, in that case, the wolves wait until you're dead before they munch out. Of course, I just might set your leg on fire, which would put you into shock and you'd die from that. Or, I could shoot your feet off, apply tourniquets, and let you hoof it back to town, emphasis on the word 'hoof.' It won't do any good to cry for help, or scream in agony, either. There is nothing, absolutely nothing within ten miles of this special spot. Not even a deer stand. I know. I checked satellite images at the Rockbluff Public Library. Do you have a library card? I've heard you're a reader."

Ivan nodded his head. "I got a card."

"Good boy." I patted his cheek, hard, with my open hand.

"Now, Ivan, you are very close to your last moments on earth. Hell awaits you, and an endless parade of disgusting people with rotten teeth and putrid breath will be French kissing you for eternity. Who killed Cindy Stalking Wolf?"

He looked indecisive, resolve maybe crumbling. I took out his book of matches from my pocket, walked up to him, and lit the match. I cupped my hand around the flame, waited for the flame to steady, then brought it close to the gasoline-soaked left leg. I was going to do it with no remorse. I was tired of his recalcitrance in response to my question. His eyes were enormous.

"It's only one question, Ivan," I said. "Sorry you're not able to answer. Now *don't* try this at home."

I flipped the match onto his left leg and his jeans ignited. He began screaming and I turned away.

Then I heard him scream, "Ted Hornung killed Cindy!"

I turned back, rushed to Ivan's sweater and smothered the fire after briefly admiring it for Ivan's benefit. His leg wasn't burned too badly, but he was being a big baby about it, crying out and cursing. I tossed the sweater aside.

"Tell me everything, now, or I'll set you back on fire and not come back."

"What will you do if I snitch?" he said between gasps and looking down at his charred and smoking leg.

"I'll set you free. I'll drive away. You can make your way back, or not."

"I'll freeze to death."

"I doubt it. But that's your problem. Tell me about Cindy Stalking Wolf."

Ivan breathed deeply, looked into the darkening sky, shook his head as if amazed at what he was about to do. He said, "She was a hooker for Ted. He sold her to men who wanted an Anishinabe girl. Her age was a turn on. She liked it at first, I swear, but then she wanted out, and she was trying to talk the other girls out of the life, too. He wanted it to stop, so he decided to make her an example to the others, so he told me to get rid of her."

"You murdered her?"

"No, man, but I was supposed to. So I got this guy, Eddie , works for Ted at the club, to help me out. We were supposed to make it look like a suicide, see. So we took her and drove downstream a ways and made her take off her clothes. I was going to hold her under, then let her go when she was good and scared, you know, give her a chance to run the hell away. I liked her, she was a good kid, but I was in a spot with Eddie there. So, it's like she was fighting me while I was holding her under and she came up waving her arms around and she caught Eddie flush in the face and the next thing I know, he's got his gun out and he shoots her twice in the back of the head, 'Bang! Bang!' and I panic and let go and she slipped away from me, heading downstream. We couldn't catch up with her.

"Eddie laughed and told me to stop running around hollering 'Oh Shit!' over and over. Said it was no big deal. I thought about just taking off because I knew we were in deep shit. I thought about killing Eddie and hitting the road, but I was afraid to. Afraid not to.

"We went back to the Pony Club and reported to Ted, and Eddie was bragging about how he'd offed the girl and Ted got real quiet and said it was okay, the only good Indian is a dead Indian anyway, and Eddie's laughing and then Ted steps up to him and slides this knife between Eddie's ribs and Eddie goes slack, like all his muscles were cut and he can't talk and he just slumps away to the floor when Ted pulls the knife back. We cleaned up the office and he told me to get rid of Eddie so no one would find him. Ted grinned at me and said, 'Loose cannon' and went back to his desk. Then he said we'd have to get that bitch's body because no one would believe she was a suicide now, with two bullets in her brain. We'd have to watch the news and read the papers to find out who'd find her.

"So when he found out the girl showed up in Rockbluff, he sent me and another guy to take care of that, you know, get the body back and make the coroner dude fake the death as a suicide."

"What happened to the coroner and his wife, Ivan?" I wanted to shoot him right then.

"Me and this other guy just took him. He won't be found. Ever."

"You killed him. You killed his wife, too, right?"

"Yeah. Now, will you let me go?"

"What did you do with Cindy's body, Ivan?"

"We took it, man. What do you think?"

"I want the name of the guy who was with you in Rockbluff."

Ivan looked troubled, then his expression was of one who had just given up. "His name's Ray Old Turtle, but he ain't old. Works at the club. That Indian with you busted him up some with the tire iron."

"Where are the bodies buried, Ivan?"

"They ain't buried. They was ground up and fed to the fish."

Oh, Lord, I thought, a girl and a fine married couple all murdered because the girl didn't want to be a sex slave. I put the shotgun barrel up under Ivan's chin and seriously considered blowing his head off. He was a despicable human being, acting under orders of another despicable human being, and then I realized some of the things I'd done in the past in the interests of national security, or for the safety of private clients, could be considered despicable by the other side. It was all about perspective. Sometimes I'd rather do without perspective. It can gum up things I want to do.

Ivan's eyes were wide with fear as he sensed I was about to pull the trigger. But I backed off and lowered the gun. What popped into my heard right then was this line from the Bible somewhere, Carl Heisler had preached about it, from the Book of James, I think. It goes, "Mercy triumphs over judgment" and it just smacked into my head right then. Go figure. I was not in a merciful mood. I looked at Ivan and then I looked at my shotgun. He gulped and I saw tears in his eyes. I made a decision about Ivan.

I walked around the area until I found a good chunk of wood, a fallen tree limb about a yard long, thick enough to get a two-handed grip on it. Then I approached Ivan, standing to one side. I planned to break his legs as a reminder not to go around killing people. But I couldn't do it. I tossed the weapon away. Then I saw Cindy Stalking Wolf, and I was feeling the bullet holes in the back of the child's head, and I nearly changed my mind, mercy fading away into the heavens that had gone black with bright pinpoints of light, buds of burning magnesium, stars far away and indifferent.

I strode over to the truck, pulled out the heavy hooded sweatshirt, tossed it on the ground. I picked up Ivan's heavy, charred sweater and dropped it at his feet. I took out my knife.

"Now what are you going to do, man? I told you the truth about that girl," Ivan moaned. All ferocity was gone. "I'm sorry about what I did. I shoulda stopped it! I shoulda let her go!"

"The 'girl' was Cynthia Stalking Wolf, Ivan. Now, I'm going to cut you a break." I sliced through the duct tape holding him to the tree. He fell to the ground, then struggled to his feet. "Put on your sweater and that sweatshirt. Sorry about the bare leg, but that won't kill you. I'm going to drive you back to town, drop you off, and park your truck in the parking lot at Mike's Asylum, keys in the ignition. I don't know why I'm not going to kill you, what you did to Cindy, the Jarlssons, but I am *such* a good guy, I find it hard to believe it myself.

"Now," I said, walking up to him, shotgun at the ready, "get in the back of your truck and sit down. If you go to Ted Hornung and tell him what happened, I'll kill you. If you tell the cops that I was involved in this, I'll kill you. You don't know who it was, maybe someone mad at one of Hornung's prostitutes. The guy didn't speak and he wore a ski mask. And finally, Ivan, if I ever see *you* again, I'll kill you. Understand?"

"Yes, sir," he muttered, sniffing. In his pain and despair, the big Indian looked like a child. He said, "But don't worry, I ain't never gonna see Ted Hornung again. He'll kill me now no matter what. When I get in my truck, I'm going to get the hell out of Chalaka. Get the hell out of *Minnesota*. Go far away. Hide." Then he put on his sweater and hoodie and got in the back of the truck and sat down with his back against the cab. He pulled the hoodie up over his head, then drew his legs, one bare, up to his chest and wrapped his arms around them.

I returned my knife to its sheath and walked over to Ivan's truck and, still pointing the shotgun at Ivan, got in behind the wheel and locked the doors. The Chevy started on the first try. Good truck. I directed the heater to my feet and the windshield and sat there for a moment, looking at Ivan looking at me, as if he expected me to renege, drag him out of the truck bed, and kill him.

When I could feel the heat coming into the cab, I pulled away.

I plunged on into the night, down lonely roads there on the rez and finally found myself approaching town again. I pulled over on the side of the road, got out, motioned for a completely docile Ivan to get out, to step down over the lift gate. He did. I kept Elsie pointed at his gut and he noticed. I drove the three miles to Chalaka and parked the truck where I told Ivan I would, then walked briskly the few blocks to the edge of the village and the side street where my own truck waited.

The cab was cold. I got the engine going, took off my gloves, snapped my seat belt into place, and turned on my headlights, slowly moving down the darkened street to the main road out of town and off the reservation, into southeastern Minnesota, across the border and into Iowa, the only vehicle on the road in the dark night, alone with my thoughts. I passed farm houses with yard lights burning like lonely sentinels, and other, abandoned, farms where no lights would ever again burn. Finally, I entered a deserted Rockbluff. I paused by Christ the King Church, then drove on, happy for the Heislers and their fine family.

Next, I went stupid and cruised slowly by Liv Olson's cottage, all the lights out, the beautiful woman asleep in her bed, her body warm and relaxed. If I could have gone inside her home and stepped into her bedroom and awakened her with a kiss, I would have. But I knew Milton would start barking, and I knew Liv always had her gun nearby. When I finished torturing myself, I crossed over the iconic bridge without looking into the river. And on out of town, headed for my place.

When I approached my house, I was surprised to see several lights on, upstairs and down. I parked my truck, eased out the door, leaving my bag on the seat, but with Elsie in hand. I paused at the front door, knowing I had not left the lights on, yet puzzled because I had seen no vehicles along the drive and there were no vehicles parked out front. What the hell? I worried about Gotcha.

Bringing the shotgun up, holding it close to my body, I opened the front door and stepped quickly inside, holding Elsie with both hands and playing the business end across the foyer, left and right, sweeping into sight every possible place where someone might be standing, waiting to kill me. I pushed the door shut with my left elbow.

"Is that you, dear?" someone said, a false high, feminine voice coming from the living room.

I lowered Elsie and strode into the living room and beheld Clancy Dominguez reclining in a recliner. Gotcha was flopped out on his lap.

"What took you so long?" I asked.

Gotcha jumped down and danced over to me and I went down on one knee, roughed her up, then got her a biscuit which she sucked in immediately. Clancy watched with amusement.

"Quite a watchdog you got there, Irish."

"She only bites bad people. Candy-asses are secure. So how the hell did you get in here?"

Clancy shifted the chair to an upright position and stood. He said, "Can you say 'doggy door'? I didn't want to screw up your locks, or break a window, so I decided to take the obvious opening. Your attack dog nearly licked my face completely to the bone before I could squiggle inside. She really does like those Milk Bones, doesn't she?"

"Jerk," I said.

"Failure."

And then we shook hands vigorously. We did not hug.

"Let's talk," Clancy said.

"It's in the cabinet over the sink."

I hung up my coat, stored my knife, pulled off my hoodie and draped it over a chair. I locked the front door and took my shotgun into the bedroom and set it by the bed, then I joined Clancy at the kitchen table. He'd found the Myer's Rum, untouched for over a year, since the day of Horace Norris's funeral. To be taken only on special occasions. Clancy had poured each of us four fingers of rum.

"You look older," he said.

"It's been over twenty years, pissant. What did you expect?"

"Sorry about your family. Bad shit."

"Yes."

"Despite that bit of gray at the temples, you look pretty good. Bigger. Not fatter."

"I do the best I can with what I have. You look pretty good, too."

"I know. It's the work, but we can talk about that later," Clancy said. "Despite the added muscle mass, you look like you've been livin' on the left side of 'Empty.' Let's catch up later this morning."

I looked at the clock. It was 2:15.

"I guess you've moved in," I said.

"Damn straight. You have a nice place here. I'm upstairs. Brought along a few things that might be helpful in bailing out your sorry ass. Right now, I need some rack time. See you in the morning, Irish."

With that, Clancy Dominguez drained off his rum, made a face, got up, and headed upstairs.

Ten minutes later I was in bed, Gotcha the Attack Dog snoring on her tuffet on the floor at the foot of the bed. I fell asleep with thoughts of old missions with Clancy, dreams of Olivia Olson sleeping in her bed, and an eagerness for tomorrow.

Chapter Twenty-Two

"It is better to be good than evil, but one
achieves goodness at a terrific cost."

—*Stephen King*—

The next day began with a feast at my kitchen table. Clancy came downstairs shortly after I took care of Gotcha's needs and had started a full pot of coffee. I was scrambling twelve eggs with some shredded sharp cheddar cheese and a few minced onions. The remaining stack of whole wheat pancakes from Jan Timmons was in the microwave. A handful of linked sausages was beginning to cook in a second Teflon frying pan and I was just reaching for the last few slabs of hash browns in the freezer when I heard him on the steps.

"Great God Almighty, but I slept like a war horse last night," he roared, striding into the kitchen. "Great mattress! And I woke up with the smell of coffee and other delights. You know how to start the day, Irish, and that's a fact," he said, slapping me on the back on his way to the cupboard. He pulled out a big, black mug with yellow "IOWA" on the side and poured coffee.

"Bailey's in the cupboard," I said.

"I'll save that for the morning after we get your situation straightened out," he said, and immediately began to tend to the sausages, taking a wooden spatula out of a big mug with other cooking tools and easing the chunks of hash browns gently alongside the cooking meat.

We took a long time to eat a fine breakfast and start in on a second pot of coffee. Exercising restraint from Clancy's example, I dropped a mere dollop of Bailey's into my cup as I filled Clancy in on what happened to my family, the troubles with the Soderstroms after I came back to Iowa, and everything I knew about Cindy Stalking Wolf's murder. I briefed him on what I had learned about the opposition from Jurgen Clontz and Martin Rodman from Mike's Asylum. I told him it all took place under the auspices of "Mulehoff's Initiative." I explained that I learned it from Mike, and that calling it "Mulehoff's Initiative" sounded better than just saying I did something because I wanted to. More intellectual.

"I like the concept. Now, I must say," he said, sliding his chair back from the table, coffee mug in hand, patting his stomach with the other, "you've been busy, but it's now time to get busier, now that I'm here. We've got some serious work to do. I'm glad you rang me up. I need to meet this Lunatic Mooning dude."

"First, you need to answer a question—why you didn't answer last night."

"Which was?"

"What the hell took you so long? It's been *eight days*, Clancy."

He smiled a quick smile, got up and topped of his mug of coffee, sat back down. He said, "I was on a fifty-five metre sailing yacht, not mine, a client's, mine's not quite that big, about eighty miles off the coast of East Africa when I got the word. I own a private security service company. Here's my card," he said, twisting in his chair, pulling his wallet out from his hip pocket, and extracting a business card. It read:

Clancy Dominguez, ex-Navy SEAL

Private Protection Specialists

We SEAL the Deal!

There was a SEAL trident, an 800 number, and a FAX number. The printing on the card was Navy blue on a white background. I groaned.

"What?"

"'We SEAL the Deal!'?"

Clancy shrugged his shoulders. "People say they remember it. Pays to have a slogan."

"So, congratulations. You've gone public. No more 'black ops' like the old days?"

"Done with that. Not enough pay. You need to memorize those numbers, then destroy the card."

I raised my eyebrows and gave him a look of skepticism.

"Or put it where a search warrant won't find it. I'm not bullshitting about that."

"Aye aye," I said. "Will do."

"Good man," he said. "Now, to answer your question. You know, I tried to retire, but I got itchy. I did a little local work there in Costa Rica, but it wasn't enough to make me happy, and there wasn't any woman to hold me. So I branched out. I have five guys working for me now, all former special forces dudes, tough and smart and a lot of fun. In fact, we'd just had some fun when I got your message."

"And what sort of fun was that? I'm afraid to ask, really, but go ahead."

"See, we were out there off the coast, south of Djibouti, eight or nine hours from Navy support, when these pirates came rushing up in their speedboat, making a pass before starting their attack. Hell, I'd seen them coming a mile away, so I had Jonny and Eric get our clients out of sight below, make sure they stayed there, and then get ready. The skinnies came right at us, then, firing away with AK47s and a couple of RPGs that weren't very accurate. They shot up the yacht a bit on their first pass, speeding by about twenty, thirty yards away. Then they turned and started to come at us again. I had seen grappling hooks and a ladder in the back of their speedboat on their first turn, so it was obvious they were going to try to board us to kill us and sell the boat, or take the boat and hostages for ransom."

"I've heard that happens quite a bit out there."

"Not so much as a couple years ago, but still it's not all that unusual. Lots of pirates in the Caribbean, too, and I'm not talking about some stupid movie." Then Clancy's eyes got bright, both the blue one and the brown one as he continued.

"When they came by on their second pass, they looked serious. I knew the first pass was to intimidate – no one's that bad a shot, not even you, Irish – but the second pass was meant to kill or kidnap. Anyway, I stood up with my SAW, fully loaded, and hosed them down, just holding that trigger back and laying 775 rounds per minute on 'em. Blew 'em to pieces, chopped their speedboat all to hell, killed them all, with Jonny and Eric backing me up with their M16s.

"We decided to leave the boat like that so the mother ship, probably a dhow a couple of miles away, would eventually find them and decide maybe they didn't want to mess with our yacht anymore," he said, a smile crossing his face.

"What was their nationality?"

"My guess is Somali. Grim little country locked into poverty and war lords and all kinds of bad shit," Clancy said. "I lived there, I'd be a pirate, too. Still, there are risks. They probably think it's worth it. The ransom business is paying off for some of them. And several of those governments look the other way, too."

"I'm not surprised," I said, pouring more Bailey's into my half-empty cup. "Give me an example."

"Okay. Try this on for size. If a yacht is moored in harbor and it gets boarded, the people are beaten and robbed, it's not considered piracy. Or if it's at anchored in the harbor of some of these countries, and it gets boarded and the people beaten or killed, robbed, boat stolen, it's not piracy."

"What do they call it, 'Workplace Violence'?"

"I don't know. Maybe it's just a domestic squabble to them. Might be some money changing hands somewhere."

I laughed. "You think?"

"I don't know. But our clients were sure happy they'd hired us. Offered nice bonuses, which we accepted with gratitude. Told them we would appreciate recommendations for our services when they had cocktails with their friends down the road in Newport or West Palm. So when I got your message my guys dropped me off at Mombasa and went on their way. So I chartered a single-prop to get me to Nairobi, then flew to London, London to Chicago to Cedar Rapids, then got some guy off the street to drop me off down the road a piece so I wouldn't reveal that I was in this village before you wanted me to. And here I am. That's what took me so long. But I'm here now and at your service. When do we start?"

"Did you make your bed?"

Clancy smiled and said, "Of course, and you can bounce a dime off it, too, loser."

"Let me clean up and then let's go. I need to bring Moon up to date."

"I suppose he'll want to be in on the mission since it was his niece that got greased," Clancy said.

"Wouldn't have it any other way."

"Is he trained?"

"As far as I know, and he's a bit secretive, no, but once you meet him you won't worry about it."

I tidied up the kitchen while Clancy stormed back upstairs, taking the steps two or three at a time. Twenty minutes later we were in the truck and speeding into Rockbluff. The late morning was clear and achingly cold. I wondered about Ivan for a couple of minutes, then moved on in my mind.

I pointed out several sights to Clancy: Arvid's house and his penchant for playing dead, the Whitetail River and the double-arched limestone bridge where I had seen Cindy's body, Mike Mulehoff's Earthen Vessel Barbell Club and Video Store.

"Doesn't he know videos are out and DVD's are in?" he asked.

"Of course. He's just not interested in changing his sign with every technological breakthrough. We're now approaching the Grain o' Truth Bar and Grill, home of the famous Loony Burger and its creator, Lunatic Mooning."

I pulled into the parking lot next to his '51 Packard, now rehabilitated back into mint condition. Clancy commented favorably on the vehicle as we got out and walked across the lot, across the slate entryway, and through the heavy oak front doors. Inside, he looked around and smiled appreciatively. It was ten-thirty now, half an hour after The Grain opens for business, which explained the sparse crowd on a Tuesday morning.

I caught Moon's eye as we headed his way. I noticed that his blue sling was gone. He nodded, then jerked his head towards a booth across the room and to our right. Harmon Payne was in a booth with two men in suits. Harmon looked miserable.

We came up to the bar and I introduced Moon and Clancy. They shook hands. I said to Moon, "Clancy's here to help us. He has certain talents we can use to get to the bottom of Cindy's murder, so you can skip the laconic Indian routine you usually save for newbies. I have some information we need to share with you, Moon. Can we talk somewhere private?"

Moon called Rachel Bergman over and asked her to take over. I noticed a display of fresh, home-made doughnuts from Holy Grounds Coffee Shop and mentioned it to Moon.

"Geez, I said, "you start selling doughnuts and the place gets filthy with cops." I nodded in toward the booth with Harmon and the suits. "When did this happen?"

"Last week. In business," Moon said, "one must be constantly improving. Doughnuts go well with coffee in the morning before the lunch crowd picks up. I've started attracting fresh clientele. Mostly retired people; farmers and schoolteachers. Besides, I was lacking stimulation waiting around for my arm to heal. Which it has. I'm ready to go back to the rez."

"Me, too," I said. "Let's talk about what I learned yesterday. On the rez."

"Follow me," he said, and we went around the bar and headed down to his office. We followed him inside. Moon pulled out a couple of stacked, beige metal folding chairs and handed them over to us. We opened them up and sat down as he settled into his desk chair. There was a computer on his desk, a few photos of the establishment, a calendar. A gray metal file cabinet and a coat tree with a leather jacket hanging from a hook.

"Who're the suits?" I asked.

"State boys. They'll want to talk to you," Moon said.

"Harmon doesn't look too happy," I said.

"Some bad medicine going down. Don't know what. So you went

up to the rez last night? Without me?" The tone was accusatory.

"It was useful, an information-gathering excursion. Here's what I learned."

For the next fifteen minutes I filled Moon in on Ted Hornung's involvement in Cindy Stalking Wolf's murder, the actual murderers, my sources, and the magnetic ambiance of Mike's Asylum.

"Mike's sounds like one of the dives we've been in," Clancy said.

"Mike's is a five-star establishment compared to a couple of the dives we've been in," I said, thinking of one outside Clark Air Base in Angeles City, Philippines. We were there Temporary Duty, kicking back after completing a minor mission when a rat ran across the bar and knocked Clancy's beer into his lap. He snagged the rat, bit off its head, spit it out, threw the body against the mirror behind the bar, and told the bartender to clean up the joint. Ah, memories.

Moon leaned forward in his chair, the leather creaking. "So the man who shot Cindy is dead. What about the man with him, the one who told you what happened?"

"I spared his life. Part of the deal. We'll never see him again. Ted Hornung is the one who ordered Cindy's murder."

Moon and I locked eyes. He said nothing. I said nothing. There was an edgy look there at first, but it faded, and a sense of resignation and acceptance replaced it. Finally, he gave a short nod and leaned back in his chair. He said, "Let's go kill Ted Hornung then. And anyone who tries to stop us."

"Now you're talkin'," Clancy said, "but we need intel and a plan. I'm here to help. One way I can do that is go up on my own to the reservation, take a fresh look, hang in the casino, listen a lot, go into the Pony Club and check out their security. I can acquire additional sources. I can do that. And I can definitely fade into the background.

Then I'll come back and we can put together a mission that will get us this Hornung asshole, any of his buddies stupid enough to take us on, and a clean exit strategy when we've got him, or he's dead."

"Or both," Moon said.

A knock on the door interrupted our meeting. It was Rachel, poking her head in and saying, "Moon, those men from the State Bureau of Investigation want to talk to you. And you, too," she said, nodding at me.

Moon nodded and stood up. Clancy and I stood, too. On the way out, I introduced Clancy to Rachel in a multicultural exchange rare in Rockbluff – a half Dominican, half Irishman meeting a Jewish German waitress supervisor. Oh, the joys of diversity. Maybe I could get a grant from the government to perpetuate the moment.

We followed Moon down the short hallway from his office to behind the bar as Clancy and I stepped into the ambiance of The Grain. I turned to say something to Clancy, but he had slipped away, maybe to the men's room. I grabbed a jelly doughnut, looked at Rachel and, when she said "One dollar," I dug into my pocket and came up with four quarters and dropped them into her hand.

The agents looked over at Moon and me and signaled for us to come over. I waived back at them and smiled, then waived some more with great exuberance, as if I had just recognized them from across the room at a high school reunion. I raised up on my tippy-toes a couple of times in false delight. They were not amused. One stood and came our way. He was in his forties, I'd say, fit looking, and wearing a nice suit with a lovely paisley tie. Dark hair cut close, parted on the left side, clean-shaven. Cold blue eyes. Perfect teeth as far as I could tell.

"I'm Special Agent Kelvin Massey," he said, "State Bureau of Investigation. Would you please join us." It was not a question.

I took a bite out of my jelly doughnut and some of the raspberry filling oozed out. I grabbed a napkin from the neat stack next to the Holy Grounds Coffee Shop display and dabbed at my mouth, then followed Massey and Moon over to the booth, finishing off the doughnut on the way. Moon slid in next to Sheriff Payne and I sat next to the other agent, a black guy with a shaved head and a spare frame. He said his name was Hector Ortiz. His suit was well cut and his red tie matched his suit handkerchief. Married, obviously. Maybe fifty, fifty-five. He was not smiling. Massey brought a chair over and set it at the end of the booth's table.

"I need to see some I.D. before we talk," I said, smiling and licking traces of raspberry filling from my fingers.

The men sighed, looked at each other and held out their little leather badge holders, flipped them open, snapped them shut right away. I said, "I need to *see* some identification. Those could be Secret Decoder Badges from the Intergalactic Observatory. Come on, guys."

The classy little holders came out again from breast pockets, flipped open, and held out for me to see. I grinned and nodded. The men returned the badges to their coat pockets. This was fun.

I looked from Massey to Ortiz, to Payne, over to Moon, and back to Massey, on my right. "Now, what can I do for you *Special Agents* this fine Iowa winter morning?"

"You can start by telling us everything about your involvement in the Cynthia Stalking Wolf case from the time you saw the body until you came back from Chalaka last night," Ortiz said.

"Sorry. I don't talk with Special Agents without my lawyer. Basic common sense. Don't you guys ever watch 'Law and Order'?"

Steely glares.

"'Castle'?"

"Tell us about the alleged bullet holes in the girl's head," Massey said.

"'Closer' re-runs? That's one of my faves. Don't you guys ever watch *any* crime shows on television? I mean," I said in false exasperation, "the perp always blabs without an attorney present and practically hangs himself. One of my friends, an attorney, once told me, 'Thomas, don't ever answer questions in any investigation, even if you're totally innocent, without an attorney there to counsel you.'"

"Are you a perp?" Ortiz asked.

More glares.

"Look, guys. I'm sure you're fine people with beautiful families. You probably even have minty breath and coach a variety of team sports for little boys and girls when you're not out making the world safe for the rest of us, but I'm through talking with you. But I do recommend the Loony Burger, if you decide to stay for lunch. Sniptious good, as one of my Georgia friends would say."

Ortiz turned to Moon. "What were you doing up in Chalaka on November 26th, eleven days ago? We already know your arm was broken. What happened?"

Moon's face was impassive. He gestured toward me. "I'm with him," he said, and folded his arms across his broad chest.

Ortiz took a deep breath and let it out slowly. "Gentlemen, we've been chatting with Sheriff Payne here. All of us have been speaking with former deputy Stephen Doltch. Sheriff, would you like to tell these men what we discovered?"

Payne looked sad and broken. He pressed his lips together and said, "Stephen Doltch has been going up to Chalaka on a regular basis on his time off, partying at The Pony Club, frequenting prostitutes, and gambling at the casino. He was in deep at the casino, enormous debts he could not repay. Ted Hornung approached him and offered to buy his debt. All Stephen had to do was, um . . . "

At this point my mind was racing as Harmon choked on his words. So Bunza Steele had been right—Doltch was gambling and losing, a lot. I was afraid to hear what was next from Harmon, but I was also drawn to it.

"Anyway," Harmon said, shrugging his shoulders and sighing, "all Stephen had to do to be free of debt to the casino was to give Hornung the photos and the fingerprints taken by Dr. Jarlsson on the night of November 18th. Stephen took them from the evidence room at the department. I should have suspected one of my people, Stoltenberg or Altemieer, or one of the others, but I didn't think, I mean, um . . . "

Ortiz stepped in. "Stephen Doltch has been arrested and placed in custody. The charges are obvious. He's cooperating fully. He confessed. He's remorseful. He will be spending his best years in prison. Sheriff Payne is fully cooperating and working with us to get to the bottom of Cynthia Stalking Wolf's murder."

I looked at Harmon. He would not look at me. Doltch and I had not exactly been best buddies, but I was still surprised. And I was sorry for Harmon. His judgment had gone bad and I was thinking he would be ready to resign out of shame and humiliation. It was right under his nose and he didn't see it. I had, all along, suspected some outsider connected to the murder and kidnappings was behind the disappearance of that evidence. Human nature knocks me down again, but not as hard as it hit Harmon. You'd think I'd learn.

Massey turned to me and leaned forward. "I understand you have a history of sticking your nose in official law enforcement investigations, Mr. O'Shea, and I am pretty sure you're into it again, and I'm telling you, don't do it. Stop now and get the hell out of our way or you will be very, very sorry. I promise."

"I'll bet you put two exclamation points after big points in your written reports," I said.

"What does that mean?" Massey asked.

"Anyone who says 'very, very' is obviously overdoing it. One 'very' is enough. I get the point," I said. I smiled my best smile but it did not melt Massey's look of disapproval.

"I also heard you were a bit of a wiseguy," he said, leaning closer, his face barely a foot from mine, "and I'm warning you to butt out."

I clapped my hands and grinned. "You DO have minty breath! I just knew it!"

Massey sat back and continued to glare. I said, "Come on, Moon, let's go."

I stood and Moon stood, but not before placing his hand on Harmon's shoulder, an out-of-character display of affection and concern that had me wondering about Lunatic's testosterone levels. I said to Harmon, "Let me know what I can do to help you, *Sheriff*," emphasizing the designation of his profession to let him know that's what he was, and is. Moon stood and we walked away, back to the bar, where Clancy was chatting up Rachel.

"Is it too late for lunch?" he asked. I looked at the clock behind the bar. It read almost 11:30. "I'd like to try one of those Loony Burgers Irish brags about."

All three of us agreed to have lunch right then, and Rachel set to filling our nutritional needs. We walked over to a booth as far as we could get from the one where Payne was sitting and I realized I was living in Rockbluff, Iowa, major crimes capital of the world. Something they could add to the signs coming into town. All kinds of things to investigate – murder, fraud, kidnapping, more murders. All we need now is a serial killer and a race war, but since there's only one race, that probably won't happen.

We conversed for a little while about my information gathering trip, Clancy asking plenty of questions as his mind began formulating strategies for our mission, and Moon listening intently. I knew he was disappointed that someone else had killed his niece's killer, but it was clear to me that he had moved on to dealing with Ted Hornung, the one behind it all.

Rachel brought us our Loony Burgers and fries, then asked for drink orders. I suggested Clancy try Three Philosophers, so that's what we ordered. Moon ordered a Sam Adams Boston Lager. Rachel had them for us quickly. Clancy sipped the Three Philosophers and nodded at me in appreciation, then held up his tulip glass and said, "Here's to our mission, and less complicated lives!"

We all drank to that and then, by means of destroying the efficacy of his toast, Suzanne Highsmith made an entrance, looked around, and headed for our booth.

Chapter Twenty-Three

"Flirting is a woman's trade, one
must keep in practice."

- Charlotte Bronte, Jane Eyre

"**T**homas, I am *so* sorry about last week!" she said, sliding into the booth, bumping Moon farther over with her hip. He made room. She reached across the table and touched my hand. "I am *so* ashamed of myself, that's why I've been keeping to my rooms and just writing. Please forgive me. That wasn't me the other night. Embarrassing."

"Sure looked like you."

Suzanne was wearing an unbuttoned violet cardigan with a white blouse underneath, unbuttoned three down. Her throat was lovely and delicious-looking. She was lightly flushed in memory of her attempted seduction.

"What caused you such shame, beautiful lady?" Clancy asked.

I looked over at him and saw that look I had seen a few times before, when Clancy Dominguez was on the precipice of a deep and long-lasting love affair that would terminate in three weeks, more or less. He was, frankly, staring at her.

"Excuse my shocking lack of manners," I said, looking from Clancy to Suzanne and seeing a look on her face that indicated her first impression of Clancy would lead to private, adult interactions. I couldn't believe it. From him, yes. But reciprocated? Love at first sight. Oh, boy! I continued and introduced them.

"No need to go into specifics about what happened last week, Clancy," I said. "Suzanne's a lady, and always will be. Besides, that wasn't Suzanne who told me she wasn't wearing any underthings, frilly or otherwise. And that wasn't me who didn't follow up."

"You are *such* a gentleman, Thomas," she said, her voice sweet and sincere, her eyes locked on Clancy. "Such a gentleman," she repeated. "And what brings you to Rockbluff, Mr. Dominguez?" Her eyes might as well have been the hands of a private masseuse.

"Please call me Clancy," he said, "and I'm here because I am into private protection services, and you most certainly look like the kind of stunningly-beautiful woman who would benefit from my profession. Did I just say 'stunningly beautiful'?"

He'd just added "stunningly" to his second "beautiful" reference in less than thirty seconds. I thought I would throw up, but I kept that to myself. I knew where this was going.

"Clancy's an old friend of mine from back in the day when we were spending our nights at the library translating Serbo-Croation poetry. Lots of war stories about verbs and antecedents," I said.

"I'll bet you'd be better translating French poetry," she said. I was feeling invisible and thrilled, when we were interrupted by a question from Lunatic Mooning.

"Would you like something to eat?" he asked.

Suzanne looked startled. "Oh, yes, please. I'm *starving*. May I have a chef's salad and a Perrier? Thank you, Moon."

Moon turned to gesture but Rachel was already there. She took Suzanne's order and hurried away. Clancy and Suzanne were staring and oblivious again. Moon and I exchanged glances. He responded with a nearly-imperceptible shaking of his head. I had to smile. He had seen it coming, too, even though he didn't know Clancy.

"I was about to ask you what kind of work you do," Clancy began, his eyes moving all over Suzanne's face, taking her in. "But then I thought, you probably don't have to really *do*, but merely *be*, and improve everything around you by your very presence, as you are now, Suzanne. And I love that name."

At that point I was overtly rolling my eyes and turning my attention to my Loony Burger and Belgian ale. Suzanne was enthralled. "Thank you, Clancy, but I *do* do something. I am a professional writer," she said, her hand slipping into her purse and extracting her business card which she slid across the table, maneuvering it around the food and drink and pushing it toward Clancy with her right index finger with the deep red polish. He picked up the card after brushing his hand across hers.

"What do you write about?" he asked.

"Dangerous men in dangerous situations. I even wrote a book about Thomas here, and some unpleasantness last year that he corrected. It's called *Something's Rotten in Rockbluff,* and you can pick up a copy down at Bednarik's Books. I'd be glad to sign it for you."

"You *should* write about *Clancy*," I said, able to restrain myself but unwilling to do so. "He's a for *real* former SEAL. All kinds of adventures."

"A SEAL?" Suzanne asked, her wide eyes widening even more, threatening prolapse. "So you used to be what they call a snake-eater?"

"Some people called us that," he said, "but not so much anymore. And I never ate a snake, although I know how."

"Clancy, show Suzanne your scar from that anaconda that tried to kill you," I said. I bit into my Loony Burger and sat back to enjoy the story.

"I didn't think anacondas had teeth," Suzanne said. "I thought they just crushed people to death. Show me your scar! Where did it bite you?" She asked leaning forward in her seat. Rachel brought her chef's salad and Perrier. Since Suzanne didn't notice, I thanked Rachel, who winked at me. I love it when women wink at me.

"Irish and I were down in Southeast Asia on a mission, and it required that we approach our target through water, and there was this big river we had to cross," Clancy began. "And so we're about chest deep when this goddamn anaconda swims by. It must have been fifteen feet long. Me and Irish exchanged looks, grateful it kept going, because this was one big snake. Then it came back and went after me, and you'd be amazed at how quickly they can get a couple of loops around their prey.

"Well, I knew I was in trouble, so I grabbed for its head and the damn thing bit me in the hand and it hurt like hell and I couldn't unpry its jaws, one reason being I was losing strength because I couldn't breathe very well. The damn thing had gotten another loop around me and I could not freaking *believe* how strong it was. Every time I breathed out, it got tighter and I knew I was in some deep stuff, if you get my drift. So Irish lunges over and manages to pry its jaw open, and then the next thing I see is this guy with his candy bar in hand, cutting off the snake's head. It gave a couple of spasmodic shivers that nearly crushed my rib cage, then relaxed and floated away. And so I've got this bleeding hand wound and we hadn't even gotten into the mission yet."

Clancy slid the sleeve of his sweatshirt up and offered his right hand for inspection, turning it over so the two fang marks on top and the two fang marks on the bottom could be seen. The story was true. Suzanne was enthralled. Moon was looking at the scar, too.

She said, "Thomas, how did you cut off that snake's head with a candy bar? Are you kidding me?"

"He means a Ka-bar, a kind of military knife with a nine inch blade. Razor sharp."

Suzanne said, "Clancy, you must have lots of stories that I could write about, stories about things you did as a SEAL, and even now with your private company. We need to talk," she said, and tore into her salad. Suzanne had found someone more interesting than me, and I was thrilled.

"Ask him to tell you about killing the pirates in the Indian Ocean," I said. I turned my attention to the remains of my Loony Burger. Rachel, ever vigilant, brought me a second Three Philosophers.

"You're kidding!" Suzanne gulped, her mouth full of chef's salad. She pushed some of the lettuce back in her mouth as she talked. "Listen, if you don't mind, why don't you pick me up at my place tonight. I've rented a suite at the Rockbluff Motel. Can you come by around seven? Maybe we can go someplace, grab a bite to eat, and you can tell me about the pirates and any other adventures you've had. My room number is thirty-eight. Can you remember that, or do I need to write it down on the back of my card?"

Clancy looked down at Suzanne's chest and said, "I think I can remember thirty-eight, Suzanne."

She grinned, actually giggled, and went back to eating. I stifled my gag reflex.

"How are you going to pick her up, Clancy?" I asked, "since you have no car."

"May I borrow your truck, Irish. I'll be good."

"*I* wouldn't do it," Moon said.

"Will you be back early?" I asked. "You know there's a curfew that goes with the keys."

"Hard to say," Suzanne interjected. "I think Clancy and I have a lot of communicating to do."

For the next few minutes, Moon and I ate and drank silently, allowing Clancy and Suzanne to entertain us with their double entendres and witty ripostes. And then she was finishing her meal, such as it was, and sliding out of the booth and establishing when Clancy would pick her up all over again. Seven o'clock.

After she left, Clancy said to me, "That is some kind of woman, Irish."

"You can say that again," I muttered.

"Oh! It just occurred to me! She isn't, wasn't, I mean, . . . "

"Fear not, dude, she isn't, wasn't and never will be, you know, my cuddle-bunny." Moon snorted and I smiled at his snorting. "She's all yours to pursue and conquer."

"I am relieved," Clancy said, noticeably relaxing. "So, let's talk about the next couple of days. To review, if it's okay with you guys, I'll go up and hang around Chalaka for a day or two, see what I can learn, come back and get debriefed. Then, depending on a lot of variables, we'll make a plan where the end game is to kill or capture, or *both*," he said, nodding at Lunatic, "Ted Hornung and bring him to justice. Anybody else hanging with him, too. A cleanup job that will leave no evidence who did it but leave the clear message that this was because of the murder of Cindy Stalking Wolf. Agreed?"

We agreed, finished eating, and left, after my leaving a nice tip for Rachel and Moon telling us all four meals were on the house. I wasn't sure why he was in such a generous mood, unless he was just grateful for our help going after his niece's killers, and encouraged about cleaning up Ted Hornung's gang.

"You leave first, Irish, and I'll saunter out in a little bit. Those guys really haven't taken notice of me, yet, and I don't want me to be linked with you," Clancy said, indicating with a nod the Special Agents still interrogating Harmon.

I left and ambled out the front door. I strode straight to my truck and drove slowly around the parking lot until Clancy appeared and hopped in, ducking down as he did. We drove back to my place. It was only one-thirty in the afternoon.

"What did the SBI guys want to know, Irish?" Clancy asked as we got out of the truck and headed for the front door of my home.

"Everything," I said, opening the door and going inside, Clancy right behind me.

"What did you tell them?"

"Nothing. After I asked to closely examine their identification."

Clancy laughed. "Good. You haven't lost a thing, man. By the way, I enjoyed your prompting that story about the anaconda. I've had a couple of bad dreams about that since it happened. They show up at weird times. Probably have another one tonight."

"Suzanne ate it up."

"That, she did. I'm glad she's not your woman, man, but I don't understand why not. Apparently she tried to knock you over a few days ago and you declined."

"She was drunk."

"She's an adult."

"*I* wasn't drunk. Sometimes I suffer from annoying attacks of conscience."

Clancy smiled. "You and that Jesus thing, I guess."

"Probably. Thank God."

"Seriously? You're glad you didn't have sex with Suzanne?"

We dumped our coats on chairs and flopped down in the twin recliners in front of the dormant fireplace. It was stacked with gray wood and needing only a match to start a nice fire on a cold winter's day in northeast Iowa.

"Here's the thing," I said. "I thought about how I'd feel the next day if I did sleep with Suzanne, her being drunk and all. And I thought about how I'd feel the next day if I just tucked her safely in her bed and came home. Very quickly, I chose the latter."

"That's what I like about you, Irish. Besides the skill set that obviously I've witnessed and benefitted from, you have scruples, and you're surprising. I'm thinking, since you're a Christian, you could just go ahead and enjoy that woman and then ask the good Lord to forgive you. I'm no theologian, but wouldn't that work?"

"God knows our hearts, Clancy."

He shrugged his shoulders. "Whatever. Guess that's why I could never be a Christian. No freaking fun."

"It's *more* fun than ever. Hard to explain, but I'll try sometime."

"You're welcome to it," he said, "but for now, I think a nice little nap will put me in a good mood for my visit with Suzanne tonight. She is a writer, isn't she?"

"Yes, and a good one, too, though she sometimes tends to exaggerate."

"Like all fiction writers. I understand. Maybe I'll pick up her book at that book store she mentioned."

"Bednarik's Books," I said. "And I think I'll take a nap, too. I don't seem to bounce back from clandestine activities like I used to."

"What clandestine activities? I thought you just went up to Chalaka to ask questions."

I told him about my interview with Ivan. Clancy broke into a grin. "I hate to admit it, Irish, but you might even be better than I am. Good work. Anyway, I'm off to a nap. See you in a while."

And I took my nap. We both woke up around four that afternoon, refreshed. Clancy declined dinner, figuring he would have dinner with Suzanne. I wasn't particularly hungry, either, more in the mood to read and think for a while until I had more information, and that was Clancy's department.

He watched television and I read, and so the afternoon slipped into darkness and early night. I could see that he was getting ready to leave, so I fished out an extra set of truck and house keys from the junk drawer in the kitchen and tossed them his way. He caught them and started for the door.

"Thanks, Irish. Much appreciated. And I wouldn't wait up for me if I were you."

"You have a ten PM curfew unless you want to be grounded."

"But Suzanne doesn't have a curfew, I don't think."

"Go away, and please give my regards to Ms. Highsmith," I said.

Clancy grinned, popped a quick salute, and was out the door. I settled back and read a little Bonhoeffer, then picked up a Warren Moore III noir novel and read, the vivid imagery disturbing in an existential way. I turned on the TV and stumbled onto an Iowa-Indiana State game I had completely forgotten about, surprising myself. I watched the Hawkeyes pull it out with perfect free throw shooting in overtime.

I buttoned off the set, poured myself a tall glass of white merlot, drank it too quickly, and went to bed after locking the doors and sliding the steel sleeve into the doggy door after taking Gotcha out to perform her nightly duties. As soon as she came in she headed for the big pillow on the floor at the foot of the bed and plopped down, arranged her thick body, and flung out her tongue for better breathing. The dog knows how to chill.

I undressed, slipping into my black boxers, and fell asleep thinking about Olivia Olson, even with a major mission on the near horizon. Sometimes I surprise myself.

Clancy showed up a little after eight the next morning with a self-satisfied smile on his face that reminded me of our big golden retriever when I was a kid. His name was Barney and he was a good dog, but on occasion he would dig under the fence in our back yard in Clinton and slink off to visit a lady friend somewhere who had "come into season," as my mother had delicately put it. He would show up the next morning, exhausted and with a sheepish look on his face, eat a big breakfast, and take a lengthy nap.

A few weeks later there would be puppies in the neighborhood with at least one that looked like Barney. I wondered if there would be little Clancy-like baby boys in nine months wherever Suzanne Highsmith was living. I hoped not. The visual was not appealing at the moment.

"Did you have a good time, Clancy?" I asked as he joined me at the breakfast table. "I waited up for you, worried sick. At least you could have called," I said in a high voice, trying to sound like a worried mother.

He looked at me over his coffee and eggs I had fixed for us both and just dished up.

"Suzanne Highsmith is a classy broad," he said, slowly nodding his head.

"Indeed."

"I think I'm in love."

"That's spelled l-u-s-t."

"You might be right, but I'd be a fool not to pursue the woman. She is flat out delicious."

I raised a skeptical eyebrow.

Clancy recovered from his reverie long enough to come back to the moment and say, "Of course, she will have to wait, my friend. We have work to do."

"We're waiting on *you*, Clancy," I said, getting up and dishing fried Spam slices onto a platter and placing the food on the table. I sat down.

"Fried Spam?"

"I like to touch base with my boyhood every now and then," I said, forking three slices onto my plate.

"Any more bacon and eggs?"

"Help yourself." Clancy got up and moved over to the stove and helped himself.

"I'm heading for Chalaka as soon as I can shower and shave and change clothes. I've reserved a rental for the drive. That monster truck of yours might look familiar to people up on the reservation. Drop me off?"

He was back downstairs in twenty minutes.

I dropped him off at the Shell station that also rented cars on the side. Not a chain. The three years old, gray Ford Taurus was ready to go. And so was Clancy, without another reference to his night with Suzanne. I saw in his eyes and overall affect the old focus coming into play, and smiled inside.

And then he was climbing into the Taurus and driving away, heading north out of town, his recon mission about to unfold.

Chapter Twenty-Four

"Action is eloquence."

—*William Shakespeare*—

We were headed north out of Rockbluff, Clancy Dominguez, Lunatic Mooning, and me, riding in silence in Moon's perfect Packard in a dark Iowa winter mid-morning. A snowstorm was coming, but Clancy said that was good. It added to our advantage of surprise.

He had come back with a plan after two days in Chalaka, and we were going to carry it out. There was some risk, but that's what fueled our collective adrenalin, slowly surging and maintaining our edge. Clancy had learned that Hornung had regular meetings with his security staff on Friday nights after hours, and that they would all be there, including the two shooters he'd brought in from Chicago. Marty Rodman's intel had held up. I was beginning to have a soft spot in my heart for the pimp.

We would enter the Pony Club after it closed down and the customers left. We would kill everyone there in Hornung's office, making sure they knew why we were there. We would set fire to the place and leave. No fingerprints. We would drive back to Rockbluff, Clancy would disappear, and Moon and I would go about our normal business.

I had attended to Gotcha's needs that morning and made the doggy door available by placing the flexible, fringed plastic slide in the sleeve. Clancy and I both skipped breakfast, but split a pot of coffee, then placed our gear in the truck. For the first time, I got a good look at the duffle bag he had brought. I didn't ask what was inside. I guessed explosives and an array of firearms useful to our purpose. Maybe an inflatable armored personnel carrier.

We were riding in silence, Moon because he is a silent person most of the time anyway, me because I was focusing and praying for the task ahead, and Clancy because Moon and I were silent. Usually exuberant and charged before a mission, at least as I knew him from the past, he was oddly subdued but restless nevertheless, jumpy as a caffeinated squirrel at the side of the road. He kept looking out both side windows, then out the back, then back to the side windows again, taking in information, his brain like a small computer. Observation had been one of his many strong points when we worked together, and he was clearly at it again. One never knows when a pineapple tree might show up – an opportunity for fresh fruit if we were cut off from supplies.

It was growing darker and darker, and I could sense the storm on the way. The weather woman on the Dubuque TV station last night was predicting eight or nine inches. That did not worry me because I knew Moon would have no trouble driving in the storm. His Packard weighed about ten tons and had snow tires. Also, I knew there would be little traffic on that road, sparsely travelled in ordinary circumstances, it would be nearly deserted with that storm approaching, even though it was a Friday.

Nearly deserted, because just as the first flurries came fluttering our way, a big SUV met us on the road and passed, heading south, toward Rockbluff.

"Shit!" Clancy said, squirming around in the back seat and staring out the back window.

"What?" I asked.

"They're hitting the brakes and slowing down. They've made us!"

"WHO made us!" I asked.

"I'm guessing it's the bad guys from Chalaka. They looked like a rough bunch," Clancy answered, muttering

"How could they make us?" I asked.

"Did you guys take this car when you went up to Chalaka to pound on those jerks?" Clancy asked, a touch of sarcasm in his tone.

"Oh," I said. "They identified the car. Not many of these around."

Moon said, "And I recognized them, too. The driver. Man who broke my windshield. We made eye contact just now. He seemed to recognize me."

"They're turning around and coming back this way," Clancy said. "Now they have the advantage, being behind us. Better step on it, Moon."

The big car surged forward and I unzipped the backpack at my feet and withdrew Elsie. She was loaded. I took off the safety.

"That's an Escalade, boys. I don't think we can outrun her. She's already gaining."

"How many?" Moon asked, glancing in his rearview mirror. I looked at him. He did not look concerned. He did look focused, however.

"I think six," Clancy said. "You know what that means."

"What?" Moon asked.

"We win. Follow my instructions now. There's a deserted farm about half a mile ahead on your left. Pull in and we'll take them on there. You'll have to bust through a gate. No time to get out and swing it open. They're closer and closer, really roaring along now. Come on, come on! Let's roll!" he said, staring out the back window.

Clancy was right. Powers of observation on his trip to Chalaka had paid off. The deserted farm was on a small hill, and as we came up the drive, Moon hauled left, hard, skidding a bit on the blacktop, tires chirping. The gate loomed up about twenty yards in and we blasted through it as if it were aluminum foil and drove over a livestock grate. Moon said nothing about the damage to his Packard.

"Head for that barn," Clancy said, now speaking softly and with authority. I had heard that tone before, and it was a comfort. The man was unflappable when it came to the business at hand. I had never seen him otherwise in any other situation. I smiled inside, glad he was with us.

Moon drove up next to the barn and turned the big car around, facing to the left and downhill. The barn, one of those with a passage right down the middle and out the other side, and stalls on each side and a hayloft above, was in serious disrepair, but a formidable gate prevented us from taking the car inside. The two-story farmhouse stood alone and decaying a good fifty yards beyond. Moon cut the engine and we all clambered out.

"If they're any good, they'll disable the car so we can't get away," Clancy said. "If we're any good, we'll kill them anyway. They don't know we're *not* going to try to get away. But they'll wish *they* had before this day is over. I'm hoping they're overconfident but I doubt it if it's true Hornung hired two pros from Chicago. Guess we'll see just how professional they are soon enough."

The Escalade slowed down and crept up the lane, then veered off to the left, edging closer and closer and finally stopped about forty yards away, blocking the road down to the highway. The snowstorm had grown serious, giving up on flurries and heading fully into serious snowfall, pounding away at an angle and reducing visibility.

The three of us huddled behind a concrete water trough as Clancy zipped open his duffel bag, reached in, and pulled out a small pair of binoculars while Moon and I checked our shotguns and peered over the top of the barrier. We could see people scrambling out from the Escalade as Clancy brought the binocs up to his eyes and studied the gang down the hill from us.

"Five, no six targets. And one of those suckers is a giant," he said. He dropped the glasses down and turned to me. "Didn't you say your contact was a big Indian? With a bald head and tats on his skull?"

I muttered and said, "That lying son of a bitch. Said he was going to take off and flee the state."

Clancy shook his head and grinned. "He did. He's in *Iowa* now. You've lost your edge, Irish. You know you should've killed him when you had the chance. He's a loose end, and now he just might end up putting a round in your butt. Never fails."

I didn't say anything, but just took the binocs when Clancy handed them to me. I looked as the men in the Escalade began to spread out. It wasn't hard to pick up Ivan.

"He's the one with Cindy when she was murdered?" Moon asked.

"Yes," I said.

"Good to know," he replied.

I handed the field glasses back to Clancy, who took another look, then whistled, grabbed his bag, and said, "Let's get to the barn right *now*."

We were barely inside the relative safety of the sagging, faded-red barn before our pursuers cut loose with every kind of firearm in their arsenal, and from the sounds of it, both handguns and automatic weapons had come into play. The sound was steady and furious and then it was not. None of us were touched, but that was because we weren't the targets, yet.

We peeked out from behind one of the barn doors and saw that the target was Lunatic Mooning's Packard, and it was a ruin. The tires were shredded, the windows blown out, liquid dripping from under the engine, sending up steam. I imagined the opposite side was pockmarked from the hundreds of rounds fired. I could not look at Moon.

"They'll come for us now," Clancy said, "probably from both ends of the barn, so let's set up. The old three-point position. You remember the drill, Irish?"

I nodded and we deployed after Clancy gave each of us a handgun to supplement the shotguns. Mine was a .44 Magnum Colt Anaconda ("for old times' sake) he said, and Moon took a Glock 9mm, which he reluctantly accepted, then stuffed inside his belt behind his back. Clancy had an M-16 in one hand and another Anaconda in the other. And then we spread out in the barn, each of us with a different angle that would generate an efficient and deadly crossfire with little chance of friendly fire.

I plopped down behind a few rotting bales of hay that had fallen through from the hayloft when the floor boards collapsed. My position placed me about ten yards from the closest barn opening. Clancy was down at the other end, blending into some old, rusted machinery, and Moon took up position in the hayloft, treading carefully over creaking boards until he found solid footing, where he crouched.

It was quiet in the barn for a few minutes, time enough for me to pray for strength and direction, and to assess our situation. I felt good about it. The boys from Chalaka were obviously heavily-armed. But we had me. And Clancy. Two guys who had been in worse situations and come through okay.

When it comes to a firefight, the person who is willing to think clearly and fire calmly is the one who will most likely survive while the other guys, inexperienced or untrained or both, panicked or came damn near to it, influencing their aim and their thinking. I was actually looking forward to cleaning up the mess generated by the murders of Cindy Stalking Wolf and Preston and Julia Jarlsson.

I heard voices, laughter, and people running, the heavy snow muting the sounds. I made sure the safety was off and the Anaconda was within easy reach. I had used the big revolver with the 8-inch barrel long ago, pleasantly surprised that the aftershock was so well absorbed into the gun's design. Heavy but accurate, it could create mayhem with just one slug. Too bad it went out of production in '99.

They came into the barn cautiously, from two directions, as expected. Two distinct groupings, too. At my end, there were two of the black security guards from the Pony Club; the leader, along with the man whose finger I had broken. At the other end, I saw one Indian, he who had smashed in the Packard's windshield in the club's parking lot. That would be Ray Old Turtle, who helped Ivan take Cindy's body and who killed the Jarlssons. Another Indian emerged behind Ray Old Turtle. It was Ivan, lingering cautiously near the barn door's frame, looking nervous.

I immediately gave credit to the shooters from Chicago. Relying on the old technique of miners taking canaries into the mines to let the workers know if there were poisonous gasses inside, they were using the local help for the same purpose. The Indians and blacks, ignorant of the dynamics of battle, might as well have been wearing Big Bird outfits with "Shoot Me" signs on their chests. I ignored those down at Clancy's end of the barn and directed my attention to the two at my end.

They stepped boldly into the doorway, the taller guy with a shotgun and the other man with a small handgun of some kind. They walked in a few feet and called for us to surrender, that they wouldn't hurt us, that they just wanted to work out an agreement. They had smirks on their young faces and I realized they didn't think we were armed, probably assured of that lie by the Chicago shooters. After all, we had been unarmed at the Pony Club. The younger man giggled a little and said, "Come out here, muthafuckers!" and waved his pistol around, aiming it sideways. Pathetic.

As close to me as they were, I used my shotgun to drop the man with the broken finger, standing up and pumping two rounds into his torso, the majority of the pellets in a snug grouping that blew his chest open, the force of the impact lifting him up and slamming him backward onto the dirt floor of the barn. His pal cut loose with his shotgun in my direction, firing wildly, but I had already ducked down behind the hay bales, which took on the blasts, two of which went into the hay. Another blast, wild and panicky, peppered the wall high up behind me to no effect.

After the third discharge, I stood up and, extending my hand with the Anaconda in it, calmly squeezed off one round that struck the man in the face, dropping him backward to the ground. Both men were dead, and just as I fired the .44 Magnum, gunfire broke out at the other end as the two Indians began firing at me, rounds going everywhere from their handguns. I could hear one round buzz by my head and I was suddenly taken back to an episode in the Sudan which had turned out well, despite some serious opposition. It was a sound I never got used to, but I have learned to accept and consider the bright side, which was that they had missed.

It made me angry, and Clancy moreso as he shot Ray Old Turtle, the one who had ruined the Packard's windshield. The short burst from the M-16 stenciled his chest and he slumped to the ground, dead. Ivan disappeared around the door. Clancy approached the dead man and made sure he was dead. I heard Moon drop down from the hayloft and take off out the door at the other end of the barn, Clancy having moved and gone down on one knee just inside the door, providing cover outside as Moon left the building.

Thinking maybe Ivan was going to get away to the Escalade and escape, I headed back out the door at my end of the barn, popping my head around the corner of the barn door, but Ivan was nowhere in sight at my end of the barn. Maybe he was just going to try to escape into the snowstorm that was now looking like another Iowa blizzard. There were only three of the bad guys left and our odds were looking better and better. I could hear pistol shots far off to my right in the direction Ivan had taken, with Moon in pursuit. Then I heard a shotgun blast.

I wondered where the two professionals were, but I didn't have to wonder long. Deep in the depths of the snowstorm, halfway between the Escalade and the barn in a small stand of trees off to my left, there was a muzzle flash and a searing, hot pain in my right side. Another muzzle flash nicked me in the same place on the other side and I dropped to the ground, Anaconda in one hand and Elsie in the other.

So I was wounded, but at least I knew where one of the shooters was. But where was the other? What was he doing? Was he seeking out Clancy or Moon? I lay there, breathing heavily, not taking time to glance at my wounds as the snow pelted down, knowing I had to move before any more shots were fired in my direction.

And then I heard the boom of Clancy's hand cannon, far behind me and to the left, near a collapsed outbuilding, a moan softened by the wind and snow, and then another shot from the Anaconda. Then, nothing.

I knew now there was just Ivan and the second shooter, and I felt pretty confident that Moon was going to be doing his duty by Ivan, who had done nothing to stop Cindy's murder. Ivan was a liar and a manipulator, and he had manipulated me. If I got the chance, I promised myself I would take away his privileges for a while. All his privileges. Permanently. Then Clancy called out, his voice to my left.

"You okay, Irish?"

"Never felt better. Isn't this fun?" I called back, pain stabbing me at both sides.

"You need to get down to their Escalade. There's one I can't pinpoint yet, and he's got to understand that it's all over unless he can escape, so cut him off if you can. With extreme prejudice, understand?"

"Aye aye sir!" I said.

Two more shots came very close to my position, whistling over my head, and I began scooting as fast as I could to my right, fighting off the pain from my wounds, crawling toward the Escalade. I risked one quick look down and saw that I was leaving a rather vivid red trail as the blood from my gunshot wounds had soaked through my clothes. I decided we could deal with that later. Nothing major had been hit, although I knew that "nothing major" always referenced other people's wounds. I put my wounds aside, blocking everything from my mind but that last shooter from Chicago.

It was nearly impossible to see the big SUV since the snowstorm had, improbably, gotten even thicker and heavier. It was a full-blown blizzard now, and I nearly missed the figure to my left, crouching, looking around furtively, and slowly edging toward the big vehicle.

I came to my feet and began trotting toward the Escalade, my angle working to cut off the man from his objective.

My sides were screaming, pulling me to a bent over position, but I sucked it up and kept on until I was immediately in the man's path. I could hear him breathing hard and crunching along in the snow, and then he appeared, at first a ghost in a white universe, then a dark shape, vague and indistinct, then a man. And then he saw me.

He stopped, looking surprised, then began to bring up his pistol. I shot him, pumping two shotgun rounds into the big target, the torso, nearly cutting him in half. He stood there, wavering, dead on his feet, and I wondered what incredible strength he must have had to keep his feet after a double shotgun blast. He was a big man, wide and thick and swarthy, and he stared at me with surprise as he wobbled. I pumped another round into the chamber of my shotgun and fired again and he just blew apart, bloodsplatter spraying all over the snow around him. When he fell, he made a heavy, soft, thumping sound. Clancy showed up right behind him in less than ten seconds.

He looked at me, looked at my side, then looked at the dead man, rolling him over, then back, the snow going red where the body lay. He walked up and said, "You okay?"

"I'm fine. Just a scratch. Two scratches. Did you know John Wayne was from Iowa?"

Clancy rolled his eyes and said, "Let's go find Moon. I count five dead bodies and so far none of them are us, although you look like you might have tried pretty hard. He's hunting down the Indian."

"Ivan," I said. "Let's go."

To his credit, Clancy did not ask me if I was "up to it." He just grinned and nodded and we set off for the barn again, loping along in the whiteout conditions, eyes on the ground ahead of us. At the far side of the barn we found two sets of tracks rapidly being obliterated by the snow, then, farther on, we found spots of blood that indicated a non-fatal wound. We crossed through a field and down into a low spot and then there was another pistol shot followed by another shotgun blast. And another blast, separated by just a few seconds. No more pistol shots.

We found Lunatic Mooning standing over Ivan's body, the giant Indian collapsed half in a brief stream of gurgling water, his face gone. Moon was just standing there, staring. When he heard us he turned toward us and looked. At me. At my bloody clothes.

"Gun go off by accident?" he asked.

"Something like that. Now, since you almost let this one get away, let's get that hulk back to the barn."

"What the hell for?" Clancy asked. "I wouldn't mind leaving him here for the critters. No one will find him."

"Let's make this look like something it isn't," I said. "We'll collect the bodies and their weapons, put them in the Escalade, push it into the barn, then push the Packard in there, too. Make it look like a drug deal gone bad, or a racial thing, or anything but what we were actually doing. What do you think?"

"Ugh," Moon said, nodding his head.

"A man with a plan," Clancy said. Then he and Moon picked up Ivan and his gun and we trudged back into the whiteness of the blizzard, back to the barn. We dumped Ivan's body next to the barn along with the two men I killed and the one Clancy took out. Then Clancy went to get the professional I shot on his way to the Escalade and the other pro he killed by the decaying outbuilding.

Moon and I walked over to the far side of what remained of the Packard. It was as I expected, peppered with gunshot holes. The car was a total loss, but I wanted it moved inside the barn, so Moon got behind the wheel and I brought the Escalade around and drove it inside the barn. They had left the keys in the ignition. The engine sputtered and caught and white smoke poured out from under the hood, but Moon was able to get it to edge along while I got behind the big Packard and pushed, my sides screaming with the effort, Moon steering it for the last time. Together, we got the car into the barn. Moon cut the engine and just sat there for a while, behind the wheel, his head down. Then he got out, no expression on his face.

Clancy showed up with the last two shooters, the Chicago boys, one black and one white, dragging each one by the collar on his coat. We put the three black men in the Packard and the Indians and the white shooter in the Escalade and drove it inside the barn. Then we closed the barn doors and sat down in the barn while the blizzard kicked ass outside.

"Now what?" I said.

"I think your plan needs tweaking," Clancy said. "Let me think."

And then we all fell silent, each of us alone for the moment, each of us thinking our own thoughts.

And as I looked around at the rotting barn, the destroyed Packard, knowing the dead bodies were in the two cars, knowing that I was twice shot, something broke inside of me, and all I wanted in my life was to be with Liv Olson, but I knew she wouldn't have me and then I realized I thought of her instead of Karen and I was ashamed and then I thought again of Liv and I wasn't ashamed that time. Just lonely.

CHAPTER TWENTY-FIVE

**"My therapist told me the way to achieve true inner peace is
to finish what I start. So today I have finished 2 bags
of M&M's and a chocolate cake. I feel better already."**

- Dave Barry

It was quiet for a moment there in the pitch-black confines of the decrepit barn. Then I spoke up. "First thing, Crazy Horse, is you've got to report your car stolen," I said.

"Got a cell phone, Moon?" Clancy asked.

Lunatic gave Clancy a look.

"Oh, so it's like that," Clancy said. "Good point, though, Irish. But we've got to finish what we started."

"What do you call this?" I asked, then I knew.

"Ted Hornung lives," Moon said. "Unacceptable."

Clancy looked at Moon. "Would you be satisfied with taking out Ivan as long as Hornung assumes room temperature? I mean, he was there when your niece was murdered. Hornung ordered it, but he didn't do it himself."

Moon thought for a moment, nodded his head yes. "Hornung must pay."

Clancy climbed to his feet, grunting with the effort. "You two stay here. Moon, take a look at Irish's injuries. I'll be back in less than an hour. We can't waste time."

"Where you going?" I asked.

"After I remove the GPS tracking device in that Escalade and take it with me, I'm gonna get us some transportation. There's a working farm about two miles from here, on the right side of the road, and they have half a dozen vehicles, most of them boring, which is good. I'll be right back. Now, give me the handguns I gave you, drop them in my duffel."

Clancy opened his duffel bag, reached in and handed out two flashlights. Then he held the bag out in front of each of us in turn and we dropped our guns inside. I thought I saw a SAW in there, and other bits of metal, but it was pretty dark. Who knows? Clancy plans well. With our handguns secured, he pulled his gloves tight and reached in and pulled out two clear plastic packages with white powdery-looking substances inside. I gave him a look. He just smiled, walked over to the front passenger's door of the Escalade, opened it, and threw the package inside, bursting it against the steering wheel, scattering white powder everywhere in the illumination from the dome light.

He said, "Some people would rather have the drugs than the money. It can come in handy." Then he tossed the other bag on the floor of the back seat, shut the door, and eased himself under the SUV, and muttered under there for a while. Then he came out and grinned. "They already took it out. No tracking."

With that, he closed up his duffle bag, hung it by its strap over his shoulder, and slipped out the front door into the early afternoon blizzard. He was wearing a black turtleneck sweater, a black leather waist-length leather jacket, bluejeans and hiking boots. He pulled a stocking cap out of his jacket pocket and pulled it over his ears as he edged out the front door of the barn.

When he left, Moon said, "Let me take a look at your scratches, Thomas."

I slipped off my pea coat and pulled up my sweatshirt, then tugged my heavy t-shirt free from being tucked inside my levi's. I rose up from the barn floor and came to my knees. Moon flicked on his flashlight. There was a lot of blood. Moon looked at the front of my belly, then my back. He touched the wounds and I smiled very, very hard.

With a deep sigh, he turned off the flashlight and announced, "One round went right through you. Clean. You are fortunate. Another just singed away a little of your left lovehandle. No one will ever know. Maybe Olivia Olson if you two ever wise up."

"I'm planning on surviving," I said, ignoring the Liv Olson remark.

"But you would be wise to get some medical attention. Maybe Clancy can help you out with that when we get back. Antiseptic, bandage. You've ruined your clothes. Blood everywhere," he said, in what amounted to a filibuster in Congress.

"Can't go to a doctor," I said. "They have to report gunshot wounds."

Moon flicked off his flashlight, returning us to relative darkness. The white snow outside helped with visibility, but not much. So we sat there in the dark, silent.

I tried to figure out what to do next. Moon would call in his stolen car when we got back to Rockbluff. With luck, the blizzard would obliterate the tracks around the farmyard. We could make sure the gate was closed as we left, and maybe no one would notice for days and weeks that there were two cars in the dilapidated barn with six dead bodies in them. No reason to look in the barn of an abandoned homestead.

Hornung would be waiting for a report, either on cell phone or in person, about how his men had fared, so it would be important to deal with him quickly. He would be suspicious and more wary than usual if he didn't hear anything.

I had no regrets about the gunfight. It was self-defense. They came to kill us before we could kill them, but I knew that wouldn't fly in a court of law unless we had an outstanding defense lawyer. But even if we won, the publicity would mess up our lives for a long time, although Suzanne Highsmith would be delighted with the story.

Forty-five minutes later, we heard a car approaching. Moon helped me to my feet and, shotguns in hand, we peered outside, bending the barn door a little to afford a sightline to the blacktop road. A barely-visible gray Toyota Camry eased its way up the drive, obscured by the snowstorm. It had no headlights beaming. It coasted up to the barn. The engine stopped and Clancy Dominguez emerged from behind the steering wheel and came over to us, a smile on his face.

"I want you two to head back to Rockbluff and, pardon the expression, chill. Wear your gloves at all times when you're in this luxury vehicle. Get your stories straight. Moon, what's the deal with Irish's wounds?"

"He won't need to go to a doctor. Could use some minor attention."

"Can you arrange for someone to help him and be discreet?" Clancy asked.

"Yes."

"Okay, now, I have to ask you guys something. Can you trust me to take care of Hornung today?" Clancy said.

"You plan on going up there alone?" I asked.

"He knows what you two look like. If he sees you, he'll know something's up. But he doesn't know me. He's never seen me. I'm boring-looking. I doubt the club will be open due to the weather. The forecast is for much more snow, up to ten inches. I heard that on the radio just now. With your blessing, I'll go ahead and complete the mission."

"What about where you got the car? How'd that go?" I asked, stalling. Clancy's plan made sense. I knew he could follow through, but I wanted to go with him, out of the question for the very reasons he gave, plus I was feeling a little light-headed from loss of blood and my adrenalin easing off.

"No problem. The people who live at the farm aren't home, or at least it didn't look like it. But this storm is getting noisy and it's hard to see more than a few yards. The keys were in the ignition of this beauty and I just drove it away. I doubt they noticed even if they were home. I'm going back for my own ride now, got my eyes on a silver Accord, then on to Chalaka. Farm people, keys in ignitions." Clancy shook his head.

"Iowan hospitality for strangers," I said.

"Okay then," Clancy said. "Moon, you got anything?"

"May The Great Spirit watch over you," Moon said.

Clancy nodded, looked at me. "Irish? Any words of advice?"

"Keep your powder dry, Clancy. I know you won't keep in touch, but I do want to say thanks. Can we give you a ride down to the farmhouse?"

"No need. Control the variables. I gotta get going," he said. He shook Moon's hand, then mine, and disappeared once again into the blizzard that had added howling winds to its repertoire.

Not wasting any time, we climbed into the car Clancy had provided. I bumped against the side of the door as I got in. I suppressed a cry of pain, allowing myself a grunt. Moon noticed. "Let's get you back home," he said.

The drive to Rockbluff was silent, of course. Lunatic Mooning and I had overdrawn our verbal banks back at the barn, and now there was nothing more to say. He had to focus on driving right down the middle of the road, fences on either side of the road barely visible to help him navigate. The Toyota's heater was working well but the windshield wipers could do little more than shove chunks of accumulated snow to the side. The clock read 2:30 but it was dark enough outside to be the middle of the night.

On several occasions the car slipped sideways, but Moon's experience in Iowa winter driving conditions came in handy. We never drove more than fifteen miles per hour. We did not meet any cars. No cars passed us. By the time we knocked off the last thirty miles to Rockbluff, it was close to 5 PM. But I must admit, despite my pain, I was enjoying the beauty of the snow-covered land. Rockbluff itself looked like some kind of Christmas village with Christmas day just a little over two weeks away.

Rachel had closed down The Grain o' Truth Bar & Grill, its night lighting reflected on the snow. There had to be six or seven inches already with no sign of letting up. We pulled into the parking lot, empty except for my big pickup truck.

"Can you make it home by yourself. I'll drive you if you want," Moon said.

"Then you'd walk back here? In a blizzard?"

"Not difficult."

"I'll be alright. What are you going to do with this stolen car?"

"I have ways and means."

"I suspect you do, Moon. So," I said, easing out of the Camry and onto the parking lot, "how did you spend your day?"

A faint smile flickered across the big Ojibwa's face. "I spent it at home with one of my wives in one of my homes that no one knows about. You?"

"Home alone, watching TV, reading a little, playing with Gotcha."

"Your imaginary Bulldog?"

Moon had never seen Gotcha, despite inviting me to bring her to The Grain anytime for free beer and burgers. "Yes, that one. Don't forget to file the stolen vehicle report."

I got out of the car and shoved the door shut and watched as Lunatic Mooning eased his ride carefully out of the parking lot and down the street, then took a left across the double-arched limestone bridge that spanned the Whitetail River where everything had started less than a month ago. I could barely see the car's headlights and taillights, and then it was gone.

The drive home wasn't bad, and it was shortly after watching Moon drive away that I pulled into my gravel parking area. Home looked awfully good, and when Gotcha greeted me inside with her grinning mug and wiggly tail, I was truly blessed. I slipped gingerly out of my coat and sweatshirt and placed them on a chair. I knelt down and grunted and roughed up my friend as much as my discomfort would allow, but she was more interested in smelling the blood on my t-shirt. I rose to my feet, fetched her a giant Milk Bone, and handed it over. She took it and ambled over to the rug in front of the fireplace and set to work.

My plan was to rest for just a minute and then tend to my wounds. That plan appealed to me as I realized how tired I was, how lonely I felt, and the magnitude of what we had done that day. Six dead men, and all who needed killing. Still . . .

The wind picked up and the sound of snowflakes being flung even harder against my windows gave me some comfort as I appreciated the home I had and the privacy it afforded. I stepped over to the fireplace, around Gotcha, and knelt down, yelping a bit from my sore right side. Gotcha stopped eating for a moment, looked at me, then went back to work on her treat that I had substituted for her dinner.

I had set a fire the day before, and all I had to do was strike one of the long fireplace matches and touch it to the twists of paper I had built the fire around. The flame caught and caught again and the fire began. I tossed the match into the fire, then, placing my hands on my knees, I worked my way up to an upright position, bent a little at the middle.

My body was stiffening and the pain was setting in as if it intended to stay a while, look over the neighborhood, and linger. I should have attended to it. I knew better, I trained better, and my experiences had taught me to attend to wounds as soon as feasible. But I was so tired. I stumbled into the kitchen, removed a Three Philosophers from the refrigerator and a tulip glass from the cabinet over the sink, and poured. I rummaged around a little in another cabinet and found a couple of Banana Flips, which I removed from their cellophane wrappers, and ate standing up. After that, I found a recliner, fetched a blanket from the sofa, and wrapped it around myself. I plopped down, leaned back until the footrest came up, and drank my ale.

When I woke up, Olivia Olson was standing next to me, looking down.

"I must be dreaming," was the wittiest thing I could come up with. That's because it didn't compute; Liv Olson in my house, the same Liv who had given up on me, given up on *us*, thought of me as a dangerous liar and a fraud?

"That's the best you can come up with?" she asked, raising an eyebrow.

"You're an answer to prayer," I said softly.

"Moon said you needed help," she replied, shrugging off my statement. "He wasn't specific, but I knew that if he wanted me to help you, it had to be serious. You look a little gray around the gills, Thomas. Now, get up and let me take a look at you. Can you walk?"

"Of course I can walk," I said, sitting up in the chair, placing my hands on the arms, and coming to my feet.

"That look on your face indicates pain," she said.

When I stood up, the blanket fell away and Liv's eyes shifted from my face to my t-shirt, black with dried blood.

"What happened, Thomas?"

"I cut myself shaving."

"Come with me," she said, taking my hand. "Which way to the bathroom?"

"But I don't have to go," I said in a fake-whiney voice.

"Thomas," she said, perfect eye contact from her perfect blue, intelligent eyes, "can we *both* be adults for a while?"

"The bathroom's this way," I said, nodding in the right direction, and we started off, her first, me following, hunched over. "And, to answer your question, I've been shot. Twice. Each side once."

Liv stopped dead in mid-stride and turned to face me. "Here we go again, Thomas."

"But this time I'm the only one who's been shot."

"Come," she said, and we walked into the bathroom where she flipped on every light in the place and even the exhaust.

"How did you get up here? It's terrible out there," I said.

"You forget I have a Subaru 4-wheel drive."

"I didn't forget. I didn't know. Never seen you driving it," I said.

"Well, I do," she said. "Now, let's get that shirt off."

Together, and very carefully, we worked to pull my blood-soaked shirt over my head, the fabric tugging firmly where the wounds were. I grimaced as the shirt pulled loose. The tugging pulled dried blood away from the entry wound and the bleeding began again. I heard Liv take in a huge breath and slowly exhale.

"Is the bullet still in there?" she asked.

To answer, I turned around and showed her the exit wound. She rubbed her left hand over her mouth and then there were tears in her eyes and her right hand went behind my neck and she pulled my face down to her and she kissed my lips and I almost forgot my pain. Then she excused herself for a moment and came back with a book bag that she had set next to my recliner when she first came in. It was filled with medical supplies. And then she went to work, cleaning me, pouring hydrogen peroxide into the wounds, applying antiseptic, then bandaging me with gauze and adhesive tape.

She rummaged around in her book bag and pulled out a capsule of meds, shook out two, and gave them to me. "For pain," she said. "Take them with food."

"I just ate a little while ago."

"What did you eat?"

I ignored her questioning skepticism and told her the truth. She shook her head and said, "Oh, Thomas, you just might be a lost cause. Go ahead, then, take the pills."

"With Bailey's?"

"With water, dear."

I tossed the pills back and drank water.

"I'm feeling better already," I said, "and the pain is ebbing."

"Good. I have another instruction for you," she said, repeating her previous topography of pulling my head down and kissing my mouth, her tongue exploring. She reached over and turned out the lights there in the bathroom.

"What instruction is that?" I asked when we came up for air.

"Undress me, Thomas," she whispered.

I can follow instructions.

Chapter Twenty-Six

"A very small degree of hope is sufficient
to cause the birth of love."

- Stendahl

In the morning, I awakened first, and tried to collect my thoughts. And when I had collected them, I thought I was mistaken. Just to make sure my thoughts were real, I glanced to my left to see if the warmth next to my body was Gotcha. It was not. It was Olivia Olson, a much better face, all things considered.

She was still asleep, at my left side, turned toward me, her short blonde hair a brief penumbra of light on the pillow, her lovely face in repose more beautiful than when she is awake. She looked as content as I felt. Liv Olson, sleeping next to me. Imagine that, I said to myself. This was something I had only allowed myself to hope for in brief moments of feeling sorry for myself over the last year plus. I stared at her face, memorizing every line, every little wrinkle around her eyes, her defiant chin, her lips.

It was still snowing outside, the wind gusting and howling and showing its strength. And I was fine with that. I could hear Gotcha softly snoring from her tuffet on the floor at the foot of the bed. I raised my head and saw that Liv's body was covered up to her neck. It was toasty under the covers, and then I realized her left hand was draped across my chest. I put my head back down and reviewed the day before and the night and the beginning of our morning. *Our* morning.

It seemed surreal in retrospect, as it always did in debriefings in my past when we critiqued missions filled with violence and death, gunfire and explosions, silent killings from knife or garrote. All that, so long ago, now revisited in the blood and smell of gunpowder boiling up in the middle of an Iowa blizzard in December. I wondered about Clancy Dominguez, stealing off to appropriate another car and head to Chalaka and the Pony Club, his mission agreed upon, knowing that, if he were successful, he would disappear and it might then be another twenty years before I saw him again. Clancy was a little crazy, but I knew that when I put out my plea for help. But his craziness was controlled, focused, and, to be candid, useful. I would go to him if he ever asked but, given his current business and those of his associates, I doubted, though, if he would ever need the likes of me to back him up.

Thinking on that, I realized I am too old for this kind of work, this kind of mission, and I found myself silently praying that the Lord would keep such things from me for the rest of my life. And then I wondered why He had me driving by the Soderstrom farm right after the "accident" there, and why was I the one to find Cindy Stalking Wolf in the Whitetail River? Why did He have me suffering from insomnia the very night her body had snagged on something in the river?

Liv shifted a little next to me and as I gazed upon her face, her eyelids fluttered and then those blue eyes, deep and intelligent, saw me. She smiled, and my heart soared, truly.

I kissed her forehead, her eyes, her nose, her chin. Her mouth. She kissed me back, moving under the covers a little so that my left arm, under which she had snuggled, slipped down across her shoulders. She was nude and warm and soft under my touch.

"Sleep well?" I asked.

"I think it's called slumber," she murmured.

Karen and I called it that when we slept together, slumber being a higher, better descriptor of that benefit of being next to the one you love in the marriage bed. But this wasn't Karen, and this wasn't the marriage bed. I decided to let those things go.

"How did you sleep, Thomas?" she asked, her hand gliding across my chest and back again.

"Like I was shot," I said before I realized my words. Then I laughed, felt a strong twinge in my side, the pain mitigated by Liv's laughter.

"Astute simile," she said. "And with that, maybe I should take a look at those wounds." She pulled the bedding down from me.

"Oops!" she said, "you're not wearing anything but bandages!"

"How'd that happen?" I asked. "Did someone take advantage of my weakened state?"

"Damn right," she said, coming to her knees in order to examine me. With that, the covers fell away from her body and I nearly gasped. Lovely in every way, erotic in her unselfconscious candor as she touched the gauze on the main bullet hole, lifting the bandage which had bled through.

"You did a good job last night. I appreciate your doctoring."

"They wouldn't have bled through if you had been quiet."

"As I recall, neither one of us were quiet. Some thrashing about ensued."

Liv blushed, God love her. She said, "But I thought I did most of the work, on purpose!"

"If what we did be work, I'm about to become a workaholic," I said, pulling her my way again.

Later, after both of us dozed a bit, we woke up at the same time.

The storm was still buffeting the windows. "Time to get going," she said, kissing me quickly and scooching out of our bed and dashing, naked, for the bathroom.

"You have an exquisite derriere," I called out, just before she closed the door, saying, "Oh, you!" The door slammed.

I started to scooch out of bed, too, but sharp pains on both sides of me stopped my progress. I recalibrated and eased out of bed, into my briefs at the side of the bed, then a clean t-shirt, levi's, and sweatshirt. I stepped into slippers and, with Gotcha rousing herself and following me, headed for the kitchen. I let her out and let her back in quickly, fed and medicated her, the sound of my shower blasting away around the corner. It was odd, hearing my shower going with me in the kitchen, and I liked it almost as much as seeing the yellow Subaru out front when I let Gotcha out.

I set a full pot of caffeine going in my Mr. Coffee machine and then, wondering if there was any news that might have come our way from Chalaka, turned on the radio on the kitchen counter. I looked at the clock. It was exactly 9 AM, so I was hoping for some local news after the national non-news of fraud, graft, rot, and corruption in politics. The local news started with the weather, informing me that it would snow all day and maybe into the night. A twelve-inch snowfall was expected, with nine already on the ground.

The local news then morphed into a brief report about a rash of stolen cars, naming Lunatic Mooning and a farm couple from the next county north of us all reporting stolen vehicles. The announcer went on to say, "And this from Chalaka, Minnesota."

My ears perked up.

"Speaking of stolen cars, and this might all be understood somehow once we connect the dots, not only was there still another stolen car report—in this weather?—the infamous Pony Club, a Chalaka nightspot famous for adult entertainment and nefarious activities, was utterly destroyed late last night by what appears to have been an explosion and fire. There was only one fatality, the owner and operator, Ted Hornung, whose body was found in the establishment, badly burned and identifiable only by dental records. The blizzard, even worse in Chalaka than here in Rockbluff, apparently was responsible for the club closing early, according to local reports. Chalaka Police and Minnesota Bureau of Investigation officers are treating the explosion and fire as 'suspicious.' At this time, there are no persons of interest. Moving on, due to the storm, tonight's basketball game between Rockbluff High School boys' and girls' teams at Strawberry Point are cancelled. Likewise, the Flannel Masters Crafts Club, the Future Farmers of America meeting, and the Lutheran women's Pole-Dancing Class will not meet. Just about everything else, too." The announcer went on to list every activity imaginable being cancelled or rescheduled.

I had to smile. Dominguez had followed through after driving the farmer's stolen car to Chalaka, then stole another car to get away into the night. By now, I imagined, he was probably on a flight headed for London, then Nairobi, and eventually back to his crew on the yacht. He had been in town exactly six days.

I withdrew his card from my billfold, finished memorizing the key numbers, and set it in the fireplace, where I started another fire. Liv's voice startled me. I hadn't realized the shower had shut off. She was standing in the doorway to the living room, breathtaking in a t-shirt and a pair of well-worn slacks that clung to her in a way that accentuated her attributes.

"Thomas, I want you to know that I was with you all day yesterday, last night, and into the weekend. Snowbound."

I nodded, looked back at the fire where Clancy's business card had fallen into flames, then looked back at Liv. I rose to my feet, winced in spite of myself, and went to her. She folded herself into my arms and I just held her.

"Thomas, I was terrified last night when Moon called me. I didn't know what had happened to you. My imagination ran wild."

"I'm delighted you came over," I said. "Worth getting shot twice. Now we both have entry and exit wounds from shootings."

"Matched set," she said.

"I'm glad Moon called you. Clancy asked him if he could get me some help and he said yes, but I honestly didn't think you'd be involved."

"You're lucky it wasn't a school night."

We both laughed, even though it snagged my sides. "Lucky, indeed. I might have bled to death on my sheets while your red pen was bleeding all over student papers."

"Being shot is probably preferable to the pain I inflict with my pen on young skulls full of social media," she said. "Now, let's go into the bathroom so I can eyeball your marvelous physique and see about those bandages. They definitely need to be changed."

I followed her again into the bathroom, pulled up my sweatshirt and t-shirt while Liv bent down, kissed my belly, and gently pulled the bandages away. They stuck a little, and she said there was some blood ooze, but no sign of infection. She cleaned the major wound, entry and exit, in my right side and rebandaged, then checked my other side where I had been nicked. It was already beginning to scab over, so she just placed a big adhesive strip on it and pulled down my t-shirt and sweatshirt.

"I wonder how it was he shot you on each side. Weird," she said as we walked back into the kitchen.

"Most shooters with any experience typically fire off two-shot bursts, then another two-shot burst, and so on," I explained. "Maybe he overcompensated against a second shot going up and missing, and forced the second shot to the right, to be sure he got his grouping in the bigger part of the target."

"Your belly is not big. On the contrary," she said, patting me there.

"Thank you. Anyway, that's my guess."

"Thomas?"

"Yes?"

"Sometime I'll ask you what happened yesterday. But I don't want to know just now. I may *never* want to know. What I do know is that you and Moon and some third person, an old friend of yours, went up to Minnesota to deal with those responsible for killing Cindy Stalking Wolf. And I know you were wounded, Moon was not, and the third person did not come back. I don't need to know any more, okay?"

"Suits me," I said. "Coffee?"

We drank coffee and waited while I prepared a subdued breakfast, by my standards. I scrambled a few eggs and a conservative number of bacon strips and even made cheese grits for the first time. Jan Timmons had taught Karen years ago, and Karen had shown me how shortly after we moved to Georgia. While the grits were cooking, Liv asked me what grits tasted like.

"If you have cheese grits, they taste like cheese. If you have buttered grits, they taste like butter."

"What do they taste like plain?"

"Plain? They taste like spoon."

She laughed, which encouraged me as I worked at the stove. After we ate, we bundled up and stepped out on the deck and watched the blizzard for a while, without Gotcha, who felt as if she needed to protect the interior of the house. The wind had died down a bit, and the snow was no longer falling at an angle, just coming down straight and steady and softly and going about the business of covering everything with big, pristine flakes. We could not see the Whitetail River Valley due to the storm, never mind the Mississippi River Valley beyond. But the view was beautiful, and the company extraordinary.

"I've never been out on this deck," Liv said. "It's a wonderful place, and wonderful year 'round, I expect."

"In warmer weather, Gotcha and I sit out here and engage in philosophical drinking. By the way, who's taking care of Milton?"

"A colleague of mine whom I trust. She's done it before. They're good buddies. I told her I had a family emergency I needed to handle and she was good enough to not ask questions. She'll cover."

"Good friend."

"Indeed."

"It's nice out here, and I'm glad you like it. But you know, you haven't seen the whole house yet. Gotcha and I like it a lot. It suits us. Would you like a tour?"

Liv nodded and we went inside. I took her upstairs and showed her the two guest bedrooms and the bath. She approved of my decorating, but I knew she would have done it differently, probably not going with "The Magician's Nephew" theme. But she kept it to herself. Downstairs, she paused and looked at the pictures in the den of Karen, Michelle, and Annie.

"Beautiful family, Thomas," she said softly, fingering the frames, not moving the photos.

"Yes, they were, Liv. But they're gone now, they're not walking through that door, ever, and I truly believe they are in heaven, which is even better than Iowa."

"That line's from *Field of Dreams*, isn't it?"

"Something like that. Anyway, I am ready to go forward with my life. With you, if you want." Sometimes I surprise myself. I hadn't planned on saying that, but it just came out. I told myself to shut up.

"I haven't been fair to you, Thomas. I've been judgmental, narrow, accusatory. And I'm sorry. I've made you out to be some kind of vigilante lunatic, ignoring the fact that you led an exemplary and peaceful life for a long, long time after you married, after you left the military, after you left your private security business. Not fair."

"But to be fair to you, in just a little over two years you've seen me involved in the Soderstrom mess and now this with Moon's niece, so maybe you're seeing a pattern, right?"

"Good point, I guess. Yes, you *do* make a good point," she said, reflecting. "But there's something else I've noticed. You just seem more alive when you're fighting, involved in shootouts. I think it helps shake you from the depression that comes with the loss of your family. Keeps you from being alone and inevitably feeling sorry for yourself, for which you have reason. Not judging, Thomas. Just seems logical now that I think about it."

"It makes the time go faster, too. Moves me closer to the day when I move up to what Bonhoeffer calls 'the true country.' Beats macramé classes and Zumba. Helps me deal with being alone."

"But Thomas, now I understand that I *cannot* leave you alone. I just can't. I fear for you sometimes. I want you to be happy, and you haven't been happy for years, hiding behind your sense of humor."

"I was happy in your bed the night of the gunfight in this house."

Liv smiled. She was supposed to say, "Me, too!"

"And I'm happy right now, Liv, with you here. Much happier than the last time you were here and told me to kiss your ass, and when I asked you to please prepare that lovely surface for that specific act of affection, you reneged and stalked off."

"The day of Horace's funeral."

"Yes. And I deserved your rebuke. It worked."

"You came to the funeral."

"Half in the bag."

"But you were there."

"Indeed, and blessed by Carl's eulogy."

"Me, too. And by the way," Liv said, a playful smile crossing her face, "feel free to kiss my ass anytime, or any other part of my body that pleases you."

I grinned. I couldn't help it. I said, "Denuded of obstacles, such as clothing?"

She said, "I think we're at the point where there should be no obstacles between us. What say you?"

"I'm in full agreement."

We passed the rest of the day comfortably, watching the storm slow down, sputter, and die after leaving fifteen inches of snow in Rockbluff before it stopped. I couldn't help but be grateful that the abandoned farmhouse with Moon's Packard and the thugs' Escalade would probably be safe from any inquiring minds for a long, long time. There would be no tracks, and the way I had rigged the gate to make it look locked would likely discourage anyone remotely curious about the place where six dead men, a load of drugs, and uncounted bullet holes waited.

It seemed to get dark early with the cloud cover, but outside it remained light because of the white comforter of snow covering everything. An occasional gust of snow would blow in from time to time, but the storm was spent, moving on into Illinois and southwestern Wisconsin, flexing its muscles there.

Liv fixed ham and cheese sandwiches on whole wheat bread, smoothed over with horseradish, a sandwich like that demanding a cold beer to take the edge away. I kept the fire going until well after dark, and we sat together wedged into one recliner while Gotcha appropriated the other. We dozed off together and woke up when a log broke and settled in the fireplace. I glanced at the clock over the fireplace. It read six-thirty.

"You hungry?" I asked.

"A little. May I fix you something? Steak tartar, blackened redfish, roast duckling?"

I said, "How 'bout a fine red wine, for the antioxidants, of course, and some healthful snack food?"

Liv turned in the chair so that she could look me in the eye. "I'm skeptical of your definition of 'healthful.'"

"Let me surprise you," I said as we slid out of the chair. My side grabbed at me a little. Liv noticed and said maybe we should check those bandages, which we did. She changed them after telling me I looked like a fast healer. I said it was her nursing skills that were the key factor.

"Tender loving care," she said, and then we both kind of caught on that "loving" word and mutually and silently moved on. Deep territory.

So I poured us each a glass of merlot and then put together some almonds, cheese sticks, and dried apricots to munch on. Liv gave me an approving look as I brought the wooden bowl to her in front of the fire and set it on an end table where we could both reach it. We spent the next few minutes in small talk, sipping the wine, and enjoying the food and the fire.

"You know, Thomas, I don't know very much about you. I know what you've lost, but nothing about your mom and dad. Are they still living?"

That stopped me, but I should have known the topic would eventually come up, at least in any decent relationship, which I was hoping would be the case with Olivia. I finished my glass of wine, got up, went into the kitchen, and brought out the bottle. It was nearly empty, so I made sure I had a second bottle and a corkscrew with me. She held her glass to me and I topped it off, finished my glass, decanted the second bottle, poured myself a glass. I drank half of it.

"That bad?" she asked, her voice sympathetic.

"Probably."

"Let's skip it, then. Topic for another day. Don't let me spoil our time together."

"My mother was a saint, but she made bad choices. The man she married, for one. She wanted children, but I am an only child. Her husband didn't want any more, and he made sure."

"Oh. Your father made sure."

"He didn't like me, and I can understand that. I was pretty rebellious all through junior high and high school, couldn't wait to go away to college, couldn't wait to join the Navy, both to get away from him.

"He got emphysema. Chain smoker. Told me he smoked because of me. Said I was a failure and an embarrassment. He was a successful insurance executive, married to his job. When he was in the hospital, on his deathbed, my mother insisted that I come home from the University of Iowa and say my goodbyes. I wouldn't have except that it was her request. So I went to see him. You know what his last words were? Kind of funny, in a way."

"Go on, Thomas."

"Well, you know the old saying that no one, at their death, ever said 'I wish I'd spent more time at the office'?"

Liv face paled. She was shaking her head and tears were starting to jerk down her cheeks.

"That old saying is a lie because that's exactly what he said. He looked angry when I stepped into his room. I said hello, and he looked at me and smiled a little, disgusted smile, more a smirk, and said, 'I wish I'd spent more time at the office and less around you.' Then he turned his head away and said, 'Now get out.' And those were his last words."

At this point Liv was openly weeping, and I felt badly that I had let that little episode in my past slip out. I never told anyone before, not even my mother. So, what's wrong with me that I'd spill my guts to someone I'd only known a couple of years? Something about Olivia Olson, I believe. I went on.

"Now, my mom was another story. After a life chained to a man who allowed her little contact outside of the house, she took to her new situation. I sold the house and she moved into an apartment complex with people of all ages, and she just took off socially. Made lots of friends, starting going to church, even dated a couple of nice widowers. Then, when Karen and I got married and moved to Georgia, we took her along. She lived half a mile from us. She died eleven years ago, a happy woman."

Liv was now smiling through a tear-streaked face. I finished my glass of wine. She finished hers and stood up. "I'm happy about your mom, but so sorry about your dad."

"Not a dad by any definition. My mother's husband."

Liv nodded. "So much pain," she said, "but I think I can help you with that. Let me take you to bed."

And so she did, and the pain floated away that night in our bed in our snowbound house, floated away like woodsmoke on the wind.

Chapter Twenty-Seven

**"We must learn to regard people less in light of
what they do or omit to do; but more
in the light of their suffering."**

- Dietrich Bonhoeffer

I wept after we made love that night, but only a little. Honest. Liv wept after we made love, too. Quite a bit. You've never seen such wet pillows. We each woke twice during the night and were good to each other. We slept and dozed and slept some more and it was good.

Sunday morning I felt clean and light inside my heart and my head, and I thought, by God, *by God*, I just might be able to live again.

"Don't tell anyone I blubbered," I said.

"I won't. That is something *we* have. No one else has a right to it. It's just between us."

"You couldn't get a cigarette paper between us last night."

"Stop. You'll make me blush."

"You couldn't get a cigarette paper between us last night," I repeated. Liv gooched me in the ribs, avoiding my wound, but when I flinched I could feel the injuries.

I looked at her head on the pillow, her blonde hair, short as it was, framing her face. I said, "You look as lovely as a whitecap on a glassy lake."

Liv smiled, obviously pleased, and then said, "You're very Irish sometimes, Thomas O'Shea."

"And you love it, Olivia Olson."

"I confess, I do."

She kissed me and slipped out of bed and I admired her backside again as she jounced off to the bathroom. I heard the sound of water in the shower and eased myself to a sitting position, then stood and dressed. My wound nipped at my side, but a nip was better than a painful pull. Progress.

It was cloudy and gray outside the window, but not in my spirit, as I made the bed, walking around Gotcha on her tuffet. When I finished, she got up and plodded into the kitchen and on to the front door. I let her out and she hesitated, the door pushing away snow that had stacked up overnight. Gotcha gave me a look and waddled out.

I closed the door and set coffee to brewing while fixing a hearty breakfast of sausage patties, hash browns, scrambled eggs with bits of onion and chopped ham mixed in, and a few buckwheat pancakes. As I reached for the maple syrup in a cabinet above the stove, I heard Liv come into the room. I looked up. She was naked as the truth, but much more alluring. I think my mouth dropped open.

"I got out of the shower and thought, why get dressed? I'd just have to get undressed again because you appeal to me very much when I hear you cooking and I want you right now, Thomas. Put the burners on simmer. I'm up for a quickie, just for the joy of it."

I nearly knocked over two Teflon pans following Liv's instructions.

"Great breakfast!" she said later. "One must wonder at the impetus to appetite provided by a roll in the hay with a real man."

"I've never had that exact experience," I said as I tidied, wiping down the breakfast table, loading the dishwasher and setting it going.

I glanced at Liv. "What's on your agenda for today, Beautiful?"

"Well," she said, getting up from the table and coming to me, embracing me with her hands high up on my back, avoiding my wounds, "sadly, I will need to get back home. I'm sure the snowplows will have done their duty by this afternoon and we'll likely have classes tomorrow. But I'd like to stay here with you until I have to go."

"Stay as long as you want. I wish you didn't have to go. Ever."

Liv leaned back from my arms and smiled a brief, sad smile, and said, "Me, too. So, what's in *your* plans for the day?"

My answer was delayed when we heard a hard scratching at the front door. I had forgotten about Gotcha and left the steel sleeve in the doggy door. No wonder, considering the glorious distractions of Liv.

When I opened the door the chunky Bulldog glared at me. Snow was all over her back and the top of her head. Apparently she'd plowed through the fresh snow to get to her place to perform her duties, and she hadn't liked it. She put her head down, hunched past me, and shook the snow off. Then she gave me an accusatory glance and walked into the kitchen and stood by her food and water dishes, turned, and looked at me. Olivia was laughing.

I attended to Gotcha and then continued my conversation with Liv. "You asked about my plans. Well, I've got to get down to The Grain and talk to Moon, and be prepared to be questioned by Harmon and maybe some state cop types. They'll be back. I know that's coming."

"You have a great alibi in me," she said, letting go, going over to the kitchen counter, and sweeping a few crumbs into her hands. She dumped the crumbs in the trash can under the sink and brushed her hands off. She looked at me and smiled. Such a smile!

"I hope it doesn't come to that."

"I don't care, really. They can question me all they want. I came up here Friday right after second lunch when they let us out early and stayed through Sunday afternoon. We never left."

"I didn't know they let you out a little early. That's unusual, isn't it?"

"Yes, but the weather reports were very clear the storm was going to be a whopper, and we have lots of kids from rural areas who need to ride the busses, so that dictated early release, and the postponing of the play."

My hated cell phone rang, playing "Three Blind Mice," the theme song of The Three Stooges. I checked. It was Ernie Timmins. I buttoned on the phone. "Hello, Ernie."

"So, I'm guessing you're behind that building in Minnesota being blown up."

"What's the weather like down there in Belue, Georgia?"

"Sixty-one degrees, blue skies, and the golf courses are calling me to action. Are you okay? Is Lunatic Mooning okay?"

"It's Sunday morning. Why aren't you preaching."

"I'm off this Sunday. We have a visiting pastor."

"Jeez Louise, you guys work one day a week and then you get a Sunday off, too?"

Ernie said, "So I'm guessing you're behind that explosion over the northern border. Y'all okay there?"

"All good. We just got a ton of snow. A real blizzard. Nearly twice as much snow as the puny storm you and Jan got to experience. How are the boys?"

"Is Olivia Olson okay? Jan wanted me to ask."

"Liv's outstanding," I said, turning and smiling at her.

"You need to call her. You need to get back together with her. Jan's orders."

"Will do. Talk to you later, Ernie."

"I'll be keeping an eye on news from up your way. Seems like there's going to be lots more. Blessings on you and Olivia Olson," he said, and hung up.

Sunday passed gently as we read together, sat together and watched wood burn in the fireplace, had a light lunch, read some more, watched more fire in the fireplace, and played a little with Gotcha, who had forgiven me, as dogs do.

When it was time to go, Liv replaced my old bandages with new, kissed me on the lips, and left after I walked her to her bright yellow Subaru, got her in her car, and sent her on her way, the vehicle firm on the driveway. We had heard snowplows throughout the day, confident that, as Liv drove home in the fading daylight, she would be fine. She promised to let me know when she got home safely, and twenty minutes later, she called.

The house seemed empty, and so did I, yet I was content. A rare thing. I liked it.

On the TV news that night, it was reported that schools throughout the county would operate on their normal schedule Monday, businesses and organizations would be back to regular hours, and there was no sign of more snow. Then there was a live, on-site report from Chalaka, Minnesota that I found worthy of my attention. The reporter, bundled up and squinting in the glare of the mobile unit's lights, was standing in front of what was left of The Pony Club, which appeared to be nothing but a charred ruin. Not even a wall had been left standing. I had to grin at Clancy's handiwork. He hadn't lost his touch.

The reporter, a girl who might have been fifteen, said the authorities were treating the demolition as a crime scene and the investigation was ongoing. Then she gave a number to call with tips and added, "Police are saying what happened Friday night here at The Pony Club is the work of a professional demolitions expert. Back to you, Nils." Nils moved on to news about hog futures.

Just as I was preparing to see what might be on ESPN, there was a hard knock on my front door. It sounded urgent. I took Elsie out of the coat closet on the way and opened the door a crack, shotgun ready in my right hand. It was Harmon. I decided not to shoot him.

"Come on in, Harmon. It's cold out there," I said, slipping the shotgun back into the closet.

He gave me a look and stepped inside the foyer.

"I have some questions for you, Thomas." I gestured for him to come on in to the living room.

"Have a seat in front of the fire, Harmon. Can I get you something to drink?"

"I'm on duty."

I sat down in a wingback chair next to the recliner where Payne was now sitting. "Go ahead. Shoot."

He gave me a look when I said "shoot."

"Thomas, you and Moon and that Dominguez guy went up to Chalaka on Friday and blew up The Pony Club, then came back here in that storm. Revenge for Cindy Stalking Wolf's murder."

"That's a statement. You said you had questions."

"Okay, Thomas. Did you go up to Chalaka Friday night, with Moon and Dominguez, and blow up The Pony Club, killing Ted Hornung?"

"No, and I mean that, Harmon. We did not."

"I've talked to Moon and he has an ironclad alibi that is pure bullshit."

"Where were you Friday night?"

"Here."

"Anyone verify that?"

"Yes."

"Who would that be?"

"Can't say."

Payne shook his head. "You mean, *won't* say."

"That's right."

"I noticed fresh tire tracks leading away from here since the storm stopped."

"You *are* a trained law enforcement professional. Hot damn!"

Payne sighed, looked around the room, unzipped his parka and leaned forward. "Okay, Thomas, then, where is Clancy Dominguez? I expected to find him here. This is where he's been staying every night?"

"Yes, I mean, well, this is where he's been staying except for one night."

Payne looked at me.

"He spent one night allegedly with Suzanne Highsmith at the Rockbluff Motel."

"She spend Friday and Saturday and today with you?"

"Nope. She is not my type."

"More bullshit. Thomas, it's getting deep in here. Glad I wore my boots."

"Sure I can't answer any more questions? Come on, Harmon, take off your coat and stay awhile. Can I fix you some Irish coffee, a glass of wine, some Myer's Rum?"

Payne stood, slipped off his coat and laid it over a chair. He took out his radio and called in, said, "Landsberger, I'm officially off duty as of now," looking at his watch, "at six-thirty PM. Call me if you need me, Deputy." He put away the radio and sighed, sat back down. "I'll take a beer if you've got something strong."

"Three Philosophers?" I asked, standing.

"Never tried it."

"I'll get you one. More to follow. If you don't like it, I'll drink it and get you a Sam Adams."

Payne nodded. I fetched the ale for him and a tall glass half full of Jameson's Irish Whiskey over ice cubes for me. Harmon sipped the dark ale, looked thoughtful, and took a drink. "That's good."

I smiled and sat down with my Jameson's.

"I need to talk to you, Thomas. Straight up. No bullshit."

"Fine. Off the record?"

Payne made a face, nodded his head, said, "Off the record, dammit!" and took another drink.

"I know you and Moon and Dominguez went up to Minnesota and blew up the Pony Club, killing Ted Hornung in revenge for whatever role he had in Moon's niece's murder. I know that."

"No, you don't. That's not true."

"Okay, okay. Then somehow *you* were involved in the blowing up of that joint."

I shook my head. "I wasn't even there."

Payne gave me a cautious look. "Then, somehow, Moon was involved in the blowing up of The Pony Club."

"He wasn't there, either."

A light went on in Payne's eyes. "Then, somehow, Clancy *Dominguez* was involved in the blowing up of The Pony Club."

I said nothing.

"I *knew* you brought that sucker into my county for a reason other than old time's sake! Where is Dominguez now?"

I looked at my watch. "London? Kenya?"

"Sonuvabitch! So, how can I get in touch with him?"

I said nothing. Payne knew nothing about Clancy except his name, what he looked like, and that he had somehow been involved. He would never find him. And if he did, he wouldn't get a word out of the man.

Payne said, "Thomas, the state's Major Crimes Unit is on my ass about this, and they're going to meet with me at my office at ten tomorrow morning. It won't be pleasant. I don't know what to tell them, but you could help me. They'll probably want to talk to you and Moon. And Dominguez."

"Tell them the rules about jurisdiction."

"They're already aware. They're in contact with the Minnesota BCI and the Chalaka Police Department. This is not going to be a fun interview."

"More like an interrogation, I'd say. Same agents from last week?"

"Yes."

I sipped some whiskey and leaned forward and said, "Harmon, they will *never* solve this one. They won't. They'll get nothing from me, or Moon, or Clancy if they ever find him, which is unlikely. If they get even *close* to him, and I suppose it's possible, he'll disappear until they get tired of looking for him. Besides, they won't go to the trouble of extraditing him from whatever country he happens to be in at the time."

"Thanks for that. But there's the other thing on my butt, and it ain't going away, Thomas."

"Doltch?"

"Right under my nose. My own willing ignorance, refusing to believe."

"Welcome to the human race, Harmon. It's icky most of the time. Our sin nature, man."

"And there's the other thing, even worse, personally."

"You and Altemier."

"Yes."

"That was weak, Harmon, but you're not the first man to fall for a pretty young thing, especially if she comes on to you, which I suspect she did, and especially if the man is twice her age. What's her problem, anyway?"

"She has abnormally strong urges, is all I can think. Oversexed." He shrugged his shoulders. "It's bad enough that I slept with a woman under my professional authority. That's despicable. But the fact the Olivia found us together is more painful than you can imagine."

"I'm pretty good at imagining pain. But why in the world, if you and Olivia were going so well, would you jeopardize that for Altemier? I don't get it."

"There was an opportunity for sex and I took it. I haven't exactly been a monk since Pam divorced me nine years ago."

"But didn't you and Olivia, I mean . . . ?"

"No need to go there, Thomas. Olivia and I never slept together. She would be strong, and when she wavered, I would be strong. She is a virtuous woman."

I thought it would be wise to move on. Quickly. "So, Harmon, what are you going to do? About all this?"

"When we conclude all of these investigations, the murder of Cindy, the disappearance and likely murders of the Prentice and Julia, the Chalaka business, I'm going to take professional leave for three months and see if I can, or even should, continue as Sheriff of Rockbluff County. I need to get away to think it through. Deputy Altemier has resigned to take another position back home in Dubuque. She's a good kid, Thomas. But what happened was my fault as much as hers. Just an old man wanting to feel young again with a mere girl."

"An old, old story. At least you're not wearing neck bling, or unbuttoning your shirt three buttons down to expose your tanned, hairy chest. But for what it's worth, I think I'd like to have you as my sheriff for a long time. For what it's worth," I repeated.

"I appreciate that." Payne finished his Belgian ale, smacked his lips, and remarked that he would be a regular imbibing that brand from now on.

"Who's going to take over during your absence as sheriff?"

"Landsberger. I have no qualms about him. I've often thought he'd succeed me when I retire someday. This will be good experience. If I come back, he'll be okay with it. If I don't, City Council will likely promote him, with my full recommendation. Doltch is going to prison. My fault."

"Not your fault. He made his own decisions."

Harmon and I both stood up. I took his empty glass while he slipped on his coat. He turned to leave, paused, looked me in the eye. "It's Olivia, isn't it?"

I knew what he meant. I said, "Yes."

Harmon Payne's eyes went sad. He nodded his head slowly, looked away, looked back. And then he turned and let himself out and slogged across the snow to his cruiser. The sound of his tires crunching on the white gravel under the white snow was a lonely sound there in the darkness of an Iowa December night in rural Rockbluff.

Chapter Twenty-Eight

"I have absolutely no pleasure in the stimulants in which I sometimes so madly indulge. It has not been in the pursuit of pleasure that I have periled life and reputation and reason. It has been the desperate attempt to escape from torturing memories, from a sense of insupportable loneliness and a dread of some strange impending doom."

- Edgar Allan Poe

Monday morning broke lonely, austere, bleak, and bereft of joy. Liv was not beside me when I woke up at seven-thirty. What woke me up was Gotcha having a dream, yelping and crying and snorting. Maybe she was dreaming that Liv was gone, too. But my reality was greater than her dream.

I sat up in bed. The movement woke up the Bulldog and she came around to me with a sheepish look on her face, as if she were ashamed of her dreaming out loud. I roughed up her goozle and gave her a kiss on top of her blunt skull and eased to a standing position with minimal discomfort. I looked down at my bandages. The one on my left passion handle had fallen off, revealing a nearly-healed scab. I fought the urge to scrape off the itchy thing, but decided to engage self-restraint and let it fall off on its own. On my right, the bandage was there, but there had been no blood ooze. Progress on both sides.

I left the bed unmade, perhaps in some vain hope that Liv Olson would come hopping out of the shower and pull me onto the white sheets.

Gotcha followed me to the front door, which I opened for her. She trotted out and I closed the door, set the coffee pot going, pulled down some Bailey's from the cabinet. Even though I had heard snowplows last night on the blacktop at the foot of my gravel driveway, I decided not to run. I was too tired, grumpy, depressed, and irritable to do anything constructive. No Olivia.

For a change, I wasn't interested in cooking a real man's breakfast. I could survive without protein for a while, or at least until I could eat lunch at The Grain. I decided on the spur of the moment to treat myself to the delicacies from the bakery of Holy Grounds.

I let Gotcha back in, dipped a soup spoon into a jar of natural peanut butter, slipped her meds into the middle of the gooey mess, folded the spread over, and held the spoon for her while she licked it clean. Then I fed her, enjoying the fervor and ferocity with which she attacked her breakfast. I watched her eat. Finished, she looked at me, belched softly, and plodded into the living room and jumped up on her preferred recliner, pushed it back into a nearly-prone position, stretched out, and looked at me. Then she plopped her tongue out to facilitate better breathing, and fell asleep. A lot to like about that dog's life, I thought.

After I showered and inexpertly replaced the old bandage with a new one, I dressed in jeans, black t-shirt, black sweatshirt with gold I-O-W-A letters across the chest, slipped into heavy socks and hiking boots, and sat down to a cup of coffee. I selected my big Harley-Davidson mug, filled it one-third with coffee, then topped it off with some Bailey's Irish Cream. I wouldn't have gone to the trouble since they do have good coffee at Holy Grounds, but I thought they might object to my BYOB –

Bring Your Own Bailey's. I drank coffee, my mind on Liv Olson, Chalaka, what we had done at that abandoned farm, whether we would ever be caught. I had a second cup, buttoned off the Mr. Coffee machine, and headed for the front door after giving the Bulldog a small Milk Bone to help assuage her separation anxieties upon my leaving. I had to wake her up to give it to her, she was so troubled.

Outside, I couldn't help but notice Liv's tire tracks, and also Harmon's, and how their paths were no longer parallel. Bad luck for Harmon. Great favor for me.

I stepped into my truck and started up. The information center on the dashboard revealed that it was eighteen degrees, colder than I thought. I tuned in the local radio station and headed for town, learning along the way that one of the stolen cars from last Friday, belonging to an Iowa farmer, had turned up in Chalaka. Also in Chalaka, another car had gone missing Saturday morning and was recovered last night near Des Moines. No suspects have been identified yet, the reporter said before moving on to the local "Help Your Neighbor" club dedicated to helping your neighbor advertise overpriced items they didn't want. I nearly called in to buy an 18-inch ceramic King Kong sculpture, but I didn't have my cell phone. I knew it would get snapped up before I could get to a phone, and that made me even grumpier. Nothing like booze and a King Kong statuette to get a guy through a tough night.

I thought some more about Liv and realized I needed her. I didn't know if she needed me, or ever would, which makes for worry lines around my mouth and eyes that will go away as soon as I order Pierre's Anti-Aging Cream from the Home Shopping Network. Second jar is free if I order quickly.

Driving by Arvid's house, I noticed him face down in a big snowdrift in his front yard, just a few feet from his steps leading up to the porch.

I honked and proceeded without any acknowledgement from the Lutheran Brotherhood Insurance man enjoying his performance art. On into downtown, I crossed over the iconic bridge and refused to look at the river, turned right, and parked in front of Holy Grounds. Inside, I took up residence in a booth near the kitchen so I could enjoy the smells of bacon cooking and delicacies being baked. Holy Grounds had a good crowd, especially considering the storm, with conversations buzzing, an occasional loud laugh, the sounds from the kitchen wafting out onto groups and individuals enjoying the fragrant ambiance and promise of nectar and ambrosia, Iowa style.

Margo, my favorite waitress, came over to take my order, greeting me with a "Good morning, Thomas! Great day to be alive in the Lord."

I nodded in a desultory way and ordered coffee, wishing that, even as I felt the Bailey's easing into my system, I could still benefit from more caffeine. I ordered two bear claws, an asiago cheese bagel, and four fruit-filled doughnuts – two lemon and two blueberry. Fruit servings for my nutritional balance. Carbo loading for my afternoon workout.

While I was waiting for Margo to come back, I looked around the place and noticed, with a bit of a start, two men looking at me. They were my friends from the Iowa Major Crimes Unit, Special Agents Kelvin Massey and Hector Ortiz. Our eye contact lingered, and I observed their lack of smiles while they observed my sullen visage. Ortiz got up and came over to my booth. He did not sit down and I was fine with that.

"Special Agent Massey and I would like to see you in Sheriff's Payne's office this morning at ten." Ortiz stood over me like a suspicious schoolteacher.

"And a top o' the morning to you, sir! Thanks for your kind and warm and heartfelt greeting this fine Iowa mornin'," I said in my best Irish brogue. "But I believe you're interviewing the good sheriff at ten, also. You really *must* get yourself a Blackberry to organize your schedule, Special Agent Ortiz."

He frowned. "You can wait."

"And you can kiss my ass."

"Oh, my!" Margo said, her face almost as red as her hair as she appeared at my place. "Excuse me. I'll come back when you two gentlemen are through talking."

"You're fine, Margo," I said. "Special Agent Ortiz was just now heading back to his booth where I hope he's drinking a cup of hemlock."

"We don't have that kind of coffee here," she said.

"Indeed, this is Holy Grounds, is it not?" I said. She placed my order in front of me and scurried away.

"Make it ten-thirty then," Ortiz said. He turned away and walked back across the room, shaking his head. He forgot to say "please," but I decided not to hold it against him. And I felt a little bit sorry I'd told him to kiss my ass, a reflection of my snippy mood. It was Olivia's fault for not staying over last night. If I had awakened next to her, I would have been nicer to everyone. The ripple effect of interpersonal harmony.

Massey and Ortiz left and I settled into my high-carb breakfast, enjoying every bite. When I finished, I left a nice tip for Margo and paid at the cash register. She said, as she always does, "Have a blessed day." With some people, that's just a rote expression to let you know they're spiritual. In Margo's case, it always feels heartfelt.

Outside, it was still bitter cold, and an hour before my meeting with Ortiz and Massey, if I decided to go. I walked a few yards and entered Bednarik's Books. The little bell over the door tinkled, and somehow that delicate sound helped calm me down. That and the world of books I had just entered, sanctuaries against the vicissitudes of life.

"Mornin', Thomas O'Shea!" Boots said. "And look who's here to greet you, other than myself!"

Suzanne Highsmith turned around and smiled. I smiled back, surprised to see her. She was lovely as always, but somehow a little off. Her makeup was missing, her long braid appeared to have been done quickly, and she was wearing frumpy clothes – faded bluejeans, scuffed cowboy boots, and a gray sweater. No accessories, either. She came to me and gave me a brief, hard hug. Which hurt. I yelped.

She stepped away quickly, startled, her head cocked and a quizzical look on her face. "Are you okay, Thomas?"

"I am," I said, "but I pulled a small muscle in my back when I was working out last week. It's getting better, though. Still a little tender."

"I have some Advil in my purse," she said, turning toward the counter where Boots watched us with genuine interest.

"I do, too, but not in my purse," Boots said.

"I just took some at home," I said, and they both stopped their searches. "So, Suzanne, what are you and Boots cooking up this morning?"

"Well," she said, smiling conspiratorially at Boots and then me, "we're going to have another book signing for *Something's Rotten in Rockbluff* now that it looks like something *else* is rotten in Rockbluff. I'm referring to the dead girl in the river."

"Cynthia Stalking Wolf."

"Yes, Cindy. Anyway, we think that will generate some more sales of my book. A-a-and," she said, drawing it out and smiling over her shoulder at Boots, "I'm going to do a short reading as a teaser for my novel."

"What novel?"

"The novel I am writing right now, a thriller based on what's happened here over the last month. I realized that I'm not getting anywhere with Cindy's case – no suspects, no action, no arrests, no help from you or Harmon or Moon, so I'm just going to make it up on the fly."

"And how is that different from your first book?"

"Oooh! Mean-spirited! The first book was truthful. That's called non-fiction. This one will be fiction. I'll *make up* the story based on what little I know about Cindy's death. Unless you want to pry open the real story that's going on, which I must say, is fucking *impossible* to get to."

"You sound frustrated."

"I am."

"I'd like to help you, but I don't want to. And won't. If that case is ever solved, and I doubt it will be, you'll be the first to know about it, I'm sure. So, why are you so irritable this morning, Suzanne?" I wondered how she hadn't connected her worries with the story breaking just north of us.

She made an angry face. "Any idea where your friend, Clancy Dominguez might be?"

"I have a general idea. He's probably not in this hemisphere. Why?"

"You know why. We had a wonderful time together. He promised we would continue to have a wonderful time together. Into perpetuity. All over the world – Cannes, Puerta Vallarta, South Beach."

"You didn't hold out for two weeks in Strawberry Point?"

"I haven't seen him since last Tuesday. I haven't even *heard* from him. No phone call, email, text. Nothing."

"I can't speak for Clancy. He's a grown, mature man. You're a grown woman, working on being mature. You both make adult decisions most of the time. What do you want from me?"

"Well, for openers, is he always like this, taking advantage of women after he wins them over with his charm, his stories of adventures, and his bedside manner?"

It sounded like Suzanne was describing the main character in *Othello*, not Clancy Dominguez, although Clancy does have those attributes Miss Highsmith was listing. I had seen him in action many times, and the guy is catnip for cuties. I think I heard Boots lean forward to eavesdrop more effectively.

"That's a question only Clancy can answer. You'll have to ask him."

"I have no idea *how* to ask him, dammit! That's the damn problem, *Thomas*. So if you're not going to be any good helping me out with Clancy, let's just drop the subject, okay? Move on. The prick."

"But the two of you will always have Rockbluff."

"And you'll always have Olivia Olson," she replied, bitterness dripping from her lovely, gloss-free lips.

"One can only hope. Now, if you'll excuse me, I need to buy a book or two. Something with derring-do, action, violence, and subterfuge. Something to bring a little excitement into my plebian, boring existence. Boots, got any new Brad Thor novels? Lee Child? Vince Flynn's last two?"

Boots just smiled and pointed. Suzanne glared at me and approached Boots, I guess to continue with plans for her book signing and teaser about her novel. I bought two Flynn novels, a Lee Child, and a new Warren Moore III gem, and left, waving to Boots and Suzanne. Boots waved back. By then it was time to head over to the courthouse and the Rockbluff County Sheriff's Offices.

I drove over, parked, edged down the stone steps and turned into the offices of Harmon Payne. I nodded at Landsberger, who was covering the phones while he read the morning paper. He nodded. I nodded back. He did not ask if I wanted a cup of coffee or a Diet Coke. I missed Penny Altemier already.

I waited until eleven-fifteen and left. Back in the day when I still had regular physical exams, at Karen's and the girls' insistence, I had been escorted into a waiting room for patients thirty minutes after the time of my appointment, which was nine-thirty. Sitting around in the silly, open-backed hospital gown, I had waited another thirty minutes with no contact from the outside world, not even to apologize for my having to wait or a guess as to when the doctor might drop by to see me on his way to meeting with his financial advisor on the first tee. Not even a month-old *Iowegian Magazine* for me to read. I figured an hour was plenty of time to allow for emergencies. So I changed back into my clothes and left. And never, ever went back to a physician. I've saved lots of money and feel great, understanding deep in the core of my being that, if I go see a doctor again, he or she will tell me something I don't want to hear, making it come true. By ignoring physicians, I avoid bad news.

One caveat is that a few times, in emergencies, I have succumbed to their expertise, if you want to call it that. Broken legs in SEALS training, a torn knee ligament jumping from a Blackhawk helicopter, and a couple of gunshot wounds, a knife slashing, and a boo-boo on my elbow when I fell-down-went-boom.

So, why go to a doctor and pay them when one is feeling great? That's what I thought. And that goes for others who do not meet appointments on time. But I digress.

As I was leaving Payne's offices, Ortiz and Massey emerged from the interview room and called out to me. I kept walking, on out the door, up the smooth limestone steps to the street, into my truck, and across the bridge and up the hill to The Grain o' Truth Bar & Grill, the Mount Olympus of domestic pubs.

Moon was behind the bar, and I must say that there is something comforting about that fact. Moon behind the bar, Rachel waiting on customers, and Ethel Waters singing "Stormy Weather" in the background reassured me that God was in His heaven and all was right with the world, especially after having had Olivia Olson in my arms again, at least for now. Time for lunch.

"Hello, Lunatic," I said, enjoying calling him by his first name for a change.

"Chatty this morning."

"Yes. Caffeine."

"The usual?"

"Yes."

Moon turned and set to my order of two Looney Burgers and an order of fries along with a Three Philosophers, on tap since I had come to town. He drew the dark liquid into a tulip glass and set it before me as I seated myself at the bar. I said, "Migwech."

Moon's stoic face shifted a little into what appeared to be a slight smile. He nodded.

"A little Anishinabe lingo for you," I said "I bought the 'Anishinabe for Morons' tapes."

"Good match."

"So," I said, expertly shifting away from the emotional, which surprised me, to the personal, "any news on your Packard?"

Moon's eyes darkened a little. He said, "No." He glanced around, said, "But it was worth it. I'll get another vehicle."

But, I thought, my friend would never get another niece to replace Cynthia Stalking Wolf.

I ate silently as Moon worked filling orders as customers drifted in on a Monday lunchtime with Rockbluff coming back to life. I drank my second ale and looked around. I drank my third ale, taking it with me to an empty booth in the far corner of the room. I thought about Olivia.

A look from a woman can be a prayer. A glance from a woman can be a dissertation. A smile from a woman can open the doors to glory, and her frown can close them all. So far, I realized, the doors to glory had opened a little, but there were impediments to the sustainability of that glory. And as I contemplated the future and Liv Olson, the idea of marriage came to me for the first time.

Sometimes I surprise myself.

Chapter Twenty-Nine

"When a train goes through a tunnel and it gets dark,
you don't throw away the ticket and jump off.
You sit still and trust the engineer."

- Corrie Ten Boom

Things died down. I was interviewed at The Grain o' Truth Bar & Grill by Special Agents Ortiz and Massey. It was a cold day, and my responses were even colder. They were polite, even confessing that it was their fault we got off to a bad start. Give them credit for a little class if you will, but I saw it as an attempt to nudge me into dropping my guard and cooperating. I had the sense that I wouldn't see them again. They seemed dispirited and a little off their game. I think they knew nothing would come of their investigation.

Maybe next spring there would be a discovery made in a crumbling barn on a lonely, deserted farm in northeast Iowa, and they would hear about the Packard, and they'd drift back and ask a few questions, maybe with renewed vigor. It wouldn't help.

I could teach them a few things about interrogation, and none of them have anything to do with their questions for me that December afternoon in a pleasant pub in Rockbluff, run by an Ojibwa Indian, and with Judy Garland singing "Have Yourself A Merry Little Christmas" in the background, the joint festooned with tasteful holiday decorations — mostly greenery and red ribbons.

My interrogations, both given and received, more often included batteries, water, and pliers. Sometimes, in special situations, the speeches of Richard Nixon were played over and over again. Once, when I was interrogated in a tropical country, I was placed in a bare ten-foot by six foot room, whomped on the soles of my feet with a bamboo shaft while being asked sensitive questions that I refused to answer. Giving up on that approach, my interviewers left the room, tossing a puff adder in as they exited.

When I saw the highly-venomous snake, I began singing, "You Are My Sunshine" to my captors while I calmed the creature, picked it up, and broke its neck. Those evil little men behind my torture thought I had lost my mind. I had.

That was easy compared to being interrogated by experts using strappudo equipment. I enjoyed that experience in the region of the Tigris and Euphrates Rivers, the cradle of civilization. That was the one where those asking the questions tied my arms behind my back, tied a rope to my wrists, and suspended me in the air. I am afraid I said hateful things to those guys. Vigorous and creative epithets I am proud of to this day. I did manage to retaliate when I got loose, but my shoulders still ache on cold nights. Warm nights, too. And sometimes in-between nights. But I prefer to let bygones be bygones. The glorious grace of my life with Karen, with Annie and Michelle more than made up for the horrors of my history. Talk about redemption.

With school back in session through the beginning of next week, Olivia was not very accessible. There were renewed rehearsals for *Our Town*, the play's December dates set back due to the disruption wrought by the blizzard but now revived for three performances in January. She had those ubiquitous papers to grade and research papers to laugh at.

So I only saw her sporadically, the joys of our snowbound weekend together gathering silvery, fragile cobwebs in the night.

As for me, I reverted to my old, solitary habits of running in the mornings now that the roads were clear, going to Mulehoff's gym to work upper body on Mondays, Wednesdays, and Fridays and legs on Tuesdays, Thursdays, and Saturdays. My wounds were healing fast, but not completely, so I avoided side bends holding a 45-pound plate, grimacing through certain other exercises that tapped me on the shoulder to ask, "Hurt much?"

In the middle of that week after my interviews with Massey and Ortiz, several conversations with Harmon Payne, who was going on "paid administrative leave" approved by the city council, and brief nightly chats with Liv, I had a visitor.

It was a Thursday mid-morning. I had run, ministered to Gotcha, absorbed several protein-rich breakfast items, drunk Bailey's-free cups of coffee (with various other sweetening additives added), and was just about to head out the door when there was a knock. Three sharp, forceful, raps. Military style.

I picked up my shotgun in my right hand and opened the door with my left. A well dressed man, maybe mid-30's stood there, a polite smile on his face. I said good morning, looking at his hands first, which were empty, then his face. "May I come in?" he asked.

It was cold outside, but he was not wearing an overcoat. He was dressed in a tasteful, tailored, pin-striped charcoal suit, sparkling white shirt, and a pale blue silk necktie with a perfectly-tied Windsor knot. His black dress shoes looked expensive, even with a bit of snow on the edges. Behind him was a black Mercedes-Benz CL 600, a vehicle that I knew cost well into six figures. The man smiled a little brighter and tilted his head to the side and asked again, "May I come in?"

"I'm thinking," I said. Then, "Okay."

I stepped aside and gestured for him to come in. The man looked at my shotgun in hand, nodded deferentially, and stepped by me and into my home, looking around. Gotcha came up to him and growled. There was no wiggle to her warped little root of a tail. Surprised me.

The man said, "Is your Bulldog controlled?"

I said yes and offered him a seat in the living room while I corrected Gotcha and brought her to my side. Gotcha is more discerning when it comes to human nature than her owner, and I wondered what was up. Usually she bites only bad people, having done it just that once, a bit over a year ago. Growling is not her style. I decided she was taking a position one step back from chomping on my visitor's leg.

The man took a seat in one of the recliners, smiled, and draped one leg over the other in a sure sign of ease and comfort. He glanced down and removed a dog hair from the bottom of a trouser leg.

"What do you want?" I asked.

"I want to offer you an arrangement. Call it a gift," he said, turning his full attention to me as I sat across from him in my wingback chair. I set my shotgun across my legs, keeping my right hand on the trigger guard.

I said, "Oh, goody! I love gifts! What is it?"

"It's valuable, but not tangible."

"You obviously know who I am. Who the hell are *you*? I was taught by my mother not to accept gifts from strangers. Are you one of those perverts who cruises around in a windowless van, stopping by elementary schools and asking little girls and boys if they'd like to see your puppy?"

The man laughed. "No, I am not that kind of person. I restrict my sexual orientation to adult females."

"I repeat. *Who* are you?"

The man shifted in his seat, uncrossed his legs. "My name is irrelevant."

"What *is* relevant? I mean, you got all dressed up to come see me."

"I dress like this every day. Not the point, Mr. O'Shea."

"Can we get on with this? I'm a little edgy this morning. I'd hate to have to shoot you simply because you teased me about a gift." I brought up Elsie and rested her stock on my right knee, her barrel pointed at the ceiling.

"Oh, please," he said, rolling his eyes.

"Come to the point, sir, before I throw you out into the snow. On your head."

"Okay then. I represent certain interests, financial interests, who are well aware that you and your Indian friend and your other friend are responsible for the death of Ted Hornung, the destruction of The Pony Club in Chalaka, and the disappearance of several of Mr. Hornung's associates."

"I don't think you can prove that." I wondered how many of Hornung's associates Clancy had disappeared in addition to those at the deserted farm shootout. I grinned inside my brain.

"I don't need to prove it. We both know it's true. Getting *on*, as you so impatiently desire, I am here to give you a gift, but there is a caveat, a *condition*, of that gift, which is substantial."

"I knew it."

"The financial interests I represent considered taking your life. Not a problem. You and I both know that a trained sniper could kill you at any moment, given time and the right situation, despite your impressive skill set. But, we are not going to do that. That's the gift. Your life."

He was right. Anyone can have anyone killed, and often get away with it. I know that from my own experience. "What's the condition? Oh, I got that out of sequence. I accept your gift and most likely the condition, under the circumstances."

The man smiled, this time genuinely. "I can see why Olivia Olson might be infatuated with you. You are quite humorous." He shifted a bit in the chair. "Anyway, the condition is that you leave everything as it is, that you no longer interfere with my employers' business interests, and that you completely drop your nosing around in the Cynthia Stalking Wolf case. Considering that everyone directly connected with that stupid mistake is now dead, that part of the gift should be easy."

I started to ask him how he knew Liv liked me, more than a little, too, but then I dropped the idea. Some things are obvious. These people have more information on me than the NSA.

"Why the offer? Why don't you just pick me off anyway without giving anything?"

The man smiled again, touched his hand to his heart, and said, "Because you did us a favor. Mr. Hornung had become a liability. He was skimming from our profits from The Pony Club, he was dipping his toe in entertainment venues we do not condone, and he ignored our strongly-worded communications to cease and desist. In local parlance, he was too big for his britches. In our parlance, he had become a negative asset. We were going to go beyond strongly-worded communications with him, but that would have led to a dot-connecting possibly incriminating my employers. Of course, those dots could likely be erased with incentives to key individuals to go dumb or become forgetful."

"You'd have to bribe and threaten authorities to lose their focus."

"Exactly, but we resist the word 'bribe.' We prefer 'business inducements' instead. Fits our mission statement better. Now, what *you've* done is save us the trouble, sending law enforcement professionals in a totally different direction. I believe there was light applause at corporate when we learned that The Pony Club had gone 'poof.'

"Now the heat's on *you*," he said, "but I doubt it will be very warm. Our sources tell us that your operation will not likely yield any traceable evidence. The trail is already cold, no pun intended, and so we may all sleep well as a result of your actions, and the fact that you will not get caught. We congratulate you on a job well done."

"Thank you," I said, keeping my shotgun pointing toward the ceiling and Gotcha at my feet, alert and, from time to time, trembling. I put my left hand on her thick shoulders and rubbed. She wanted a piece of the man. "But what we did was not a job, it was personal."

"Yes, of course. An important distinction. Now, one other thing," he said.

"Which is?"

"Your friend. Not the Indian. We know a little bit about Dominguez. And his associates. Not much, but we are inclined to believe he would take offense if something happened to you, and we are inclined to believe he would bring unorthodox resources to discover what happened, and we are inclined to believe it would turn out expensively and unpleasantly for everyone that I represent."

"And I am inclined to believe he would feed you your livers before setting you on fire," I said. God, I love Clancy Dominguez.

"So?" he asked, shrugging his shoulders.

"So?"

"*So*, do you accept the gift? We allow you to live, you back off completely from anything related to the sadness around Cynthia

Stalking Wolf's death, and life goes on for you and also for my employers."

"Yes." I'm glad he used the word "sadness" with regard to Cynthia's murder. Otherwise, I was thinking about breaking his nose for him.

"Most excellent," he said, coming to his feet. Gotcha growled. He looked down. "Even though your dog doesn't like me, I confess I like her. Substantial, intelligent, loyal. A fine canine, Mr. O'Shea."

I rose, keeping my shotgun in hand and walking to the front door with the man, Gotcha at my side. I was beginning to like him better than Suzanne Highsmith, who thought Gotcha was "icky."

Outside, on the stoop, he turned and offered his hand. I said, "I don't think so. No offense intended. It's not personal."

"Philosophical? Ethical dilemma?"

It was my turn to laugh. He put his hand down, turned and strode away, confident in every gesture, called out, "Merry Christmas, Mr. O'Shea!" got in his super duper sedan, and drove away and down my drive, beeping his horn once. Nice touch. I noticed that the Mercedes had Minnesota plates. Of course.

I found myself relaxing, not realizing how I had been tensing my neck and back muscles. It felt good to breathe a deep breath. I closed the door and went back to my recliner. Gotcha flopped down at my side and I said to her, "You booger. You're the best."

She wiggled her root.

I sat there for a while, realizing that, truly, the man's employers had given me a gift. And I was grateful, to be candid. They had given me a gift, but they had received something in return, being spared the wrath of Clancy Dominguez and his associates who would cut off the head of the snake, and then the rest of it, too, piece by piece. Clancy and

I owed each other our lives. I wondered if I would ever see him again, made up my mind that I would, and headed for the gym after giving my Bulldog a jumbo Milk Bone, just for being discerning.

CHAPTER THIRTY

"One act of obedience is worth one hundred sermons."

- Dietrich Bonhoeffer

For a small town, little more than a village, an astounding number of parties emerged that week before Christmas. I was invited to, and accepted invitations for, parties at Mike Mulelhoff's, The Grain o' Truth Bar & Grill, and, on Christmas Eve, the Heisler's. I turned down an offer to engage in festivities at Shlop's Roadhouse (courtesy of Bunza). So tempting.

The party at Mike and Gabby Mulehoff's stone house was for the members of his Men's Bible Study group and their wives, plus a few others I got to know over several cups of Mike's high-octane eggnog. Harmon Payne was there and we exchanged a few pleasantries over the soft background of Christmas carols, both Christian and secular. His countenance was better than I had seen it since I found Cindy Stalking Wolf in the Whitetail River. He seemed resigned to the fact that there just might not be closure on the case, and that he had not been successful in arresting and convicting the perps. I told him the Iowa Major Crimes Unit had been unsuccessful, too, and that seemed to assuage his guilt. He left early. I felt no compunction to tell him the truth.

After being as outgoing as I am capable, which included speaking briefly yet personally with everyone at the party and complementing Gabby on her heavy hor's d'ouvres, I left, taking with me a substantial paper bag filled with samples of her cooking. Gotcha enjoyed her share shortly after I got home and poured myself a glass of pinot grigio.

Two days later Lunatic Mooning closed down The Grain early, an action announced in advance by word of mouth and also a notice taped to his front door for a week preceding. At 9 PM, only his closest friends were inside. The Mulehoff's, Julie and Gunther Schmidt, Clara and Arvid Pendergast, the Heislers, Harvey Goodell, owner of the Rockbluff Motel, and Rachel Bergman were all in attendance. Liv Olson was my guest, and we showed up at precisely nine, just a few minutes before Harmon Payne arrived with his date – Suzanne Highsmith.

As soon as they were inside and had shed their coats, Harmon strode over to Moon and shook his hand and engaged in a conversation. Suzanne, wearing a scoop-neck sweater that revealed enough cleavage to spur apoplexy in every man there, rushed over to me, threw her arms around my neck, and before I could resist, planted a hot kiss on my mouth, the tip of her tongue gliding quickly along my lower lip.

She pushed back from her hearty clinch and said, "Merry Christmas, Thomas! You sure can kiss!"

I smiled politely and said nothing, glancing in Liv's direction. She did not look pleased, but her eyes were daggered in Suzanne's direction, not mine. The Queen of Jiggle then left me, fastened herself to Harmon's arm, and gazed up at him in total devotion as he continued his conversation with Moon, who let his eyes drift briefly from Harmon's face.

It was a good party. Plenty of hot food, cold drinks, and timely music in the background. Burl Ives was singing, "A Holly Jolly

Christmas," followed by several other secular classics of the season, including "All I Want for Christmas is My Two Front Teeth," by Spike Jones and his City Slickers, and that Anishinabe favorite, "I Yust Go Nuts at Christmas," by Yogi Jorgesson. Elvis, Brenda Lee and The Chipmunks all contributed to a vast array of seasonal delights. As the night wore on, a few of us danced slow dances, and then it was time to leave. Moon would close down The Grain for four days beginning tomorrow, a Thursday, with Christmas on Saturday.

I walked Liv home through the cold, dark night as a light snow dusted the village. When we crossed the bridge over the Whitetail River, we held hands tighter and kept our eyes straight ahead. Or at least, Liv did. I was able to get away with a quick glance on either side. At her front door, she asked me if I'd like to come in for the night, but I hadn't made arrangements for Gotcha, so I had to turn down the offer. I countered with an offer to have her come sleep with me at my place, but she hadn't made arrangements for Milton, which made me wonder briefly why neither one of us had been anticipatory and made such arrangements?

I did step inside for a few minutes, however, and what ensued reminded me of a joke told to me by a Baptist down in Belue, Georgia. He said the question was, why do Baptists frown on making love standing up, and the answer was that it looked too much like dancing. When we had calmed down and stepped back, I told Liv the joke. She laughed and laughed, a wonderful sound. Then we kissed goodnight and said sweet things to each other that we both meant, and I went on home.

Between Moon's party and the Heisler soiree, Gotcha and I made a side trip to Iowa City to do a little Christmas shopping, choosing to go out of town because some gifts need to be kept quiet, and I'm confident anything I bought in Rockbluff would be on the evening news that night. I bought a gift for Liv, an action toy and a stuffed animal for the Heisler children, and a small nativity scene carved by hand out of olive wood from Israel, that for the Heislers.

Gotcha and I both enjoyed the outing, she got some extra adoration from a few more students staying over in town through the holidays, and we both enjoyed a good bit of exercise walking around the campus and downtown. Two of the stores had clerks who raised eyebrows when I brought Gotcha inside with me, but said nothing. The others shook their heads and Gotcha was forced to sit and wait by the front door, frightening away customers who knew nothing about the breed. On the way home we drove through a light snowfall that was more poetry than problem.

On Christmas Eve, I showed up at 7 PM at the Heisler's big stone manse behind Christ the King Church. There were Christmas lights outlining the front door, electric candles in every window, and a Christmas tree prominently displayed in the front living room window. Liv was already there, having volunteered to help Molly prepare whatever needed to be prepared.

I noticed no other cars in the four-car parking area in front of their house except the two Heisler vehicles. Liv's yellow Subaru was absent. Then I remembered her telling me that Molly was going to pick her up, and she'd have to beg a ride home from me. A setup if there ever was one, but a setup I embraced.

I parked and got out. I had not asked who else was coming to the party, once being told that it was poor form to do so when invited to a gathering at someone's home. I had assumed there would be a group, but I was wrong. I gathered up my professionally-wrapped gifts and withdrew from my truck and turned toward the Heisler's residence.

Molly greeted me at the front door, ushered me in, gushed over the gifts, and put their packages under the tree. Carl appeared shortly after with Liv in tow. He shook my hand and Liv embraced me while avoiding my rapidly-healing bullet wounds, kissing my ear and whispering "It's a blessing to behold you, Thomas." Someday, when a woman winks at me, pats me on the butt, and says, "It's a blessing to behold you, Thomas," I'll turn toes up and move directly into a state of ecstasy.

The evening went well. Carl hustled their children off to bed with a promise of telling them a story. We enjoyed a fine dinner of Cornish hen, two casseroles, kale salad with bits of bacon, cold glasses of a Chilean Chardonnay, and French vanilla ice cream on top of hefty slices of mince pie for dessert. Afterwards, we adjourned to the living room with more wine and conversation.

We talked about the unsolved murder of Moon's niece, Suzanne Highsmith's appearance in town, Ernie and Jan from Belue, and the Hawkeyes' basketball season so far. We also talked about Christmas, and the real gift involved in the holiday. Then Carl got up from his wing chair, stooped down at the Christmas tree, and pulled out a bright, shiny red package with a green ribbon. "It's for you, Thomas, with our love. Please open it."

Always uncomfortable opening gifts in the presence of the givers, I proceeded to unwrap the package. I could tell it was a book. "Is this that book on men's makeup I've been talking about?" I asked.

There were short chuckles. Liv shook her head slowly and smiled at me. "Oh, Thomas" was all she said, but her voice tone and expression spoke much more and I felt warm and loved.

It was a book about the history of Hawkeye sports teams. "Thank you!" I said, "And what a relief. I was afraid it would be some deep, theological tome by someone I had never heard of but an author you were familiar with from childhood. Thanks again!" I said.

"I'll give you your gift. Later," Olivia said. Carl wiggled his eyebrows rapidly and Molly just smiled.

"It's been a wonderful evening, you guys," I said, "but I'm eager to see what Liv has for me, so I guess we need to be on our way. Don't want to overstay our welcome."

"You can't do that with us, Thomas," Carl said.

"Maybe not, but you haven't seen me in the morning," I replied.

"But I . . . " Liv started to say, caught herself, restarted, "but I don't think we should test it," she said. I was impressed with her recovery that fooled no one.

We said our good nights, sleep wells, and Merry Christmases and made our way to the truck. I helped Liv inside, went around and got in, and started the engine. She scooted over, leaned across the console, and kissed me full on the mouth. It was a wonderful kiss, sensuous, warm, slightly eager. I kissed her back, with feeling.

"Now, wasn't that better than Suzanne Highsmith's kiss?" she asked, a tease in her voice. She sat back and let her left hand rest high up on my right thigh.

"No comparison, but you understand that I didn't kiss Suzanne. She kissed me. And I did not kiss her back."

"I'll bet Harmon kissed more than her back later that night."

"I hope he understands that she's only coming on to him because she wants to squeeze information for her next book," I said, backing out of my parking place, turning the truck, and driving on out to the street.

"I'm sure he does. He is not stupid. But she needs to understand that her, um, *enticements* will not bear fruit. He won't divulge anything.

I think he's probably recommitted to going by the book. I *know* he is. He's that kind of man."

"I agree."

I drove slowly up the street from Christ the King, passing the bridge on my right, then on up the street after a left turn right after we passed Blossom's Bistro, closed for the night. I parked in front of Liv's house and cut the engine and doused the headlights.

"Would you like to come in for a nightcap?"

"I thought you'd never ask."

Inside, Milton came up and sniffed my pantleg. He was wagging his tail now that we were friends. Liv walked with him to the back door, let him out, waited for a minute, let him in, and secured him in his crate. She gave him a treat and rejoined me in the living room. We sat on her sofa, Olivia to my right, where our affair had begun over a year ago. And died shortly after that. A single Craftsman stained glass lamp was the only illumination in the room resulting in a soft, dim, roseate glow to our evening.

I was holding the ring box in my hand. It was black velvet on the outside and had a tiny red bow. Olivia saw it and stared. Then she looked at me and there were tears in her eyes.

"Don't jump to conclusions, Liv. It's not my high school ring and I'm not going to ask you to go steady. But I am going to ask you a question, corny as it may sound when I say it."

I had her full, moist attention. I took her left hand in my left and said, "Ernie Timmons once said to me, after Karen died, 'Thomas, I believe there'll come a time when you'll find a woman you can't walk away from, and you will need to be with her.' And now, Liv, although I hate to make a prophet out of Ernie, there *is* you. And I can't walk away. I just can't."

In a tiny voice, she said, "Thank you, Thomas, but . . . "

I kissed her so that she would stop talking and she did. I let go of her hand and opened the box and extended it to her, revealing a simple, one-carat diamond ring nestled in a white satin setting.

I said, "I love you, Liv, and I'm asking you to marry me and make me happier than an Iowa win in the Rose Bowl. *Much* happier than that. A profound and enduring happiness, and I'll do everything I can to make you even happier."

Liv looked at me, tears streaming down her face, and then she reached out, slowly closed the lid to the box, and folded my fingers around the gift. The tiny red bow fell off. She pushed my hand away.

"Thomas, I love you, too. I do. More than you know. But the truth is, someone's going to kill you someday, Thomas. They will. I'm a selfish person and I don't think I have it in me to wake up alone in your bed in your lovely home, knowing that I have lost you to some evil, malignant, crazy person you've somehow brought into your life, *our* life. I can't do that. I won't. But I want to be with you and love you and kiss you and touch you as time permits, when we can steal away and love, knowing that it could end in an instant.

"Thomas, I want you to tell me now what happened with you and Moon and Clancy. I told you I would want to know, that I would ask. Please do not lie. There's a calm, a stillness around Cindy's death since Clancy left. Moon's car was stolen, you've been shot twice. Tell me."

I did, leaving nothing out. She was trembling when I finished.

"So," she said, "you were on your way to Chalaka to kill those men when you met them on the road?"

"Yes, and they were on their way to kill us. They fired first. Self defense."

"And that's your justification for killing six men?"

"I only killed three."

"You think that's funny? My God, I doubt if you even knew their names."

"It's simpler that way."

"Thank you for not lying to me, Thomas. That's something to build on there, my love, my heart," she said. And then she broke down, falling against me and sobbing. I stroked her golden hair and kissed the top of her head. When she stopped, she looked up and said, "Let's just be as we are now, Thomas. We are good together, aren't we?"

"Yes, of course. But," I said, pausing, gathering my courage to say something that was harder than facing those killers at that deserted barn two weeks ago, "I don't want to continue as we are. I do, but I want more. I want *deeper*. I want to be your husband. I want you to be my wife. I want to do the right thing."

Silently, Liv's tears came from deep within her as she lifted her tear-streaked face to me, mascara running and her nose dripping. She looked beautiful. "Thomas, you honor me, and I am so sorry that we can't, that I can't do what you want. I want to give my heart and soul to you, but you continue to frighten me. There is death around you, Thomas. There is murder, revenge, danger over and over and over again. It will never stop as long as you live."

"Would you have me ignore Cindy murdered in the river? Would you have me let Moon try to bring justice all by himself? I can't be like that."

Liv sniffed and dabbed her free hand across her nose. "And there's the rub, Thomas O'Shea, and I love you for it. You can't stay away from trouble. This is done, the Soderstrom violence is done, but there will be more. It's who you are."

"All of those things were in self defense, Liv. Understand that."

"I do understand, but Thomas, everything in life is, really, self-defense one way or another, but you go *look* for opportunities to defend yourself. And one day it won't work, and I'm not going to be there to bewail the loss of my one love in my life, my husband. I'll weep at your funeral, Thomas, but not as your wife. Lover? Yes. Wife? I can't."

I rose to my feet, pulling her up with me. And I kissed her lips and she kissed me back and I left her, sobbing again, the ring in its box back in my pocket. I went outside and heard Liv's door close softly behind me. I sat in the truck for a moment and nearly went back to the woman and the night and her body. Then I cursed principles, cursed myself, cursed the night. I started the engine and pulled away, turned around at the next corner, and drove.

As I crossed the bridge it began snowing again, hard. I stopped the truck and got out, leaving the engine running and the door open. It was cold. There was no traffic, so many people asleep in their beds on this Christmas eve, children hoping Christmas morning would hurry up so they could head for the gifts under the tree, which reminded me that I hadn't collected Liv's gift for *me*. Darn.

I put my elbows on the parapet and looked down at the north side of the river rushing beneath the bridge, to the spillway, and beyond, where its waters would merge with the Mississippi and continue on south, past Clinton and Davenport, St. Louis and below to New Orleans and the Gulf of Mexico.

I stood up and took out the little black velvet box and removed the ring. I stared at it for a moment, admiring its pristine, simple setting. I held it out over the black water for a long moment, then put it back in the box and into my pocket again.

Someday I would place that ring on Olivia Olson's finger. Someday I would marry her. In the meantime, I would go home, not so lonely when I think about it. After all, Gotcha was waiting for me, and there was a refrigerator with multiple bottles of Three Philosophers, Bailey's Irish Crème in the cabinet keeping the Myer's Rum company. That wasn't so bad.

I climbed back in the truck, suddenly weary. The snow picked up a bit, and I drove on home peering into beautiful flakes blowing about ahead of me, startlingly white in my headlights that would lead me to the house on the bluff overlooking two river valleys, deep and immutable in the dark of the storm.

About the Author

John Carenen, a native of Clinton, Iowa, graduated with an M.F.A. in Fiction Writing from the prestigious University of Iowa Writers Workshop. His work has appeared in numerous popular and literary magazines, and he has been a featured humor columnist in newspapers in North and South Carolina. A novel, *Son-up, Son-down* was published by the National Institute of Mental Health.

A Far Gone Night is the second in his series of mysteries with the darkly humorous protagonist Thomas O'Shea, and a uniquely Midwestern cast of quirky characters hanging out in the picturesque village of Rockbluff, Iowa.

John recently retired from his years as an English professor at Newberry College in Newberry, South Carolina. He and his long-suffering wife live in their cozy cottage down a quiet lane just north of Greenville, South Carolina. He is a big fan of his family (wife and two published daughters), the Iowa Hawkeyes, and the Boston Red Sox.

CPSIA information can be obtained
at www.ICGtesting.com
Printed in the USA
LVHW041548110621
689976LV00002B/153